NATHANIEL HAWTHORNE

SELECTED STORIES

INTRODUCTION BY BRENDA WINEAPPLE

JOHN
HARVARD
LIBRARY

T0339389

THE BELKNAP PRESS OF HARVARD UNIVERSITY PRESS

Cambridge, Massachusetts, and London, England 2011

Printed in the United States of America

Library of Congress Cataloging-in-Publication Data

Hawthorne, Nathaniel, 1804–1864.
[Short stories. Selections]
Selected stories / Nathaniel Hawthorne;
[selected and] introduction by Brenda Wineapple.
p.   cm.—(The John Harvard library)
Includes bibliographical references.
ISBN 978-0-674-05022-8 (pbk.)
I. Wineapple, Brenda.   II. Title.
PS1853.W56 2011
813'.3—dc22   2011000197

THE JOHN HARVARD LIBRARY

The John Harvard Library, founded in 1959, publishes essential American writings, including novels, poetry, memoirs, criticism, and works of social and political history, representing all periods, from the beginning of settlement in America to the twenty-first century. The purpose of The John Harvard Library is to make these works available to scholars and general readers in affordable, authoritative editions.

JOHN
HARVARD
LIBRARY

Contents

Introduction

"I HAVE WASTED FAR TOO much of my life, and done myself more than enough of moral and intellectual harm, with scribbling sketches for Magazines," Nathaniel Hawthorne once confided to a friend.[1] And yet his short stories are American koans—elegant, dense, memorable—and the form in which he most consistently excelled. In fact, Hawthorne initially conceived *The Scarlet Letter* (1850), his canonical tour de force, as part of a collection of stories to be titled "Old-Time Legends, Together with Sketches Experimental and Ideal," but his savvy publisher, James T. Fields, who understood the exceptional nature of the tale, urged Hawthorne to complete the story as a novel, which Fields promised to publish.

The House of the Seven Gables (1851) was also likely conceived as a series of briefer works. The novel certainly can be read that way; for instance, the chapter about Matthew Maule's hold over Alice Pyncheon seems not to fit into the novel at all and may have been composed far earlier than 1851. And despite the quirky brilliance of *The Blithedale Romance* (1852) and *The Marble Faun* (1860), Hawthorne's astonishingly modernist novels, their virtuosity is their limitation; one could argue that they hesitate and finally falter.

But it is in the short stories that Hawthorne is at his stylistic best. Though constrained by the exigencies of publication early in his career, his execution is perfect. A master at timing, suspense, and the fearsomeness of the unsaid, Hawthorne knows how to keep and to reveal secrets most succinctly in a short form. Nothing, however trifling, escapes his scrutiny. As Henry James remarked, Hawthorne was "an inveterate observer of small things."[2]

Take Hawthorne's "Night Sketches." James cogently noted that the Night Sketches are simply the light, familiar record of a walk under an umbrella, at the end of a long, dull, rainy day, through the sloppy, ill-paved streets of a country town, where the rare gas-lamps twinkle in the large puddles, and the blue jars in the druggist's window shine through the vulgar drizzle. One would say that the inspiration of such a theme could have had no great force, and such doubtless was the case; but out of the Salem puddles, nevertheless, springs, flower-like, a charming and natural piece of prose.[3]

If the trivial did not pass Hawthorne unnoticed, neither did the profound. Two of his very early stories, "Roger Malvin's Burial" and "My Uncle Molineux" (the latter was published as "My Kinsman, Major Molineux") rank among Hawthorne's most outstanding. Written when or before Hawthorne was twenty-five, these tales spring full-blown, as if from a mature writer certain of his subject matter: the incandescent, nuanced examination of innocence coming ambiguously of age. And he had already perfected a signature style: phrases and clauses well calibrated and modulated into sentences, sentences expanded into paragraphs, each grammatical component—and ultimately the whole tale—accruing meaning far beyond the literal. "It was near nine o'clock of a moonlight evening, when a boat crossed the ferry with a single passenger, who had obtained his conveyance, at that unusual hour, by the promise of an extra fare," Hawthorne writes, modulating each phrase, in the opening paragraphs of "My Kinsman, Major Molineux." Half buried in a tale about a young man's initiation into history, that of his own and of the country's, the classical allusions shift the story from the psychological and social to the mythic with a rhetorical sleight of hand. "Deep as Dante," Melville would characterize Hawthorne's odd, evocative tales.[4]

Who was the man who seemed, in his twenties, to have cultivated a style, a sensibility, and a voice so emphatically individual? Born in 1804 in the once-thriving seaport of Salem, Massachusetts, where ships bound for the Far East returned to port laden with Sumatran pepper, Cantonese tea, Indian cotton, and nuts, figs, and Arabian coffee, Hawthorne was less the inheritor of the wealth that transformed Puritans into Boston Brahmins than the beneficiary of its bleak hour, 1692, when men like Hawthorne's ancestor, John Hathorne, sentenced more than one hundred people, women mostly, to hang as witches on Gallows Hill.

Thus descended from the notorious judge and a far less notorious young sea captain, his father, who died in Surinam when Hawthorne was a boy, young Hawthorne (born Nathaniel Hathorne, he would change the spelling of his name when he turned twenty-one), listened with care to what he called "chimney-corner" accounts of the deeds, ignominious and otherwise, of his forebears. For more information, he also scoured the local organizations and libraries recently established to conserve—and create—a history of the new republic. And Hawthorne read such histories of New England as Cotton Mather's *Magnalia Christi Americana* and William Sewell's *History of the Quakers,* to name just two sources. As a consequence, when first published, Hawthorne's own collected tales, drawing on the past, were appropriately called "twice-told." But as he explained, "a license must be assumed"; that is, he brightened "the materials which time has rusted, and in tracing out the half-obliterated inscriptions on the columns of antiquity, fancy must throw her reviving light on the faded incidents that indicate character."[5] Not an antiquarian, Hawthorne wanted to be a poet.

And he was. Sketches such as "The Haunted Mind" limn the confusions and pleasures of waking in the night, looking out the window at the frosty sky and frozen street, and then letting the mind wander over the deeds undone; he evokes the wintry gloom of an itchy conscience, which is Hawthorne's forte. For he seems to write from an inner core—what he later called the "Inmost Me"—which is the fundamentally lonely and self-doubting part of him. But with extraordinary clarity he then depicts the shadows and fantasies that arrange and deepen and trouble night. Again, as Henry James perspicaciously remarked, Hawthorne had the eyes of a cat; he could see in the dark.

Yet Hawthorne was also a satirist. Not only had he read John Bunyan and Sir Walter Scott, he had studied Swift, Voltaire, Montaigne, and Mandeville and did not hesitate to mock America, its unliterary citizens, or its ambitious authors. Such is the thrust of the revenge fantasy in "The Devil in Manuscript," where the neglected author converts his despair into rage and avenges himself in his writing. "My brain has set the town on fire!" he cries. There is something demonic in Hawthorne's work; to him there is something demonic about ambition, art, and indeed creation itself. He thus tells tales of bourgeois anomie—like "Wakefield," which can be interpreted as a parable of the artist as somebody who is different from the whole damned bunch, or so it seems, and who pays a high price for that difference: "amid the seeming confusion of our mysterious world, individuals are so nicely adjusted to a system, and systems to one another, and to a whole, that by stepping aside for a moment, a man exposes himself to a fearful risk of losing his place forever." This outside man is also, as Hawthorne calls him, "a crafty nincompoop."

Though Hawthorne is often presented as the animator of American history, he is also the scourge of the American present, and he satirizes the present by satirizing himself. As in "Wakefield," self-mocking wit is at the core of "A Virtuoso's Collection," in which the virtuoso, or artist, is "cut off from natural sympathies, and blasted with a doom that had been inflicted on no other human being, and by the result of which he had ceased to be human." But well-meaning reformers besotted with their own goodness are also the object of Hawthorne's gentle ridicule. In "Earth's Holocaust," he imagines a huge bonfire into which zealots toss civilization's rubbish: everything from yesterday's newspapers and last season's hats to the crests of once-illustrious families and barrels of booze, crops of tobacco, bags of coffee, and stores of guns. As muskets and swords melt into a puddle of metal, an onlooker sneers: "When Cain wished to slay his brother, he was at no loss for a weapon." Books are set ablaze, from Shakespeare to Mother Goose; the benighted narrator approves, asking, "Is not Nature better than a book?"

This is Hawthorne's critique of Ralph Waldo Emerson, whose transcendentalist manifesto, *Nature*, had appeared eight years earlier. For, unlike Emerson, Hawthorne was an inveterate skeptic. Ironically, though, he had come of age during one of the most optimistic eras in American history. Educated at Bowdoin College, he met lifelong friends there—other Jacksonian Democrats like himself, such as Franklin Pierce, later elected as the fourteenth president of the United States. But despite the manifest destiny, spread-eagle confidence, and territorial expansion of an exhilarated Jacksonian America, despite the upswing of Protestant evangelism, despite such radical technological changes as wrought by the telegraph, the railroad, and the daguerreotype, and despite innovations in printing, America was not kind to her writers. Hawthorne chose to enter a profession that in America, as he later wrote, "ranked me with the tavern-haunters and town-paupers,—with the drunken poet, who hawked his own fourth of July odes,—and the broken soldier who had been good for nothing since the last war."[6]

He persisted. Influenced not just by Milton, Shakespeare, and Shelley, Hawthorne heeded the call of the brash American novelist John Neal, whose call for an indigenous literature was as loud, if not louder, than that of Hawthorne's Bowdoin classmate, poet Henry Wadsworth Longfellow (whose father had told him to seek another line of work). After graduating, Hawthorne composed a Gothic college novel, *Fanshawe* (1828), which he published anonymously in Boston and at his own expense. Shortly after *Fanshawe*'s appearance, according to his sister, Hawthorne insisted on destroying all copies; in later life he proudly pretended it did not exist.

Hawthorne returned to the short story, for his aim was a fiction steeped, as he put it, in the superstitions of New England. This first collection would be called *Seven Tales of My Native Land*. One of the stories intended for it may have been the atmospheric set-piece "The Hollow of Three Hills," which appeared in Hawthorne's hometown newspaper, the *Salem Gazette,* in 1830. But the road to publication was strewn with rejection. Devastated by the rebuffs of the several men to whom he'd sent his collection—one publisher didn't even bother to read it—Hawthorne later claimed to have set fire to *Seven Tales.* (This Hawthornian motif, fire, is a recurring one.) In another version of events, Hawthorne presented his stories to the *Salem Gazette*'s owner, Ferdinand Andrews, and, both optimistic and naïve, he expected Andrews to print them without hesitation. When Andrews temporized, Hawthorne asked for his manuscript back and torched it. Again, fire.

By 1829, a year after *Fanshawe* had appeared, Hawthorne was submitting such tales as "Roger Malvin's Burial" to Samuel Griswold Goodrich, a self-made publisher known for his children's books and the Christmas annual *The Token and Atlantic Souvenir.* Hawthorne hoped Griswold might help him find a publisher for the collection, whose working title was now *Provincial Tales of My Native Land,* and which included "My Kinsman, Major Molineux," "Roger Malvin's Burial," and possibly "Young Goodman Brown" and "The Minister's Black Veil."[7] When the book did not materialize—another dreadful disappointment—he conceived of yet another set of interconnected tales, this time called "The Story Teller," a series of sketches linked via the persona of an itinerant storyteller, who is part entertainer and part spectator. ("The Devil in Manuscript" and "The Ambitious Guest" may have been part of this series.) Again, failure: no one was interested, and he published the tales individually.

Hawthorne's stories were beginning to appear under one or another pseudonym, or anonymously, in the *Token* or in such magazines as the *Knickerbocker* or the *New England Magazine,* but it was not until 1837 that *Twice-told Tales* saw the light of day. Unbeknownst to him, another college friend, Horatio Bridge, had contacted Griswold and volunteered to underwrite it. Priced at one dollar, this first edition of *Twice-told Tales* included some of Hawthorne's finest forays into the peculiar, like the baffling "Minister's Black Veil" as well as such psychological landscapes as "The Hollow of the Three Hills." Curiously, Hawthorne excluded the early and incomparable stories "My Kinsman, Major Molineux," "Roger Malvin's Burial," and "Young Goodman Brown."

He may have held them back because these three stories, taken together, cut too close to the bone. In each, a young man encounters himself and his country's history in stark, unappealing terms: Robin Molineux discovers the cruelty at the heart of a people's so-called revolution and his own complicity in that cruelty; Young Goodman

Brown loses his faith not just because we may all be children of the devil but because we have no confidence in one another. And in "Roger Malvin's Burial," Hawthorne creates in the aftermath of a forgotten historical incident, the massacre at Lovewell's Pond in 1725, a story of fathers displaced, of origins reconstituted, and of the blood spilled to build a nation.

According to the literary critic Michael J. Colacurcio, Hawthorne's early stories are those of a moral historian who scrupulously peers through America's nationalistic myth of origins—as promulgated, for instance, by the Democratic historian George Bancroft—to expose a spotted past, not the providential story of messianic destiny. Readers unfamiliar with the battle at Lovewell's Pond and the vicissitudes of eighteenth-century America still discover in tales like "Roger Malvin's Burial" stories of self-deception, obsessive guilt, and of self-love. The compulsive psychology of the tale is dead-on, and the consequences of the small lie, told to oneself, bewilder and bewitch. Hawthorne's stories, once read, are unforgettable.

Sales of *Twice-told Tales* were dismal. The book had been published during the debilitating panic of 1837, and though reviews were favorable (Longfellow had said that Hawthorne was a new star), his publisher went bankrupt and the book was remaindered. Hawthorne managed to republish the collection in 1842 with a different firm and as a two-volume second edition, which now included "The Haunted Mind," "The Ambitious Guest," and "Night Sketches." That edition sold no better.

The same year, Hawthorne, who had just married, rented an old parsonage in Concord, Massachusetts, from Emerson's great-grandfather. These two events—his marriage and the move to Concord—demonstrably affected Hawthorne's new batch of stories. For

in Concord, Emerson held transcendental court over such bona fide
eccentrics as Bronson Alcott, recently returned with his family, including daughter Louisa May, from the collapsed vegan paradise
known as "Fruitlands"; the young naturalist writer Henry David Thoreau; and the oddball poet Ellery Channing. To a certain extent, it was
a village that attracted the like-minded, except for Hawthorne, who
skirted on the edge of this group, which he gently mocked as "bores,"
he said, "of a very intense water."

Emerson had his own reservations about his new neighbor. When
a friend gave him a story of Hawthorne's, Emerson had complained
that "there was no inside to it."[8] Later Emerson confided to his journals that "N. Hawthorn's reputation as a writer is a very pleasing fact,
because his writing is not good for anything, and this is a tribute to
the man."[9] But the men were friends, of a sort. In his sketch "The Old
Manse," Hawthorne said of Emerson that he had never met a man "so
quiet, so simple, so without pretension, encountering each man alive
as if expecting to receive more than he could impart."

But what better place than Concord for Hawthorne, the chronicler
of America's past? Near Concord's North Bridge, on April 18, 1775,
embattled farmers, in the first skirmishes of the American Revolution, fired the shots, as Emerson had written, "heard round the world."
But Hawthorne had (ambivalently) declared his independence from
"ancestral superstitions." In his tale "Old Esther Dudley," the redoubt-
able Governor Hancock exclaims, "We are no longer children of the
Past!" Hawthorne was now a citizen of the present, a happily married
man, composing a new set of linked stories (never finished) to be
called "Allegories of the Heart."

Written largely for the Democratic party's literary magazine, the
Democratic Review, one of these allegories, "Egotism; or, the Bosom-
Serpent," was included in Hawthorne's new volume, *Mosses from an
Old Manse* (1846). Thus, while *Mosses* contains at last stories such as

"Young Goodman Brown" and "Roger Malvin's Burial" that reflect his abiding interest in history, which Hawthorne renders psychologically —his gift—it also includes stories about the present, which is to say the reformers and do-gooders of Concord.

"We are all a little wild here with numberless projects of social reform," Emerson had enthusiastically written to Thomas Carlyle.[10] Yet Hawthorne's sense of reform was decidedly unlike Emerson's; for Emerson, improvement begins at home in the self-reliant individualism buttressed by a benign, immanent divinity. "If the single man plant himself indomitably on his instincts, and there abide," Emerson had instructed in "The American Scholar," "the huge world will come round to him."[11] Emerson was a spiritual idealist and pantheist; Hawthorne considered himself, at least when compared to some of his Concord neighbors, a hard-headed realist. And he knew whereof he spoke, having joined (for less than six months) the Brook Farm experiment in communal living in West Roxbury. "Persons of marked individuality—crooked sticks, as some of us might be called—are not exactly the easiest to bind up into a faggot," he quipped.[12] Hawthorne's self-reliant characters are lonely individualists bound for a fall. Their motives mixed, their intentions crossed, these Hawthornian individualists knock into other people and the truth, as he writes in "The Birth-mark," "against which all seekers sooner or later stumble, that our great creative Mother, while she amuses us with apparently working in the broadest sunshine, is yet severely careful to keep her own secrets, and, in spite of her pretended openness, shows us nothing but results." Hawthorne's world is enigmatic and unknowable.

It must have irked him to read Edgar Allan Poe's anti-Concord review of *Mosses:* "Get a bottle of visible ink, come out from the Old Manse, cut Mr. Alcott, [and] hang (if possible) the editor of *The Dial.*"[13] Poe's criticism notwithstanding, Hawthorne remained heir to the Puritans, not to Mr. Alcott. With this legacy of guilt and sorrow ever in full view, Hawthorne embedded a tragic vision—that our ends seldom match our aims—into his nimble prose and showed how expectation is inevitably disappointed by human frailty. As "The Birthmark" demonstrates, humans are forever fallible and flawed. Yet Hawthorne provides more than a broken world and stupid self: a poet of imperfection, he chronicles with compassion our yearning after the ineffable and reminds us that "the reward of all high performance," as he writes in "The Artist of the Beautiful," "must be sought within itself, or sought in vain."

Though largely praised, *Mosses from an Old Manse* enlarged neither Hawthorne's audience nor his wallet. With his penchant for mock self-deprecation, he had called himself "the obscurest man of letters" in America, anticipating Poe's observation that Hawthorne was "*the* example, *par excellence,* in this country, of the privately admired and publicly unappreciated man of genius."[14] Similarly, in the prologue to "Rappaccini's Daughter," Hawthorne pretends to be a voluminous but neglected French writer, who occupies "an unfortunate position between the Transcendentalists (who, under one name or another, have their share in all the current literature of the world), and the great body of pen-and-ink men who address the intellect and sympathies of the multitude." And the narrator? A nowhere man, Hawthorne acknowledges, who writes tales "sometimes historical, sometimes of the present day, and sometimes, so far as can be discovered, [that] have little or no reference either to time or space."

Yet when Herman Melville read *Mosses,* he comprehended it as no other reviewer had, and when he praised *Mosses* in the *Literary Review,* the former seaman confirmed that under Hawthorne's "mild moonlight of contemplative humor" lay "a great, deep intellect, which drops down into the universe like a plummet." For in "spite of all the

Indian-summer sunlight on the hither side of Hawthorne's soul," wrote Melville, "the other side—like the dark half of the physical sphere—is shrouded in a blackness, ten times black."[15]

Hawthorne's subversive wit, his ability to unsettle moral convictions and his willingness to negate, not affirm, the status quo appealed to Melville, who admired "Young Goodman Brown" as well as "Egotism; or, the Bosom Serpent." And in tales like "The Birth-mark" and "Rappaccini's Daughter," Hawthorne explores the vehemences of love (which is frequently self-love) and the sexual anxieties besetting his male protagonists, who, demanding purity and perfection from their beloveds, destroy them. "I would fain have been loved, not feared," mutters Beatrice, the main character of "Rappaccini's Daughter," as she sinks into death. There is no perfection in this world. One loves one's crooked neighbor with one's crooked heart.

Or in spite of one's birthmark. Birthmarks blighting the body or bosom-serpents dwelling within it highlight Hawthorne's obsession with exposure, with what can be hidden, masked, and kept at bay— and what can not. Secrets and the uncertain revelation of them propel his tales; they would later shape *The Scarlet Letter* and they inspire the marvelous essay "The Old Manse," which Hawthorne wrote as a preface to *Mosses*. "So far as I am a man of really individual attributes," he says, "I veil my face; nor am I, nor have ever been, one of those supremely hospitable people, who serve up their own hearts delicately fried, with brain-sauce, as a tidbit for their beloved public."

"The Old Manse" is a delightful tour of Hawthorne's Concord house and grounds and as such it is a statement of artistic method. In rendering his abode, Hawthorne affects to lift the veil and step outside his stories, which shimmer with ambiguity, and introduce us to the Hawthorne whom we identify as neighbor, gardener, author. Yet here too he conceals even as he reveals, and he reveals only *that* he conceals, for secrets, he suggests, are the *sine qua non* of suspense. As Dan McCall, a literary critic, once said, "the closer you get to Hawthorne the farther he moves away."[16]

Hawthorne's autobiographical self is something of a dissociated presence, just the kind that defines characters such as Robin Molineux (in "My Kinsman, Major Molineux") and Parson Hooper (in "The Minister's Black Veil") and Owen Warland (in "The Artist of the Beautiful"). Each of them, including Hawthorne, is painfully conscious of the disparity between conception and accomplishment— that "when we see how little we can express," as Hawthorne wrote in his notebooks, "it is a wonder that any man ever takes up a pen a second time."[17] And this disturbs the autobiographical narrator of "The Old Manse," who never quite bridges the distance between the self that writes and the written self on the page. The writer lives in a historical time which, as Hawthorne says in *The House of the Seven Gables,* is always flitting away from us. "I wish there was something in the intellectual world analogous to the Daguerreotype (is that the name of it?) in the visible—something which should print off our deepest, and subtlest, and delicatest thoughts and feelings, as minutely and accurately as the above-mentioned instrument paints the various aspects of Nature," he once lamented.[18] But no mechanical invention can reproduce consciousness. That is the writer's task.

Hawthorne asserts that each autobiographical act implies an audience and that the imagined audience brings the writer into closer communion with others. "My theory is, that there is less indelicacy in speaking out your highest, deepest, tenderest emotions to the world at large, than to almost any individual," he explained to a friend. "You may be mistaken in the individual; but you cannot be mistaken in thinking that, somewhere among your fellow-creatures, there is a heart that will receive yours into itself."[19] And so there was that heart.

Hawthorne dedicated his last collection of stories, *The Snow-Image and Other Twice-told Tales* (1852) to Horatio Bridge, who had backed and paid for Hawthorne's first volume of stories. "If anybody is responsible for my being at this day an author," Hawthorne wrote, "it is you yourself."

In 1853, his friend Franklin Pierce, then president of the United States, appointed Hawthorne the American Consul in Liverpool, England, and Hawthorne and his family spent the next seven years abroad. He did write another novel, *The Marble Faun,* but no more stories—unless one considers his essays about life in England as nonfiction tales. ("A life of much smoulder, but scanty fire," he mordantly characterized his output.[20]) "The Old Manse" had forecast this shift to nonfiction, and had Hawthorne lived, and had he valued his nonfiction as dearly as he had his romances and tales, he would have become a premier American essayist, or so suggests his superb and coruscating "Chiefly about War Matters, by a Peaceable Man," published in the *Atlantic Monthly* in the second year of the Civil War. The short form remained his métier. But Hawthorne died two years later, in 1864.

The Snow-Image had included new tales like "Ethan Brand," about another seeker, along with previously uncollected ones like, at last, "My Kinsman, Major Molineux" and "The Devil in Manuscript." "The Devil in Manuscript," which Horatio Bridge doubtless remembered, aptly concludes Hawthorne's career as a storyteller, for the town that the author had inadvertently set ablaze might well now be Hawthorne's own audience, readers ignited and illumined, from Horatio Bridge to Henry James, from Herman Melville to Willa Cather, from Poe to Flannery O'Connor, from Robert Lowell to Paul Auster, from Louisa May Alcott to H. P. Lovecraft, from Ivan Turgenev to Virginia Woolf, from William Faulkner to Bharati Mukherjee, from George Eliot to Toni Morrison, from Edith Wharton to John Hawkes, from

Emerson to Borges to us. Emboldened by Hawthorne, inspired by him, we look to him, albeit through a glass, darkly, and hence keep reading and rereading those tales, twice and thrice and many times told, tales that, as Emily Dickinson said, entice, appall. And they beguile, they glow, they linger.

Notes

1. Nathaniel Hawthorne, *The Centenary Edition of the Works of Nathaniel Hawthorne*, ed. William Charvat et al., 23 vols. (Columbus: Ohio State University Press, 1962–1997), VI, p. 612. Future references to the *Centenary Edition* will appear as *CE*, followed by the volume and page number.

2. Henry James, *Hawthorne* (London: Macmillan and Co., 1879), p. 39.

3. Ibid., p. 40.

4. Herman Melville, "Hawthorne and His Mosses," in *The Northwestern-Newberry Edition of the Writings of Herman Melville,* vol. IX, *The Piazza Tales and Other Prose Pieces, 1839–1860,* ed. Harrison Hayford, Alma A. MacDougall, and G. Thomas Tanselle (Evanston, Ill.: Northwestern University Press, 1987), p. 251.

5. "Sir William Phips," *CE,* XXII, p. 59.

6. "Passages from a Relinquished Work," *CE,* X, p. 407.

7. See Lea Bertani Vozar Newman, "One-Hundred-and-Fifty Years of Looking At, Into, Through, Behind, Beyond, and Around 'The Minister's Black Veil,'" *Nathaniel Hawthorne Review* 13:2 (Fall 1987), pp. 5–12.

8. Ralph Waldo Emerson, *Emerson in His Journals,* ed. Joel Porte (Cambridge: Harvard University Press, 1982), p. 288.

9. Ibid.

10. Joseph Slater, ed., *The Correspondence of Emerson and Carlyle* (New York: Columbia University Press, 1964), pp. 283–284.

11. Ralph Waldo Emerson, *Emerson: Essays and Lectures,* ed. Joel Porte (New York: Library of America, 1983), p. 70.

12. *CE,* III, p. 63.

13. Edgar Allan Poe, "Tale-Writing—Nathaniel Hawthorne," *Godey's Magazine and Lady's Book* 35 (Nov. 1847), pp, 252–256, quoted in *Nathaniel Hawthorne: The Contemporary Reviews,* ed. John Idol, Jr., and Buford Jones (New York: Cambridge University Press, 1994), p. 104.

14. *CE,* IX, p. 3; Poe, "Tale-Writing," op. cit., p. 98.

15. Melville, "Hawthorne and His Mosses," op. cit., pp. 241, 243.

16. Dan McCall, *Citizens of Somewhere Else: Nathaniel Hawthorne and Henry James* (Ithaca: Cornell University Press, 1998), p. 182.

17. *CE,* VIII, p. 250.

18. *CE,* CXV, p. 384.

19. *CE,* VI, p. 324.

20. *CE,* XVIII, p. 641.

Note on the Text

THE TEXTS OF ALL the stories printed here follow those established by *The Centenary Edition of the Works of Nathaniel Hawthorne* (Columbus: Ohio State University Press, 1974), edited by William Charvat, Roy Harvey Pearce, Claude M. Simpson, Fredson Bowers, Matthew J. Bruccoli, and L. Neal Smith. The editors of the Centenary Edition employ as copy-texts Hawthorne's manuscripts wherever possible. For the larger balance of the short fiction, the editors use the first printings as copy-texts. In some cases, Hawthorne made alterations to his tales and sketches when collecting them for book publication; the editors of the Centenary Edition judge substantive emendations "by the authority of their sources." For a more detailed explanation of these substantive changes, readers should consult the relevant Centenary volumes. In the Centenary Edition, the copy-texts have general authority for accidentals. A full explanation of editorial principles is found in the first four volumes of the Centenary Edition. In the John Harvard Library edition, selections of the tales and sketches are arranged chronologically by the date of their first appearance in serial or book form.

Chronology of Nathaniel Hawthorne's Life

1804   Born July 4, Salem, Massachusetts, second of three children of Nathaniel and Elizabeth Manning Hathorne (the author will add a *w* to the family name after college graduation). Descended on paternal side from the Puritan William Hathorne, who emigrated from England in 1632. Hathorne's son John was one of three judges who presided over the Salem witch trials in 1692.

1808   Father, a sea captain, dies in Surinam; family moves in with mother's parents, the Manning family of Salem.

1813–1815   Taught at home by lexicographer Joseph Emerson Worcester (a rival to Noah Webster).

1818   Family moves to Manning property in Raymond, Maine: Hawthorne briefly allowed to run "quite wild."

1819–1821   Back in Salem with Manning relatives, prepares for college under the direction of a Salem lawyer, Benjamin Lynde Oliver.

1821–1825   Attends Bowdoin College (Brunswick, Maine), where he is an average student with an interest in authorship. Classmates include the future poet Henry Wadsworth Longfellow and Franklin Pierce, who would serve as U.S. president from 1853 to 1857.

1825–1838 SALEM PERIOD: Returning from Bowdoin to the Manning house on Herbert Street in Salem, embarks on literary career. Here, in the "dismal chamber" of a house that Salemites have failed to preserve, "fame was won."

1827 Unable to find a publisher for "Seven Tales of My Native Land" (concerned with "witchcraft and the sea"). The manuscript includes "Hollow of the Three Hills," a version of "Alice Doane's Appeal," and possibly "Wives of the Dead."

1828 Publishes *Fanshawe* anonymously and at his own expense; almost immediately disowns it. Begins serious archival study of New England history.

1829 Fails to find a publisher for "Provincial Tales," which includes "The Gentle Boy," "Roger Malvin's Burial," and "My Kinsman, Major Molineux."

1830–1831 Publishes, unsigned, several historical sketches in the *Salem Gazette*, including "Mrs. Hutchinson."

1832 Publishes (separately, anonymously) "The Gentle Boy," "Roger Malvin's Burial," and "My Kinsman, Major Molineux." On a long summer trip to Vermont and New Hampshire (taken by himself), conceives a set of frame stories involving a wandering Narrator, evoking scenes and telling tales related to the places visited.

1833 Works on two-volume set of frame stories to be called "The Story-Teller."

1834 New publisher rejects "The Story-Teller."

1834–1836 Along with its narrative beginning—"Passages from a Relinquished Work" and "Mr. Higginbotham's Catastrophe"—the dislocated (and still unsigned) tales and sketches of "The Story-Teller" flood the magazines; e.g., "The Notch of the White Mountains," "The Ambitious Guest," "The Great Carbuncle," "Alice Doane's Appeal," "Young Goodman Brown," "The Minister's Black Veil," "Endicott and the Red Cross," "The May-Pole of Merry Mount."

1836 In Boston, aided by sister Elizabeth in Salem, edits the *American Magazine of Useful and Entertaining Knowledge* (a self-improvement periodical that founders after two issues).

1837 Publishes *Twice-told Tales* (a miscellany of eighteen tales and sketches) silently financed by Bowdoin classmate Horatio Bridge. Opening an "intercourse with the world," this first signed work introduces Hawthorne to the Peabody sisters of Salem.

1838   Four "Legends of the Province House" reprise the ideology of the American Revolution and begin the author's association with John O'Sullivan's *Democratic Review*.

1839–1842   INTERLUDE ONE: Boston and West Roxbury.

1839–1840   With help from Elizabeth Peabody—and the patronage of George Bancroft—secures a "day job" in the Boston Custom House. Becomes engaged, writes love letters to Sophia Peabody.

1840   Publishes *Grandfather's Chair* (framed stories of New England History for children).

1841   Resigns from Boston Custom House. In April joins George Ripley's utopian commune in West Roxbury, Massachusetts (Brook Farm); feeling the strains of communal living, resigns membership and leaves at the end of October.

1842   Married to Sophia Peabody on July 9, five days after celebrating his thirty-eighth birthday; moves with his bride to the "Old Manse" in Concord, Massachusetts. New and enlarged edition of *Twice-told Tales* published (adds seventeen items).

1842–1845   OLD MANSE PERIOD: Friendship with Emerson, Alcott, Thoreau, Fuller, Ellery Channing, etc. Writes about two dozen new tales and sketches of contemporaneous ("Transcendentalist") interest.

1842   Publishes "A Virtuoso's Collection."

1843   Publishes "The Hall of Fantasy," "The New Adam and Eve," "The Birth-mark," "The Celestial Rail-road," "Egotism; or, the Bosom-Serpent."

1844   Publishes "The Christmas Banquet," "Earth's Holocaust," "The Artist of the Beautiful," "Rappaccini's Daughter." Daughter Una born.

1845–1849   INTERLUDE TWO: Return to Salem; Surveyor in the Custom House.

1845   Hawthornes, financially strapped, move in with mother and sisters, back in Salem.

1846   With the help of Bridge, Pierce, and other influential friends in the Democratic party, secures lucrative appointment of Surveyor in the Salem Custom House. For three and a half "numbing" hours every morning, gives a share of his life to "Uncle Sam." Publishes new and other (previously uncollected) tales and sketches in *Mosses from an Old Manse*, its preface entitled "The Old Manse." Son Julian born.

1847   Hawthornes rent a small house in Salem (18 Chestnut Street); then, two months later, move to larger quarters (14 Mall Street), where his mother and sister live in a separate apartment on the second floor.

1849–1852   MAJOR PHASE: In addition to several new tales and sketches and a volume of myth stories framed for children, publishes the three "American Romances."

1849   Publishes "Ethan Brand" and "Main-street"; dismissed from Salem Custom House by new Whig administration. Mother dies in July; begins writing *The Scarlet Letter*.

1850   Publishes *The Scarlet Letter* (whose preface, "The Custom-House," contains reference to an "article entitled 'Main Street,' included in the present volume"). Moves from Salem to Lenox in the Berkshires; meets Melville, whose belated review of *Mosses from an Old Manse* appears in *Literary World* for August.

1851   Publishes *The House of the Seven Gables* and *A Wonder-Book for Girls and Boys* (myth stories for children, with a narrative frame). Friendship with Melville (Hawthorne's letters to Melville destroyed). Third edition of *Twice-told Tales* appears, the preface recalling early years as the "obscurest man of letters in America." Daughter Rose born.

1852   Publishes *The Blithedale Romance* (recalling Brook Farm experience). Buys the Wayside (the Alcotts' home) and returns to Concord; sister Louisa killed in steamboat accident. Campaign biography of Franklin Pierce defends "compromise" with the slave South.

1853–1857   INTERLUDE THREE: Consul to Liverpool.

1853   Publishes *Tanglewood Tales* (more myth-stories for children, without frame). Thanks to the Pierce biography, appointed American Consul to Liverpool; begins *English Notebooks*.

1854   Second edition of *Mosses from an Old Manse* appears.

1856–1857   In Liverpool, last of two meetings with a "much overshadowed" Melville, on his way to and returning from a trip to the Holy Land. Resigns Consulship in February 1857, stays on till October.

1858–1859   Travels in France and Italy; keeps *French and Italian Notebooks*.

1859   Returns to England with family; begins *The Marble Faun*; then, with reluctance, moves back to the Wayside in Concord early in the following year.

1860–1864 LAST PHASE: Several romances started but left incomplete.

1860 Publishes *The Marble Faun*, his last completed romance (an international novel that comes out of his *French and Italian Notebooks*).

1861–1863 Takes up and puts aside several romances: American Claimant Manuscripts explore American fascination with, and attraction to, England through a particular American's claim to an English estate; Elixir of Life Manuscripts examine the effects of an individual's search for elongated mortal life.

1862 Essay "Chiefly about War Matters" appears in the *Atlantic Monthly*.

1863 *Our Old Home*, major essays on English culture, published.

1864 Deteriorating health: dies May 19, on a New Hampshire trip undertaken with Pierce. Buried in Concord's Sleepy Hollow Cemetery, near Emerson, Thoreau, and Louisa May Alcott. Melville notes his death in poem "Monody." Posthumous publication of "Scenes from 'The Dolliver Romance.'"

SELECTED STORIES

The Hollow of the Three Hills

IN THOSE STRANGE OLD TIMES, when fantastic dreams and madmen's reveries were realized among the actual circumstances of life, two persons met together at an appointed hour and place. One was a lady, graceful in form and fair of feature, though pale and troubled, and smitten with an untimely blight in what should have been the fullest bloom of her years; the other was an ancient and meanly dressed woman, of ill-favored aspect, and so withered, shrunken and decrepit, that even the space since she began to decay must have exceeded the ordinary term of human existence. In the spot where they encountered, no mortal could observe them. Three little hills stood near each other, and down in the midst of them sunk a hollow basin, almost mathematically circular, two or three hundred feet in breadth, and of such depth that a stately cedar might but just be visible above the sides. Dwarf pines were numerous upon the hills, and partly fringed the outer verge of the intermediate hollow; within which there was nothing but the brown grass of October, and here and there a tree-trunk, that had fallen long ago, and lay mouldering with no green successor from its roots. One of these masses of decaying wood, formerly a majestic oak, rested close beside a pool of green and sluggish water at the bottom of the basin. Such scenes as this (so gray tradition tells) were once the resort of a Power of Evil and his plighted subjects; and here, at midnight or on the dim verge of evening, they were said to stand round the mantling pool, disturbing its putrid waters in the performance of an impious baptismal rite. The chill beauty of an autumnal sunset was now gilding the three hill-tops, whence a paler tint stole down their sides into the hollow.

"Here is our pleasant meeting come to pass," said the aged crone, "according as thou hast desired. Say quickly what thou wouldst have of me, for there is but a short hour that we may tarry here."

As the old withered woman spoke, a smile glimmered on her countenance, like lamplight on the wall of a sepulchre. The lady trembled, and cast her eyes upward to the verge of the basin, as if meditating to return with her purpose unaccomplished. But it was not so ordained.

"I am stranger in this land, as you know," said she at length. "Whence I come it matters not;—but I have left those behind me with whom my fate was intimately bound, and from whom I am cut off forever. There is a weight in my bosom that I cannot away with, and I have come hither to inquire of their welfare."

"And who is there by this green pool, that can bring thee news from the ends of the Earth?" cried the old woman, peering into the lady's face. "Not from my lips mayst thou hear these tidings; yet, be thou bold, and the daylight shall not pass away from yonder hill-top, before thy wish be granted."

"I will do your bidding though I die," replied the lady desperately.

The old woman seated herself on the trunk of the fallen tree, threw aside the hood that shrouded her gray locks, and beckoned her companion to draw near.

"Kneel down," she said, "and lay your forehead on my knees."

She hesitated a moment, but the anxiety, that had long been kindling, burned fiercely up within her. As she knelt down, the border of her garment was dipped into the pool; she laid her forehead on the old woman's knees, and the latter drew a cloak about the lady's face, so that she was in darkness. Then she heard the muttered words of a prayer, in the midst of which she started, and would have arisen.

"Let me flee,—let me flee and hide myself, that they may not look upon me!" she cried. But, with returning recollection, she hushed herself, and was still as death.

For it seemed as if other voices—familiar in infancy, and unforgotten through many wanderings, and in all the vicissitudes of her heart and fortune—were mingling with the accents of the prayer. At first the words were faint and indistinct, not rendered so by distance, but rather resembling the dim pages of a book, which we strive to read by an imperfect and gradually brightening light. In such a manner, as the prayer proceeded, did those voices strengthen upon the ear; till at length the petition ended, and the conversation of an aged man, and of a woman broken and decayed like himself, became distinctly audible to the lady as she knelt. But those strangers appeared not to stand in the hollow depth between the three hills. Their voices were encompassed and re-echoed by the walls of a chamber, the windows of which were rattling in the breeze; the regular vibration of a clock, the crackling of a fire, and the tinkling of the embers as they fell among the ashes, rendered the scene almost as vivid as if painted to the eye. By a melancholy hearth sat these two old people, the man calmly despondent, the woman querulous and tearful, and their words were all of sorrow. They spoke of a daughter, a wanderer they knew not where, bearing dishonor along with her, and leaving shame and affliction to bring their gray heads to the grave. They alluded also to other and more recent woe, but in the midst of their talk, their voices seemed to melt into the sound of the wind sweeping mournfully among the autumn leaves; and when the lady lifted her eyes, there was she kneeling in the hollow between three hills.

"A weary and lonesome time yonder old couple have of it," remarked the old woman, smiling in the lady's face.

"And did you also hear them!" exclaimed she, a sense of intolerable humiliation triumphing over her agony and fear.

"Yea; and we have yet more to hear," replied the old woman. "Wherefore, cover thy face quickly."

Again the withered hag poured forth the monotonous words of a prayer that was not meant to be acceptable in Heaven; and soon, in the pauses of her breath, strange mur-murings began to thicken, gradually increasing so as to drown and overpower the charm by which they grew. Shrieks pierced through the obscurity of sound, and were succeeded by the singing of sweet female voices, which in their turn gave way to a wild roar of laughter, broken suddenly by groanings and sobs, forming altogether a ghastly confusion of terror and mourning and mirth. Chains were rattling, fierce and stern voices uttered threats, and the scourge resounded at their command. All these noises deepened and became substantial to the listener's ear, till she could distinguish every soft and dreamy accent of the love songs, that died causelessly into funeral hymns. She shuddered at the unprovoked wrath which blazed up like the spontaneous kindling of flame, and she grew faint at the fearful merriment, raging miserably around her. In the midst of this wild scene, where unbound passions jostled each other in a drunken career, there was one solemn voice of a man, and a manly and melodious voice it might once have been. He went to-and-fro continually, and his feet sounded upon the floor. In each member of that frenzied company, whose own burning thoughts had become their exclusive world, he sought an auditor for the story of his individual wrong, and interpreted their laughter and tears as his reward of scorn or pity. He spoke of woman's perfidy, of a wife who had broken her holiest vows, of a home and heart made desolate. Even as he went on, the shout, the laugh, the shriek, the sob, rose up in unison, till they changed into the hollow, fitful, and uneven sound of the wind, as it fought among the pine-trees on those three lonely hills. The lady looked up, and there was the withered woman smiling in her face.

"Couldst thou have thought there were such merry times in a Mad House?" inquired the latter.

"True, true," said the lady to herself; "there is mirth within its walls, but misery, misery without."

"Wouldst thou hear more?" demanded the old woman.

"There is one other voice I would fain listen to again," replied the lady faintly.

"Then lay down thy head speedily upon my knees, that thou may'st get thee hence before the hour be past."

The golden skirts of day were yet lingering upon the hills, but deep shades obscured the hollow and the pool, as if sombre night were rising thence to overspread the world. Again that evil woman began to weave her spell. Long did it proceed unanswered, till the knolling of a bell stole in among the intervals of her words, like a clang that had travelled far over valley and rising ground, and was just ready to die in the air. The lady shook upon her companion's knees, as she heard that boding sound. Stronger it grew and sadder, and deepened into the tone of a death-bell, knolling dolefully from some ivy-mantled tower, and bearing tidings of mortality and woe to the cottage, to the hall, and to the solitary wayfarer, that all might weep for the doom appointed in turn to them. Then came a measured tread, passing slowly, slowly on, as of mourners with a coffin, their garments trailing on the ground, so that the car could measure the length of their melancholy array. Before them went the priest, reading the burial-service, while the leaves of his book were rustling in the breeze. And though no voice but his was heard to speak aloud, still there were revilings and anathemas, whispered but distinct, from women and from men, breathed against the daughter who had wrung the aged hearts of her parents,—the wife who had betrayed the trusting fondness of her husband,—the mother who had sinned against natural affection, and left her child to die. The sweeping sound of the funeral train faded away like a thin vapour, and the wind, that just before had seemed to shake the coffin-pall, moaned sadly round the verge of the Hollow between three Hills. But when the old woman stirred the kneeling lady, she lifted not her head.

"Here has been a sweet hour's sport!" said the withered crone, chuckling to herself.

My Kinsman, Major Molineux

AFTER THE KINGS OF Great Britain had assumed the right of appointing the colonial governors, the measures of the latter seldom met with the ready and general approbation, which had been paid to those of their predecessors, under the original charters. The people looked with most jealous scrutiny to the exercise of power, which did not emanate from themselves, and they usually rewarded the rulers with slender gratitude, for the compliances, by which, in softening their instructions from beyond the sea, they had incurred the reprehension of those who gave them. The annals of Massachusetts Bay will inform us, that of six governors, in the space of about forty years from the surrender of the old charter, under James II., two were imprisoned by a popular insurrection; a third, as Hutchinson inclines to believe, was driven from the province by the whizzing of a musket ball; a fourth, in the opinion of the same historian, was hastened to his grave by continual bickerings with the House of Representatives; and the remaining two, as well as their successors, till the Revolution, were favored with few and brief intervals of peaceful sway. The inferior members of the court party, in times of high political excitement, led scarcely a more desirable life. These remarks may serve as preface to the following adventures, which chanced upon a summer night, not far from a hundred years ago. The reader, in order to avoid a long and dry detail of colonial affairs, is requested to dispense with an account of the train of circumstances, that had caused much temporary inflammation of the popular mind.

It was near nine o'clock of a moonlight evening, when a boat crossed the ferry with a single passenger, who had obtained his conveyance, at that unusual hour, by the promise of an extra fare. While he stood on the landing-place, searching in either pocket for the means of fulfilling his agreement, the ferryman lifted a lantern, by the aid of which, and the newly risen moon, he took a very accurate survey of the stranger's figure. He was a youth of barely eighteen years, evidently country-bred, and now, as it should seem, upon his first visit to town. He was clad in a coarse grey coat, well worn, but in excellent repair; his under garments were durably constructed of leather, and sat tight to a pair of serviceable and well-shaped limbs; his stockings of blue yarn, were the incontrovertible handiwork of a mother or a sister; and on his head was a three-cornered hat, which in its better days had perhaps sheltered the graver brow of the lad's father. Under his left arm was a heavy cudgel, formed of an oak sapling, and retaining a part of the hardened root; and his equipment was completed by a wallet, not so abundantly stocked as to incommode the vigorous shoulders on which it hung. Brown, curly hair, well-shaped features, and bright, cheerful eyes, were nature's gifts, and worth all that art could have done for his adornment.

The youth, one of whose names was Robin, finally drew from his pocket the half of a little province-bill of five shillings, which, in the depreciation of that sort of currency, did but satisfy the ferryman's demand, with the surplus of a sexangular piece of parchment valued at three pence. He then walked forward into the town, with as light a step, as if his day's journey had not already exceeded thirty miles, and with as eager an eye, as if he were entering London city, instead of the little metropolis of a New England colony. Before Robin had proceeded far, however, it occurred to him, that he knew not whither to direct his steps; so he paused, and looked up and down the narrow street, scrutinizing the small and mean wooden buildings, that were scattered on either side.

"This low hovel cannot be my kinsman's dwelling," thought he, "nor yonder old house, where the moonlight enters at the broken casement; and truly I see none hereabouts that might be worthy of him. It would have been wise to inquire my way of the ferryman, and doubtless he would have gone with me, and earned a shilling from the Major for his pains. But the next man I meet will do as well."

He resumed his walk, and was glad to perceive that the street now became wider, and the houses more respectable in their appearance. He soon discerned a figure moving on moderately in advance, and hastened his steps to overtake it. As Robin drew nigh, he saw that the passenger was a man in years, with a full periwig of grey hair, a wide-skirted coat of dark cloth, and silk stockings rolled about his knees. He carried a long and polished cane, which he struck down perpendicularly before him, at every step; and at regular intervals he uttered two successive hems, of a peculiarly solemn and sepulchral intonation. Having made these observations, Robin laid hold of the skirt of the old man's coat, just when the light from the open door and windows of a barber's shop, fell upon both their figures.

"Good evening to you, honored Sir," said he, making a low bow, and still retaining his hold of the skirt. "I pray you to tell me whereabouts is the dwelling of my kinsman, Major Molineux?"

The youth's question was uttered very loudly; and one of the barbers, whose razor was descending on a well-soaped chin, and another who was dressing a Ramillies wig, left their occupations, and came to the door. The citizen, in the meantime, turned a long favored countenance upon Robin, and answered him in a tone of excessive anger and annoyance. His two sepulchral hems, however, broke into the very centre of his rebuke, with most singular effect, like a thought of the cold grave obtruding among wrathful passions.

"Let go my garment, fellow! I tell you, I know not the man you speak of. What! I have authority, I have—hem, hem—authority; and if this be the respect you show your betters, your feet shall be brought acquainted with the stocks, by daylight, tomorrow morning!"

Robin released the old man's skirt, and hastened away, pursued by an ill-mannered roar of laughter from the barber's shop. He was at first considerably surprised by the result of his question, but, being a shrewd youth, soon thought himself able to account for the mystery.

"This is some country representative," was his conclusion, "who has never seen the inside of my kinsman's door, and lacks the breeding to answer a stranger civilly. The man is old, or verily—I might be tempted to turn back and smite him on the nose. Ah, Robin, Robin! even the barber's boys laugh at you, for choosing such a guide! You will be wiser in time, friend Robin."

He now became entangled in a succession of crooked and narrow streets, which crossed each other, and meandered at no great distance from the water-side. The smell of tar was obvious to his nostrils, the masts of vessels pierced the moonlight above the tops of the buildings, and the numerous signs, which Robin paused to read, informed him that he was near the centre of business. But the streets were empty, the shops were closed, and lights were visible only in the second stories of a few dwelling-houses. At length, on the corner of a narrow lane, through which he was passing, he beheld the broad countenance of a British hero swinging before the door of an inn, whence proceeded the voices of many guests. The casement of one of the lower windows was thrown back, and a very thin curtain permitted Robin to distinguish a party at supper, round a well-furnished table. The fragrance of the good cheer steamed forth into the outer air, and the youth could not fail to recollect, that the last remnant of his travelling stock of provision had yielded to his morning appetite, and that noon had found, and left him, dinnerless.

"Oh, that a parchment three-penny might give me a right to sit down at yonder table," said Robin, with a sigh. "But the Major will make me welcome to the best of his victuals; so I will even step boldly in, and inquire my way to his dwelling."

He entered the tavern, and was guided by the murmur of voices, and fumes of tobacco, to the public room. It was a long and low apartment, with oaken walls, grown dark in the continual smoke, and a floor, which was thickly sanded, but of no immaculate purity. A number of persons, the larger part of whom appeared to be mariners, or in some way connected with the sea, occupied the wooden benches, or leather-bottomed chairs, conversing on various matters, and occasionally lending their attention to some topic of general interest. Three or four little groups were draining as many bowls of punch, which the great West India trade had long since made a familiar drink in the colony. Others, who had the aspect of men who lived by regular and laborious handicraft, preferred the insulated bliss of an unshared potation, and became more taciturn under its influence. Nearly all, in short, evinced a predilection for the Good Creature in some of its various shapes, for this is a vice, to which, as the Fast-day sermons of a hundred years ago will testify, we have a long hereditary claim. The only guests to whom Robin's sympathies inclined him, were two or three sheepish countrymen, who were using the inn somewhat after the fashion of a Turkish Caravansary; they had gotten themselves into the darkest corner of the room, and, heedless of the Nicotian atmosphere, were supping on the bread of their own ovens, and the bacon cured in their own chimney-smoke. But though Robin felt a sort of brotherhood with these strangers, his eyes were attracted from them, to a person who stood near the door, holding whispered conversation with a group of ill-dressed associates. His features were separately striking almost to grotesqueness, and the whole face left a deep impression in the memory. The forehead bulged out into a double prominence, with a vale between; the nose came boldly forth in an irregular curve, and its bridge was of more than a finger's breadth; the eyebrows were deep and shaggy, and the eyes glowed beneath them like fire in a cave.

While Robin deliberated of whom to inquire respecting his kinsman's dwelling, he was accosted by the innkeeper, a little man in a stained white apron, who had come to pay his professional welcome to the stranger. Being in the second generation from a French Protestant, he seemed to have inherited the courtesy of his parent nation; but no variety of circumstance was ever known to change his voice from the one shrill note in which he now addressed Robin.

"From the country, I presume, Sir?" said he, with a profound bow. "Beg to congratulate you on your arrival, and trust you intend a long stay with us. Fine town here, Sir, beautiful buildings, and much that may interest a stranger. May I hope for the honor of your commands in respect to supper?"

"The man sees a family likeness! the rogue has guessed that I am related to the Major!" thought Robin, who had hitherto experienced little superfluous civility.

All eyes were now turned on the country lad, standing at the door, in his worn three-cornered hat, grey coat, leather breeches, and blue yarn stockings, leaning on an oaken cudgel, and bearing a wallet on his back.

Robin replied to the courteous innkeeper, with such an assumption of consequence, as befitted the Major's relative.

"My honest friend," he said, I shall make it a point to patronize your house on some occasion, when—" here he could not help lowering his voice—"I may have more than a parchment three-pence in my pocket. My present business," continued he, speaking with lofty confidence, "is merely to inquire the way to the dwelling of my kinsman, Major Molineux."

There was a sudden and general movement in the room, which Robin interpreted as expressing the eagerness of each individual to become his guide. But the innkeeper turned his eyes to a written paper on the wall, which he read, or seemed to read, with occasional recurrences to the young man's figure.

"What have we here?" said he, breaking his speech into little dry fragments. " 'Left the house of the subscriber, bounden servant, Hezekiah Mudge—had on, when he went away, grey coat, leather breeches, master's third best hat. One pound currency reward to whoever shall lodge him in any jail in the province.' Better trudge, boy, better trudge!"

Robin had begun to draw his hand towards the lighter end of the oak cudgel, but a strange hostility in every countenance, induced him to relinquish his purpose of breaking the courteous innkeeper's head. As he turned to leave the room, he encountered a sneering glance from the bold-featured personage whom he had before noticed; and no sooner was he beyond the door, than he heard a general laugh, in which the innkeeper's voice might be distinguished, like the dropping of small stones into a kettle.

"Now is it not strange," thought Robin, with his usual shrewdness, "is it not strange, that the confession of an empty pocket, should outweigh the name of my kinsman, Major Molineux? Oh, if I had one of these grinning rascals in the woods, where I and my oak sapling grew up together, I would teach him that my arm is heavy, though my purse be light!"

On turning the corner of the narrow lane, Robin found himself in a spacious street, with an unbroken line of lofty houses on each side, and a steepled building at the upper end, whence the ringing of a bell announced the hour of nine. The light of the moon, and the lamps from numerous shop windows, discovered people promenading on the pavement, and amongst them, Robin hoped to recognize his hitherto inscrutable relative. The result of his former inquiries made him unwilling to hazard another, in a scene of such publicity, and he determined to walk slowly and silently up the street, thrusting his face close to that of every elderly gentleman, in search of the Major's lineaments. In his progress, Robin encountered many gay and gallant figures. Embroidered garments, of showy colors, enormous periwigs, gold-laced hats, and silver hiked swords, glided past him and dazzled his optics. Travelled youths, imitators of the European fine gentlemen of the period, trod jauntily along, half-dancing to the fashionable tunes which they hummed, and making poor Robin ashamed of his quiet and natural gait. At length, after many pauses to examine the gorgeous display of goods in the shop windows, and after suffering some rebukes for the impertinence of his scrutiny into people's faces, the Major's kinsman found himself near the steepled building, still unsuccessful in his search. As yet, however, he had seen only one side of the thronged street; so Robin crossed, and continued the same sort of inquisition down the opposite pavement, with stronger hopes than the philosopher seeking an honest man, but with no better fortune. He had arrived about midway towards the lower end, from which his course began, when he overheard the approach of some one, who struck down a cane on the flag-stones at every step, uttering, at regular intervals, two sepulchral hems.

"Mercy on us!" quoth Robin, recognizing the sound.

Turning a corner, which chanced to be close at his right hand, he hastened to pursue his researches, in some other part of the town. His patience was now wearing low, and he seemed to feel more fatigue from his rambles since he crossed the ferry, than from his journey of several days on the other side. Hunger also pleaded loudly within him, and Robin began to balance the propriety of demanding, violently and with lifted cudgel, the necessary guidance from the first solitary passenger, whom he should meet. While a resolution to this effect was gaining strength, he entered a street of mean appearance, on either side of which, a row of ill-built houses was straggling towards the harbor. The moonlight fell upon no passenger along the whole extent, but in the third domicile which Robin passed, there was a half-opened door, and his keen glance detected a woman's garment within.

"My luck may be better here," said he to himself.

Accordingly, he approached the door, and beheld it shut closer as he did so; yet an open space remained, sufficing for the fair occupant to observe the stranger, without a corresponding display on her part. All that Robin could discern was a strip of scarlet petticoat, and the occasional sparkle of an eye, as if the moonbeams were trembling on some bright thing.

"Pretty mistress,"—for I may call her so with a good conscience, thought the shrewd youth, since I know nothing to the contrary— "my sweet pretty mistress, will you be kind enough to tell me whereabouts I must seek the dwelling of my kinsman, Major Molineux?"

Robin's voice was plaintive and winning, and the female, seeing nothing to be shunned in the handsome country youth, thrust open the door, and came forth into the moonlight. She was a dainty little figure, with a white neck, round arms, and a slender waist, at the extremity of which her scarlet petticoat jutted out over a hoop, as if she were standing in a balloon. Moreover, her face was oval and pretty, her hair dark beneath the little cap, and her bright eyes possessed a sly freedom, which triumphed over those of Robin.

"Major Molineux dwells here," said this fair woman.

Now her voice was the sweetest Robin had heard that night, the airy counterpart of a stream of melted silver; yet he could not help doubting whether that sweet voice spoke Gospel truth. He looked up and down the mean street, and then surveyed the house before which they stood. It was a small, dark edifice of two stories, the second of which projected over the lower floor; and the front apartment had the aspect of a shop for petty commodities.

"Now truly I am in luck," replied Robin, cunningly, "and so indeed is my kinsman, the Major, in having so pretty a housekeeper. But I prithee trouble him to step to the door; I will deliver him a message from his friends in the country, and then go back to my lodgings at the inn."

"Nay, the Major has been a-bed this hour or more," said the lady of the scarlet petticoat; "and it would be to little purpose to disturb him to-night, seeing his evening draught was of the strongest. But he is a kind-hearted man, and it would be as much as my life's worth, to let a kinsman of his turn away from the door. You are the good old gentleman's very picture, and I could swear that was his rainy-weather hat. Also, he has garments very much resembling those leather—But come in, I pray, for I bid you hearty welcome in his name."

So saying, the fair and hospitable dame took our hero by the hand; and though the touch was light, and the force was gentleness, and though Robin read in her eyes what he did not hear in her words, yet the slender waisted woman, in the scarlet petticoat, proved stronger than the athletic country youth. She had drawn his half-willing footsteps nearly to the threshold, when the opening of a door in the neighborhood, startled the Major's housekeeper, and, leaving the Major's kinsman, she vanished speedily into her own domicile. A heavy yawn preceded the appearance of a man, who, like the Moonshine of Pyramus and Thisbe, carried a lantern, needlessly aiding his sister luminary in the heavens. As he walked sleepily up the street, he turned his broad, dull face on Robin, and displayed a long staff, spiked at the end.

"Home, vagabond, home!" said the watchman, in accents that seemed to fall asleep as soon as they were uttered. "Home, or we'll set you in the stocks by peep of day!"

"This is the second hint of the kind," thought Robin. "I wish they would end my difficulties, by setting me there to-night."

Nevertheless, the youth felt an instinctive antipathy towards the guardian of midnight order, which at first prevented him from asking his usual question. But just when the man was about to vanish behind the corner, Robin resolved not to lose the opportunity, and shouted lustily after him—

"I say, friend! will you guide me to the house of my kinsman, Major Molineux?"

The watchman made no reply, but turned the corner and was gone; yet Robin seemed to hear the sound of drowsy laughter stealing along the solitary street. At that moment, also, a pleasant titter saluted him from the open window above his head; he looked up, and caught the sparkle of a saucy eye; a round arm beckoned to him, and next he heard light footsteps descending the staircase within. But Robin, being of the household of a New England clergyman, was a good youth, as well as a shrewd one; so he resisted temptation, and fled away.

He now roamed desperately, and at random, through the town, almost ready to believe that a spell was on him, like that, by which a wizard of his country, had once kept three pursuers wandering, a whole winter night, within twenty paces of the cottage which they sought. The streets lay before him, strange and desolate, and the lights were extinguished in almost every house. Twice, however, little parties

of men, among whom Robin distinguished individuals in outlandish attire, came hurrying along, but though on both occasions they
paused to address him, such intercourse did not at all enlighten his
perplexity. They did but utter a few words in some language of which
Robin knew nothing, and perceiving his inability to answer, bestowed
a curse upon him in plain English, and hastened away. Finally, the lad
determined to knock at the door of every mansion that might appear
worthy to be occupied by his kinsman, trusting that perseverance
would overcome the fatality which had hitherto thwarted him. Firm
in this resolve, he was passing beneath the walls of a church, which
formed the corner of two streets, when, as he turned into the shade of
its steeple, he encountered a bulky stranger, muffled in a cloak. The
man was proceeding with the speed of earnest business, but Robin
planted himself full before him, holding the oak cudgel with both
hands across his body, as a bar to further passage.

"Halt, honest man, and answer me a question," said he, very resolutely. "Tell me, this instant, whereabouts is the dwelling of my kinsman, Major Molineux?"

"Keep your tongue between your teeth, fool, and let me pass," said
a deep, gruff voice, which Robin partly remembered. "Let me pass, I
say, or I'll strike you to the earth!"

"No, no, neighbor!" cried Robin, flourishing his cudgel, and then
thrusting its larger end close to the man's muffled face. "No, no, I'm
not the fool you take me for, nor do you pass, till I have an answer to
my question. Whereabouts is the dwelling of my kinsman, Major Molineux?"

The stranger, instead of attempting to force his passage, stept back
into the moonlight, unmuffled his own face and stared full into that
of Robin.

"Watch here an hour, and Major Molineux will pass by," said he.

Robin gazed with dismay and astonishment, on the unprecedented

physiognomy of the speaker. The forehead with its double prominence, the broad-hooked nose, the shaggy eyebrows, and fiery eyes,
were those which he had noticed at the inn, but the man's complexion had undergone a singular, or, more properly, a two-fold change.
One side of the face blazed of an intense red, while the other was black
as midnight, the division line being in the broad bridge of the nose;
and a mouth, which seemed to extend from ear to ear, was black or
red, in contrast to the color of the cheek. The effect was as if two individual devils, a fiend of fire and a fiend of darkness, had united
themselves to form this infernal visage. The stranger grinned in Robin's face, muffled his particolored features, and was out of sight in a
moment.

"Strange things we travellers see!" ejaculated Robin.

He seated himself, however, upon the steps of the church-door, resolving to wait the appointed time for his kinsman's appearance. A
few moments were consumed in philosophical speculations, upon
the species of the *genus homo,* who had just left him, but having settled this point shrewdly, rationally, and satisfactorily, he was compelled to look elsewhere for amusement. And first he threw his eyes
along the street; it was of more respectable appearance than most of
those into which he had wandered, and the moon, "creating, like the
imaginative power, a beautiful strangeness in familiar objects," gave
something of romance to a scene, that might not have possessed it in
the light of day. The irregular, and often quaint architecture of the
houses, some of whose roofs were broken into numerous little peaks;
while others ascended, steep and narrow, into a single point; and others again were square; the pure milk-white of some of their complexions, the aged darkness of others, and the thousand sparklings, reflected from bright substances in the plastered walls of many; these
matters engaged Robin's attention for awhile, and then began to grow
wearisome. Next he endeavored to define the forms of distant objects,

starting away with almost ghostly indistinctness, just as his eye appeared to grasp them; and finally he took a minute survey of an edifice, which stood on the opposite side of the street, directly in front of the church-door, where he was stationed. It was a large square mansion, distinguished from its neighbors by a balcony, which rested on tall pillars, and by an elaborate Gothic window, communicating therewith.

"Perhaps this is the very house I have been seeking," thought Robin.

Then he strove to speed away the time, by listening to a murmur, which swept continually along the street, yet was scarcely audible, except to an unaccustomed ear like his; it was a low, dull, dreamy sound, compounded of many noises, each of which was at too great a distance to be separately heard. Robin marvelled at this snore of a sleeping town, and marvelled more, whenever its continuity was broken, by now and then a distant shout, apparently loud where it originated. But altogether it was a sleep-inspiring sound, and to shake off its drowsy influence, Robin arose, and climbed a window-frame, that he might view the interior of the church. There the moonbeams came trembling in, and fell down upon the deserted pews, and extended along the quiet aisles. A fainter, yet more awful radiance, was hovering round the pulpit, and one solitary ray had dared to rest upon the opened page of the great Bible. Had Nature, in that deep hour, become a worshipper in the house, which man had builded? Or was that heavenly light the visible sanctity of the place, visible because no earthly and impure feet were within the walls? The scene made Robin's heart shiver with a sensation of loneliness, stronger than he had ever felt in the remotest depths of his native woods; so he turned away, and sat down again before the door. There were graves around the church, and now an uneasy thought obtruded into Robin's breast. What if the object of his search, which had been so often and so strangely thwarted, were all the time mouldering in his shroud? What if his kinsman should glide through yonder gate, and nod and smile to him in passing dimly by?

"Oh, that any breathing thing were here with me!" said Robin.

Recalling his thoughts from this uncomfortable track, he sent them over forest, hill, and stream, and attempted to imagine how that evening of ambiguity and weariness, had been spent by his father's household. He pictured them assembled at the door, beneath the tree, the great old tree, which had been spared for its huge twisted trunk, and venerable shade, when a thousand leafy brethren fell. There, at the going down of the summer sun, it was his father's custom to perform domestic worship, that the neighbors might come and join with him like brothers of the family, and that the wayfaring man might pause to drink at that fountain, and keep his heart pure by freshening the memory of home. Robin distinguished the seat of every individual of the little audience; he saw the good man in the midst, holding the Scriptures in the golden light that shone from the western clouds; he beheld him close the book, and all rise up to pray. He heard the old thanksgivings for daily mercies, the old supplications for their continuance, to which he had so often listened in weariness, but which were now among his dear remembrances. He perceived the slight inequality of his father's voice when he came to speak of the Absent One; he noted how his mother turned her face to the broad and knotted trunk; how his elder brother scorned, because the beard was rough upon his upper lip, to permit his features to be moved; how his younger sister drew down a low hanging branch before her eyes; and how the little one of all, whose sports had hitherto broken the decorum of the scene, understood the prayer for her playmate, and burst into clamorous grief. Then he saw them go in at the door; and when Robin would have entered also, the latch tinkled into its place, and he was excluded from his home.

"Am I here, or there?" cried Robin, starting; for all at once, when his thoughts had become visible and audible in a dream, the long, wide, solitary street shone out before him.

He aroused himself, and endeavored to fix his attention steadily upon the large edifice which he had surveyed before. But still his mind kept vibrating between fancy and reality; by turns, the pillars of the balcony lengthened into the tall, bare stems of pines, dwindled down to human figures, settled again in their true shape and size, and then commenced a new succession of changes. For a single moment, when he deemed himself awake, he could have sworn that a visage, one which he seemed to remember, yet could not absolutely name as his kinsman's, was looking towards him from the Gothic window. A deeper sleep wrestled with, and nearly overcame him, but fled at the sound of footsteps along the opposite pavement. Robin rubbed his eyes, discerned a man passing at the foot of the balcony, and addressed him in a loud, peevish, and lamentable cry.

"Halloo, friend! must I wait here all night for my kinsman, Major Molineux?"

The sleeping echoes awoke, and answered the voice; and the passenger, barely able to discern a figure sitting in the oblique shade of the steeple, traversed the street to obtain a nearer view. He was himself a gentleman in his prime, of open, intelligent, cheerful, and altogether prepossessing countenance. Perceiving a country youth, apparently homeless and without friends, he accosted him in a tone of real kindness, which had become strange to Robin's ears.

"Well, my good lad, why are you sitting here?" inquired he. "Can I be of service to you in any way?"

"I am afraid not, Sir," replied Robin, despondingly; "yet I shall take it kindly, if you'll answer me a single question. I've been searching half the night for one Major Molineux; now, Sir, is there really such a person in these parts, or am I dreaming?"

"Major Molineux! The name is not altogether strange to me," said the gentleman, smiling. "Have you any objection to telling me the nature of your business with him?"

Then Robin briefly related that his father was a clergyman, settled on a small salary, at a long distance back in the country, and that he and Major Molineux were brothers' children. The Major, having inherited riches, and acquired civil and military rank, had visited his cousin in great pomp a year or two before; had manifested much interest in Robin and an elder brother, and, being childless himself, had thrown out hints respecting the future establishment of one of them in life. The elder brother was destined to succeed to the farm, which his father cultivated, in the interval of sacred duties; it was therefore determined that Robin should profit by his kinsman's generous intentions, especially as he had seemed to be rather the favorite, and was thought to possess other necessary endowments.

"For I have the name of being a shrewd youth," observed Robin, in this part of his story.

"I doubt not you deserve it," replied his new friend, good naturedly; "but pray proceed."

"Well, Sir, being nearly eighteen years old, and well grown, as you see," continued Robin, raising himself to his full height, "I thought it high time to begin the world. So my mother and sister put me in handsome trim, and my father gave me half the remnant of his last year's salary, and five days ago I started for this place, to pay the Major a visit. But would you believe it, Sir? I crossed the ferry a little after dusk, and have yet found nobody that would show me the way to his dwelling; only an hour or two since, I was told to wait here, and Major Molineux would pass by."

"Can you describe the man who told you this?" inquired the gentleman.

"Oh, he was a very ill-favored fellow, Sir," replied Robin, "with two great bumps on his forehead, a hook nose, fiery eyes, and, what struck me as the strangest, his face was of two different colors. Do you happen to know such a man, Sir?"

"Not intimately," answered the stranger, "but I chanced to meet him a little time previous to your stopping me. I believe you may trust his word, and that the Major will very shortly pass through this street. In the mean time, as I have a singular curiosity to witness your meeting, I will sit down here upon the steps, and bear you company."

He seated himself accordingly, and soon engaged his companion in animated discourse. It was but of brief continuance, however, for a noise of shouting, which had long been remotely audible, drew so much nearer, that Robin inquired its cause.

"What may be the meaning of this uproar?" asked he. "Truly, if your town be always as noisy, I shall find little sleep, while I am an inhabitant."

"Why, indeed, friend Robin, there do appear to be three or four riotous fellows abroad to-night," replied the gentleman. "You must not expect all the stillness of your native woods, here in our streets. But the watch will shortly be at the heels of these lads, and—"

"Aye, and set them in the stocks by peep of day," interrupted Robin, recollecting his own encounter with the drowsy lantern-bearer. "But, dear Sir, if I may trust my ears, an army of watchmen would never make head against such a multitude of rioters. There were at least a thousand voices went to make up that one shout."

"May not one man have several voices, Robin, as well as two complexions?" said his friend.

"Perhaps a man may; but Heaven forbid that a woman should!" responded the shrewd youth, thinking of the seductive tones of the Major's housekeeper.

The sounds of a trumpet in some neighboring street now became so evident and continual, that Robin's curiosity was strongly excited.

In addition to the shouts, he heard frequent bursts from many instruments of discord, and a wild and confused laughter filled up the intervals. Robin rose from the steps, and looked wistfully towards a point, whither several people seemed to be hastening.

"Surely some prodigious merrymaking is going on," exclaimed he. "I have laughed very little since I left home, Sir, and should be sorry to lose an opportunity. Shall we just step round the comer by that darkish house, and take our share of the fun?"

"Sit down again, sit down, good Robin," replied the gentleman, laying his hand on the skirt of the grey coat. "You forget that we must wait here for your kinsman; and there is reason to believe that he will pass by, in the course of a very few moments."

The near approach of the uproar had now disturbed the neighborhood; windows flew open on all sides; and many heads, in the attire of the pillow, and confused by sleep suddenly broken, were protruded to the gaze of whoever had leisure to observe them. Eager voices hailed each other from house to house, all demanding the explanation, which not a soul could give. Half-dressed men hurried towards the unknown commotion, stumbling as they went over the stone steps, that thrust themselves into the narrow foot-walk. The shouts, the laughter, and the tuneless bray, the antipodes of music, came onward with increasing din, till scattered individuals, and then denser bodies, began to appear round a corner, at the distance of a hundred yards.

"Will you recognize your kinsman, Robin, if he passes in this crowd?" inquired the gentleman.

"Indeed, I can't warrant it, Sir; but I'll take my stand here, and keep a bright look out," answered Robin, descending to the outer edge of the pavement.

A mighty stream of people now emptied into the street, and came rolling slowly towards the church. A single horseman wheeled the

corner in the midst of them, and close behind him came a band of
fearful wind-instruments, sending forth a fresher discord, now that
no intervening buildings kept it from the ear. Then a redder light
disturbed the moonbeams, and a dense multitude of torches shone
along the street, concealing by their glare whatever object they illuminated. The single horseman, clad in a military dress, and bearing
a drawn sword, rode onward as the leader, and, by his fierce and variegated countenance, appeared like war personified; the red of one
cheek was an emblem of fire and sword; the blackness of the other
betokened the mourning which attends them. In his train, were wild
figures in the Indian dress, and many fantastic shapes without a
model, giving the whole march a visionary air, as if a dream had broken forth from some feverish brain, and were sweeping visibly
through the midnight streets. A mass of people, inactive, except as applauding spectators, hemmed the procession in, and several women
ran along the sidewalks, piercing the confusion of heavier sounds,
with their shrill voices of mirth or terror.

"The double-faced fellow has his eye upon me," muttered Robin,
with an indefinite but uncomfortable idea, that he was himself to bear
a part in the pageantry.

The leader turned himself in the saddle, and fixed his glance full
upon the country youth, as the steed went slowly by. When Robin had
freed his eyes from those fiery ones, the musicians were passing before him, and the torches were close at hand; but the unsteady brightness of the latter formed a veil which he could not penetrate. The
rattling of wheels over the stones sometimes found its way to his ear,
and confused traces of a human form appeared at intervals, and then
melted into the vivid light. A moment more, and the leader thundered a command to halt; the trumpets vomited a horrid breath, and
held their peace; the shouts and laughter of the people died away, and

there remained only a universal hum, nearly allied to silence. Right before Robin's eyes was an uncovered cart. There the torches blazed the brightest, there the moon shone out like day, and there, in tar-and-feathery dignity, sate his kinsman, Major Molineux!

He was an elderly man, of large and majestic person, and strong, square features, betokening a steady soul; but steady as it was, his enemies had found the means to shake it. His face was pale as death, and far more ghastly; the broad forehead was contracted in his agony, so that his eyebrows formed one grizzled line; his eyes were red and wild, and the foam hung white upon his quivering lip. His whole frame was agitated by a quick, and continual tremor, which his pride strove to quell, even in those circumstances of overwhelming humiliation. But perhaps the bitterest pang of all was when his eyes met those of Robin; for he evidently knew him on the instant, as the youth stood witnessing the foul disgrace of a head that had grown grey in honor. They stared at each other in silence, and Robin's knees shook, and his hair bristled, with a mixture of pity and terror. Soon, however, a bewildering excitement began to seize upon his mind; the preceding adventures of the night, the unexpected appearance of the crowd, the torches, the confused din, and the hush that followed, the spectre of his kinsman reviled by that great multitude, all this, and more than all, a perception of tremendous ridicule in the whole scene, affected him with a sort of mental inebriety. At that moment a voice of sluggish merriment saluted Robin's ears; he turned instinctively, and just behind the corner of the church stood the lantern-bearer, rubbing his eyes, and drowsily enjoying the lad's amazement. Then he heard a peal of laughter like the ringing of silvery bells; a woman twitched his arm, a saucy eye met his, and he saw the lady of the scarlet petticoat. A sharp, dry cachinnation appealed to his memory, and, standing on tiptoe in the crowd, with his white apron over his head, he beheld the courteous little innkeeper. And lastly, there sailed over the heads of the multitude a great, broad laugh, broken in the midst by two sepulchral hems; thus—

"Haw, haw, haw—hem, hem—haw, haw, haw, haw!"

The sound proceeded from the balcony of the opposite edifice, and thither Robin turned his eyes. In front of the Gothic window stood the old citizen, wrapped in a wide gown, his grey periwig exchanged for a nightcap, which was thrust back from his forehead, and his silk stockings hanging down about his legs. He supported himself on his polished cane in a fit of convulsive merriment, which manifested itself on his solemn old features, like a funny inscription on a tombstone. Then Robin seemed to hear the voices of the barbers; of the guests of the inn; and of all who had made sport of him that night. The contagion was spreading among the multitude, when, all at once, it seized upon Robin, and he sent forth a shout of laughter that echoed through the street; every man shook his sides, every man emptied his lungs, but Robin's shout was the loudest there. The cloud-spirits peeped from their silvery islands, as the congregated mirth went roaring up the sky! The Man in the Moon heard the far bellow; "Oho," quoth he, "the old Earth is frolicsome to-night!"

When there was a momentary calm in that tempestuous sea of sound, the leader gave the sign, the procession resumed its march. On they went, like fiends that throng in mockery round some dead potentate, mighty no more, but majestic still in his agony. On they went, in counterfeited pomp, in senseless uproar, in frenzied merriment, trampling all on an old man's heart. On swept the tumult, and left a silent street behind.

"Well, Robin, are you dreaming?" inquired the gentleman, laying his hand on the youth's shoulder.

Robin started, and withdrew his arm from the stone post, to which he had instinctively clung, while the living stream rolled by him. His cheek was somewhat pale, and his eye not quite so lively as in the earlier part of the evening.

"Will you be kind enough to show me the way to the ferry?" said he, after a moment's pause.

"You have then adopted a new subject of inquiry?" observed his companion, with a smile.

"Why, yes, Sir," replied Robin, rather dryly. "Thanks to you, and to my other friends, I have at last met my kinsman, and he will scarce desire to see my face again. I begin to grow weary of a town life, Sir. Will you show me the way to the ferry?"

"No, my good friend Robin, not to-night, at least," said the gentleman. "Some few days hence, if you continue to wish it, I will speed you on your journey. Or, if you prefer to remain with us, perhaps, as you are a shrewd youth, you may rise in the world, without the help of your kinsman, Major Molineux."

Roger Malvin's Burial

ONE OF THE FEW incidents of Indian warfare, naturally susceptible of the moonlight of romance, was that expedition, undertaken, for the defence of the frontiers, in the year 1725, which resulted in the well-remembered "Lovell's Fight." Imagination, by casting certain circumstances judiciously into the shade, may see much to admire in the heroism of a little band, who gave battle to twice their number in the heart of the enemy's country. The open bravery displayed by both parties was in accordance with civilized ideas of valor, and chivalry itself might not blush to record the deeds of one or two individuals. The battle, though so fatal to those who fought, was not unfortunate in its consequences to the country; for it broke the strength of a tribe, and conduced to the peace which subsisted during several ensuing years. History and tradition are unusually minute in their memorials of this affair; and the captain of a scouting party of frontier-men has acquired as actual a military renown, as many a victorious leader of thousands. Some of the incidents contained in the following pages will be recognized, notwithstanding the substitution of fictitious names, by such as have heard, from old men's lips, the fate of the few combatants who were in a condition to retreat, after "Lovell's Fight."

The early sunbeams hovered cheerfully upon the tree-tops, beneath which two weary and wounded men had stretched their limbs the night before. Their bed of withered oak-leaves was strewn upon the small level space, at the foot of a rock, situated near the summit of one of the gentle swells, by which the face of the country is there diversified. The mass of granite, rearing its smooth, flat surface, fifteen or twenty feet above their heads, was not unlike a gigantic gravestone, upon which the veins seemed to form an inscription in forgotten characters. On a tract of several acres around this rock, oaks and other hard-wood trees had supplied the place of the pines, which were the usual growth of the land; and a young and vigorous sapling stood close beside the travellers.

The severe wound of the elder man had probably deprived him of sleep; for, so soon as the first ray of sunshine rested on the top of the highest tree, he reared himself painfully from his recumbent posture, and sat erect. The deep lines of his countenance, and the scattered grey of his hair, marked him as past the middle age; but his muscular frame would, but for the effects of his wound, have been as capable of sustaining fatigue, as in the early vigor of life. Languor and exhaustion now sat upon his haggard features, and the despairing glance which he sent forward through the depths of the forest, proved his own conviction that his pilgrimage was at an end. He next turned his eyes to the companion, who reclined by his side. The youth, for he had scarcely attained the years of manhood, lay, with his head upon his arm, in the embrace of an unquiet sleep, which a thrill of pain from his wounds seemed each moment on the point of breaking. His right hand grasped a musket, and, to judge from the violent action of his features, his slumbers were bringing back a vision of the conflict, of which he was one of the few survivors. A shout,—deep and loud to his dreaming fancy,—found its way in an imperfect murmur to his lips, and, starting even at the slight sound of his own voice, he suddenly awoke. The first act of reviving recollection, was to make anxious inquiries respecting the condition of his wounded fellow traveller. The latter shook his head.

"Reuben, my boy," said he, "this rock, beneath which we sit, will serve for an old hunter's grave-stone. There is many and many a long mile of howling wilderness before us yet; nor would it avail me anything, if the smoke of my own chimney were but on the other side of that swell of land. The Indian bullet was deadlier than I thought."

"You are weary with our three days' travel," replied the youth, "and a little longer rest will recruit you. Sit you here, while I search the woods for the herbs and roots, that must be our sustenance; and having eaten, you shall lean on me, and we will turn our faces homeward. I doubt not, that, with my help, you can attain to some one of the frontier garrisons."

"There is not two days' life in me, Reuben," said the other, calmly, "and I will no longer burthen you with my useless body, when you can scarcely support your own. Your wounds are deep, and your strength is failing fast; yet, if you hasten onward alone, you may be preserved. For me there is no hope; and I will await death here."

"If it must be so, I will remain and watch by you," said Reuben, resolutely.

"No, my son, no," rejoined his companion. "Let the wish of a dying man have weight with you; give me one grasp of your hand, and get you hence. Think you that my last moments will be eased by the thought, that I leave you to die a more lingering death? I have loved you like a father, Reuben, and, at a time like this, I should have something of a father's authority. I charge you to be gone, that I may die in peace."

"And because you have been a father to me, should I therefore leave you to perish, and to lie unburied in the wilderness?" exclaimed the youth. "No; if your end be in truth approaching, I will watch by you, and receive your parting words. I will dig a grave here by the rock, in which, if my weakness overcome me, we will rest together; or, if Heaven gives me strength, I will seek my way home."

"In the cities, and wherever men dwell," replied the other, "they bury their dead in the earth; they hide them from the sight of the living; but here, where no step may pass, perhaps for a hundred years, wherefore should I not rest beneath the open sky, covered only by the oak-leaves, when the autumn, winds shall strew them? And for a monument, here is this grey rock, on which my dying hand shall carve the name of Roger Malvin; and the traveller in days to come will know, that here sleeps a hunter and a warrior. Tarry not, then, for a folly like this, but hasten away, if not for your own sake, for hers who will else be desolate."

Malvin spoke the last few words in a faultering voice, and their effect upon his companion was strongly visible. They reminded him that there were other, and less questionable duties, than that of sharing the fate of a man whom his death could not benefit. Nor can it be affirmed that no selfish feeling strove to enter Reuben's heart, though the consciousness made him more earnestly resist his companion's entreaties.

"How terrible, to wait the slow approach of death, in this solitude!" exclaimed he. "A brave man does not shrink in the battle, and, when friends stand round the bed, even women may die composedly; but here—"

"I shall not shrink, even here, Reuben Bourne," interrupted Malvin. "I am a man of no weak heart; and, if I were, there is a surer support than that of earthly friends. You are young, and life is dear to you. Your last moments will need comfort far more than mine; and when you have laid me in the earth, and are alone, and night is settling on the forest, you will feel all the bitterness of the death that may now be escaped. But I will urge no selfish motive to your generous nature. Leave me for my sake; that, having said a prayer for your safety, I may have space to settle my account, undisturbed by worldly sorrows."

"And your daughter! How shall I dare to meet her eye?" exclaimed Reuben. "She will ask the fate of her father, whose life I vowed to defend with my own. Must I tell her, that he travelled three days' march with me from the field of battle, and that then I left him to perish in the wilderness? Were it not better to lie down and die by your side, than to return safe, and say this to Dorcas?"

"Tell my daughter," said Roger Malvin, "that, though yourself sore wounded, and weak, and weary, you led my tottering footsteps many a mile, and left me only at my earnest entreaty, because I would not have your blood upon my soul. Tell her, that through pain and danger you were faithful, and that, if your life-blood could have saved me, it would have flowed to its last drop. And tell her, that you will be something dearer than a father, and that my blessing is with you both, and that my dying eyes can see a long and pleasant path, in which you will journey together."

As Malvin spoke, he almost raised himself from the ground, and the energy of his concluding words seemed to fill the wild and lonely forest with a vision of happiness. But when he sank exhausted upon his bed of oak-leaves, the light, which had kindled in Reuben's eye, was quenched. He felt as if it were both sin and folly to think of hap-

piness at such a moment. His companion watched his changing countenance, and sought, with generous art, to wile him to his own good.

"Perhaps I deceive myself in regard to the time I have to live," he
resumed. "It may be, that, with speedy assistance, I might recover of
my wound. The foremost fugitives must, ere this, have carried tidings
of our fatal battle to the frontiers, and parties will be out to succour
those in like condition with ourselves. Should you meet one of these,
and guide them hither, who can tell but that I may sit by my own fireside again?"

A mournful smile strayed across the features of the dying man, as
he insinuated that unfounded hope; which, however, was not without
its effect on Reuben. No merely selfish motive, nor even the desolate
condition of Dorcas, could have induced him to desert his companion, at such a moment. But his wishes seized upon the thought, that
Malvin's life might be preserved, and his sanguine nature heightened,
almost to certainty, the remote possibility of procuring human aid.

"Surely there is reason, weighty reason, to hope that friends are not
far distant," he said, half aloud. There fled one coward, unwounded,
in the beginning of the fight, and most probably he made good speed.
Every true man on the frontier would shoulder his musket, at the
news; and though no party may range so far into the woods as this, I
shall perhaps encounter them in one day's march. Counsel me faithfully," he added, turning to Malvin, in distrust of his own motives.
"Were your situation mine, would you desert me while life remained?"

"It is now twenty years," replied Roger Malvin, sighing, however,
as he secretly acknowledged the wide dissimilarity between the two
cases,—"it is now twenty years, since I escaped, with one dear friend,
from Indian captivity, near Montreal. We journeyed many days
through the woods, till at length, overcome with hunger and weariness, my friend lay down, and besought me to leave him; for he knew,

that, if I remained, we both must perish. And, with but little hope of obtaining succour, I heaped a pillow of dry leaves beneath his head, and hastened on."

"And did you return in time to save him?" asked Reuben, hanging on Malvin's words, as if they were to be prophetic of his own success.

"I did," answered the other. "I came upon the camp of a hunting party, before sunset of the same day. I guided them to the spot where my comrade was expecting death; and he is now a hale and hearty man, upon his own farm, far within the frontiers, while I lie wounded here, in the depths of the wilderness."

This example, powerful in effecting Reuben's decision, was aided, unconsciously to himself, by the hidden strength of many another motive. Roger Malvin perceived that the victory was nearly won.

"Now go, my son, and Heaven prosper you!" he said. "Turn not back with our friends, when you meet them, lest your wounds and weariness overcome you; but send hitherward two or three, that may be spared, to search for me. And believe me, Reuben, my heart will be lighter with every step you take towards home." Yet there was perhaps a change, both in his countenance and voice, as he spoke thus; for, after all, it was a ghastly fate, to be left expiring in the wilderness.

Reuben Bourne, but half convinced that he was acting rightly, at length raised himself from the ground, and prepared himself for his departure. And first, though contrary to Malvin's wishes, he collected a stock of roots and herbs, which had been their only food during the last two days. This useless supply he placed within reach of the dying man, for whom, also, he swept together a fresh bed of dry oak-leaves. Then, climbing to the summit of the rock, which on one side was rough and broken, he bent the oak-sapling downward, and bound his handkerchief to the topmost branch. This precaution was not unnecessary, to direct any who might come in search of Malvin; for every part of the rock, except its broad, smooth front, was concealed, at a little distance, by the dense undergrowth of the forest. The handkerchief had been the bandage of a wound upon Reuben's arm; and, as he bound it to the tree, he vowed, by the blood that stained it, that he would return, either to save his companion's life, or to lay his body in the grave. He then descended, and stood, with downcast eyes, to receive Roger Malvin's parting words.

The experience of the latter suggested much and minute advice, respecting the youth's journey through the trackless forest. Upon this subject he spoke with calm earnestness, as if he were sending Reuben to the battle or the chase, while he himself remained secure at home; and not as if the human countenance, that was about to leave him, were the last he would ever behold. But his firmness was shaken, before he concluded.

"Carry my blessing to Dorcas, and say that my last prayer shall be for her and you. Bid her have no hard thoughts because you left me here"—Reuben's heart smote him—"for that your life would not have weighed with you, if its sacrifice could have done me good. She will marry you, after she has mourned a little while for her father; and Heaven grant you long and happy days! and may your children's children stand round your death-bed! And, Reuben," added he, as the weakness of mortality made its way at last, "return, when your wounds are healed and your weariness refreshed, return to this wild rock, and lay my bones in the grave, and say a prayer over them."

An almost superstitious regard, arising perhaps from the customs of the Indians, whose war was with the dead, as well as the living, was paid by the frontier inhabitants to the rites of sepulture; and there are many instances of the sacrifice of life, in the attempt to bury those who had fallen by the "sword of the wilderness." Reuben, therefore, felt the full importance of the promise, which he most solemnly made, to return, and perform Roger Malvin's obsequies. It was remarkable, that the latter, speaking his whole heart in his parting

words, no longer endeavored to persuade the youth, that even the
speediest succour might avail to the preservation of his life. Reuben
was internally convinced, that he should see Malvin's living face no
more. His generous nature would fain have delayed him, at whatever
risk, till the dying scene were past; but the desire of existence, and the
hope of happiness had strengthened in his heart, and he was unable
to resist them.

"It is enough," said Roger Malvin, having listened to Reuben's
promise. "Go, and God speed you!"

The youth pressed his hand in silence, turned, and was departing.
His slow and faultering steps, however, had borne him but a little way,
before Malvin's voice recalled him.

"Reuben, Reuben," said he, faintly; and Reuben returned and knelt
down by the dying man.

"Raise me, and let me lean against the rock," was his last request.
"My face will be turned towards home, and I shall see you a moment
longer, as you pass among the trees."

Reuben, having made the desired alteration in his companion's
posture, again began his solitary pilgrimage. He walked more hastily at first, than was consistent with his strength; for a sort of guilty
feeling, which sometimes torments men in their most justifiable acts,
caused him to seek concealment from Malvin's eyes. But, after he had
trodden far upon the rustling forest-leaves, he crept back, impelled
by a wild and painful curiosity, and, sheltered by the earthy roots of
an uptorn tree, gazed earnestly at the desolate man. The morning sun
was unclouded, and the trees and shrubs imbibed the sweet air of
the month of May; yet there seemed a gloom on Nature's face, as if
she sympathized with mortal pain and sorrow. Roger Malvin's hands
were uplifted in a fervent prayer, some of the words of which stole
through the stillness of the woods, and entered Reuben's heart, torturing it with an unutterable pang. They were the broken accents of a

petition for his own happiness and that of Dorcas; and, as the youth listened, conscience, or something in its similitude, pleaded strongly with him to return, and lie down again by the rock. He felt how hard was the doom of the kind and generous being whom he had deserted in his extremity. Death would come, like the slow approach of a corpse, stealing gradually towards him through the forest, and showing its ghastly and motionless features from behind a nearer, and yet a nearer tree. But such must have been Reuben's own fate, had he tarried another sunset; and who shall impute blame to him, if he shrank from so useless a sacrifice? As he gave a parting look, a breeze waved the little banner upon the sapling-oak, and reminded Reuben of his vow.

Many circumstances contributed to retard the wounded traveller, in his way to the frontiers. On the second day, the clouds, gathering densely over the sky, precluded the possibility of regulating his course by the position of the sun; and he knew not but that every effort of his almost exhausted strength, was removing him farther from the home he sought. His scanty sustenance was supplied by the berries, and other spontaneous products of the forest. Herds of deer, it is true, sometimes bounded past him, and partridges frequently whirred up before his footsteps; but his ammunition had been expended in the fight, and he had no means of slaying them. His wounds, irritated by the constant exertion in which lay the only hope of life, wore away his strength, and at intervals confused his reason. But, even in the wanderings of intellect, Reuben's young heart clung strongly to existence, and it was only through absolute incapacity of motion, that he at last sank down beneath a tree, compelled there to await death. In this situation he was discovered by a party, who, upon the first intelligence of the fight, had been despatched to the relief of the survivors. They conveyed him to the nearest settlement, which chanced to be that of his own residence.

Dorcas, in the simplicity of the olden time, watched by the bedside of her wounded lover, and administered all those comforts, that are in the sole gift of woman's heart and hand. During several days, Reuben's recollection strayed drowsily among the perils and hardships through which he had passed, and he was incapable of returning definite answers to the inquiries, with which many were eager to harass him. No authentic particulars of the battle had yet been circulated; nor could mothers, wives, and children tell, whether their loved ones were detained by captivity, or by the stronger chain of death. Dorcas nourished her apprehensions in silence, till one afternoon, when Reuben awoke from an unquiet sleep, and seemed to recognize her more perfectly than at any previous time. She saw that his intellect had become composed, and she could no longer restrain her filial anxiety.

"My father, Reuben?" she began; but the change in her lover's countenance made her pause.

The youth shrank, as if with a bitter pain, and the blood gushed vividly into his wan and hollow cheeks. His first impulse was to cover his face; but, apparently with a desperate effort, he half raised himself, and spoke vehemently, defending himself against an imaginary accusation.

"Your father was sore wounded in the battle, Dorcas, and he bade me not burthen myself with him, but only to lead him to the lakeside, that he might quench his thirst and die. But I would not desert the old man in his extremity, and, though bleeding myself, I supported him; I gave him half my strength, and led him away with me. For three days we journeyed on together, and your father was sustained beyond my hopes; but, awaking at sunrise on the fourth day, I found him faint and exhausted,—he was unable to proceed,—his life had ebbed away fast,—and—"

"He died!" exclaimed Dorcas, faintly.

Reuben felt it impossible to acknowledge, that his selfish love of life had hurried him away, before her father's fate was decided. He spoke not; he only bowed his head; and, between shame and exhaustion, sank back and hid his face in the pillow. Dorcas wept, when her fears were thus confirmed; but the shock, as it had been long anticipated, was on that account the less violent.

"You dug a grave for my poor father, in the wilderness, Reuben?" was the question by which her filial piety manifested itself.

"My hands were weak, but I did what I could," replied the youth in a smothered tone. There stands a noble tomb-stone above his head, and I would to Heaven I slept as soundly as he!"

Dorcas, perceiving the wildness of his latter words, inquired no further at the time; but her heart found ease in the thought, that Roger Malvin had not lacked such funeral rites as it was possible to bestow. The tale of Reuben's courage and fidelity lost nothing, when she communicated it to her friends; and the poor youth, tottering from his sick chamber to breathe the sunny air, experienced from every tongue the miserable and humiliating torture of unmerited praise. All acknowledged that he might worthily demand the hand of the fair maiden, to whose father he had been "faithful unto death"; and, as my tale is not of love, it shall suffice to say, that, in the space of a few months, Reuben became the husband of Dorcas Malvin. During the marriage ceremony, the bride was covered with blushes, but the bridegroom's face was pale.

There was now in the breast of Reuben Bourne an incommunicable thought; something which he was to conceal most heedfully from her whom he most loved and trusted. He regretted, deeply and bitterly, the moral cowardice that had restrained his words, when he was about to disclose the truth to Dorcas; but pride, the fear of losing her affection, the dread of universal scorn, forbade him to rectify this falsehood. He felt, that, for leaving Roger Malvin, he deserved no censure. His presence, the gratuitous sacrifice of his own life, would have added only another, and a needless agony to the last moments of the dying man. But concealment had imparted to a justifiable act, much of the secret effect of guilt; and Reuben, while reason told him that he had done right, experienced, in no small degree, the mental horrors, which punish the perpetrator of undiscovered crime. By a certain association of ideas, he at times almost imagined himself a murderer. For years, also, a thought would occasionally recur, which, though he perceived all its folly and extravagance, he had not power to banish from his mind; it was a haunting and torturing fancy, that his father-in-law was yet sitting at the foot of the rock, on the withered forest-leaves, alive, and awaiting his pledged assistance. These mental deceptions, however, came and went, nor did he ever mistake them for realities; but in the calmest and clearest moods of his mind, he was conscious that he had a deep vow unredeemed, and that an unburied corpse was calling to him, out of the wilderness. Yet, such was the consequence of his prevarication, that he could not obey the call. It was now too late to require the assistance of Roger Malvin's friends, in performing his long-deferred sepulture; and superstitious fears, of which none were more susceptible than the people of the outward settlements, forbade Reuben to go alone. Neither did he know where, in the pathless and illimitable forest, to seek that smooth and lettered rock, at the base of which the body lay; his remembrance of every portion of his travel thence was indistinct, and the latter part had left no impression upon his mind. There was, however, a continual impulse, a voice audible only to himself, commanding him to go forth and redeem his vow; and he had a strange impression, that, were he to make the trial, he would be led straight to Malvin's bones. But, year after year, that summons, unheard but felt, was disobeyed. His one secret thought, became like a chain, binding down his spirit, and, like a serpent, gnawing into his heart; and he was transformed into a sad and downcast, yet irritable man.

In the course of a few years after their marriage, changes began to be visible in the external prosperity of Reuben and Dorcas. The only riches of the former had been his stout heart and strong arm; but the latter, her father's sole heiress, had made her husband master of a farm, under older cultivation, larger, and better stocked than most of the frontier establishments. Reuben Bourne, however, was a neglectful husbandman; and while the lands of the other settlers became annually more fruitful, his deteriorated in the same proportion. The discouragements to agriculture were greatly lessened by the cessation of Indian war, during which men held the plough in one hand, and the musket in the other; and were fortunate if the products of their dangerous labor were not destroyed, either in the field or in the barn, by the savage enemy. But Reuben did not profit by the altered condition of the country; nor can it be denied, that his intervals of industrious attention to his affairs were but scantily rewarded with success. The irritability, by which he had recently become distinguished, was another cause of his declining prosperity, as it occasioned frequent quarrels, in his unavoidable intercourse with the neighboring settlers. The results of these were innumerable law-suits; for the people of New England, in the earliest stages and wildest circumstances of the country, adopted, whenever attainable, the legal mode of deciding their differences. To be brief, the world did not go well with Reuben Bourne, and, though not till many years after his marriage, he was finally a ruined man, with but one remaining expedient against the evil fate that had pursued him. He was to throw sunlight into some deep recess of the forest, and seek subsistence from the virgin bosom of the wilderness.

The only child of Reuben and Dorcas was a son, now arrived at the age of fifteen years, beautiful in youth, and giving promise of a glorious manhood. He was peculiarly qualified for, and already began to excel in, the wild accomplishments of frontier life. His foot was fleet, his aim true, his apprehension quick, his heart glad and high; and all, who anticipated the return of Indian war, spoke of Cyrus Bourne as a future leader in the land. The boy was loved by his father, with a deep and silent strength, as if whatever was good and happy in his own nature had been transferred to his child, carrying his affections with it. Even Dorcas, though loving and beloved, was far less dear to him; for Reuben's secret thoughts and insulated emotions had gradually made him a selfish man; and he could no longer love deeply, except where he saw, or imagined, some reflection or likeness of his own mind. In Cyrus he recognized what he had himself been in other days; and at intervals he seemed to partake of the boy's spirit, and to be revived with a fresh and happy life. Reuben was accompanied by his son in the expedition, for the purpose of selecting a tract of land, and felling and burning the timber, which necessarily preceded the removal of the household gods. Two months of autumn were thus occupied; after which Reuben Bourne and his young hunter returned, to spend their last winter in the settlements.

It was early in the month of May, that the little family snapped asunder whatever tendrils of affection had clung to inanimate objects, and bade farewell to the few, who, in the blight of fortune, called themselves their friends. The sadness of the parting moment had, to each of the pilgrims, its peculiar alleviations. Reuben, a moody man, and misanthropic because unhappy, strode onward, with his usual stern brow and downcast eye, feeling few regrets, and disdaining to acknowledge any. Dorcas, while she wept abundantly over the broken ties by which her simple and affectionate nature had bound itself to everything, felt that the inhabitants of her inmost heart moved on with her, and that all else would be supplied wherever she might go. And the boy dashed one tear-drop from his eye, and thought of the adventurous pleasures of the untrodden forest. Oh! who, in the enthusiasm of a day-dream, has not wished that he were a wanderer in a world of summer wilderness, with one fair and gentle being hanging lightly on his arm? In youth, his free and exulting step would know no barrier but the rolling ocean or the snow-topt mountains; calmer manhood would choose a home, where Nature had strewn a double wealth, in the vale of some transparent stream; and when hoary age, after long, long years of that pure life, stole on and found him there, it would find him the father of a race, the patriarch of a people, the founder of a mighty nation yet to be. When death, like the sweet sleep which we welcome after a day of happiness, came over him, his far descendants would mourn over the venerated dust. Enveloped by tradition in mysterious attributes, the men of future generations would call him godlike; and remote posterity would see him standing, dimly glorious, far up the valley of a hundred centuries!

The tangled and gloomy forest, through which the personages of my tale were wandering, differed widely from the dreamer's Land of Fantasie; yet there was something in their way of life that Nature asserted as her own; and the gnawing cares, which went with them from the world, were all that now obstructed their happiness. One stout and shaggy steed, the bearer of all their wealth, did not shrink from the added weight of Dorcas; although her hardy breeding sustained her, during the latter part of each day's journey, by her husband's side. Reuben and his son, their muskets on their shoulders, and their axes slung behind them, kept an unwearied pace, each watching with a hunter's eye for the game that supplied their food. When hunger bade, they halted and prepared their meal on the bank of some un-polluted forest-brook, which, as they knelt down with thirsty lips to drink, murmured a sweet unwillingness, like a maiden, at love's first kiss. They slept beneath a hut of branches, and awoke at peep of light, refreshed for the toils of another day. Dorcas and the boy went on joyously, and even Reuben's spirit shone at intervals with an outward gladness; but inwardly there was a cold, cold sorrow, which he com-pared to the snow-drifts, lying deep in the glens and hollows of the rivulets, while the leaves were brightly green above.

Cyrus Bourne was sufficiently skilled in the travel of the woods, to observe, that his father did not adhere to the course they had pur-sued, in their expedition of the preceding autumn. They were now keeping farther to the north, striking out more directly from the set-tlements, and into a region, of which savage beasts and savage men were as yet the sole possessors. The boy sometimes hinted his opin-ions upon the subject, and Reuben listened attentively, and once or twice altered the direction of their march in accordance with his son's counsel. But having so done, he seemed ill at ease. His quick and wan-dering glances were sent forward, apparently in search of enemies lurking behind the tree-trunks; and seeing nothing there, he would cast his eyes backward, as if in fear of some pursuer. Cyrus, perceiving that his father gradually resumed the old direction, forbore to inter-fere; nor, though something began to weigh upon his heart, did his adventurous nature permit him to regret the increased length and the mystery of their way.

On the afternoon of the fifth day, they halted and made their simple encampment, nearly an hour before sunset. The face of the country, for the last few miles, had been diversified by swells of land, resembling huge waves of a petrified sea; and in one of the corresponding hollows, a wild and romantic spot, had the family reared their hut, and kindled their fire. There is something chilling, and yet heart-warming, in the thought of these three, united by strong bands of love, and insulated from all that breathe beside. The dark and gloomy pines looked down upon them, and, as the wind swept through their tops, a pitying sound was heard in the forest; or did those old trees groan, in fear that men were come to lay the axe to their roots at last? Reuben and his son, while Dorcas made ready their meal, proposed to wander out in search of game, of which that day's march had afforded no supply. The boy, promising not to quit the vicinity of the encampment, bounded off with a step as light and elastic as that of the deer he hoped to slay; while his father, feeling a transient happiness as he gazed after him, was about to pursue an opposite direction. Dorcas, in the meanwhile, had seated herself near their fire of fallen branches, upon the moss-grown and mouldering trunk of a tree, uprooted years before. Her employment, diversified by an occasional glance at the pot, now beginning to simmer over the blaze, was the perusal of the current year's Massachusetts Almanac, which, with the exception of an old black-letter Bible, comprised all the literary wealth of the family. None pay a greater regard to arbitrary divisions of time, than those who are excluded from society; and Dorcas mentioned, as if the information were of importance, that it was now the twelfth of May. Her husband started.

"The twelfth of May! I should remember it well," muttered he, while many thoughts occasioned a momentary confusion in his mind. "Where am I? Whither am I wandering? Where did I leave him?"

Dorcas, too well accustomed to her husband's wayward moods to note any peculiarity of demeanor, now laid aside the Almanac, and addressed him in that mournful tone, which the tender-hearted appropriate to griefs long cold and dead.

"It was near this time of the month, eighteen years ago, that my poor father left this world for a better. He had a kind arm to hold his head, and a kind voice to cheer him, Reuben, in his last moments; and the thought of the faithful care you took of him, has comforted me, many a time since. Oh! death would have been awful to a solitary man, in a wild place like this!"

"Pray Heaven, Dorcas," said Reuben, in a broken voice, "pray Heaven, that neither of us three die solitary, and lie unburied, in this howling wilderness!" And he hastened away, leaving her to watch the fire, beneath the gloomy pines.

Reuben Bourne's rapid pace gradually slackened, as the pang, unintentionally inflicted by the words of Dorcas, became less acute. Many strange reflections, however, thronged upon him; and, straying onward, rather like a sleep-walker than a hunter, it was attributable to no care of his own, that his devious course kept him in the vicinity of the encampment. His steps were imperceptibly led almost in a circle, nor did he observe that he was on the verge of a tract of land heavily timbered, but not with pine-trees. The place of the latter was here supplied by oaks, and other of the harder woods; and around their roots clustered a dense and bushy undergrowth, leaving, however, barren spaces between the trees, thick-strewn with withered leaves. Whenever the rustling of the branches, or the creaking of the trunks made a sound, as if the forest were waking from slumber, Reuben instinctively raised the musket that rested on his arm, and cast a quick, sharp glance on every side; but, convinced by a partial observation that no animal was near, he would again give himself up to his thoughts. He was musing on the strange influence, that had led him away from his premeditated course, and so far into the depths of the wilderness. Unable to penetrate to the secret place of his soul, where his motives lay hidden, he believed that a supernatural voice had called him onward, and that a supernatural power had obstructed his retreat. He trusted that it was Heaven's intent to afford him an opportunity of expiating his sin; he hoped that he might find the bones, so long unburied; and that, having laid the earth over them, peace would throw its sunlight into the sepulchre of his heart. From these thoughts he was aroused by a rustling in the forest, at some distance from the spot to which he had wandered. Perceiving the motion of some object behind a thick veil of undergrowth, he fired, with the instinct of a hunter, and the aim of a practised marksman. A low moan, which told his success, and by which even animals can express their dying agony, was unheeded by Reuben Bourne. What were the recollections now breaking upon him?

The thicket, into which Reuben had fired, was near the summit of a swell of land, and was clustered around the base of a rock, which, in the shape and smoothness of one of its surfaces, was not unlike a gigantic grave-stone. As if reflected in a mirror, its likeness was in Reuben's memory. He even recognized the veins which seemed to form an inscription in forgotten characters; everything remained the same, except that a thick covert of bushes shrouded the lower part of the rock, and would have hidden Roger Malvin, had he still been sitting there. Yet, in the next moment, Reuben's eye was caught by another change, that time had effected, since he last stood, where he was now standing again, behind the earthy roots of the uptorn tree. The sapling, to which he had bound the blood-stained symbol of his vow, had increased and strengthened into an oak, far indeed from its maturity, but with no mean spread of shadowy branches. There was one singularity, observable in this tree, which made Reuben tremble. The middle and lower branches were in luxuriant life, and an excess of vegetation had fringed the trunk, almost to the ground; but a blight had apparently stricken the upper part of the oak, and the very topmost bough was withered, sapless, and utterly dead. Reuben remembered how the little banner had fluttered on the topmost bough, when it was green and lovely, eighteen years before. Whose guilt had blasted it?

Dorcas, after the departure of the two hunters, continued her preparations for their evening repast. Her sylvan table was the moss-covered trunk of a large fallen tree, on the broadest part of which she had spread a snow-white cloth, and arranged what were left of the bright pewter vessels, that had been her pride in the settlements. It had a strange aspect—that one little spot of homely comfort, in the desolate heart of Nature. The sunshine yet lingered upon the higher branches of the trees that grew on rising ground; but the shades of evening had deepened into the hollow, where the encampment was made; and the fire-light began to redden as it gleamed up the tall trunks of the pines, or hovered on the dense and obscure mass of foliage, that circled round the spot. The heart of Dorcas was not sad; for she felt that it was better to journey in the wilderness, with two whom she loved, than to be a lonely woman in a crowd that cared not for her. As she busied herself in arranging seats of mouldering wood, covered with leaves, for Reuben and her son, her voice danced through the gloomy forest, in the measure of a song that she had learned in youth. The rude melody, the production of a bard who won no name, was descriptive of a winter evening in a frontier-cottage, when, secured from savage inroad by the high-piled snow-drifts, the family rejoiced by their own fireside. The whole song possessed that nameless charm, peculiar to unborrowed thought; but four continually-recurring lines shone out from the rest, like the blaze of the hearth whose joys they celebrated. Into them, working magic with a few simple words, the poet had instilled the very essence of domestic love and household happiness, and they were poetry and picture joined in one.

As Dorcas sang, the walls of her forsaken home seemed to encircle her; she no longer saw the gloomy pines, nor heard the wind, which still, as she began each verse, sent a heavy breath through the branches, and died away in a hollow moan, from the burthen of the song. She was aroused by the report of a gun, in the vicinity of the encampment; and either the sudden sound, or her loneliness by the glowing fire, caused her to tremble violently. The next moment, she laughed in the pride of a mothers heart.

"My beautiful young hunter! my boy has slain a deer!" she exclaimed, recollecting that, in the direction whence the shot proceeded, Cyrus had gone to the chase.

She waited a reasonable time, to hear her son's light step bounding over the rustling leaves, to tell of his success. But he did not immediately appear, and she sent her cheerful voice among the trees, in search of him.

"Cyrus! Cyrus!"

His coming was still delayed, and she determined, as the report had apparently been very near, to seek for him in person. Her assistance, also, might be necessary in bringing home the venison, which she flattered herself he had obtained. She therefore set forward, directing her steps by the long-past sound, and singing as she went, in order that the boy might be aware of her approach, and run to meet her. From behind the trunk of every tree, and from every hiding place in the thick foliage of the undergrowth, she hoped to discover the countenance of her son, laughing with the sportive mischief that is born of affection. The sun was now beneath the horizon, and the light that came down among the trees was sufficiently dim to create many illusions in her expecting fancy. Several times she seemed indistinctly to see his face gazing out from among the leaves; and once she imagined that he stood beckoning to her, at the base of a craggy rock. Keeping her eyes on this object, however, it proved to be no more than the trunk of an oak, fringed to the very ground with little branches, one of which, thrust out farther than the rest, was shaken by the breeze. Making her way round the foot of the rock, she suddenly found herself close to her husband, who had approached in another direction. Leaning upon the butt of his gun, the muzzle of which rested upon the withered leaves, he was apparently absorbed in the contemplation of some object at his feet.

"How is this, Reuben? Have you slain the deer, and fallen asleep over him?" exclaimed Dorcas, laughing cheerfully, on her first slight observation of his posture and appearance.

He stirred not, neither did he turn his eyes towards her; and a cold, shuddering fear, indefinite in its source and object, began to creep into her blood. She now perceived that her husband's face was ghastly pale, and his features were rigid, as if incapable of assuming any other expression than the strong despair which had hardened upon them. He gave not the slightest evidence that he was aware of her approach.

"For the love of Heaven, Reuben, speak to me!" cried Dorcas, and the strange sound of her own voice affrighted her even more than the dead silence.

Her husband started, stared into her face; drew her to the front of the rock, and pointed with his finger.

Oh! there lay the boy, asleep, but dreamless, upon the fallen forest-leaves! his cheek rested upon his arm, his curled locks were thrown back from his brow, his limbs were slightly relaxed. Had a sudden weariness overcome the youthful hunter? Would his mother's voice arouse him? She knew that it was death.

"This broad rock is the grave-stone of your near kindred, Dorcas," said her husband. "Your tears will fall at once over your father and your son."

She heard him not. With one wild shriek, that seemed to force its way from the sufferer's inmost soul, she sank insensible by the side of her dead boy. At that moment, the withered topmost bough of the oak loosened itself, in the stilly air, and fell in soft, light fragments upon the rock, upon the leaves, upon Reuben, upon his wife and child, and upon Roger Malvin's bones. Then Reuben's heart was stricken, and the tears gushed out like water from a rock. The vow that the wounded youth had made, the blighted man had come to redeem. His sin was expiated, the curse was gone from him; and, in the hour, when he had shed blood dearer to him than his own, a prayer, the first for years, went up to Heaven from the lips of Reuben Bourne.

The Haunted Mind

WHAT A SINGULAR MOMENT is the first one, when you have hardly begun to recollect yourself, after starting from midnight slumber! By unclosing your eyes so suddenly, you seem to have surprised the personages of your dream in full convocation round your bed, and catch one broad glance at them before they can flit into obscurity. Or, to vary the metaphor, you find yourself, for a single instant, wide awake in that realm of illusions, whither sleep has been the passport, and behold its ghostly inhabitants and wondrous scenery, with a perception of their strangeness, such as you never attain while the dream is undisturbed. The distant sound of a church clock is borne faintly on the wind. You question with yourself, half seriously, whether it has stolen to your waking ear from some gray tower, that stood within the precincts of your dream. While yet in suspense, another clock flings its heavy clang over the slumbering town, with so full and distinct a sound, and such a long murmur in the neighboring air, that you are certain it must proceed from the steeple at the nearest corner. You count the strokes—one—two—and there they cease, with a booming sound, like the gathering of a third stroke within the bell.

If you could choose an hour of wakefulness out of the whole night, it would be this. Since your sober bedtime, at eleven, you have had rest enough to take off the pressure of yesterday's fatigue; while before you, till the sun comes from 'far Cathay' to brighten your window, there is almost the space of a summer night; one hour to be spent in thought, with the mind's eye half shut, and two in pleasant dreams, and two in that strangest of enjoyments, the forgetfulness alike of joy and woe. The moment of rising belongs to another period of time, and appears so distant, that the plunge out of a warm bed into the frosty air cannot yet be anticipated with dismay. Yesterday has already vanished among the shadows of the past; to-morrow has not yet emerged from the future. You have found an intermediate space, where the business of life does not intrude; where the passing moment lingers, and becomes truly the present; a spot where Father Time, when he thinks nobody is watching him, sits down by the way side to take breath. Oh, that he would fall asleep, and let mortals live on without growing older!

Hitherto you have lain perfectly still, because the slightest motion would dissipate the fragments of your slumber. Now, being irrevocably awake, you peep through the half drawn window curtain, and observe that the glass is ornamented with fanciful devices in frost work, and that each pane presents something like a frozen dream. There will be time enough to trace out the analogy, while waiting the summons to breakfast. Seen through the clear portion of the glass, where the silvery mountain peaks of the frost scenery do not ascend, the most conspicuous object is the steeple; the white spire of which directs you to the wintry lustre of the firmament. You may almost distinguish the figures on the clock that has just told the hour. Such a frosty sky, and the snow covered roofs, and the long vista of the frozen street, all white, and the distant water hardened into rock, might make you shiver, even under four blankets and a woolen comforter. Yet look at that one glorious star! Its beams are distinguishable from all the rest, and actually cast the shadow of the casement on the bed, with a radiance of deeper hue than moonlight, though not so accurate an outline.

You sink down and muffle your head in the clothes, shivering all the while, but less from bodily chill, than the bare idea of a polar atmosphere. It is too cold even for the thoughts to venture abroad. You speculate on the luxury of wearing out a whole existence in bed, like an oyster in its shell, content with the sluggish ecstasy of inaction, and drowsily conscious of nothing but delicious warmth, such as you now feel again. Ah! that idea has brought a hideous one in its train. You think how the dead are lying in their cold shrouds and narrow coffins, through the drear winter of the grave, and cannot persuade your fancy that they neither shrink nor shiver, when the snow is drifting over their little hillocks, and the bitter blast howls against the door of the tomb. That gloomy thought will collect a gloomy multitude, and throw its complexion over your wakeful hour.

In the depths of every heart, there is a tomb and a dungeon, though the lights, the music, and revelry above may cause us to forget their existence, and the buried ones, or prisoners whom they hide. But sometimes, and oftenest at midnight, those dark receptacles are flung wide open. In an hour like this, when the mind has a passive sensibility, but no active strength; when the imagination is a mirror, imparting vividness to all ideas, without the power of selecting or controlling them; then pray that your griefs may slumber, and the brotherhood of remorse not break their chain. It is too late! A funeral train comes gliding by your bed, in which Passion and Feeling assume bodily shape, and things of the mind become dim spectres to the eye. There is your earliest Sorrow, a pale young mourner, wearing a sister's likeness to first love, sadly beautiful, with a hallowed sweetness in her melancholy features, and grace in the flow of her sable robe. Next appears a shade of ruined loveliness, with dust among her golden hair, and her bright garments all faded and defaced, stealing from your glance with drooping head, as fearful of reproach; she was your fondest Hope, but a delusive one; so call her Disappointment now. A sterner form succeeds, with a brow of wrinkles, a look and gesture of iron authority; there is no name for him unless it be Fatality, an emblem of the evil influence that rules your fortunes; a demon to whom you subjected yourself by some error at the outset of life, and were bound his slave forever, by once obeying him. See! those fiendish lineaments graven on the darkness, the writhed lip of scorn, the mockery of that living eye, the pointed finger, touching the sore place in your heart! Do you remember any act of enormous folly, at which you would blush, even in the remotest cavern of the earth? Then recognize your Shame.

Pass, wretched band! Well for the wakeful one, if, riotously miserable, a fiercer tribe do not surround him, the devils of a guilty heart, that holds its hell within itself. What if Remorse should assume the features of an injured friend? What if the fiend should come in woman's garments, with a pale beauty amid sin and desolation, and lie down by your side? What if he should stand at your bed's foot, in the likeness of a corpse, with a bloody stain upon the shroud? Sufficient without such guilt, is this nightmare of the soul; this heavy, heavy sinking of the spirits; this wintry gloom about the heart; this indistinct horror of the mind, blending itself with the darkness of the chamber.

By a desperate effort, you start upright, breaking from a sort of conscious sleep, and gazing wildly round the bed, as if the fiends were any where but in your haunted mind. At the same moment, the slumbering embers on the hearth send forth a gleam which palely illuminates the whole outer room, and flickers through the door of the bedchamber, but cannot quite dispel its obscurity. Your eye searches for whatever may remind you of the living world. With eager minuteness, you take note of the table near the fire-place, the book with an ivory knife between its leaves, the unfolded letter, the hat and the fallen glove. Soon the flame vanishes, and with it the whole scene is gone, though its image remains an instant in your mind's eye, when darkness has swallowed the reality. Throughout the chamber, there is the same obscurity as before, but not the same gloom within your breast. As your head falls back upon the pillow, you think—in a whisper be it spoken—how pleasant in these night solitudes, would be the rise and fall of a softer breathing than your own, the slight pressure of a tenderer bosom, the quiet throb of a purer heart, imparting its peacefulness to your troubled one, as if the fond sleeper were involving you in her dream.

Her influence is over you, though she have no existence but in that momentary image. You sink down in a flowery spot, on the borders of sleep and wakefulness, while your thoughts rise before you in pictures, all disconnected, yet all assimilated by a pervading gladsomeness and beauty. The wheeling of gorgeous squadrons, that glitter in the sun, is succeeded by the merriment of children round the door of a school-house, beneath the glimmering shadow of old trees, at the corner of a rustic lane. You stand in the sunny rain of a summer shower, and wander among the sunny trees of an autumnal wood, and look upward at the brightest of all rainbows, over-arching the unbroken sheet of snow, on the American side of Niagara. Your mind struggles pleasantly between the dancing radiance round the hearth of a young man and his recent bride, and the twittering flight of birds in spring, about their new-made nest. You feel the merry bounding of a ship before the breeze; and watch the tuneful feet of rosy girls, as they twine their last and merriest dance, in a splendid ball room; and find yourself in the brilliant circle of a crowded theatre, as the curtain falls over a light and airy scene.

With an involuntary start, you seize hold on consciousness, and prove yourself but half awake, by running a doubtful parallel between human life and the hour which has now elapsed. In both you emerge from mystery, pass through a vicissitude that you can but imperfectly control, and are borne onward to another mystery. Now comes the peal of the distant clock, with fainter and fainter strokes as you plunge farther into the wilderness of sleep. It is the knell of a temporary death. Your spirit has departed, and strays like a free citizen, among the people of a shadowy world, beholding strange sights, yet without wonder or dismay. So calm, perhaps, will be the final change; so undisturbed, as if among familiar things, the entrance of the soul to its Eternal home!

Young Goodman Brown

YOUNG GOODMAN BROWN CAME FORTH, at sunset, into the street of Salem village, but put his head back, after crossing the threshold, to exchange a parting kiss with his young wife. And Faith, as the wife was aptly named, thrust her own pretty head into the street, letting the wind play with the pink ribbons of her cap, while she called to Goodman Brown.

"Dearest heart," whispered she, softly and rather sadly, when her lips were close to his ear, "pr'y thee, put off your journey until sunrise, and sleep in your own bed to-night. A lone woman is troubled with such dreams and such thoughts, that she's afeard of herself, sometimes. Pray, tarry with me this night, dear husband, of all nights in the year!"

"My love and my Faith," replied young Goodman Brown, "of all nights in the year, this one night must I tarry away from thee. My journey, as thou callest it, forth and back again, must needs be done 'twixt now and sunrise. What, my sweet, pretty wife, dost thou doubt me already, and we but three months married!"

"Then, God bless you!" said Faith, with the pink ribbons, "and may you find all well, when you come back."

"Amen!" cried Goodman Brown. "Say thy prayers, dear Faith, and go to bed at dusk, and no harm will come to thee."

So they parted; and the young man pursued his way, until, being about to turn the corner by the meeting-house, he looked back, and saw the head of Faith still peeping after him, with a melancholy air, in spite of her pink ribbons.

"Poor little Faith!" thought he, for his heart smote him. "What a wretch am I, to leave her on such an errand! She talks of dreams, too. Methought, as she spoke, there was trouble in her face, as if a dream had warned her what work is to be done to-night. But, no, no! 'twould kill her to think it. Well; she's a blessed angel on earth; and after this one night, I'll cling to her skirts and follow her to Heaven."

With this excellent resolve for the future, Goodman Brown felt himself justified in making more haste on his present evil purpose. He had taken a dreary road, darkened by all the gloomiest trees of the forest, which barely stood aside to let the narrow path creep through, and closed immediately behind. It was all as lonely as could be; and there is this peculiarity in such a solitude, that the traveller knows not who may be concealed by the innumerable trunks and the thick boughs overhead; so that, with lonely footsteps, he may yet be passing through an unseen multitude.

"There may be a devilish Indian behind every tree," said Goodman Brown, to himself; and he glanced fearfully behind him, as he added, "What if the devil himself should be at my very elbow!"

His head being turned back, he passed a crook of the road, and looking forward again, beheld the figure of a man, in grave and decent attire, seated at the foot of an old tree. He arose, at Goodman Brown's approach, and walked onward, side by side with him.

"You are late, Goodman Brown," said he. "The clock of the Old South was striking as I came through Boston; and that is full fifteen minutes agone."

"Faith kept me back awhile," replied the young man, with a tremor in his voice, caused by the sudden appearance of his companion, though not wholly unexpected.

It was now deep dusk in the forest, and deepest in that part of it where these two were journeying. As nearly as could be discerned, the second traveller was about fifty years old, apparently in the same rank of life as Goodman Brown, and bearing a considerable resemblance to him, though perhaps more in expression than features. Still, they might have been taken for father and son. And yet, though the elder person was as simply clad as the younger, and as simple in manner too, he had an indescribable air of one who knew the world, and would not have felt abashed at the governor's dinner-table, or in King William's court, were it possible that his affairs should call him thither. But the only thing about him, that could be fixed upon as remarkable, was his staff, which bore the likeness of a great black snake, so curiously wrought, that it might almost be seen to twist and wriggle itself, like a living serpent. This, of course, must have been an ocular deception, assisted by the uncertain light.

"Come, Goodman Brown!" cried his fellow-traveller, "this is a dull pace for the beginning of a journey. Take my staff, if you are so soon weary."

"Friend," said the other, exchanging his slow pace for a full stop, "having kept covenant by meeting thee here, it is my purpose now to return whence I came. I have scruples, touching the matter thou wot'st of."

"Sayest thou so?" replied he of the serpent, smiling apart. "Let us walk on, nevertheless, reasoning as we go, and if I convince thee not, thou shalt turn back. We are but a little way in the forest, yet."

"Too far, too far!" exclaimed the goodman, unconsciously resuming his walk. "My father never went into the woods on such an errand, nor his father before him. We have been a race of honest men and good Christians, since the days of the martyrs. And shall I be the first of the name of Brown, that ever took this path, and kept—"

"Such company, thou wouldst say," observed the elder person, interpreting his pause. "Well said, Goodman Brown! I have been as well acquainted with your family as with ever a one among the Puritans; and that's no trifle to say. I helped your grandfather, the constable, when he lashed the Quaker woman so smartly through the streets of Salem. And it was I that brought your father a pitch-pine knot, kindled at my own hearth, to set fire to an Indian village, in King Philip's war. They were my good friends, both; and many a pleasant walk have we had along this path, and returned merrily after midnight. I would fain be friends with you, for their sake."

"If it be as thou sayest," replied Goodman Brown, "I marvel they never spoke of these matters. Or, verily, I marvel not, seeing that the least rumor of the sort would have driven them from New-England. We are a people of prayer, and good works, to boot, and abide no such wickedness."

"Wickedness or not," said the traveller with the twisted staff, "I have a very general acquaintance here in New-England. The deacons of many a church have drunk the communion wine with me; the selectmen, of divers towns, make me their chairman; and a majority of the Great and General Court are firm supporters of my interest. The governor and I, too—but these are state-secrets."

"Can this be so!" cried Goodman Brown, with a stare of amazement at his undisturbed companion. "Howbeit, I have nothing to do with the governor and council; they have their own ways, and are no rule for a simple husbandman, like me. But, were I to go on with thee, how should I meet the eye of that good old man, our minister, at Salem village? Oh, his voice would make me tremble, both Sabbath-day and lecture-day!"

Thus far, the elder traveller had listened with due gravity, but now burst into a fit of irrepressible mirth, shaking himself so violently, that his snake-like staff actually seemed to wriggle in sympathy.

"Ha! ha! ha!" shouted he, again and again; then composing himself, "Well, go on, Goodman Brown, go on; but pr'y thee, don't kill me with laughing!"

"Well, then, to end the matter at once," said Goodman Brown, considerably nettled, "there is my wife, Faith. It would break her dear little heart; and I'd rather break my own!"

"Nay, if that be the case," answered the other, "e'en go thy ways, Goodman Brown. I would not, for twenty old women like the one hobbling before us, that Faith should come to any harm."

As he spoke, he pointed his staff at a female figure on the path, in whom Goodman Brown recognized a very pious and exemplary dame, who had taught him his catechism, in youth, and was still his moral and spiritual adviser, jointly with the minister and Deacon Gookin.

"A marvel, truly, that Goody Cloyse should be so far in the wilderness, at night-fall!" said he. "But, with your leave, friend, I shall take a cut through the woods, until we have left this Christian woman behind. Being a stranger to you, she might ask whom I was consorting with, and whither I was going."

"Be it so," said his fellow-traveller. "Betake you to the woods, and let me keep the path."

Accordingly, the young man turned aside, but took care to watch his companion, who advanced softly along the road, until he had come within a staff's length of the old dame. She, meanwhile, was making the best of her way, with singular speed for so aged a woman, and mumbling some indistinct words, a prayer, doubtless, as she went. The traveller put forth his staff, and touched her withered neck with what seemed the serpent's tail.

"The devil!" screamed the pious old lady.

"Then Goody Cloyse knows her old friend?" observed the traveller, confronting her, and leaning on his writhing stick.

"Ah, forsooth, and is it your worship, indeed?" cried the good dame. "Yea, truly is it, and in the very image of my old gossip, Goodman Brown, the grandfather of the silly fellow that now is. But— would your worship believe it?—my broomstick hath strangely disappeared, stolen, as I suspect, by that unhanged witch, Goody Cory, and that, too, when I was all anointed with the juice of smallage and cinque-foil and wolf's-bane—"

"Mingled with fine wheat and the fat of a new-born babe," said the shape of old Goodman Brown.

"Ah, your worship knows the receipt," cried the old lady, cackling aloud. "So, as I was saying, being all ready for the meeting, and no horse to ride on, I made up my mind to foot it; for they tell me, there is a nice young man to be taken into communion to-night. But now your good worship will lend me your arm, and we shall be there in a twinkling."

"That can hardly be," answered her friend. "I may not spare you my arm, Goody Cloyse, but here is my staff, if you will."

So saying, he threw it down at her feet, where, perhaps, it assumed life, being one of the rods which its owner had formerly lent to the Egyptian Magi. Of this fact, however, Goodman Brown could not take cognizance. He had cast up his eyes in astonishment, and looking down again, beheld neither Goody Cloyse nor the serpentine staff, but his fellow-traveller alone, who waited for him as calmly as if nothing had happened.

"That old woman taught me my catechism!" said the young man; and there was a world of meaning in this simple comment.

They continued to walk onward, while the elder traveller exhorted his companion to make good speed and persevere in the path, discoursing so aptly, that his arguments seemed rather to spring up in the bosom of his auditor, than to be suggested by himself. As they went, he plucked a branch of maple, to serve for a walking-stick, and began to strip it of the twigs and little boughs, which were wet with evening dew. The moment his fingers touched them, they became strangely withered and dried up, as with a week's sunshine. Thus the pair proceeded, at a good free pace, until suddenly, in a gloomy hollow of the road, Goodman Brown sat himself down on the stump of a tree, and refused to go any farther.

"Friend," said he, stubbornly, "my mind is made up. Not another step will I budge on this errand. What if a wretched old woman do choose to go to the devil, when I thought she was going to Heaven! Is that any reason why I should quit my dear Faith, and go after her?"

"You will think better of this, by-and-by," said his acquaintance, composedly. "Sit here and rest yourself awhile; and when you feel like moving again, there is my staff to help you along."

Without more words, he threw his companion the maple stick, and was as speedily out of sight, as if he had vanished into the deepening gloom. The young man sat a few moments, by the road-side, applauding himself greatly, and thinking with how clear a conscience he should meet the minister, in his morning-walk, nor shrink from the eye of good old Deacon Gookin. And what calm sleep would be his, that very night, which was to have been spent so wickedly, but purely and sweetly now, in the arms of Faith! Amidst these pleasant and praiseworthy meditations, Goodman Brown heard the tramp of horses along the road, and deemed it advisable to conceal himself within the verge of the forest, conscious of the guilty purpose that had brought him thither, though now so happily turned, from it.

On came the hoof-tramps and the voices of the riders, two grave old voices, conversing soberly as they drew near. These mingled sounds appeared to pass along the road, within a few yards of the young man's hiding-place; but owing, doubtless, to the depth of the gloom, at that particular spot, neither the travellers nor their steeds were visible. Though their figures brushed the small boughs by the way-side, it could not be seen that they intercepted, even for a moment, the faint gleam from the strip of bright sky, athwart which they must have passed. Goodman Brown alternately crouched and stood on tip-toe, pulling aside the branches, and thrusting forth his head as far as he durst, without discerning so much as a shadow. It vexed him the more, because he could have sworn, were such a thing possible, that he recognized the voices of the minister and Deacon Gookin, jogging along quietly, as they were wont to do, when bound to some ordination or ecclesiastical council. While yet within hearing, one of the riders stopped to pluck a switch.

"Of the two, reverend Sir," said the voice like the deacon's, "I had rather miss an ordination-dinner than to-night's meeting. They tell me that some of our community are to be here from Falmouth and beyond, and others from Connecticut and Rhode-Island; besides several of the Indian powows, who, after their fashion, know almost as much deviltry as the best of us. Moreover, there is a goodly young woman to be taken into communion."

"Mighty well, Deacon Gookin!" replied the solemn old tones of the minister. "Spur up, or we shall be late. Nothing can be done, you know, until I get on the ground."

The hoofs clattered again, and the voices, talking so strangely in the empty air, passed on through the forest, where no church had ever been gathered, nor solitary Christian prayed. Whither, then, could these holy men be journeying, so deep into the heathen wilderness? Young Goodman Brown caught hold of a tree, for support, being ready to sink down on the ground, faint and overburthened with the heavy sickness of his heart. He looked up to the sky, doubting whether there really was a Heaven above him. Yet, there was the blue arch, and the stars brightening in it.

"With Heaven above, and Faith below, I will yet stand firm against the devil!" cried Goodman Brown.

While he still gazed upward, into the deep arch of the firmament, and had lifted his hands to pray, a cloud, though no wind was stirring, hurried across the zenith, and hid the brightening stars. The blue sky was still visible, except directly overhead, where this black mass of cloud was sweeping swiftly northward. Aloft in the air, as if from the depths of the cloud, came a confused and doubtful sound of voices. Once, the listener fancied that he could distinguish the accents of town's-people of his own, men and women, both pious and ungodly, many of whom he had met at the communion-table, and had seen others rioting at the tavern. The next moment, so indistinct were the sounds, he doubted whether he had heard aught but the murmur of the old forest, whispering without a wind. Then came a stronger swell of those familiar tones, heard daily in the sunshine, at Salem village, but never, until now, from a cloud of night. There was one voice, of a young woman, uttering lamentations, yet with an uncertain sorrow, and entreating for some favor, which, perhaps, it would grieve her to obtain. And all the unseen multitude, both saints and sinners, seemed to encourage her onward.

"Faith!" shouted Goodman Brown, in a voice of agony and desperation; and the echoes of the forest mocked him, crying—"Faith!

Faith!" as if bewildered wretches were seeking her, all through the wilderness.

The cry of grief, rage, and terror, was yet piercing the night, when the unhappy husband held his breath for a response. There was a scream, drowned immediately in a louder murmur of voices, fading into far-off laughter, as the dark cloud swept away, leaving the clear and silent sky above Goodman Brown. But something fluttered lightly down through the air, and caught on the branch of a tree. The young man seized it, and beheld a pink ribbon.

"My Faith is gone!" cried he, after one stupefied moment. "There is no good on earth; and sin is but a name. Come, devil! for to thee is this world given."

And maddened with despair, so that he laughed loud and long, did Goodman Brown grasp his staff and set forth again, at such a rate, that he seemed to fly along the forest-path, rather than to walk or run. The road grew wilder and drearier, and more faintly traced, and vanished at length, leaving him in the heart of the dark wilderness, still rushing onward, with the instinct that guides mortal man to evil. The whole forest was peopled with frightful sounds; the creaking of the trees, the howling of wild beasts, and the yell of Indians; while, sometimes, the wind tolled like a distant church-bell, and sometimes gave a broad roar around the traveller, as if all Nature were laughing him to scorn. But he was himself the chief horror of the scene, and shrank not from its other horrors.

"Ha! ha! ha!" roared Goodman Brown, when the wind laughed at him. "Let us hear which will laugh loudest! Think not to frighten me with your deviltry! Come witch, come wizard, come Indian powow, come devil himself! and here comes Goodman Brown. You may as well fear him as he fear you!"

In truth, all through the haunted forest, there could be nothing more frightful than the figure of Goodman Brown. On he flew, among the black pines, brandishing his staff with frenzied gestures, now giving vent to an inspiration of horrid blasphemy, and now shouting forth such laughter, as set all the echoes of the forest laughing like demons around him. The fiend in his own shape is less hideous, than when he rages in the breast of man. Thus sped the demoniac on his course, until, quivering among the trees, he saw a red light before him, as when the felled trunks and branches of a clearing have been set on fire, and throw up their lurid blaze against the sky, at the hour of midnight. He paused, in a lull of the tempest that had driven him onward, and heard the swell of what seemed a hymn, rolling solemnly from a distance, with the weight of many voices. He knew the tune; it was a familiar one in the choir of the village meetinghouse. The verse died heavily away, and was lengthened by a chorus, not of human voices, but of all the sounds of the benighted wilderness, pealing in awful harmony together. Goodman Brown cried out; and his cry was lost to his own ear, by its unison with the cry of the desert.

In the interval of silence, he stole forward, until the light glared full upon his eyes. At one extremity of an open space, hemmed in by the dark wall of the forest, arose a rock, bearing some rude, natural resemblance either to an altar or a pulpit, and surrounded by four blazing pines, their tops aflame, their stems untouched, like candles at an evening meeting. The mass of foliage, that had overgrown the summit of the rock, was all on fire, blazing high into the night, and fitfully illuminating the whole field. Each pendent twig and leafy festoon was in a blaze. As the red light arose and fell, a numerous congregation alternately shone forth, then disappeared in shadow, and again grew, as it were, out of the darkness, peopling the heart of the solitary woods at once.

"A grave and dark-clad company!" quoth Goodman Brown.

In truth, they were such. Among them, quivering to-and-fro, between gloom and splendor, appeared faces that would be seen, next day, at the council-board of the province, and others which, Sabbath after Sabbath, looked devoutly heavenward, and benignantly over the crowded pews, from the holiest pulpits in the land. Some affirm, that the lady of the governor was there. At least, there were high dames well known to her, and wives of honored husbands, and widows, a great multitude, and ancient maidens, all of excellent repute, and fair young girls, who trembled, lest their mothers should espy them. Either the sudden gleams of light, flashing over the obscure field, bedazzled Goodman Brown, or he recognized a score of the church-members of Salem village, famous for their especial sanctity. Good old Deacon Gookin had arrived, and waited at the skirts of that venerable saint, his revered pastor. But, irreverently consorting with these grave, reputable, and pious people, these elders of the church, these chaste dames and dewy virgins, there were men of dissolute lives and women of spotted fame, wretches given over to all mean and filthy vice, and suspected even of horrid crimes. It was strange to see, that the good shrank not from the wicked, nor were the sinners abashed by the saints. Scattered, also, among their pale-faced enemies, were the Indian priests, or powows, who had often scared their native forest with more hideous incantations than any known to English witchcraft.

"But, where is Faith?" thought Goodman Brown; and, as hope came into his heart, he trembled.

Another verse of the hymn arose, a slow and mournful strain, such as the pious love, but joined to words which expressed all that our nature can conceive of sin, and darkly hinted at far more. Unfathomable to mere mortals is the lore of fiends. Verse after verse was sung, and still the chorus of the desert swelled between, like the deepest tone of a mighty organ. And, with the final peal of that dreadful anthem, there came a sound, as if the roaring wind, the rushing streams, the howling beasts, and every other voice of the unconverted wilderness, were mingling and according with the voice of guilty man, in homage to the prince of all. The four blazing pines threw up a loftier flame, and obscurely discovered shapes and visages of horror on the smoke-wreaths, above the impious assembly. At the same moment, the fire on the rock shot redly forth, and formed a glowing arch above its base, where now appeared a figure. With reverence be it spoken, the figure bore no slight similitude, both in garb and manner, to some grave divine of the New-England churches.

"Bring forth the converts!" cried a voice, that echoed through the field and rolled into the forest.

At the word, Goodman Brown stept forth from the shadow of the trees, and approached the congregation, with whom he felt a loathful brotherhood, by the sympathy of all that was wicked in his heart. He could have well nigh sworn, that the shape of his own dead father beckoned him to advance, looking downward from a smoke-wreath, while a woman, with dim features of despair, threw out her hand to warn him back. Was it his mother? But he had no power to retreat one step, nor to resist, even in thought, when the minister and good old Deacon Gookin seized his arms, and led him to the blazing rock. Thither came also the slender form of a veiled female, led between Goody Cloyse, that pious teacher of the catechism, and Martha Carrier, who had received the devil's promise to be queen of hell. A rampant hag was she! And there stood the proselytes, beneath the canopy of fire.

"Welcome, my children," said the dark figure, "to the communion of your race! Ye have found, thus young, your nature and your destiny. My children, look behind you!"

They turned; and flashing forth, as it were, in a sheet of flame, the fiend-worshippers were seen; the smile of welcome gleamed darkly on every visage.

"There," resumed the sable form, "are all whom ye have reverenced from youth. Ye deemed them holier than yourselves, and shrank from your own sin, contrasting it with their lives of righteousness, and prayerful aspirations heavenward. Yet, here are they all, in my worshipping assembly! This night it shall be granted you to know their secret deeds; how hoary-bearded elders of the church have whispered wanton words to the young maids of their households; how many a woman, eager for widow's weeds, has given her husband a drink at bed-time, and let him sleep his last sleep in her bosom; how beardless youths have made haste to inherit their fathers' wealth; and how fair damsels—blush not, sweet ones!—have dug little graves in the garden, and bidden me, the sole guest, to an infant's funeral. By the sympathy of your human hearts for sin, ye shall scent out all the places—whether in church, bed-chamber, street, field, or forest—where crime has been committed, and shall exult to behold the whole earth one stain of guilt, one mighty blood-spot. Far more than this! It shall be yours to penetrate, in every bosom, the deep mystery of sin, the fountain of all wicked arts, and which inexhaustibly supplies more evil impulses than human power—than my power, at its utmost!—can make manifest in deeds. And now, my children, look upon each other."

They did so; and, by the blaze of the hell-kindled torches, the wretched man beheld his Faith, and the wife her husband, trembling before that unhallowed altar.

"Lo! there ye stand, my children," said the figure, in a deep and solemn tone, almost sad, with its despairing awful-ness, as if his once angelic nature could yet mourn for our miserable race. "Depending upon one another's hearts, ye had still hoped, that virtue were not all a dream. Now are ye undeceived! Evil is the nature of mankind. Evil must be your only happiness. Welcome, again, my children, to the communion of your race!"

"Welcome!" repeated the fiend-worshippers, in one cry of despair and triumph.

And there they stood, the only pair, as it seemed, who were yet hesitating on the verge of wickedness, in this dark world. A basin was hollowed, naturally, in the rock. Did it contain water, reddened by the lurid light? or was it blood? or, perchance, a liquid flame? Herein did the Shape of Evil dip his hand, and prepare to lay the mark of baptism upon their foreheads, that they might be partakers of the mystery of sin, more conscious of the secret guilt of others, both in deed and thought, than they could now be of their own. The husband cast one look at his pale wife, and Faith at him. What polluted wretches would the next glance shew them to each other, shuddering alike at what they disclosed and what they saw!

"Faith! Faith!" cried the husband. "Look up to Heaven, and resist the Wicked One!"

Whether Faith obeyed, he knew not. Hardly had he spoken, when he found himself amid calm night and solitude, listening to a roar of the wind, which died heavily away through the forest. He staggered against the rock and felt it chill and damp, while a hanging twig, that had been all on fire, besprinkled his cheek with the coldest dew.

The next morning, young Goodman Brown came slowly into the street of Salem village, staring around him like a bewildered man. The good old minister was taking a walk along the grave-yard, to get an appetite for breakfast and meditate his sermon, and bestowed a blessing, as he passed, on Goodman Brown. He shrank from the venerable saint, as if to avoid an anathema. Old Deacon Gookin was at domestic worship, and the holy words of his prayer were heard through the open window. "What God doth the wizard pray to?" quoth Goodman Brown. Goody Cloyse, that excellent old Christian, stood in the early sunshine, at her own lattice, catechising a little girl, who had brought her a pint of morning's milk. Goodman Brown snatched away the child, as from the grasp of the fiend himself. Turning the corner by the meeting-house, he spied the head of Faith, with the pink ribbons, gazing anxiously forth, and bursting into such joy at sight of him, that she skipt along the street, and almost kissed her husband before the whole village. But, Goodman Brown looked sternly and sadly into her face, and passed on without a greeting.

Had Goodman Brown fallen asleep in the forest, and only dreamed a wild dream of a witch-meeting?

Be it so, if you will. But, alas! it was a dream of evil omen for young Goodman Brown. A stern, a sad, a darkly meditative, a distrustful, if not a desperate man, did he become, from the night of that fearful dream. On the Sabbath-day, when the congregation were singing a holy psalm, he could not listen, because an anthem of sin rushed loudly upon his ear, and drowned all the blessed strain. When the minister spoke from the pulpit, with power and fervid eloquence, and, with his hand on the open Bible, of the sacred truths of our religion, and of saint-like lives and triumphant deaths, and of future bliss or misery unutterable, then did Goodman Brown turn pale, dreading, lest the roof should thunder down upon the gray blasphemer and his hearers. Often, awakening suddenly at midnight, he shrank from the bosom of Faith, and at morning or eventide, when the family knelt down at prayer, he scowled, and muttered to himself, and gazed sternly at his wife, and turned away. And when he had lived long, and was borne to his grave, a hoary corpse, followed by Faith, an aged woman, and children and grandchildren, a goodly procession, besides neighbors, not a few, they carved no hopeful verse upon his tomb-stone; for his dying hour was gloom.

Wakefield

IN SOME OLD MAGAZINE or newspaper, I recollect a story, told as truth, of a man—let us call him Wakefield—who absented himself for a long time, from his wife. The fact, thus abstractedly stated, is not very uncommon, nor—without a proper distinction of circumstances—to be condemned either as naughty or nonsensical. Howbeit, this, though far from the most aggravated, is perhaps the strangest instance, on record, of marital delinquency; and, moreover, as remarkable a freak as may be found in the whole list of human oddities. The wedded couple lived in London. The man, under pretence of going a journey, took lodgings in the next street to his own house, and there, unheard of by his wife or friends, and without the shadow of a reason for such self-banishment, dwelt upwards of twenty years. During that period, he beheld his home every day, and frequently the forlorn Mrs. Wakefield. And after so great a gap in his matrimonial felicity—when his death was reckoned certain, his estate settled, his name dismissed from memory, and his wife, long, long ago, resigned to her autumnal widowhood—he entered the door one evening, quietly, as from a day's absence, and became a loving spouse till death.

This outline is all that I remember. But the incident, though of the purest originality, unexampled, and probably never to be repeated, is one, I think, which appeals to the general sympathies of mankind. We know, each for himself, that none of us would perpetrate such a folly, yet feel as if some other might. To my own contemplations, at least, it has often recurred, always exciting wonder, but with a sense that the story must be true, and a conception of its hero's character. Whenever any subject so forcibly affects the mind, time is well spent in thinking of it. If the reader choose, let him do his own meditation; or if he prefer to ramble with me through the twenty years of Wakefield's vagary, I bid him welcome; trusting that there will be a pervading spirit and a moral, even should we fail to find them, done up neatly, and condensed into the final sentence. Thought has always its efficacy, and every striking incident its moral.

What sort of a man was Wakefield? We are free to shape out our own idea, and call it by his name. He was now in the meridian of life; his matrimonial affections, never violent, were sobered into a calm, habitual sentiment; of all husbands, he was likely to be the most constant, because a certain sluggishness would keep his heart at rest, wherever it might be placed. He was intellectual, but not actively so; his mind occupied itself in long and lazy musings, that tended to no purpose, or had not vigor to attain it; his thoughts were seldom so energetic as to seize hold of words. Imagination, in the proper meaning of the term, made no part of Wakefield's gifts. With a cold, but not depraved nor wandering heart, and a mind never feverish with riotous thoughts, nor perplexed with originality, who could have anticipated, that our friend would entitle himself to a foremost place among the doers of eccentric deeds? Had his acquaintances been asked, who was the man in London, the surest to perform nothing to-day which should be remembered on the morrow, they would have thought of Wakefield. Only the wife of his bosom might have hesitated. She, without having analyzed his character, was partly aware of a quiet selfishness, that had rusted into his inactive mind—of a peculiar sort of vanity, the most uneasy attribute about him—of a disposition to craft, which had seldom produced more positive effects than the keeping of petty secrets, hardly worth revealing—and, lastly, of what she called a little strangeness, sometimes, in the good man. This latter quality is indefinable, and perhaps non-existent.

Let us now imagine Wakefield bidding adieu to his wife. It is the dusk of an October evening. His equipment is a drab great-coat, a hat covered with an oil-cloth, top-boots, an umbrella in one hand and a small portmanteau in the other. He has informed Mrs. Wakefield that he is to take the night-coach into the country. She would fain inquire the length of his journey, its object, and the probable time of his return; but, indulgent to his harmless love of mystery, interrogates him only by a look. He tells her not to expect him positively by the return coach, nor to be alarmed should he tarry three or four days; but, at all events, to look for him at supper on Friday evening. Wakefield himself, be it considered, has no suspicion of what is before him. He holds out his hand; she gives her own, and meets his parting kiss, in the matter-of-course way of a ten years' matrimony; and forth goes the middle-aged Mr. Wakefield, almost resolved to perplex his good lady by a whole week's absence. After the door has closed behind him, she perceives it thrust partly open, and a vision of her husband's face, through the aperture, smiling on her, and gone in a moment. For the time, this little incident is dismissed without a thought. But, long afterwards, when she has been more years a widow than a wife, that smile recurs, and flickers across all her reminiscences of Wakefield's visage. In her many musings, she surrounds the original smile with a multitude of fantasies, which make it strange and awful; as, for instance, if she imagines him in a coffin, that parting look is frozen on his pale features; or, if she dreams of him in Heaven, still his blessed spirit wears a quiet and crafty smile. Yet, for its sake, when all others have given him up for dead, she sometimes doubts whether she is a widow.

But, our business is with the husband. We must hurry after him, along the street, ere he lose his individuality, and melt into the great mass of London life. It would be vain searching for him there. Let us follow close at his heels, therefore, until, after several superfluous turns and doublings, we find him comfortably established by the fireside of a small apartment, previously bespoken. He is in the next street to his own, and at his journey's end. He can scarcely trust his good fortune, in having got thither unperceived—recollecting that, at one time, he was delayed by the throng, in the very focus of a lighted lantern; and, again, there were footsteps, that seemed to tread behind his own, distinct from the multitudinous tramp around him; and, anon, he heard a voice shouting afar, and fancied that it called his name. Doubtless, a dozen busy-bodies had been watching him, and told his wife the whole affair. Poor Wakefield! Little knowest thou thine own insignificance in this great world! No mortal eye but mine has traced thee. Go quietly to thy bed, foolish man; and, on the morrow, if thou wilt be wise, get thee home to good Mrs. Wakefield, and tell her the truth. Remove not thyself, even for a little week, from thy place in her chaste bosom. Were she, for a single moment, to deem thee dead, or lost, or lastingly divided from her, thou wouldst be woefully conscious of a change in thy true wife, forever after. It is perilous to make a chasm in human affections; not that they gape so long and wide—but so quickly close again!

Almost repenting of his frolic, or whatever it may be termed,

Wakefield lies down betimes, and starting from his first nap, spreads forth his arms into the wide and solitary waste of the unaccustomed bed. "No"—thinks he, gathering the bed-clothes about him—"I will not sleep alone another night."

In the morning, he rises earlier than usual, and sets himself to consider what he really means to do. Such are his loose and rambling modes of thought, that he has taken this very singular step, with the consciousness of a purpose, indeed, but without being able to define it sufficiently for his own contemplation. The vagueness of the project, and the convulsive effort with which he plunges into the execution of it, are equally characteristic of a feeble-minded man. Wakefield sifts his ideas, however, as minutely as he may, and finds himself curious to know the progress of matters at home—how his exemplary wife will endure her widowhood, of a week; and, briefly, how the little sphere of creatures and circumstances, in which he was a central object, will be affected by his removal. A morbid vanity, therefore, lies nearest the bottom of the affair. But, how is he to attain his ends? Not, certainly, by keeping close in this comfortable lodging, where, though he slept and awoke in the next street to his home, he is as effectually abroad, as if the stage-coach had been whirling him away all night. Yet, should he reappear, the whole project is knocked in the head. His poor brains being hopelessly puzzled with this dilemma, he at length ventures out, partly resolving to cross the head of the street, and send one hasty glance towards his forsaken domicile. Habit—for he is a man of habits—takes him by the hand, and guides him, wholly unaware, to his own door, where, just at the critical moment, he is aroused by the scraping of his foot upon the step. Wakefield! whither are you going?

At that instant, his fate was turning on the pivot. Little dreaming of the doom to which his first backward step devotes him, he hurries away, breathless with agitation hitherto unfelt, and hardly dares turn his head, at the distant corner. Can it be, that nobody caught sight of him? Will not the whole household—the decent Mrs. Wakefield, the smart maid-servant, and the dirty little foot-boy—raise a hue-and-cry, through London streets, in pursuit of their fugitive lord and master? Wonderful escape! He gathers courage to pause and look homeward, but is perplexed with a sense of change about the familiar edifice, such as affects us all, when, after a separation of months or years, we again see some hill or lake, or work of art, with which we were friends, of old. In ordinary cases, this indescribable impression is caused by the comparison and contrast between our imperfect reminiscences and the reality. In Wakefield, the magic of a single night has wrought a similar transformation, because, in that brief period, a great moral change has been effected. But this is a secret from himself. Before leaving the spot, he catches a far and momentary glimpse of his wife, passing athwart the front window, with her face turned towards the head of the street. The crafty nincompoop takes to his heels, scared with the idea, that, among a thousand such atoms of mortality, her eye must have detected him. Right glad is his heart, though his brain be somewhat dizzy, when he finds himself by the coal-fire of his lodgings.

So much for the commencement of this long whim-wham. After the initial conception, and the stirring up of the man's sluggish temperament to put it in practice, the whole matter evolves itself in a natural train. We may suppose him, as the result of deep deliberation, buying a new wig, of reddish hair, and selecting sundry garments, in a fashion unlike his customary suit of brown, from a Jew's old-clothes bag. It is accomplished. Wakefield is another man. The new system being now established, a retrograde movement to the old would be almost as difficult as the step that placed him in his unparalleled position. Furthermore, he is rendered obstinate by a sulkiness, occasionally incident to his temper, and brought on, at present, by the inadequate sensation which he conceives to have been produced in the bosom of Mrs. Wakefield. He will not go back until she be frightened half to death. Well, twice or thrice has she passed before his sight, each time with a heavier step, a paler cheek, and more anxious brow; and, in the third week of his non-appearance, he detects a portent of evil entering the house, in the guise of an apothecary. Next day, the knocker is muffled. Towards night-fall, comes the chariot of a physician, and deposits its big-wigged and solemn burthen at Wakefield's door, whence, after a quarter of an hour's visit, he emerges, perchance the herald of a funeral. Dear woman! Will she die? By this time, Wakefield is excited to something like energy of feeling, but still lingers away from his wife's bedside, pleading with his conscience, that she must not be disturbed at such a juncture. If aught else restrains him, he does not know it. In the course of a few weeks, she gradually recovers; the crisis is over; her heart is sad, perhaps, but quiet; and, let him return soon or late, it will never be feverish for him again. Such ideas glimmer through the mist of Wakefield's mind, and render him indistinctly conscious, that an almost impassable gulf divides his hired apartment from his former home. "It is but in the next street!" he sometimes says. Fool! it is in another world. Hitherto, he has put off his return from one particular day to another; henceforward, he leaves the precise time undetermined. Not to-morrow—probably next week—pretty soon. Poor man! The dead have nearly as much chance of re-visiting their earthly homes, as the self-banished Wakefield.

Would that I had a folio to write, instead of an article of a dozen pages! Then might I exemplify how an influence, beyond our control, lays its strong hand on every deed which we do, and weaves its consequences into an iron tissue of necessity. Wakefield is spell-bound. We must leave him, for ten years or so, to haunt around his house, without once crossing the threshold, and to be faithful to his wife, with all the affection of which his heart is capable, while he is slowly fading out of hers. Long since, it must be remarked, he has lost the perception of singularity in his conduct.

Now for a scene! Amid the throng of a London street, we distinguish a man, now waxing elderly, with few characteristics to attract careless observers, yet bearing, in his whole aspect, the hand-writing of no common fate, for such as have the skill to read it. He is meagre; his low and narrow forehead is deeply wrinkled; his eyes, small and lustreless, sometimes wander apprehensively about him, but oftener seem to look inward. He bends his head, but moves with an indescribable obliquity of gait, as if unwilling to display his full front to the world. Watch him, long enough to see what we have described, and you will allow, that circumstances—which often produce remarkable men from nature's ordinary handiwork—have produced one such here. Next, leaving him to sidle along the foot-walk, cast your eyes in the opposite direction, where a portly female, considerably in the wane of life, with a prayer-book in her hand, is proceeding to yonder church. She has the placid mien of settled widowhood. Her regrets have either died away, or have become so essential to her heart, that they would be poorly exchanged for joy. Just as the lean man and well conditioned woman are passing, a slight obstruction occurs, and brings these two figures directly in contact. Their hands touch; the pressure of the crowd forces her bosom against his shoulder; they stand, face to face, staring into each other's eyes. After a ten years' separation, thus Wakefield meets his wife!

The throng eddies away, and carries them asunder. The sober widow, resuming her former pace, proceeds to church, but pauses in the portal, and throws a perplexed glance along the street. She passes in, however, opening her prayer-book as she goes. And the man? With so wild a face, that busy and selfish London stands to gaze after him, he hurries to his lodgings, bolts the door, and throws himself upon the bed. The latent feelings of years break out; his feeble mind acquires a brief energy from their strength; all the miserable strangeness of his life is revealed to him at a glance; and he cries out, passionately—"Wakefield! Wakefield! You are mad!"

Perhaps he was so. The singularity of his situation must have so moulded him to itself, that, considered in regard to his fellow-creatures and the business of life, he could not be said to possess his right mind. He had contrived, or rather he had happened, to dissever himself from the world—to vanish—to give up his place and privileges with living men, without being admitted among the dead. The life of a hermit is nowise parallel to his. He was in the bustle of the city, as of old; but the crowd swept by, and saw him not; he was, we may figuratively say, always beside his wife, and at his hearth, yet must never feel the warmth of the one, nor the affection of the other. It was Wakefield's unprecedented fate, to retain his original share of human sympathies, and to be still involved in human interests, while he had lost his reciprocal influence on them. It would be a most curious speculation, to trace out the effect of such circumstances on his heart and intellect, separately, and in unison. Yet, changed as he was, he would seldom be conscious of it, but deem himself the same man as ever; glimpses of the truth, indeed, would come, but only for the moment; and still he would keep saying—"I shall soon go back!"—nor reflect, that he had been saying so for twenty years.

I conceive, also, that these twenty years would appear, in the retrospect, scarcely longer than the week to which Wakefield had at first limited his absence. He would look on the affair as no more than an interlude in the main business of his life. When, after a little while more, he should deem it time to re-enter his parlor, his wife would clap her hands for joy, on beholding the middle-aged Mr. Wakefield.

Alas, what a mistake! Would Time but await the close of our favorite follies, we should be young men, all of us, and till Doom's Day.

One evening, in the twentieth year since he vanished, Wakefield is taking his customary walk towards the dwelling which he still calls his own. It is a gusty night of autumn, with frequent showers, that patter down upon the pavement, and are gone, before a man can put up his umbrella. Pausing near the house, Wakefield discerns, through the parlor-windows of the second floor, the red glow, and the glimmer and fitful flash, of a comfortable fire. On the ceiling, appears a grotesque shadow of good Mrs. Wakefield. The cap, the nose and chin, and the broad waist, form an admirable caricature, which dances, moreover, with the up-flickering and down-sinking blaze, almost too merrily for the shade of an elderly widow. At this instant, a shower chances to fall, and is driven, by the unmannerly gust, full into Wakefield's face and bosom. He is quite penetrated with its autumnal chill. Shall he stand, wet and shivering here, when his own hearth has a good fire to warm him, and his own wife will run to fetch the gray coat and small-clothes, which, doubtless, she has kept carefully in the closet of their bed-chamber? No! Wakefield is no such fool. He ascends the steps—heavily!—for twenty years have stiffened his legs, since he came down—but he knows it not. Stay, Wakefield! Would you go to the sole home that is left you? Then step into your grave! The door opens. As he passes in, we have a parting glimpse of his visage, and recognize the crafty smile, which was the precursor of the little joke, that he has ever since been playing off at his wife's expense. How unmercifully has he quizzed the poor woman! Well; a good night's rest to Wakefield!

This happy event—supposing it to be such—could only have occurred at an unpremeditated moment. We will not follow our friend across the threshold. He has left us much food for thought, a portion of which shall lend its wisdom to a moral; and be shaped into a figure.

Amid the seeming confusion of our mysterious world, individuals are so nicely adjusted to a system, and systems to one another, and to a whole, that, by stepping aside for a moment, a man exposes himself to a fearful risk of losing his place forever. Like Wakefield, he may become, as it were, the Outcast of the Universe.

The Ambitious Guest

O NE SEPTEMBER NIGHT, a family had gathered round their hearth, and piled it high with the driftwood of mountain-streams, the dry cones of the pine, and the splintered ruins of great trees, that had come crashing down the precipice. Up the chimney roared the fire, and brightened the room with its broad blaze. The faces of the father and mother had a sober gladness; the children laughed; the eldest daughter was the image of Happiness at seventeen; and the aged grandmother, who sat knitting in the warmest place, was the image of Happiness grown old. They had found the "herb, heart's ease," in the bleakest spot of all New-England. This family were situated in the Notch of the White Hills, where the wind was sharp throughout the year, and pitilessly cold in the winter—giving their cottage all its fresh inclemency, before it descended on the valley of the Saco. They dwelt in a cold spot and a dangerous one; for a mountain towered above their heads, so steep, that the stones would often rumble down its sides, and startle them at midnight.

The daughter had just uttered some simple jest, that filled them all with mirth, when the wind came through the Notch and seemed to pause before their cottage—rattling the door, with a sound of wailing and lamentation, before it passed into the valley. For a moment, it saddened them, though there was nothing unusual in the tones. But the family were glad again, when they perceived that the latch was lifted by some traveller, whose footsteps had been unheard amid the dreary blast, which heralded his approach, and wailed as he was entering, and went moaning away from the door.

Though they dwelt in such a solitude, these people held daily converse with the world. The romantic pass of the Notch is a great artery, through which the life-blood of internal commerce is continually throbbing, between Maine, on one side, and the Green Mountains and the shores of the St. Lawrence on the other. The stage-coach always drew up before the door of the cottage. The wayfarer, with no companion but his staff, paused here to exchange a word, that the sense of loneliness might not utterly overcome him, ere he could pass through the cleft of the mountain, or reach the first house in the valley. And here the teamster, on his way to Portland market, would put up for the night—and, if a bachelor, might sit an hour beyond the usual bed-time, and steal a kiss from the mountain-maid, at parting. It was one of those primitive taverns, where the traveller pays only for food and lodging, but meets with a homely kindness, beyond all price. When the footsteps were heard, therefore, between the outer door and the inner one, the whole family rose up, grandmother, children, and all, as if about to welcome some one who belonged to them, and whose fate was linked with theirs.

The door was opened by a young man. His face at first wore the melancholy expression, almost despondency, of one who travels a wild and bleak road, at night-fall and alone, but soon brightened up, when he saw the kindly warmth of his reception. He felt his heart spring forward to meet them all, from the old woman, who wiped a chair with her apron, to the little child that held out its arms to him. One glance and smile placed the stranger on a footing of innocent familiarity with the eldest daughter.

"Ah, this fire is the right thing!" cried he; "especially when there is such a pleasant circle round it. I am quite benumbed; for the Notch is just like the pipe of a great pair of bellows; it has blown a terrible blast in my face, all the way from Bartlett."

"Then you are going towards Vermont?" said the master of the house, as he helped to take a light knapsack off the young man's shoulders.

"Yes; to Burlington, and far enough beyond," replied he. "I meant to have been at Ethan Crawford's, to-night; but a pedestrian lingers along such a road as this. It is no matter; for, when I saw this good fire, and all your cheerful faces, I felt as if you had kindled it on purpose for me, and were waiting my arrival. So I shall sit down among you, and make myself at home."

The frank-hearted stranger had just drawn his chair to the fire, when something like a heavy footstep was heard without, rushing down the steep side of the mountain, as with long and rapid strides, and taking such a leap, in passing the cottage, as to strike the opposite precipice. The family held their breath, because they knew the sound, and their guest held his, by instinct.

"The old Mountain has thrown a stone at us, for fear we should forget him," said the landlord, recovering himself. "He sometimes nods his head, and threatens to come down; but we are old neighbors, and agree together pretty well, upon the whole. Besides, we have a sure place of refuge, hard by, if he should be coming in good earnest."

Let us now suppose the stranger to have finished his supper of bear's meat; and, by his natural felicity of manner, to have placed himself on a footing of kindness with the whole family—so that they talked as freely together, as if he belonged to their mountain brood. He was of a proud, yet gentle spirit—haughty and reserved among the rich and great; but ever ready to stoop his head to the lowly cottage door, and be like a brother or a son at the poor man's fireside. In the household of the Notch, he found warmth and simplicity of feeling, the pervading intelligence of New-England, and a poetry, of native growth, which they had gathered, when they little thought of it, from the mountain-peaks and chasms, and at the very threshold of their romantic and dangerous abode. He had travelled far and alone; his whole life, indeed, had been a solitary path; for, with the lofty caution of his nature, he had kept himself apart from those who might otherwise have been his companions. The family, too, though so kind and hospitable, had that consciousness of unity among themselves, and separation from the world at large, which, in every domestic circle, should still keep a holy place, where no stranger may intrude. But, this evening, a prophetic sympathy impelled the refined and educated youth to pour out his heart before the simple mountaineers, and constrained them to answer him with the same free confidence. And thus it should have been. Is not the kindred of a common fate a closer tie than that of birth?

The secret of the young man's character was, a high and abstracted ambition. He could have borne to live an undistinguished life, but not to be forgotten in the grave. Yearning desire had been transformed to hope; and hope, long cherished, had become like certainty, that, obscurely as he journeyed now, a glory was to beam on all his pathway—though not, perhaps, while he was treading it. But, when posterity should gaze back into the gloom of what was now the present, they would trace the brightness of his footsteps, brightening as meaner glories faded, and confess, that a gifted one had passed from his cradle to his tomb, with none to recognize him.

"As yet," cried the stranger—his cheek glowing and his eye flashing with enthusiasm—"as yet, I have done nothing. Were I to vanish from the earth to-morrow, none would know so much of me as you; that a nameless youth came up, at night-fall, from the valley of the Saco, and opened his heart to you in the evening, and passed through the Notch, by sunrise, and was seen no more. Not a soul would ask— 'Who was he?—Whither did the wanderer go?' But, I cannot die till I have achieved my destiny. Then, let Death come! I shall have built my monument!"

There was a continual flow of natural emotion, gushing forth amid abstracted reverie, which enabled the family to understand this young man's sentiments, though so foreign from their own. With quick sensibility of the ludicrous, he blushed at the ardor into which he had been betrayed.

"You laugh at me," said he, taking the eldest daughter's hand, and laughing himself. "You think my ambition as nonsensical as if I were to freeze myself to death on the top of Mount Washington, only that people might spy at me from the country roundabout. And truly, that would be a noble pedestal for a man's statue!"

"It is better to sit here, by this fire," answered the girl, blushing, "and be comfortable and contented, though nobody thinks about us."

"I suppose," said her father, after a fit of musing, "there is something natural in what the young man says; and if my mind had been turned that way, I might have felt just the same. It is strange, wife, how his talk has set my head running on things, that are pretty certain never to come to pass."

"Perhaps they may," observed the wife. "Is the man thinking what he will do when he is a widower?"

"No, no!" cried he, repelling the idea with reproachful kindness. "When I think of your death, Esther, I think of mine, too. But I was wishing we had a good farm, in Bartlett, or Bethlehem, or Littleton, or some other township round the White Mountains; but not where they could tumble on our heads. I should want to stand well with my neighbors, and be called 'Squire, and sent to General Court, for a term or two; for a, plain, honest man may do as much good there as a lawyer. And when I should be grown quite an old man, and you an old woman, so as not to be long apart, I might die happy enough in my bed, and leave you all crying around me. A slate grave-stone would suit me as well as a marble one—with just my name and age, and a verse of a hymn, and something to let people know, that I lived an honest man and died a Christian."

"There now!" exclaimed the stranger; "it is our nature to desire a monument, be it slate, or marble, or a pillar of granite, or a glorious memory in the universal heart of man."

"We're in a strange way, to-night," said the wife, with tears in her eyes. "They say it's a sign of something, when folks' minds go a wandering so. Hark to the children!"

They listened accordingly. The younger children had been put to bed in another room, but with an open door between, so that they could be heard talking busily among themselves. One and all seemed to have caught the infection from the fireside circle, and were outvying each other, in wild wishes, and childish projects of what they would do, when they came to be men and women. At length, a little boy, instead of addressing his brothers and sisters, called out to his mother.

"I'll tell you what I wish, mother," cried he. "I want you and father and grandma'm, and all of us, and the stranger too, to start right away, and go and take a drink out of the basin of the Flume!"

Nobody could help laughing at the child's notion of leaving a warm bed, and dragging them from a cheerful fire, to visit the basin of the Flume—a brook, which tumbles over the precipice, deep within the Notch. The boy had hardly spoken, when a wagon rattled along the road, and stopped a moment before the door. It appeared to contain two or three men, who were cheering their hearts with the rough chorus of a song, which resounded, in broken notes, between the cliffs, while the singers hesitated whether to continue their journey, or put up here for the night.

"Father," said the girl, "they are calling you by name."

But the good man doubted whether they had really called him, and was unwilling to show himself too solicitous of gain, by inviting people to patronize his house. He therefore did not hurry to the door; and the lash being soon applied, the travellers plunged into the Notch, still singing and laughing, though their music and mirth came back drearily from the heart of the mountain.

"There, mother!" cried the boy, again. "They'd have given us a ride to the Flume."

Again they laughed at the child's pertinacious fancy for a night-ramble. But it happened, that a light cloud passed over the daughter's spirit; she looked gravely into the fire, and drew a breath that was almost a sigh. It forced its way, in spite of a little struggle to repress it. Then starting and blushing, she looked quickly round the circle, as if they had caught a glimpse into her bosom. The stranger asked what she had been thinking of.

"Nothing," answered she, with a downcast smile. "Only I felt lonesome just then."

"Oh, I have always had a gift of feeling what is in other people's hearts," said he, half seriously. "Shall I tell the secrets of yours? For I know what to think, when a young girl shivers by a warm hearth, and complains of lonesomeness at her mother's side. Shall I put these feelings into words?"

"They would not be a girl's feelings any longer, if they could be put into words," replied the mountain-nymph, laughing, but avoiding his eye.

All this was said apart. Perhaps a germ of love was springing in their hearts, so pure that it might blossom in Paradise, since it could not be matured on earth; for women worship such gentle dignity as his; and the proud, contemplative, yet kindly soul is oftenest captivated by simplicity like hers. But, while they spoke softly, and he was watching the happy sadness, the lightsome shadows, the shy yearnings of a maiden's nature, the wind, through the Notch, took a deeper and dearier sound. It seemed, as the fanciful stranger said, like the choral strain of the spirits of the blast, who, in old Indian times, had their dwelling among these mountains, and made their heights and recesses a sacred region. There was a wail, along the road, as if a funeral were passing. To chase away the gloom, the family threw pine branches on their fire, till the dry leaves crackled and the flame arose, discovering once again a scene of peace and humble happiness. The light hovered about them fondly, and caressed them all. There were the little faces of the children, peeping from their bed apart, and here the father's frame of strength, the mother's subdued and careful mien, the high-browed youth, the budding girl, and the good old grandam, still knitting in the warmest place. The aged woman looked up from her task, and, with fingers ever busy, was the next to speak.

"Old folks have their notions," said she, "as well as young ones. You've been wishing and planning; and letting your heads run on one thing and another, till you've set my mind a wandering too. Now what should an old woman wish for, when she can go but a step or two before she comes to her grave? Children, it will haunt me night and day, till I tell you."

"What is it, mother?" cried the husband and wife, at once.

Then the old woman, with an air of mystery, which drew the circle closer round the fire, informed them that she had provided her grave-clothes some years before—a nice linen shroud, a cap with a muslin ruff, and everything of a finer sort than she had worn since her wedding-day. But, this evening, an old superstition had strangely re-curred to her. It used to be said, in her younger days, that, if anything were amiss with a corpse, if only the ruff were not smooth, or the cap did not set right, the corpse, in the coffin and beneath the clods, would strive to put up its cold hands and arrange it. The bare thought made her nervous.

"Don't talk so, grandmother!" said the girl, shuddering.

"Now,"—continued the old woman, with singular earnestness, yet smiling strangely at her own folly,—"I want one of you, my chil-dren—when your mother is drest, and in the coffin—I want one of you to hold a looking-glass over my face. Who knows but I may take a glimpse at myself, and see whether all's right?"

"Old and young, we dream of graves and monuments," murmured the stranger-youth. "I wonder how mariners feel, when the ship is sinking, and they, unknown and undistinguished, are to be buried to-gether in the ocean—that wide and nameless sepulchre!"

For a moment, the old woman's ghastly conception so engrossed the minds of her hearers, that a sound, abroad in the night, rising like the roar of a blast, had grown broad, deep, and terrible, before the fated group were conscious of it. The house, and all within it, trem-bled; the foundations of the earth seemed to be shaken, as if this aw-ful sound were the peal of the last trump. Young and old exchanged one wild glance, and remained an instant, pale, affrighted, without utterance, or power to move. Then the same shriek burst simultane-ously from all their lips.

"The Slide! The Slide!"

The simplest words must intimate, but not portray, the unutter-able horror of the catastrophe. The victims rushed from their cottage, and sought refuge in what they deemed a safer spot—where, in con-templation of such an emergency, a sort of barrier had been reared. Alas! they had quitted their security, and fled right into the pathway of destruction. Down came the whole side of the mountain, in a cataract of ruin. Just before it reached the house, the stream broke into two branches—shivered not a window there, but overwhelmed the whole vicinity, blocked up the road, and annihilated everything in its dreadful course. Long ere the thunder of that great Slide had ceased to roar among the mountains, the mortal agony had been endured, and the victims were at peace. Their bodies were never found.

The next morning, the light smoke was seen stealing from the cottage-chimney, up the mountain-side. Within, the fire was yet smouldering on the hearth, and the chairs in a circle round it, as if the inhabitants had but gone forth to view the devastation of the Slide, and would shortly return, to thank Heaven for their miraculous escape. All had left separate tokens, by which those, who had known the family, were made to shed a tear for each. Who has not heard their name? The story has been told far and wide, and will forever be a legend of these mountains. Poets have sung their fate.

There were circumstances, which led some to suppose that a stranger had been received into the cottage on this awful night, and had shared the catastrophe of all its inmates. Others denied that there were sufficient grounds for such a conjecture. Wo, for the high-souled youth, with his dream of Earthly Immortality! His name and person utterly unknown; his history, his way of life, his plans, a mystery never to be solved; his death and his existence, equally a doubt! Whose was the agony of that death-moment?

The Devil in Manuscript

O N A B I T T E R E V E N I N G O F December, I arrived by mail in a large town, which was then the residence of an intimate friend, one of those gifted youths who cultivate poetry and the belles lettres, and call themselves students at law. My first business, after supper, was to visit him at the office of his distinguished instructer. As I have said, it was a bitter night, clear starlight, but cold as Nova Zembla— the shop-windows along the street being frosted, so as almost to hide the lights, while the wheels of coaches thundered equally loud over frozen earth and pavements of stone. There was no snow, either on the ground or the roofs of the houses. The wind blew so violently, that I had but to spread my cloak like a mainsail, and scud along the street at the rate of ten knots, greatly envied by other navigators who were beating slowly up, with the gale right in their teeth. One of these I capsized, but was gone on the wings of the wind before he could even vociferate an oath.

After this picture of an inclement night, behold us seated by a great blazing fire, which looked so comfortable and delicious that I felt inclined to lie down and roll among the hot coals. The usual furniture of a lawyer's office was around us—rows of volumes in sheepskin, and a multitude of writs, summonses, and other legal papers, scattered over the desks and tables. But there were certain objects which seemed to intimate that we had little dread of the intrusion of clients, or of the learned counsellor himself, who, indeed, was attending court in a distant town. A tall, decanter-shaped bottle stood on the table, between two tumblers, and beside a pile of blotted manuscripts, altogether dissimilar to any law documents recognized in our courts. My friend, whom I shall call Oberon—it was a name of fancy and friendship between him and me—my friend Oberon looked at these papers with a peculiar expression of disquietude.

"I do believe," said he, soberly, "or, at least, I would believe, if I chose, that there is a devil in this pile of blotted papers. You have read them, and know what I mean—that conception, in which I endeavored to embody the character of a fiend, as represented in our traditions and the written records of witchcraft. Oh! I have a horror of what was created in my own brain, and shudder at the manuscripts in which I gave that dark idea a sort of material existence. Would they were out of my sight!"

"And of mine too," thought I.

"You remember," continued Oberon, "how the hellish thing used to suck away the happiness of those who, by a simple concession that seemed almost innocent, subjected themselves to his power. Just so my peace is gone, and all by these accursed manuscripts. Have you felt nothing of the same influence?"

"Nothing," replied I, "unless the spell be hid in a desire to turn novelist, after reading your delightful tales."

"Novelist!" exclaimed Oberon, half seriously. "Then, indeed, my

devil has his claw on you! You are gone! You cannot even pray for deliverance! But we will be the last and only victims; for this night I
mean to burn the manuscripts, and commit the fiend to his retribution in the flames."

"Burn your tales!" repeated I, startled at the desperation of the
idea.

"Even so," said the author, despondingly. "You cannot conceive
what an effect the composition of these tales has had on me. I have
become ambitious of a bubble, and careless of solid reputation. I am
surrounding myself with shadows, which bewilder me, by aping the
realities of life. They have drawn me aside from the beaten path of
the world, and led me into a strange sort of solitude—a solitude in
the midst of men—where nobody wishes for what I do, nor thinks
nor feels as I do. The tales have done all this. When they are ashes, perhaps I shall be as I was before they had existence. Moreover, the sacrifice is less than you may suppose; since nobody will publish them."

"That does make a difference, indeed," said I.

"They have been offered, by letter," continued Oberon, reddening
with vexation, "to some seventeen booksellers. It would make you
stare to read their answers; and read them you should, only that I
burnt them as fast as they arrived. One man publishes nothing but
school-books; another has five novels already under examination—"

"What a voluminous mass the unpublished literature of America
must be!" cried I.

"Oh! the Alexandrian manuscripts were nothing to it," said my
friend. "Well; another gentleman is just giving up business, on purpose, I verily believe, to escape publishing my book. Several, however,
would not absolutely decline the agency, on my advancing half the
cost of an edition, and giving bonds for the remainder, besides a high
percentage to themselves, whether the book sells or not. Another ad-
vises a subscription."

"The villain!" exclaimed I.

"A fact!" said Oberon. "In short, of all the seventeen booksellers, only one has vouchsafed even to read my tales; and he—a literary dabbler himself, I should judge—has the impertinence to criticize them, proposing what he calls vast improvements, and concluding, after a general sentence of condemnation, with the definitive assurance that he will not be concerned on any terms."

It might not be amiss to pull that fellow's nose," remarked I.

"If the whole 'trade' had one common nose, there would be some satisfaction in pulling it," answered the author. "But, there does seem to be one honest man among these seventeen unrighteous ones, and he tells me fairly, that no American publisher will meddle with an American work, seldom if by a known writer, and never if by a new one, unless at the writer's risk."

"The paltry rogues!" cried I. "Will they live by literature, and yet risk nothing for its sake? But, after all, you might publish on your own account."

"And so I might," replied Oberon. "But the devil of the business is this. These people have put me so out of conceit with the tales, that I loathe the very thought of them, and actually experience a physical sickness of the stomach, whenever I glance at them on the table. I tell you there is a demon in them! I anticipate a wild enjoyment in seeing them in the blaze; such as I should feel in taking vengeance on an enemy, or destroying something noxious."

I did not very strenuously oppose this determination, being privately of opinion, in spite of my partiality for the author, that his tales would make a more brilliant appearance in the fire than anywhere else. Before proceeding to execution, we broached the bottle of champagne, which Oberon had provided for keeping up his spirits in this doleful business. We swallowed each a tumblerfull, in sparkling commotion; it went bubbling down our throats, and brightened my eyes at once, but left my friend sad and heavy as before. He drew the tales towards him, with a mixture of natural affection and natural disgust, like a father taking a deformed infant into his arms.

"Pooh! Pish! Pshaw!" exclaimed he, holding them at arm's length. "It was Gray's idea of Heaven, to lounge on a sofa and read new novels. Now, what more appropriate torture would Dante himself have contrived, for the sinner who perpetrates a bad book, than to be continually turning over the manuscript?"

"It would fail of effect," said I, "because a bad author is always his own great admirer."

"I lack that one characteristic of my tribe, the only desirable one," observed Oberon. "But how many recollections throng upon me, as I turn over these leaves! This scene came into my fancy as I walked along a hilly road, on a starlight October evening; in the pure and bracing air, I became all soul, and felt as if I could climb the sky and run a race along the Milky Way. Here is another tale, in which I wrapt myself during a dark and dreary night-ride in the month of March, till the rattling of the wheels and the voices of my companions seemed like faint sounds of a dream, and my visions a bright reality. That scribbled page describes shadows which I summoned to my bedside at midnight; they would not depart when I bade them; the gray dawn came, and found me wide awake and feverish, the victim of my own enchantments!"

"There must have been a sort of happiness in all this," said I, smitten with a strange longing to make proof of it.

"There may be happiness in a fever fit," replied the author. "And then the various moods in which I wrote! Sometimes my ideas were like precious stones under the earth, requiring toil to dig them up, and care to polish and brighten them; but often, a delicious stream of thought would gush out upon the page at once, like water sparkling up suddenly in the desert; and when it had passed, I gnawed my pen hopelessly, or blundered on with cold and miserable toil, as if there were a wall of ice between me and my subject."

"Do you now perceive a corresponding difference," inquired I, "between the passages which you wrote so coldly, and those fervid flashes of the mind?"

"No," said Oberon, tossing the manuscripts on the table. "I find no traces of the golden pen, with which I wrote in characters of fire. My treasure of fairy coin is changed to worthless dross. My picture, painted in what seemed the loveliest hues, presents nothing but a faded and indistinguishable surface. I have been eloquent and poetical and humorous in a dream—and behold! it is all nonsense, now that I am awake."

My friend now threw sticks of wood and dry chips upon the fire, and seeing it blaze like Nebuchadnezzar's furnace, seized the champagne bottle, and drank two or three brimming bumpers, successively. The heady liquor combined with his agitation to throw him into a species of rage. He laid violent hands on the tales. In one instant more, their faults and beauties would alike have vanished in a glowing purgatory. But, all at once, I remembered passages of high imagination, deep pathos, original thoughts, and points of such varied excellence, that the vastness of the sacrifice struck me most forcibly. I caught his arm.

"Surely, you do not mean to burn them!" I exclaimed.

"Let me alone!" cried Oberon, his eyes flashing fire. "I will burn them! Not a scorched syllable shall escape! Would you have me a damned author?—To undergo sneers, taunts, abuse, and cold neglect, and faint praise, bestowed, for pity's sake, against the giver's conscience! A hissing and a laughingstock to my own traitorous thoughts! An outlaw from the protection of the grave—one whose ashes every careless foot might spurn, unhonored in life, and remembered scornfully in death! Am I to bear all this, when yonder fire will ensure me from the whole? No! There go the tales! May my hand wither when it would write another!"

The deed was done. He had thrown the manuscripts into the hottest of the fire, which at first seemed to shrink away, but soon curled around them, and made them a part of its own fervent brightness. Oberon stood gazing at the conflagration, and shortly began to soliloquize, in the wildest strain, as if Fancy resisted and became riotous, at the moment when he would have compelled her to ascend that funeral pile. His words described objects which he appeared to discern in the fire, fed by his own precious thoughts; perhaps the thousand visions, which the writer's magic had incorporated with those pages, became visible to him in the dissolving heat, brightening forth ere they vanished forever; while the smoke, the vivid sheets of flame, the ruddy and whitening coals, caught the aspect of a varied scenery.

"They blaze," said he, "as if I had steeped them in the intensest spirit of genius. There I see my lovers clasped in each other's arms. How pure the flame that bursts from their glowing hearts! And yonder the features of a villain, writhing in the fire that shall torment him to eternity. My holy men, my pious and angelic women, stand like martyrs amid the flames, their mild eyes lifted heavenward. Ring out the bells! A city is on fire. See!—destruction roars through my dark forests, while the lakes boil up in steaming billows, and the mountains are volcanoes, and the sky kindles with a lurid brightness! All elements are but one pervading flame! Ha! The fiend!"

I was somewhat startled by this latter exclamation. The tales were almost consumed, but just then threw forth a broad sheet of fire, which flickered as with laughter, making the whole room dance in its brightness, and then roared portentously up the chimney.

"You saw him? You must have seen him!" cried Oberon. "How he glared at me and laughed, in that last sheet of flame, with just the features that I imagined for him! Well! The tales are gone."

The papers were indeed reduced to a heap of black cinders, with a multitude of sparks hurrying confusedly among them, the traces of the pen being now represented by white lines, and the whole mass fluttering to and fro, in the draughts of air. The destroyer knelt down to look at them.

"What is more potent than fire!" said he, in his gloomiest tone. "Even thought, invisible and incorporeal as it is, cannot escape it. In this little time, it has annihilated the creations of long nights and days, which I could no more reproduce, in their first glow and freshness, than cause ashes and whitened bones to rise up and live. There, too, I sacrificed the unborn children of my mind. All that I had accomplished—all that I planned for future years—has perished by one common ruin, and left only this heap of embers. The deed has been my fate. And what remains? A weary and aimless life—a long repentance of this hour—and at last an obscure grave, where they will bury and forget me."

As the author concluded his dolorous moan, the extinguished embers arose and settled down and arose again, and finally flew up the chimney, like a demon with sable wings. Just as they disappeared, there was a loud and solitary cry in the street below us. "Fire! Fire!" Other voices caught up that terrible word, and it speedily became the shout of a multitude. Oberon started to his feet, in fresh excitement.

"A fire on such a night!" cried he. "The wind blows a gale, and wherever it whirls the flames, the roofs will flash up like gunpowder. Every pump is frozen up, and boiling water would turn to ice the moment it was flung from the engine. In an hour, this wooden town will be one great bonfire! What a glorious scene for my next——Pshaw!"

The street was now all alive with footsteps, and the air full of voices. We heard one engine thundering round a corner, and another rattling from a distance over the pavements. The bells of three steeples clanged out at once, spreading the alarm to many a neighboring town, and expressing hurry, confusion and terror, so inimitably that I could almost distinguish in their peal the burthen of the universal cry—"Fire! Fire! Fire!"

"What is so eloquent as their iron tongues!" exclaimed Oberon. "My heart leaps and trembles, but not with fear. And that other sound, too—deep and awful as a mighty organ—the roar and thunder of the multitude on the pavement below! Come! We are losing time. I will cry out in the loudest of the uproar, and mingle my spirit with the wildest of the confusion, and be a bubble on the top of the ferment!"

From the first outcry, my forebodings had warned me of the true object and centre of alarm. There was nothing now but uproar—above, beneath, and around us; footsteps stumbling pell-mell up the public stair-case, eager shouts and heavy thumps at the door, the whiz and dash of water from the engines, and the crash of furniture thrown upon the pavement. At once, the truth flashed upon my friend. His frenzy took the hue of joy, and, with a wild gesture of exultation, he leaped almost to the ceiling of the chamber.

"My tales!" cried Oberon. "The chimney! The roof! The Fiend has gone forth by night, and startled thousands in fear and wonder from their beds! Here I stand—a triumphant author! Huzza! Huzza! My brain has set the town on fire! Huzza!"

The Minister's Black Veil

A Parable*

T HE SEXTON STOOD IN the porch of Milford meeting-house,
pulling lustily at the bell-rope. The old people of the village
came stooping along the street. Children, with bright faces, tript merrily beside their parents, or mimicked a graver gait, in the conscious
dignity of their Sunday clothes. Spruce bachelors looked sidelong at
the pretty maidens, and fancied that the Sabbath sunshine made them
prettier than on week-days. When the throng had mostly streamed
into the porch, the sexton began to toll the bell, keeping his eye on the
Reverend Mr. Hooper's door. The first glimpse of the clergyman's figure was the signal for the bell to cease its summons.

*Another clergyman in New England, Mr. Joseph Moody, of York, Maine, who
died about eighty years since, made himself remarkable by the same eccentricity that
is here related of the Reverend Mr. Hooper. In his case, however, the symbol had a different import. In early life he had accidentally killed a beloved friend; and from that
day till the hour of his own death, he hid his face from men.

"But what has good Parson Hooper got upon his face?" cried the sexton in astonishment.

All within hearing immediately turned about, and beheld the semblance of Mr. Hooper, pacing slowly his meditative way towards the meeting-house. With one accord they started, expressing more wonder than if some strange minister were coming to dust the cushions of Mr. Hooper's pulpit.

"Are you sure it is our parson?" inquired Goodman Gray of the sexton.

"Of a certainty it is good Mr. Hooper," replied the sexton. "He was to have exchanged pulpits with Parson Shute of Westbury; but Parson Shute sent to excuse himself yesterday, being to preach a funeral sermon."

The cause of so much amazement may appear sufficiently slight. Mr. Hooper, a gentlemanly person of about thirty, though still a bachelor, was dressed with due clerical neatness, as if a careful wife had starched his band, and brushed the weekly dust from his Sunday's garb. There was but one thing remarkable in his appearance. Swathed about his forehead, and hanging down over his face, so low as to be shaken by his breath, Mr. Hooper had on a black veil. On a nearer view, it seemed to consist of two folds of crape, which entirely concealed his features, except the mouth and chin, but probably did not intercept his sight, farther than to give a darkened aspect to all living and inanimate things. With this gloomy shade before him, good Mr. Hooper walked onward, at a slow and quiet pace, stooping somewhat and looking on the ground, as is customary with abstracted men, yet nodding kindly to those of his parishioners who still waited on the meeting-house steps. But so wonder-struck were they, that his greeting hardly met with a return.

"I can't really feel as if good Mr. Hooper's face was behind that piece of crape," said the sexton.

"I don't like it," muttered an old woman, as she hobbled into the meeting-house. "He has changed himself into something awful, only by hiding his face."

"Our parson has gone mad!" cried Goodman Gray, following him across the threshold.

A rumor of some unaccountable phenomenon had preceded Mr. Hooper into the meeting-house, and set all the congregation astir. Few could refrain from twisting their heads towards the door; many stood upright, and turned directly about; while several little boys clambered upon the seats, and came down again with a terrible racket. There was a general bustle, a rustling of the women's gowns and shuffling of the men's feet, greatly at variance with that hushed repose which should attend the entrance of the minister. But Mr. Hooper appeared not to notice the perturbation of his people. He entered with an almost noiseless step, bent his head mildly to the pews on each side, and bowed as he passed his oldest parishioner, a white-haired great-grandsire, who occupied an arm-chair in the centre of the aisle. It was strange to observe, how slowly this venerable man became conscious of something singular in the appearance of his pastor. He seemed not fully to partake of the prevailing wonder, till Mr. Hooper had ascended the stairs, and showed himself in the pulpit, face to face with his congregation, except for the black veil. That mysterious emblem was never once withdrawn. It shook with his measured breath as he gave out the psalm; it threw its obscurity between him and the holy page, as he read the Scriptures; and while he prayed, the veil lay heavily on his uplifted countenance. Did he seek to hide it from the dread Being whom he was addressing?

Such was the effect of this simple piece of crape, that more than one woman of delicate nerves was forced to leave the meeting-house. Yet perhaps the pale-faced congregation was almost as fearful a sight to the minister, as his black veil to them.

Mr. Hooper had the reputation of a good preacher, but not an energetic one: he strove to win his people heavenward, by mild persuasive influences, rather than to drive them thither, by the thunders of the Word. The sermon which he now delivered, was marked by the same characteristics of style and manner, as the general series of his pulpit oratory. But there was something, either in the sentiment of the discourse itself, or in the imagination of the auditors, which made it greatly the most powerful effort that they had ever heard from their pastor's lips. It was tinged, rather more darkly than usual, with the gentle gloom of Mr. Hooper's temperament. The subject had reference to secret sin, and those sad mysteries which we hide from our nearest and dearest, and would fain conceal from our own consciousness, even forgetting that the Omniscient can detect them. A subtle power was breathed into his words. Each member of the congregation, the most innocent girl, and the man of hardened breast, felt as if the preacher had crept upon them, behind his awful veil, and discovered their hoarded iniquity of deed or thought. Many spread their clasped hands on their bosoms. There was nothing terrible in what Mr. Hooper said; at least, no violence; and yet, with every tremor of his melancholy voice, the hearers quaked. An unsought pathos came hand in hand with awe. So sensible were the audience of some unwonted attribute in their minister, that they longed for a breath of wind to blow aside the veil, almost believing that a stranger's visage would be discovered, though the form, gesture, and voice were those of Mr. Hooper.

At the close of the services, the people hurried out with indecorous confusion, eager to communicate their pent-up amazement, and conscious of lighter spirits, the moment they lost sight of the black veil. Some gathered in little circles, huddled closely together, with their mouths all whispering in the centre; some went homeward alone, wrapt in silent meditation; some talked loudly, and profaned

the Sabbath-day with ostentatious laughter. A few shook their sagacious heads, intimating that they could penetrate the mystery; while
one or two affirmed that there was no mystery at all, but only that Mr.
Hooper's eyes were so weakened by the midnight lamp, as to require a
shade. After a brief interval, forth came good Mr. Hooper also, in the
rear of his flock. Turning his veiled face from one group to another,
he paid due reverence to the hoary heads, saluted the middle-aged
with kind dignity, as their friend and spiritual guide, greeted the
young with mingled authority and love, and laid his hands on the little children's heads to bless them. Such was always his custom on the
Sabbath-day. Strange and bewildered looks repaid him for his courtesy. None, as on former occasions, aspired to the honor of walking
by their pastor's side. Old Squire Saunders, doubtless by an accidental
lapse of memory, neglected to invite Mr. Hooper to his table, where
the good clergyman had been wont to bless the food, almost every
Sunday since his settlement. He returned, therefore, to the parsonage,
and, at the moment of closing the door, was observed to look back
upon the people, all of whom had their eyes fixed upon the minister.
A sad smile gleamed faintly from beneath the black veil, and flickered
about his mouth, glimmering as he disappeared.

"How strange," said a lady, "that a simple black veil, such as any
woman might wear on her bonnet, should become such a terrible
thing on Mr. Hooper's face!"

"Something must surely be amiss with Mr. Hooper's intellects,"
observed her husband, the physician of the village. "But the strangest
part of the affair is the effect of this vagary, even on a sober-minded
man like myself. The black veil, though it covers only our pastor's face,
throws its influence over his whole person, and makes him ghost-like
from head to foot. Do you not feel it so?"

"Truly do I," replied the lady; "and I would not be alone with him
for the world. I wonder he is not afraid to be alone with himself!"

"Men sometimes are so," said her husband.

The afternoon service was attended with similar circumstances. At its conclusion, the bell tolled for the funeral of a young lady. The relatives and friends were assembled in the house, and the more distant acquaintances stood about the door, speaking of the good qualities of the deceased, when their talk was interrupted by the appearance of Mr. Hooper, still covered with his black veil. It was now an appropriate emblem. The clergyman stepped into the room where the corpse was laid, and bent over the coffin, to take a last farewell of his deceased parishioner. As he stooped, the veil hung straight down from his forehead, so that, if her eye-lids had not been closed for ever, the dead maiden might have seen his face. Could Mr. Hooper be fearful of her glance, that he so hastily caught back the black veil? A person, who watched the interview between the dead and living, scrupled not to affirm, that, at the instant when the clergyman's features were disclosed, the corpse had slightly shuddered, rustling the shroud and muslin cap, though the countenance retained the composure of death. A superstitious old woman was the only witness of this prodigy. From the coffin, Mr. Hooper passed into the chamber of the mourners, and thence to the head of the staircase, to make the funeral prayer. It was a tender and heart-dissolving prayer, full of sorrow, yet so imbued with celestial hopes, that the music of a heavenly harp, swept by the fingers of the dead, seemed faintly to be heard among the saddest accents of the minister. The people trembled, though they but darkly understood him, when he prayed that they, and himself, and all of mortal race, might be ready, as he trusted this young maiden had been, for the dreadful hour that should snatch the veil from their faces. The bearers went heavily forth, and the mourners followed, saddening all the street, with the dead before them, and Mr. Hooper in his black veil behind.

"Why do you look back?" said one in the procession to his partner.

"I had a fancy," replied she, "that the minister and the maiden's spirit were walking hand in hand."

"And so had I, at the same moment," said the other.

That night, the handsomest couple in Milford village were to be joined in wedlock. Though reckoned a melancholy man, Mr. Hooper had a placid cheerfulness for such occasions, which often excited a sympathetic smile, where livelier merriment would have been thrown away. There was no quality of his disposition which made him more beloved than this. The company at the wedding awaited his arrival with impatience, trusting that the strange awe, which had gathered over him throughout the day, would now be dispelled. But such was not the result. When Mr. Hooper came, the first thing that their eyes rested on was the same horrible black veil, which had added deeper gloom to the funeral, and could portend nothing but evil to the wedding. Such was its immediate effect on the guests, that a cloud seemed to have rolled duskily from beneath the black crape, and dimmed the light of the candles. The bridal pair stood up before the minister. But the bride's cold fingers quivered in the tremulous hand of the bridegroom, and her death-like paleness caused a whisper, that the maiden who had been buried a few hours before, was come from her grave to be married. If ever another wedding were so dismal, it was that famous one, where they tolled the wedding-knell. After performing the ceremony, Mr. Hooper raised a glass of wine to his lips, wishing happiness to the new-married couple, in a strain of mild pleasantry that ought to have brightened the features of the guests, like a cheerful gleam from the hearth. At that instant, catching a glimpse of his figure in the looking-glass, the black veil involved his own spirit in the horror with which it overwhelmed all others. His frame shuddered—his lips grew white—he spilt the untasted wine upon the carpet—and rushed forth into the darkness. For the Earth, too, had on her Black Veil.

The next day, the whole village of Milford talked of little else than Parson Hooper's black veil. That, and the mystery concealed behind it, supplied a topic for discussion between acquaintances meeting in the street, and good women gossiping at their open windows. It was the first item of news that the tavern-keeper told to his guests. The children babbled of it on their way to school. One imitative little imp covered his face with an old black handkerchief, thereby so affrighting his playmates, that the panic seized himself, and he well nigh lost his wits by his own waggery.

It was remarkable, that, of all the busy-bodies and impertinent people in the parish, not one ventured to put the plain question to Mr. Hooper, wherefore he did this thing. Hitherto, whenever there appeared the slightest call for such interference, he had never lacked advisers, not shown himself averse to be guided by their judgment. If he erred at all, it was by so painful a degree of self-distrust, that even the mildest censure would lead him to consider an indifferent action as a crime. Yet, though so well acquainted with this amiable weakness, no individual among his parishioners chose to make the black veil a subject of friendly remonstrance. There was a feeling of dread, neither plainly confessed nor carefully concealed, which caused each to shift the responsibility upon another, till at length it was found expedient to send a deputation of the church, in order to deal with Mr. Hooper about the mystery, before it should grow into a scandal. Never did an embassy so ill discharge its duties. The minister received them with friendly courtesy, but became silent, after they were seated, leaving to his visiters the whole burthen of introducing their important business. The topic, it might be supposed, was obvious enough. There was the black veil, swathed round Mr. Hooper's forehead, and concealing every feature above his placid mouth, on which, at times, they could perceive the glimmering of a melancholy smile. But that piece of crape, to their imagination, seemed to hang down before his heart, the symbol of a fearful secret between him and them. Were the veil but cast aside, they might speak freely of it, but not till then. Thus they sat a considerable time, speechless, confused, and shrinking uneasily from Mr. Hooper's eye, which they felt to be fixed upon them with an invisible glance. Finally, the deputies returned abashed to their constituents, pronouncing the matter too weighty to be handled, except by a council of the churches, if, indeed, it might not require a general synod.

But there was one person in the village, unappalled by the awe with which the black veil had impressed all beside herself. When the deputies returned without an explanation, or even venturing to demand one, she, with the calm energy of her character, determined to chase away the strange cloud that appeared to be settling round Mr. Hooper, every moment more darkly than before. As his plighted wife, it should be her privilege to know what the black veil concealed. At the minister's first visit, therefore, she entered upon the subject, with a direct simplicity, which made the task easier both for him and her. After he had seated himself, she fixed her eyes steadfastly upon the veil, but could discern nothing of the dreadful gloom that had so overawed the multitude: it was but a double fold of crape, hanging down from his forehead to his mouth, and slightly stirring with his breath.

"No," said she aloud, and smiling, "there is nothing terrible in this piece of crape, except that it hides a face which I am always glad to look upon. Come, good sir, let the sun shine from behind the cloud. First lay aside your black veil: then tell me why you put it on."

Mr. Hooper's smile glimmered faintly.

"There is an hour to come," said he, "when all of us shall cast aside our veils. Take it not amiss, beloved friend, if I wear this piece of crape till then."

"Your words are a mystery too," returned the young lady. "Take away the veil from them, at least."

"Elizabeth, I will," said he, "so far as my vow may suffer me. Know, then, this veil is a type and a symbol, and I am bound to wear it ever, both in light and darkness, in solitude and before the gaze of multitudes, and as with strangers, so with my familiar friends. No mortal eye will see it withdrawn. This dismal shade must separate me from the world: even you, Elizabeth, can never come behind it!"

"What grievous affliction hath befallen you," she earnestly inquired, "that you should thus darken your eyes for ever?"

"If it be a sign of mourning," replied Mr. Hooper, "I, perhaps, like most other mortals, have sorrows dark enough to be typified by a black veil."

"But what if the world will not believe that it is the type of an innocent sorrow?" urged Elizabeth. "Beloved and respected as you are, there may be whispers, that you hide your face under the consciousness of secret sin. For the sake of your holy office, do away this scandal!"

The color rose into her cheeks, as she intimated the nature of the rumors that were already abroad in the village. But Mr. Hooper's mildness did not forsake him. He even smiled again—that same sad smile, which always appeared like a faint glimmering of light, proceeding from the obscurity beneath the veil.

"If I hide my face for sorrow, there is cause enough," he merely replied; "and if I cover it for secret sin, what mortal might not do the same?"

And with this gentle, but unconquerable obstinacy, did he resist all her entreaties. At length Elizabeth sat silent. For a few moments she appeared lost in thought, considering, probably, what new methods might be tried, to withdraw her lover from so dark a fantasy, which, if it had no other meaning, was perhaps a symptom of mental disease. Though of a firmer character than his own, the tears rolled down her cheeks. But, in an instant, as it were, a new feeling took the place of sorrow: her eyes were fixed insensibly on the black veil, when, like a sudden twilight in the air, its terrors fell around her. She arose, and stood trembling before him.

"And do you feel it then at last?" said he mournfully.

She made no reply, but covered her eyes with her hand, and turned to leave the room. He rushed forward and caught her arm.

"Have patience with me, Elizabeth!" cried he passionately. "Do not desert me, though this veil must be between us here on earth. Be mine, and hereafter there shall be no veil over my face, no darkness between our souls! It is but a mortal veil—it is not for eternity! Oh! you know not how lonely I am, and how frightened to be alone behind my black veil. Do not leave me in this miserable obscurity for ever!"

"Lift the veil but once, and look me in the face," said she.

"Never! It cannot be!" replied Mr. Hooper.

"Then, farewell!" said Elizabeth.

She withdrew her arm from his grasp, and slowly departed, pausing at the door, to give one long, shuddering gaze, that seemed almost to penetrate the mystery of the black veil. But, even amid his grief, Mr. Hooper smiled to think that only a material emblem had separated him from happiness, though the horrors which it shadowed forth, must be drawn darkly between the fondest of lovers.

From that time no attempts were made to remove Mr. Hooper's black veil, or, by a direct appeal, to discover the secret which it was supposed to hide. By persons who claimed a superiority to popular prejudice, it was reckoned merely an eccentric whim, such as often mingles with the sober actions of men otherwise rational, and tinges them all with its own semblance of insanity. But with the multitude, good Mr. Hooper was irreparably a bugbear. He could not walk the streets with any peace of mind, so conscious was he that the gentle and timid would turn aside to avoid him, and that others would make it a point of hardihood to throw themselves in his way. The impertinence of the latter class compelled him to give up his customary walk, at sunset, to the burial ground; for when he leaned pensively over the gate, there would always be faces behind the grave-stones, peeping at his black veil. A fable went the rounds, that the stare of the dead people drove him thence. It grieved him, to the very depth of his kind heart, to observe how the children fled from his approach, breaking up their merriest sports, while his melancholy figure was yet afar off. Their instinctive dread caused him to feel, more strongly than aught else, that a preternatural horror was interwoven with the threads of the black crape. In truth, his own antipathy to the veil was known to be so great, that he never willingly passed before a mirror, nor stooped to drink at a still fountain, lest, in its peaceful bosom, he should be affrighted by himself. This was what gave plausibility to the whispers, that Mr. Hooper's conscience tortured him for some great crime, too horrible to be entirely concealed, or otherwise than so obscurely intimated. Thus, from beneath the black veil, there rolled a cloud into the sunshine, an ambiguity of sin or sorrow, which enveloped the poor minister, so that love or sympathy could never reach him. It was said, that ghost and fiend consorted with him there. With self-shudderings and outward terrors, he walked continually in its shadow, groping darkly within his own soul, or gazing through a medium that saddened the whole world. Even the lawless wind, it was believed, respected his dreadful secret, and never blew aside the veil. But still good Mr. Hooper sadly smiled, at the pale visages of the worldly throng as he passed by.

Among all its bad influences, the black veil had the one desirable effect, of making its wearer a very efficient clergyman. By the aid of his mysterious emblem—for there was no other apparent cause—he became a man of awful power, over souls that were in agony for sin. His converts always regarded him with a dread peculiar to themselves, affirming, though but figuratively, that, before he brought them to celestial light, they had been with him behind the black veil. Its gloom, indeed, enabled him to sympathize with all dark affections. Dying sinners cried aloud for Mr. Hooper, and would not yield their breath till he appeared; though ever, as he stooped to whisper consolation, they shuddered at the veiled face so near their own. Such were the terrors of the black veil, even when Death had bared his visage! Strangers came long distances to attend service at his church, with the mere idle purpose of gazing at his figure, because it was forbidden them to behold his face. But many were made to quake ere they departed! Once, during Governor Belcher's administration, Mr. Hooper was appointed to preach the election sermon. Covered with his black veil, he stood before the chief magistrate, the council, and the representatives, and wrought so deep an impression, that the legislative measures of that year, were characterized by all the gloom and piety of our earliest ancestral sway.

In this manner Mr. Hooper spent a long life, irreproachable in outward act, yet shrouded in dismal suspicions; kind and loving, though unloved, and dimly feared; a man apart from men, shunned in their health and joy, but ever summoned to their aid in mortal anguish. As years wore on, shedding their snows above his sable veil, he acquired a name throughout the New-England churches, and they called him Father Hooper. Nearly all his parishioners, who were of mature age when he was settled, had been borne away by many a funeral: he had one congregation in the church, and a more crowded one in the church-yard; and having wrought so late into the evening, and done his work so well, it was now good Father Hooper's turn to rest.

Several persons were visible by the shaded candlelight, in the death-chamber of the old clergyman. Natural connections he had none. But there was the decorously grave, though unmoved physician, seeking only to mitigate the last pangs of the patient whom he could not save. There were the deacons, and other eminently pious members of his church. There, also, was the Reverend Mr. Clark, of Westbury, a young and zealous divine, who had ridden in haste to pray by the bed-side of the expiring minister. There was the nurse, no hired handmaiden of death, but one whose calm affection had endured thus long, in secresy, in solitude, amid the chill of age, and would not perish, even at the dying hour. Who, but Elizabeth! And there lay the hoary head of good Father Hooper upon the death-pillow, with the black veil still swathed about his brow and reaching down over his face, so that each more difficult gasp of his faint breath caused it to stir. All through life that piece of crape had hung between him and the world: it had separated him from cheerful brotherhood and woman's love, and kept him in that saddest of all prisons, his own heart; and still it lay upon his face, as if to deepen the gloom of his darksome chamber, and shade him from the sunshine of eternity.

For some time previous, his mind had been confused, wavering doubtfully between the past and the present, and hovering forward, as it were, at intervals, into the indistinctness of the world to come. There had been feverish turns, which tossed him from side to side, and wore away what little strength he had. But in his most convulsive struggles, and in the wildest vagaries of his intellect, when no other thought retained its sober influence, he still showed an awful solicitude lest the black veil should slip aside. Even if his bewildered soul could have forgotten, there was a faithful woman at his pillow, who, with averted eyes, would have covered that aged face, which she had last beheld in the comeliness of manhood. At length the death-stricken old man lay quietly in the torpor of mental and bodily exhaustion, with an imperceptible pulse, and breath that grew fainter and fainter, except when a long, deep, and irregular inspiration seemed to prelude the flight of his spirit.

The minister of Westbury approached the bedside.

"Venerable Father Hooper," said he, "the moment of your release is at hand. Are you ready for the lifting of the veil, that shuts in time from eternity?"

Father Hooper at first replied merely by a feeble motion of his head; then, apprehensive, perhaps, that his meaning might be doubtful, he exerted himself to speak.

"Yea," said he, in faint accents, "my soul hath a patient weariness until that veil be lifted."

"And is it fitting," resumed the Reverend Mr. Clark, "that a man so given to prayer, of such a blameless example, holy in deed and thought, so far as mortal judgment may pronounce; is it fitting that a father in the church should leave a shadow on his memory, that may seem to blacken a life so pure? I pray you, my venerable brother, let not this thing be! Suffer us to be gladdened by your triumphant aspect, as you go to your reward. Before the veil of eternity be lifted, let me cast aside this black veil from your face!"

And thus speaking, the Reverend Mr. Clark bent forward to reveal the mystery of so many years. But, exerting a sudden energy, that made all the beholders stand aghast, Father Hooper snatched both his hands from beneath the bed-clothes, and pressed them strongly on the black veil, resolute to struggle, if the minister of Westbury would contend with a dying man.

"Never!" cried the veiled clergyman. "On earth, never!"

"Dark old man!" exclaimed the affrighted minister, "with what horrible crime upon your soul are you now passing to the judgment?"

Father Hooper's breath heaved; it rattled in his throat; but, with a mighty effort, grasping forward with his hands, he caught hold of life, and held it back till he should speak. He even raised himself in bed; and there he sat, shivering with the arms of death around him, while the black veil hung down, awful, at that last moment, in the gathered terrors of a life-time. And yet the faint, sad smile, so often there, now seemed to glimmer from its obscurity, and linger on Father Hooper's lips.

"Why do you tremble at me alone?" cried he, turning his veiled face round the circle of pale spectators. "Tremble also at each other! Have men avoided me, and women shown no pity, and children screamed and fled, only for my black veil? What, but the mystery which it obscurely typifies, has made this piece of crape so awful? When the friend shows his inmost heart to his friend; the lover to his best-beloved; when man does not vainly shrink from the eye of his Creator, loathsomely treasuring up the secret of his sin; then deem me a monster, for the symbol beneath which I have lived, and die! I look around me, and, lo! on every visage a Black Veil!"

While his auditors shrank from one another, in mutual affright, Father Hooper fell back upon his pillow, a veiled corpse, with a faint smile lingering on the lips. Still veiled, they laid him in his coffin, and a veiled corpse they bore him to the grave. The grass of many years has sprung up and withered on that grave, the burial-stone is moss-grown, and good Mr. Hooper's face is dust; but awful is still the thought, that it mouldered beneath the Black Veil!

Night Sketches

Beneath an Umbrella

P LEASANT IS A RAINY winter's day, within doors! The best study for such a day, or the best amusement,—call it which you will,—is a book of travels, describing scenes the most unlike that sombre one, which is mistily presented through the windows. I have experienced, that fancy is then most successful in imparting distinct shapes and vivid colors to the objects which the author has spread upon his page, and that his words become magic spells to summon up a thousand varied pictures. Strange landscapes glimmer through the familiar walls of the room, and outlandish figures thrust themselves almost within the sacred precincts of the hearth. Small as my chamber is, it has space enough to contain the ocean-like circumference of an Arabian desert, its parched sands tracked by the long line of a caravan, with the camels patiently journeying through the heavy sunshine. Though my ceiling be not lofty, yet I can pile up the mountains of Central Asia beneath it, till their summits shine far above the clouds of the middle atmosphere. And, with my humble means, a wealth that is not taxable, I can transport hither the magnificent merchandise of an Oriental bazaar, and call a crowd of purchasers from distant countries, to pay a fair profit for the precious articles which are displayed on all sides. True it is, however, that, amid the bustle of traffic, or whatever else may seem to be going on around me, the rain-drops will occasionally be heard to patter against my window-panes, which look forth upon one of the quietest streets in a New England town. After a time, too, the visions vanish, and will not appear again at my bidding. Then, it being nightfall, a gloomy sense of unreality depresses my spirits, and impels me to venture out, before the clock shall strike bedtime, to satisfy myself that the world is not entirely made up of such shadowy materials, as have busied me throughout the day. A dreamer may dwell so long among fantasies, that the things without him will seem as unreal as those within.

When eve has fairly set in, therefore, I sally forth, tightly buttoning my shaggy over-coat, and hoisting my umbrella, the silken dome of which immediately resounds with the heavy drumming of the invisible rain-drops. Pausing on the lowest door-step, I contrast the warmth and cheerfulness of my deserted fireside, with the drear obscurity and chill discomfort, into which I am about to plunge. Now come fearful auguries, innumerable as the drops of rain. Did not my manhood cry shame upon me, I should turn back within doors, resume my elbow-chair, my slippers, and my book, pass such an evening of sluggish enjoyment as the day has been, and go to bed inglorious. The same shivering reluctance, no doubt, has quelled, for a moment, the adventurous spirit of many a traveller, when his feet, which were destined to measure the earth around, were leaving their last tracks in the home-paths.

In my own case, poor human nature may be allowed a few misgivings. I look upward, and discern no sky, not even an unfathomable

void, but only a black, impenetrable nothingness, as though heaven
and all its lights were blotted from the system of the universe. It is as
if Nature were dead, and the world had put on black, and the clouds
were weeping for her. With their tears upon my cheek, I turn my eyes
earthward, but find little consolation here below. A lamp is burning
dimly at the distant corner, and throws just enough of light along the
street, to show, and exaggerate by so faintly showing, the perils and
difficulties which beset my path. Yonder dingily white remnant of
a huge snowbank,—which will yet cumber the sidewalk till the latter days of March,—over or through that wintry waste must I stride
onward. Beyond, lies a certain Slough of Despond, a concoction of
mud and liquid filth, ankle-deep, leg-deep, neck-deep,—in a word, of
unknown bottom,—on which the lamplight does not even glimmer,
but which I have occasionally watched, in the gradual growth of its
horrors, from morn till nightfall. Should I flounder into its depths,
farewell to upper earth! And hark! how roughly resounds the roaring of a stream, the turbulent career of which is partially reddened
by the gleam of the lamp, but elsewhere brawls noisily through the
densest gloom. Oh, should I be swept away in fording that impetuous
and unclean torrent, the coroner will have a job with an unfortunate
gentleman, who would fain end his troubles anywhere but in a mud-
puddle!

Pshaw! I will linger not another instant at arm's length from these
dim terrors, which grow more obscurely formidable, the longer I delay to grapple with them. Now for the onset! And lo! with little dam-
age, save a dash of rain in the face and breast, a splash of mud high up
the pantaloons, and the left boot full of ice-cold water, behold me at
the corner of the street. The lamp throws down a circle of red light
around me; and, twinkling onward from corner to corner, I discern
other beacons, marshalling my way to a brighter scene. But this is a
lonesome and dreary spot. The tall edifices bid gloomy defiance to

the storm, with their blinds all closed, even as a man winks when he faces a spattering gust. How loudly tinkles the collected rain down the tin spouts! The puffs of wind are boisterous, and seem to assail me from various quarters at once. I have often observed that this corner is a haunt and loitering-place for those winds which have no work to do upon the deep, dashing ships against our iron-bound shores; nor in the forest, tearing up the sylvan giants with half a rood of soil at their vast roots. Here they amuse themselves with lesser freaks of mischief. See, at this moment, how they assail yonder poor woman, who is passing just within the verge of the lamplight! One blast struggles for her umbrella, and turns it wrong side outward; another whisks the cape of her cloak across her eyes; while a third takes most unwarrantable liberties with the lower part of her attire. Happily, the good dame is no gossamer, but a figure of rotundity and fleshly substance; else would these aerial tormentors whirl her aloft, like a witch upon a broomstick, and set her down, doubtless, in the filthiest kennel hereabout.

From hence I tread upon firm pavements into the centre of the town. Here there is almost as brilliant an illumination as when some great victory has been won, either on the battle-field or at the polls. Two rows of shops, with windows down nearly to the ground, cast a glow from side to side, while the black night hangs overhead like a canopy, and thus keeps the splendor from diffusing itself away. The wet sidewalks gleam with a broad sheet of red light. The rain-drops glitter, as if the sky were pouring down rubies. The spouts gush with fire. Methinks the scene is an emblem of the deceptive glare, which mortals throw around their footsteps in the moral world, thus bedazzling themselves, till they forget the impenetrable obscurity that hems them in, and that can be dispelled only by radiance from above. And, after all, it is a cheerless scene, and cheerless are the wanderers in it. Here comes one who has so long been familiar with tempestuous weather, that he takes the bluster of the storm for a friendly greeting, as if it should say, "How fare ye, brother?" He is a retired sea-captain, wrapped in some nameless garment of the pea-jacket order, and is now laying his course towards the Marine Insurance Office, there to spin yarns of gale and ship-wreck, with a crew of old sea-dogs like himself. The blast will put in its word among their hoarse voices, and be understood by all of them. Next I meet an unhappy slip-shod gentleman, with a cloak flung hastily over his shoulders, running a race with boisterous winds, and striving to glide between the drops of rain. Some domestic emergency or other has blown this miserable man from his warm fireside, in quest of a doctor! See that little vagabond,—how carelessly he has taken his stand right underneath a spout, while staring at some object of curiosity in a shop-window! Surely the rain is his native element; he must have fallen with it from the clouds, as frogs are supposed to do.

Here is a picture, and a pretty one. A young man and a girl, both enveloped in cloaks, and huddled beneath the scanty protection of a cotton umbrella. She wears rubber over-shoes; but he is in his dancing-pumps; and they are on their way, no doubt, to some cotillon-party, or subscription-ball at a dollar a head, refreshments included. Thus they struggle against the gloomy tempest, lured onward by a vision of festal splendor. But, ah! a most lamentable disaster. Bewildered by the red, blue, and yellow meteors in an apothecary's window, they have stepped upon a slippery remnant of ice, and are precipitated into a confluence of swollen floods, at the corner of two streets. Luckless lovers! Were it my nature to be other than a looker-on in life, I would attempt your rescue. Since that may not be, I vow, should you be drowned, to weave such a pathetic story of your fate, as shall call forth tears enough to drown you both anew. Do ye touch bottom, my young friends? Yes; they emerge like a water-nymph and a river-deity, and paddle hand-in-hand out of the depths of the dark pool. They hurry homeward, dripping, disconsolate, abashed, but with love too warm to be chilled by the cold water. They have stood a test which proves too strong for many. Faithful, though over head and ears in trouble!

Onward I go, deriving a sympathetic joy or sorrow from the varied aspect of mortal affairs, even as my figure catches a gleam from the lighted windows, or is blackened by an interval of darkness. Not that mine is altogether a chameleon spirit, with no hue of its own. Now I pass into a more retired street, where the dwellings of wealth and poverty are intermingled, presenting a range of strongly contrasted pictures. Here, too, may be found the golden mean. Through yonder casement I discern a family circle,—the grandmother, the parents, and the children,—all flickering, shadow-like, in the glow of a wood-fire. Bluster, fierce blast, and beat, thou wintry rain, against the window-panes! Ye cannot damp the enjoyment of that fireside. Surely my fate is hard, that I should be wandering homeless here, taking to my bosom night, and storm, and solitude, instead of wife and children. Peace, murmurer! Doubt not that darker guests are sitting round the hearth, though the warm blaze hides all but blissful images. Well; here is still a brighter scene. A stately mansion, illuminated for a ball, with cut-glass chandeliers and alabaster lamps in every room, and sunny landscapes hanging round the walls. See! a coach has stopped, whence emerges a slender beauty, who, canopied by two umbrellas, glides within the portal, and vanishes amid lightsome thrills of music. Will she ever feel the night-wind and the rain? Perhaps,—perhaps! And will Death and Sorrow ever enter that proud mansion? As surely as the dancers will be gay within its halls to-night. Such thoughts sadden, yet satisfy my heart; for they teach me that the poor man, in this mean, weather-beaten hovel, without a fire to cheer him, may call the rich his brother,—brethren by Sorrow, who must be an inmate of both their households,—brethren by Death, who will lead them both to other homes.

Onward, still onward, I plunge into the night. Now have I reached the utmost limits of the town, where the last lamp struggles feebly with the darkness, like the farthest star that stands sentinel on the borders of uncreated space. It is strange what sensations of sublimity may spring from a very humble source. Such are suggested by this hollow roar of a subterranean cataract, where the mighty stream of a kennel precipitates itself beneath an iron grate, and is seen no more on earth. Listen awhile to its voice of mystery; and fancy will magnify it, till you start, and smile at the illusion. And now another sound,— the rumbling of wheels,—as the mail-coach, outward bound, rolls heavily off the pavements, and splashes through the mud and water of the road. All night long, the poor passengers will be tossed to and fro between drowsy watch and troubled sleep, and will dream of their own quiet beds, and awake to find themselves still jolting onward. Happier my lot, who will straightway hie me to my familiar room, and toast myself comfortably before the fire, musing, and fitfully dozing, and fancying a strangeness in such sights as all may see. But first let me gaze at this solitary figure, who comes hitherward with a tin lantern, which throws the circular pattern of its punched holes on the ground about him. He passes fearlessly into the unknown gloom, whither I will not follow him.

This figure shall supply me with a moral, wherewith, for lack of a more appropriate one, I may wind up my sketch. He fears not to tread the dreary path before him, because his lantern, which was kindled at the fireside of his home, will light him back to that same fireside again. And thus we, night-wanderers through a stormy and dismal world, if we bear the lamp of Faith, enkindled at a celestial fire, it will surely lead us home to that Heaven whence its radiance was borrowed.

Old Esther Dudley

Legends of the Province-House IV

O UR HOST HAVING RESUMED the chair, he, as well as Mr. Tiffany and myself, expressed much eagerness to be made acquainted with the story to which the loyalist had alluded. That venerable man first of all saw fit to moisten his throat with another glass of wine, and then, turning his face towards our coal-fire, looked steadfastly for a few moments into the depths of its cheerful glow. Finally, he poured forth a great fluency of speech. The generous liquid that he had imbibed, while it warmed his age-chilled blood, likewise took off the chill from his heart and mind, and gave him an energy to think and feel, which we could hardly have expected to find beneath the snows of fourscore winters. His feelings, indeed, appeared to me more excitable than those of a younger man; or, at least, the same degree of feeling manifested itself by more visible effects, than if his judgment and will had possessed the potency of meridian life. At the pathetic passages of his narrative, he readily melted into tears. When a breath of indignation swept across his spirit, the blood flushed his withered visage even to the roots of his white hair; and he shook his clenched fist at the trio of peaceful auditors, seeming to fancy enemies in those who felt very kindly towards the desolate old soul. But ever and anon, sometimes in the midst of his most earnest talk, this ancient person's intellect would wander vaguely, losing its hold of the matter in hand, and groping for it amid misty shadows. Then would he cackle forth a feeble laugh, and express a doubt whether his wits—for by that phrase it pleased our ancient friend to signify his mental powers— were not getting a little the worse for wear.

Under these disadvantages, the old loyalist's story required more revision to render it fit for the public eye, than those of the series which have preceded it; nor should it be concealed, that the sentiment and tone of the affair may have undergone some slight, or perchance more than slight metamorphosis, in its transmission to the reader through the medium of a thorough-going democrat. The tale itself is a mere sketch, with no involution of plot, nor any great interest of events, yet possessing, if I have rehearsed it aright, that pensive influence over the mind, which the shadow of the old Province-House flings upon the loiterer in its court-yard.

The hour had come—the hour of defeat and humiliation—when Sir William Howe was to pass over the threshold of the Province-House, and embark, with no such triumphal ceremonies as he once promised himself, on board the British fleet. He bade his servants and military attendants go before him, and lingered a moment in the loneliness of the mansion, to quell the fierce emotions that struggled in his bosom as with a death-throb. Preferable, then, would he have deemed his fate, had a warrior's death left him a claim to the narrow territory of a grave, within the soil which the King had given him to defend. With an ominous perception that, as his departing footsteps echoed adown the staircase, the sway of Britain was passing forever from New England, he smote his clenched hand on his brow, and cursed the destiny that had flung the shame of a dismembered empire upon him.

"Would to God," cried he, hardly repressing his tears of rage, "that the rebels were even now at the door-step! A bloodstain upon the floor should then bear testimony that the last British ruler was faithful to his trust."

The tremulous voice of a woman replied to his exclamation.

"Heaven's cause and the King's are one," it said. "Go forth, Sir William Howe, and trust in Heaven to bring back a Royal Governor in triumph."

Subduing at once the passion to which he had yielded only in the faith that it was unwitnessed, Sir William Howe became conscious that an aged woman, leaning on a gold-headed staff, was standing betwixt him and the door. It was old Esther Dudley, who had dwelt almost immemorial years in this mansion, until her presence seemed as inseparable from it as the recollections of its history. She was the daughter of an ancient and once eminent family, which had fallen into poverty and decay, and left its last descendant no resource save the bounty of the King, nor any shelter except within the walls of the Province-House. An office in the household, with merely nominal duties, had been assigned to her as a pretext for the payment of a small pension, the greater part of which she expended in adorning herself with an antique magnificence of attire. The claims of Esther Dudley's gentle blood were acknowledged by all the successive Governors; and they treated her with the punctilious courtesy which it was her foible to demand, not always with success, from a neglectful world. The only actual share which she assumed in the business of the mansion, was to glide through its passages and public chambers, late at night, to see that the servants had dropped no fire from their flaring torches, nor left embers crackling and blazing on the hearths. Perhaps it was this invariable custom of walking her rounds in the hush of midnight, that caused the superstition of the times to invest the old woman with attributes of awe and mystery; fabling that she had entered the portal of the Province-House, none knew whence, in the train of the first Royal Governor, and that it was her fate to dwell there till the last should have departed. But Sir William Howe, if he ever heard this legend, had forgotten it.

"Mistress Dudley, why are you loitering here?" asked he, with some severity of tone. "It is my pleasure to be the last in this mansion of the King."

"Not so, if it please your Excellency," answered the time-stricken woman. "This roof has sheltered me long. I will not pass from it until they bear me to the tomb of my forefathers. What other shelter is there for old Esther Dudley, save the Province-House or the grave?"

"Now Heaven forgive me!" said Sir William Howe to himself. "I was about to leave this wretched old creature to starve or beg. Take this, good Mistress Dudley," he added, putting a purse into her hands. "King George's head on these golden guineas is sterling yet, and will continue so, I warrant you, even should the rebels crown John Hancock their king. That purse will buy a better shelter than the Province-House can now afford."

"While the burthen of life remains upon me, I will have no other shelter than this roof," persisted Esther Dudley, striking her staff upon the floor, with a gesture that expressed immovable resolve. "And when your Excellency returns in triumph, I will totter into the porch to welcome you."

"My poor old friend!" answered the British General,—and all his manly and martial pride could no longer restrain a gush of bitter tears. "This is an evil hour for you and me. The province which the King entrusted to my charge is lost. I go hence in misfortune—per-

chance in disgrace—to return no more. And you, whose present being is incorporated with the past—who have seen Governor after
Governor, in stately pageantry, ascend these steps—whose whole life
has been an observance of majestic ceremonies, and a worship of the
King—how will you endure the change? Come with us! Bid farewell
to a land that has shaken off its allegiance, and live still under a Royal
government, at Halifax."

"Never, never!" said the pertinacious old dame. "Here will I abide;
and King George shall still have one true subject in his disloyal province."

"Beshrew the old fool!" muttered Sir William Howe, growing im-
patient of her obstinacy, and ashamed of the emotion into which he
had been betrayed. "She is the very moral of old-fashioned prejudice,
and could exist nowhere but in this musty edifice. Well, then, Mistress Dudley, since you will needs tarry, I give the Province-House in
charge to you. Take this key, and keep it safe until myself, or some
other Royal Governor, shall demand it of you."

Smiling bitterly at himself and her, he took the heavy key of the
Province-House, and delivering it into the old lady's hands, drew his
cloak around him for departure. As the General glanced back at Esther Dudley's antique figure, he deemed her well-fitted for such a
charge, as being so perfect a representative of the decayed past—of an
age gone by, with its manners, opinions, faith, and feelings, all fallen
into oblivion or scorn—of what had once been a reality, but was now
merely a vision of faded magnificence. Then Sir William Howe strode
forth, smiting his clenched hands together, in the fierce anguish of his
spirit; and old Esther Dudley was left to keep watch in the lonely
Province-House, dwelling there with memory;—and if Hope ever
seemed to flit around her, still it was Memory in disguise.

The total change of affairs that ensued on the departure of the
British troops did not drive the venerable lady from her strong-hold.

There was not, for many years afterwards, a Governor of Massachusetts; and the magistrates, who had charge of such matters, saw no objection to Esther Dudley's residence in the Province-House, especially as they must otherwise have paid a hireling for taking care of the premises, which with her was a labor of love. And so they left her the undisturbed mistress of the old historic edifice. Many and strange were the fables which the gossips whispered about her, in all the chimney-corners of the town. Among the time-worn articles of furniture that had been left in the mansion, there was a tall, antique mirror, which was well worthy of a tale by itself, and perhaps may hereafter be the theme of one. The gold of its heavily-wrought frame was tarnished, and its surface so blurred, that the old woman's figure, whenever she paused before it, looked indistinct and ghostlike. But it was the general belief that Esther could cause the Governors of the overthrown dynasty, with the beautiful ladies who had once adorned their festivals, the Indian chiefs who had come up to the Province-House to hold council or swear allegiance, the grim Provincial warriors, the severe clergymen—in short, all the pageantry of gone days—all the figures that ever swept across the broad plate of glass in former times—she could cause the whole to reappear, and people the inner world of the mirror with shadows of old life. Such legends as these, together with the singularity of her isolated existence, her age, and the infirmity that each added winter flung upon her, made Mistress Dudley the object both of fear and pity; and it was partly the result of either sentiment, that, amid all the angry license of the times, neither wrong nor insult ever fell upon her unprotected head. Indeed, there was so much haughtiness in her demeanour towards intruders, among whom she reckoned all persons acting under the new authorities, that it was really an affair of no small nerve to look her in the face. And to do the people justice, stern republicans as they had now become, they were well content that the old gentlewoman, in her hoop-petticoat and faded embroidery, should still haunt the palace of ruined pride and overthrown power, the symbol of a departed system embodying a history in her person. So Esther Dudley dwelt, year after year, in the Province-House, still reverencing all that others had flung aside, still faithful to her King, who, so long as the venerable dame yet held her post, might be said to retain one true subject in New England, and one spot of the empire that had been wrested from him.

And did she dwell there in utter loneliness? Rumor said, not so. Whenever her chill and withered heart desired warmth, she was wont to summon a black slave of Governor Shirley's from the blurred mirror, and send him in search of guests who had long ago been familiar in those deserted chambers. Forth went the sable messenger, with the starlight or the moonshine gleaming through him, and did his errand in the burial-grounds, knocking at the iron doors of tombs, or upon the marble slabs that covered them, and whispering to those within: "My mistress, old Esther Dudley, bids you to the Province-House at midnight." And, punctually as the clock of the Old South told twelve, came the shadows of the Olivers, the Hutchinsons, the Dudleys, all the grandees of a by-gone generation, gliding beneath the portal into the well-known mansion, where Esther mingled with them as if she likewise were a shade. Without vouching for the truth of such traditions, it is certain that Mistress Dudley sometimes assembled a few of the staunch, though crest-fallen old tories, who had lingered in the rebel town during those days of wrath and tribulation. Out of a cobwebbed bottle, containing liquor that a Royal Governor might have smacked his lips over, they quaffed healths to the King, and babbled treason to the Republic, feeling as if the protecting shadow of the throne were still flung around them. But, draining the last drops of their liquor, they stole timorously homeward, and answered not again, if the rude mob reviled them in the street.

Yet Esther Dudley's most frequent and favored guests were the children of the town. Towards them she was never stern. A kindly and loving nature, hindered elsewhere from its free course by a thousand rocky prejudices, lavished itself upon these little ones. By bribes of gingerbread of her own making, stamped with a royal crown, she tempted their sunny sportive-ness beneath the gloomy portal of the Province-House, and would often beguile them to spend a whole play-day there, sitting in a circle round the verge of her hoop-petti-coat, greedily attentive to her stories of a dead world. And when these little boys and girls stole forth again from the dark mysterious man-sion, they went bewildered, full of old feelings that graver people had long ago forgotten, rubbing their eyes at the world around them as if they had gone astray into ancient times, and become children of the past. At home, when their parents asked where they had loitered such a weary while, and with whom they had been at play, the children would talk of all the departed worthies of the Province, as far back as Governor Belcher, and the haughty dame of Sir William Phips. It would seem as though they had been sitting on the knees of these fa-mous personages, whom the grave had hidden for half a century, and had toyed with the embroidery of their rich waistcoats, or roguishly pulled the long curls of their flowing wigs. "But Governor Belcher has been dead this many a year," would the mother say to her little boy. "And did you really see him at the Province-House?" "Oh, yes, dear mother! yes!" the half dreaming child would answer. "But when old Esther had done speaking about him he faded away out of his chair." Thus, without affrighting her little guests, she led them by the hand into the chambers of her own desolate heart, and made childhood's fancy discern the ghosts that haunted there.

Living so continually in her own circle of ideas, and never regulat-ing her mind by a proper reference to present things, Esther Dudley appears to have grown partially crazed. It was found that she had no right sense of the progress and true state of the Revolutionary war, but held a constant faith that the armies of Britain were victorious on every field, and destined to be ultimately triumphant. Whenever the town rejoiced for a battle won by Washington, or Gates, or Morgan, or Greene, the news, in passing through the door of the Province-House, as through the ivory gate of dreams, became metamorphosed into a strange tale of the prowess of Howe, Clinton, or Cornwallis. Sooner or later, it was her invincible belief, the colonies would be prostrate at the footstool of the King. Sometimes she seemed to take for granted that such was already the case. On one occasion, she startled the town's people by a brilliant illumination of the Province-House, with candles at every pane of glass, and a transparency of the King's initials and a crown of light, in the great balcony window. The figure of the aged woman, in the most gorgeous of her mildewed velvets and brocades, was seen passing from casement to casement, until she paused before the balcony, and flourished a huge key above her head. Her wrinkled visage actually gleamed with triumph, as if the soul within her were a festal lamp.

"What means this blaze of light? What does old Esther's joy portend?" whispered a spectator. "It is frightful to see her gliding about the chambers, and rejoicing there without a soul to bear her company."

"It is as if she were making merry in a tomb," said another.

"Pshaw! It is no such mystery," observed an old man, after some brief exercise of memory. "Mistress Dudley is keeping jubilee for the King of England's birth-day."

Then the people laughed aloud, and would have thrown mud against the blazing transparency of the King's crown and initials, only that they pitied the poor old dame, who was so dismally triumphant amid the wreck and ruin of the system to which she appertained.

Oftentimes it was her custom to climb the weary staircase that wound upward to the cupola, and thence strain her dimmed eyesight seaward and countryward, watching for a British fleet, or for the march of a grand procession, with the King's banner floating over it. The passengers in the street below would discern her anxious visage, and send up a shout—"When the golden Indian on the Province-House shall shoot his arrow, and when the cock on the Old South spire shall crow, then look for a Royal Governor again!"—for this had grown a by-word through the town. And at last, after long, long years, old Esther Dudley knew, or perchance she only dreamed, that a Royal Governor was on the eve of returning to the Province-House, to receive the heavy key which Sir William Howe had committed to her charge. Now it was the fact, that intelligence bearing some faint analogy to Esther's version of it, was current among the town's people. She set the mansion in the best order that her means allowed, and arraying herself in silks and tarnished gold, stood long before the blurred mirror to admire her own magnificence. As she gazed, the gray and withered lady moved her ashen lips, murmuring half aloud, talking to shapes that she saw within the mirror, to shadows of her own fantasies, to the household friends of memory, and bidding them rejoice with her, and come forth to meet the Governor. And while absorbed in this communion, Mistress Dudley heard the tramp of many footsteps in the street, and looking out at the window, beheld what she construed as the Royal Governor's arrival.

"Oh, happy day! oh, blessed, blessed hour!" she exclaimed. "Let me but bid him welcome within the portal, and my task in the Province-House, and on earth, is done!"

Then with tottering feet, which age and tremulous joy caused to tread amiss, she hurried down the grand staircase, her silks sweeping and rustling as she went, so that the sound was as if a train of spectral courtiers were thronging from the dim mirror. And Esther Dudley fancied, that as soon as the wide door should be flung open, all the pomp and splendor of by-gone times would pace majestically into the Province-House, and the gilded tapestry of the past would be brightened by the sunshine of the present. She turned the key—withdrew it from the lock—unclosed the door—and stept across the threshold. Advancing up the court-yard, appeared a person of most dignified mien, with tokens, as Esther interpreted them, of gentle blood, high rank, and long accustomed authority, even in his walk and every gesture. He was richly dressed, but wore a gouty shoe, which, however, did not lessen the stateliness of his gait. Around and behind him were people in plain civic dresses, and two or three war-worn veterans, evidently officers of rank, arrayed in a uniform of blue and buff. But Esther Dudley, firm in the belief that had fastened its roots about her heart, beheld only the principal personage, and never doubted that this was the long-looked-for Governor, to whom she was to surrender up her charge. As he approached, she involuntarily sank down on her knees, and tremblingly held forth the heavy key.

"Receive my trust! take it quickly!" cried she; "for methinks Death is striving to snatch away my triumph. But he comes too late. Thank Heaven for this blessed hour! God save King George!"

"That, Madam, is a strange prayer to be offered up at such a moment," replied the unknown guest of the Province-House, and courteously removing his hat, he offered his arm to raise the aged woman. "Yet, in reverence for your gray hairs and long-kept faith, Heaven forbid that any here should say you nay. Over the realms which still acknowledge his sceptre, God save King George!"

Esther Dudley started to her feet, and hastily clutching back the key, gazed with fearful earnestness at the stranger; and dimly and doubtfully, as if suddenly awakened from a dream, her bewildered eyes half recognized his face. Years ago, she had known him among the gentry of the Province. But the ban of the King had fallen upon him! How, then, came the doomed victim here? Proscribed, excluded from mercy, the monarch's most dreaded and hated foe, this New England merchant had stood triumphantly against a kingdom's strength; and his foot now trod upon humbled Royalty, as he ascended the steps of the Province-House, the people's chosen Governor of Massachusetts.

"Wretch, wretch that I am!" muttered the old woman, with such a heart-broken expression, that the tears gushed from the stranger's eyes. "Have I bidden a traitor welcome! Come, Death! come quickly!"

"Alas, venerable lady!" said Governor Hancock, lending her his support with all the reverence that a courtier would have shown to a queen. "Your life has been prolonged until the world has changed around you. You have treasured up all that time has rendered worthless—the principles, feelings, manners, modes of being and acting, which another generation has flung aside—and you are a symbol of the past. And I, and these around me—we represent a new race of men, living no longer in the past, scarcely in the present—but projecting our lives forward into the future. Ceasing to model ourselves on ancestral superstitions, it is our faith and principle to press onward, onward! Yet," continued he, turning to his attendants, "let us reverence, for the last time, the stately and gorgeous prejudices of the tottering Past!"

While the Republican Governor spoke, he had continued to support the helpless form of Esther Dudley; her weight grew heavier against his arm; but at last, with a sudden effort to free herself, the ancient woman sank down beside one of the pillars of the portal. The key of the Province-House fell from her grasp, and clanked against the stone.

"I have been faithful unto death," murmured she. "God save the King!"

"She hath done her office!" said Hancock solemnly. "We will follow her reverently to the tomb of her ancestors; and then, my fellow-citizens, onward—onward! We are no longer children of the Past!"

As the old loyalist concluded his narrative, the enthusiasm which had been fitfully flashing within his sunken eyes, and quivering across his wrinkled visage, faded away, as if all the lingering fire of his soul were extinguished. Just then, too, a lamp upon the mantle-piece threw out a dying gleam, which vanished as speedily, as it shot upward, compelling our eyes to grope for one another's features by the dim glow of the hearth. With such a lingering fire, methought, with such a dying gleam, had the glory of the ancient system vanished from the Province-House, when the spirit of old Esther Dudley took its flight. And now, again, the clock of the Old South threw its voice of ages on the breeze, knolling the hourly knell of the Past, crying out far and wide through the multitudinous city, and filling our ears, as we sat in the dusky chamber, with its reverberating depth of tone. In that same mansion—in that very chamber—what a volume of history had been told off into hours, by the same voice that was now trembling in the air. Many a Governor had heard those midnight accents, and longed to exchange his stately cares for slumber. And as for mine host, and Mr. Bela Tiffany, and the old loyalist, and me, we had babbled about dreams of the past, until we almost fancied that the clock was still striking in a by-gone century. Neither of us would have wondered, had a hoop-petticoated phantom of Esther Dudley tottered into the chamber, walking her rounds in the hush of midnight, as of yore, and motioned us to quench the fading embers of the fire, and leave the historic precincts to herself and her kindred shades. But as no such vision was vouchsafed, I retired unbidden, and would advise Mr. Tiffany to lay hold of another auditor, being resolved not to show my face in the Province-House for a good while hence—if ever.

A Virtuoso's Collection

THE OTHER DAY, having a leisure hour at my disposal, I stept into a new museum, to which my notice was casually drawn by a small and unobtrusive sign: "TO BE SEEN HERE, A VIRTUOSO'S COLLECTION." Such was the simple, yet not altogether unpromising announcement, that turned my steps aside, for a little while, from the sunny sidewalk of our principal thoroughfare. Mounting a sombre staircase, I pushed open a door at its summit, and found myself in the presence of a person, who mentioned the moderate sum that would entitle me to admittance:

"Three shillings, Massachusetts tenor," said he; "no, I mean half a dollar, as you reckon in these days."

While searching my pocket for the coin, I glanced at the doorkeeper, the marked character and individuality of whose aspect encouraged me to expect something not quite in the ordinary way. He wore an old-fashioned great-coat, much faded, within which his meagre person was so completely enveloped that the rest of his attire was undistinguishable. But his visage was remarkably wind-flushed, sun-burnt, and weather-worn, and had a most unquiet, nervous, and apprehensive expression. It seemed as if this man had some all-important object in view, some point of deepest interest to be decided, some momentous question to ask, might he but hope for a reply. As it was evident, however, that I could have nothing to do with his private affairs, I passed through an open door-way, which admitted me into the extensive hall of the Museum.

Directly in front of the portal was the bronze statue of a youth with winged feet. He was represented in the act of flitting away from earth, yet wore such a look of earnest invitation that it impressed me like a summons to enter the hall.

"It is the original statue of Opportunity, by the ancient sculptor Lysippus," said a gentleman who now approached me; "I place it at the entrance of my Museum, because it is not at all times that one can gain admittance to such a collection."

The speaker was a middle-aged person, of whom it was not easy to determine whether he had spent his life as a scholar, or as a man of action; in truth, all outward and obvious peculiarities had been worn away by an extensive and promiscuous intercourse with the world. There was no mark about him of profession, individual habits, or scarcely of country; although his dark complexion and high features made me conjecture that he was a native of some southern clime of Europe. At all events, he was evidently the Virtuoso in person.

"With your permission," said he, "as we have no descriptive cata-logue, I will accompany you through the Museum, and point out whatever may be most worthy of attention. In the first place, here is a choice collection of stuffed animals."

Nearest the door stood the outward semblance of a wolf, exqui-sitely prepared, it is true, and showing a very wolfish fierceness in the large glass eyes, which were inserted into its wild and crafty head. Still it was merely the skin of a wolf, with nothing to distinguish it from other individuals of that unlovely breed.

"How does this animal deserve a place in your collection?" inquired I.

"It is the wolf that devoured Little Red Riding-Hood," answered the Virtuoso; "and by his side,—with a milder and more matronly look, as you perceive,—stands the she-wolf that suckled Romulus and Remus."

"Ah, indeed!" exclaimed I. "And what lovely lamb is this, with the snow-white fleece, which seems to be of as delicate a texture as innocence itself?"

"Methinks you have but carelessly read Spenser," replied my guide, "or you would at once recognize the 'milk-white lamb' which Una led. But I set no great value upon the lamb. The next specimen is better worth our notice."

"What!" cried I, "this strange animal, with the black head of an ox upon the body of a white horse? Were it possible to suppose it, I should say that this was Alexander's steed Bucephalus."

"The same," said the Virtuoso. "And can you likewise give a name to the famous charger that stands beside him?"

Next to the renowned Bucephalus stood the mere skeleton of a horse, with the white bones peeping through its ill-conditioned hide. But, if my heart had not warmed towards that pitiful anatomy, I might as well have quitted the Museum at once. Its rarities had not been collected with pain and toil from the four quarters of the earth, and from the depths of the sea, and from the palaces and sepulchres of ages, for those who could mistake this illustrious steed.

"It is Rosinante!" exclaimed I, with enthusiasm.

And so it proved! My admiration for the noble and gallant horse caused me to glance with less interest at the other animals, although many of them might have deserved the notice of Cuvier himself. There was the donkey which Peter Bell cudgelled so soundly; and a brother of the same species, who had suffered a similar infliction from the ancient prophet Balaam. Some doubts were entertained, however, as to the authenticity of the latter beast. My guide pointed out the venerable Argus, that faithful dog of Ulysses, and also another dog, (for so the skin bespoke it,) which, though imperfectly preserved, seemed once to have had three heads. It was Cerberus. I was considerably amused at detecting, in an obscure corner, the fox that became so famous by the loss of his tail. There were several stuffed cats, which, as a dear lover of that comfortable beast, attracted my affectionate regards. One was Dr. Johnson's cat Hodge; and in the same row stood the favorite cats of Mahomet, Gray, and Walter Scott, together with Puss in Boots, and a cat of very noble aspect who had once been a deity of ancient Egypt. Byron's tame bear came next. I must not forget to mention the Erymanthean boar, the skin of St. George's Dragon, and that of the serpent Python; and another skin, with beautifully variegated hues, supposed to have been the garment of the "spirited sly snake," which tempted Eve. Against the wall were suspended the horns of the stag that Shakspeare shot; and on the floor lay the ponderous shell of the tortoise which fell upon the head of Æschylus. In one row, as natural as life, stood the sacred bull Apis, the "cow with the crumpled horn," and a very wild looking young heifer, which I guessed to be the cow that jumped over the moon. She was probably killed by the rapidity of her descent. As I turned away, my eyes fell upon an indescribable monster, which proved to be a griffin.

"I look in vain," observed I, "for the skin of an animal which might well deserve the closest study of a naturalist,—the winged horse Pegasus."

"He is not yet dead," replied the Virtuoso, "but he is so hard ridden by many young gentlemen of the day, that I hope soon to add his skin and skeleton to my collection."

We now passed to the next alcove of the hall, in which was a multitude of stuffed birds. They were very prettily arranged, some upon the branches of trees, others brooding upon nests, and others suspended by wires so artificially that they seemed in the very act of flight. Among them was a white dove, with a withered branch of olive leaves in her mouth.

"Can this be the very dove," inquired I, "that brought the message of peace and hope to the tempest-beaten passengers of the ark?"

"Even so," said my companion.

"And this raven, I suppose," continued I, "is the same that fed Elijah in the wilderness."

"The raven?—no," said the Virtuoso, "it is a bird of modern date. He belonged to one Barnaby Rudge; and many people fancied that the devil himself was disguised under his sable plumage. But poor Grip has drawn his last cork, and has been forced to 'say die' at last. This other raven, hardly less curious, is that in which the soul of King George the First revisited his lady love, the Duchess of Kendall."

My guide next pointed out Minerva's owl, and the vulture that preyed upon the liver of Prometheus. There was likewise the sacred Ibis of Egypt, and one of the Stymphalides, which Hercules shot in his sixth labor. Shelley's sky-lark, Bryant's water-fowl, and a pigeon from the belfry of the Old South Church, preserved by N. P. Willis, were placed on the same perch. I could not but shudder on beholding Coleridge's albatross, transfixed with the Ancient Mariner's crossbow shaft. Beside this bird of awful poesy stood a gray goose of very ordinary aspect.

"Stuffed goose is no such rarity," observed I. "Why do you preserve such a specimen in your Museum?"

"It is one of the flock whose cackling saved the Roman Capitol," answered the Virtuoso. "Many geese have cackled and hissed, both before and since; but none, like those, have clamored themselves into immortality."

There seemed to be little else that demanded notice in this department of the Museum, unless we except Robinson Crusoe's parrot, a live phoenix, a footless bird of Paradise, and a splendid peacock, supposed to be the same that once contained the soul of Pythagoras. I therefore passed to the next alcove, the shelves of which were covered with a miscellaneous collection of curiosities, such as are usually found in similar establishments. One of the first things that took my eye was a strange looking cap, woven of some substance that appeared to be neither woollen, cotton, nor linen.

"Is this a magician's cap?" I asked.

"No," replied the Virtuoso, "it is merely Dr. Franklin's cap of asbestos. But here is one which, perhaps, may suit you better. It is the wishing-cap of Fortunatus. Will you try it on?"

"By no means," answered I, putting it aside with my hand. "The day of wild wishes is past with me. I desire nothing that may not come in the ordinary course of Providence."

"Then, probably," returned the Virtuoso, "you will not be tempted to rub this lamp?"

While speaking, he took from the shelf an antique brass lamp, curiously wrought with embossed figures, but so covered with verdigris that the sculpture was almost eaten away.

"It is a thousand years," said he, "since the genius of this lamp constructed Aladdin's palace in a single night. But he still retains his power; and the man who rubs Aladdin's lamp, has but to desire either a palace or a cottage."

"I might desire a cottage," replied I, "but I would have it founded on sure and stable truth, not on dreams and fantasies. I have learned to look for the real and the true."

My guide next showed me Prospero's magic wand, broken into three fragments by the hand of its mighty master. On the same shelf lay the gold ring of ancient Gyges, which enabled the wearer to walk invisible. On the other side of the alcove was a tall looking-glass in a frame of ebony, but veiled with a curtain of purple silk, through the rents of which the gleam of the mirror was perceptible.

"This is Cornelius Agrippa's magic glass," observed the Virtuoso. "Draw aside the curtain, and picture any human form within your mind, and it will be reflected in the mirror."

"It is enough if I can picture it within my mind," answered I. "Why should I wish it to be repeated in the mirror? But, indeed, these works of magic have grown wearisome to me. There are so many greater wonders in the world, to those who keep their eyes open, and their sight undimmed by custom, that all the delusions of the old sorcerers seem flat and stale. Unless you can show me something really curious, I care not to look further into your Museum."

"Ah, well, then," said the Virtuoso, composedly, "perhaps you may deem some of my antiquarian rarities deserving of a glance."

He pointed out the Iron Mask, now corroded with rust; and my heart grew sick at the sight of this dreadful relic, which had shut out a human being from sympathy with his race. There was nothing half so terrible in the axe that beheaded King Charles, nor in the dagger that slew Henry of Navarre, nor in the arrow that pierced the heart of William Rufus,—all of which were shown to me. Many of the articles derived their interest, such as it was, from having been formerly in the possession of royalty. For instance, here was Charlemagne's sheepskin cloak, the flowing wig of Louis Quatorze, the spinning-wheel of Sardanapalus, and King Stephen's famous breeches, which cost him but a crown. The heart of the Bloody Mary, with the word "Calais" worn into its diseased substance, was preserved in a bottle of spirits; and near it lay the golden case in which the queen of Gustavus Adolphus treasured up that hero's heart. Among these relics and heirlooms of kings, I must not forget the long, hairy ears of Midas, and a piece of bread, which had been changed to gold by the touch of that unlucky monarch. And as Grecian Helen was a queen, it may here be mentioned, that I was permitted to take into my hand a lock of her golden hair, and the bowl which a sculptor modelled from the curve of her perfect breast. Here, likewise, was the robe that smothered Agamemnon, Nero's fiddle, the Czar Peter's brandy-bottle, the crown of Semiramis, and Canute's sceptre, which he extended over the sea. That my own land may not deem itself neglected, let me add, that I was favored with a sight of the skull of King Philip, the famous Indian chief, whose head the Puritans smote off and exhibited upon a pole.

"Show me something else," said I to the Virtuoso. "Kings are in such an artificial position, that people in the ordinary walks of life cannot feel an interest in their relics. If you could show me the straw hat of sweet little Nell, I would far rather see it than a king's golden crown."

"There it is," said my guide, pointing carelessly with his staff to the straw hat in question. "But, indeed, you are hard to please. Here are the seven-league boots. Will you try them on?"

"Our modern railroads have superseded their use," answered I; "and as to these cow-hide boots, I could show you quite as curious a pair at the transcendental community in Roxbury."

We next examined a collection of swords and other weapons, belonging to different epochs, but thrown together without much attempt at arrangement. Here was Arthur's sword Excalibar, and that of the Cid Campeador, and the sword of Brutus rusted with Caesar's blood and his own, and the sword of Joan of Arc, and that of Horatius, and that with which Virginius slew his daughter, and the one which Dionysius suspended over the head of Damocles. Here, also, was Arria's sword, which she plunged into her own breast, in order to taste of death before her husband. The crooked blade of Saladin's scimetar next attracted my notice. I know not by what chance, but so it happened that the sword of one of our own militia generals was suspended between Don Quixote's lance and the brown blade of Hudibras. My heart throbbed high at the sight of the helmet of Miltiades, and the spear that was broken in the breast of Epaminondas. I recognized the shield of Achilles, by its resemblance to the admirable cast in the possession of Professor Felton. Nothing in this department interested me more than Major Pitcairn's pistol, the discharge of which, at Lexington, began the war of the revolution, and was reverberated in thunder around the land for seven long years. The bow of Ulysses, though unstrung for ages, was placed against the wall, together with a sheaf of Robin Hood's arrows, and the rifle of Daniel Boone.

"Enough of weapons," said I, at length; "although I would gladly have seen the sacred shield which fell from Heaven in the time of Numa. And surely you should obtain the sword which Washington unsheathed at Cambridge. But the collection does you much credit. Let us pass on."

In the next alcove we saw the golden thigh of Pythagoras, which had so divine a meaning; and, by one of the queer analogies to which the Virtuoso seemed to be addicted, this ancient emblem lay on the same shelf with Peter Stuyvesant's wooden leg, that was fabled to be of silver. Here was a remnant of the Golden Fleece; and a sprig of yellow leaves that resembled the foliage of a frost-bitten elm, but was duly authenticated as a portion of the golden branch by which Æneas gained admittance to the realm of Pluto. Atalanta's golden apple, and one of the apples of discord, were wrapt in the napkin of gold which Rampsinitus brought from Hades; and the whole were deposited in the golden vase of Bias, with its inscription: "To THE WISEST."

"And how did you obtain this vase?" said I to the Virtuoso.

"It was given me long ago," replied he, with a scornful expression in his eye, "because I had learned to despise all things."

It had not escaped me that, though the Virtuoso was evidently a man of high cultivation, yet he seemed to lack sympathy with the spiritual, the sublime, and the tender. Apart from the whim that had led him to devote so much time, pains, and expense to the collection of this Museum, he impressed me as one of the hardest and coldest men of the world whom I had ever met.

"To despise all things!" repeated I. "This, at best, is the wisdom of the understanding. It is the creed of a man whose soul,—whose better and diviner part,—has never been awakened, or has died out of him."

"I did not think that you were still so young," said the Virtuoso. "Should you live to my years, you will acknowledge that the vase of Bias was not ill bestowed."

Without farther discussion of the point, he directed my attention to other curiosities. I examined Cinderella's little glass slipper, and compared it with one of Diana's sandals, and with Fanny Elssler's shoe, which bore testimony to the muscular character of her illustrious foot. On the same shelf were Thomas the Rhymer's green velvet shoes, and the brazen shoe of Empedocles, which was thrown out of Mount Ætna. Anacreon's drinking-cup was placed in apt juxtaposition with one of Tom Moore's wine-glasses and Circe's magic bowl. These were symbols of luxury and riot; but near them stood the cup whence Socrates drank his hemlock; and that which Sir Philip Sydney put from his death-parched lips to bestow the draught upon a dying soldier. Next appeared a cluster of tobacco pipes, consisting of Sir Walter Raleigh's, the earliest on record, Dr. Parr's, Charles Lamb's, and the first calumet of peace which was ever smoked between a European and an Indian. Among other musical instruments, I noticed the lyre of Orpheus, and those of Homer and Sappho, Dr. Franklin's famous whistle, the trumpet of Anthony Van Corlear, and the flute which Goldsmith played upon in his rambles through the French provinces. The staff of Peter the Hermit stood in a corner, with that of good old Bishop Jewel, and one of ivory, which had belonged to Papirius, the Roman Senator. The ponderous club of Hercules was close at hand. The Virtuoso showed me the chisel of Phidias, Claude's palette, and the brush of Apelles, observing that he intended to bestow the former either on Greenough, Crawford, or Powers, and the two latter upon Washington Allston. There was a small vase of oracular gas from Delphos, which, I trust, will be submitted to the scientific analysis of Professor Silliman. I was deeply moved on beholding a phial of the tears into which Niobe was dissolved; nor less so, on learning that a shapeless fragment of salt was a relic of that victim of despondency and sinful regrets, Lot's wife. My companion appeared to set great value upon some Egyptian darkness in a blacking jug. Several of the shelves were covered by a collection of coins; among which, however, I remember none but the Splendid Shilling, celebrated by Phillips, and a dollar's worth of the iron money of Lycurgus, weighing about fifty pounds.

Walking carelessly onward, I had nearly fallen over a huge bundle, like a pedlar's pack, done up in sackcloth and very securely strapped and corded.

"It is Christian's burthen of sin," said the Virtuoso.

"Oh, pray let us open it!" cried I. "For many a year I have longed to know its contents."

"Look into your own consciousness and memory," replied the Virtuoso. "You will there find a list of whatever it contains."

As this was an undeniable truth, I threw a melancholy look at the burthen, and passed on. A collection of old garments, hanging on pegs, was worthy of some attention, especially the shirt of Nessus,

Caesar's mantle, Joseph's coat of many colors, the Vicar of Bray's cassock, Goldsmith's peach-bloom suit, a pair of President Jefferson's scarlet breeches, John Randolph's red baize hunting-shirt, the drab small clothes of the Stout Gentleman, and the rags of the "man all tattered and torn." George Fox's hat impressed me with deep reverence, as a relic of perhaps the truest apostle that has appeared on earth for these eighteen hundred years. My eye was next attracted by an old pair of shears, which I should have taken for a memorial of some famous tailor, only that the Virtuoso pledged his veracity that they were the identical scissors of Atropos. He also showed me a broken hour-glass, which had been thrown aside by Father Time, together with the old gentleman's gray forelock, tastefully braided into a brooch. In the hour-glass was the handful of sand, the grains of which had numbered the years of the Cumaean Sibyl. I think it was in this alcove that I saw the inkstand which Luther threw at the Devil, and the ring which Essex, while under sentence of death, sent to Queen Elizabeth. And here was the blood-encrusted pen of steel with which Faust signed away his salvation.

The Virtuoso now opened the door of a closet, and showed me a lamp burning, while three others stood unlighted by its side. One of the three was the lamp of Diogenes, another that of Guy Faux, and the third that which Hero set forth to the midnight breeze in the high tower of Abydos.

"See!" said the Virtuoso, blowing with all his force at the lighted lamp.

The flame quivered and shrank away from his breath, but clung to the wick, and resumed its brilliancy as soon as the blast was exhausted.

"It is an undying lamp from the tomb of Charlemagne," observed my guide. "That flame was kindled a thousand years ago."

"How ridiculous, to kindle an unnatural light in tombs!" exclaimed

I. "We should seek to behold the dead in the light of Heaven. But what is the meaning of this chafing-dish of glowing coals?"

"That," answered the Virtuoso, "is the original fire which Prometheus stole from Heaven. Look steadfastly into it, and you will discern another curiosity."

I gazed into that fire,—which, symbolically, was the origin of all that was bright and glorious in the soul of man,—and in the midst of it, behold! a little reptile, sporting with evident enjoyment of the fervid heat. It was a salamander.

"What a sacrilege!" cried I, with inexpressible disgust. "Can you find no better use for this ethereal fire than to cherish a loathsome reptile in it? Yet there are men who abuse the sacred fire of their own souls to as foul and guilty a purpose."

The Virtuoso made no answer, except by a dry laugh, and an assurance that the salamander was the very same which Benvenuto Cellini had seen in his father's household fire. He then proceeded to show me other rarities; for this closet appeared to be the receptacle of what he considered most valuable in his collection.

"There," said he, "is the Great Carbuncle of the White Mountains."

I gazed with no little interest at this mighty gem, which it had been one of the wild projects of my youth to discover. Possibly it might have looked brighter to me in those days than now; at all events, it had not such brilliancy as to detain me long from the other articles of the Museum. The Virtuoso pointed out to me a crystalline stone, which hung by a gold chain against the wall.

"That is the Philosopher's Stone," said he.

"And have you the Elixir Vitæ, which generally accompanies it?" inquired I.

"Even so,—this urn is filled with it," he replied. "A draught would refresh you. Here is Hebe's cup,—will you quaff a health from it?"

My heart thrilled within me at the idea of such a reviving draught;

for methought I had great need of it, after travelling so far on the dusty road of life. But I know not whether it were a peculiar glance in the Virtuoso's eye, or the circumstance that this most precious liquid was contained in an antique sepulchral urn, that made me pause. Then came many a thought, with which, in the calmer and better hours of life, I had strengthened myself to feel that Death is the very friend whom, in his due season, even the happiest mortal should be willing to embrace.

"No, I desire not an earthly immortality," said I. "Were man to live longer on the earth, the spiritual would die out of him. The spark of ethereal fire would be choked by the material, the sensual. There is a celestial something within us that requires, after a certain time, the atmosphere of Heaven to preserve it from decay and ruin. I will have none of this liquid. You do well to keep it in a sepulchral urn; for it would produce death, while bestowing the shadow of life."

"All this is unintelligible to me," responded my guide, with indifference. "Life,—earthly life,—is the only good. But you refuse the draught? Well, it is not likely to be offered twice within one man's experience. Probably you have griefs which you seek to forget in death. I can enable you to forget them in life. Will you take a draught of Lethe?"

As he spoke, the Virtuoso took from the shelf a crystal vase containing a sable liquor, which caught no reflected image from the objects around.

"Not for the world!" exclaimed I, shrinking back. "I can spare none of my recollections,—not even those of error or sorrow. They are all alike the food of my spirit. As well never to have lived, as to lose them now."

Without further parley we passed to the next alcove, the shelves of which were burthened with ancient volumes, and with those rolls of papyrus, in which was treasured up the eldest wisdom of the earth.

Perhaps the most valuable work in the collection, to a bibliomaniac, was the Book of Hermes. For my part, however, I would have given a higher price for those six of the Sibyl's books which Tarquin refused to purchase, and which the Virtuoso informed me he had himself found in the cave of Trophonius. Doubtless these old volumes contain prophecies of the fate of Rome, both as respects the decline and fall of her temporal empire, and the rise of her spiritual one. Not without value, likewise, was the work of Anaxagoras on Nature, hitherto supposed to be irrecoverably lost; and the missing treatises of Longinus, by which modern criticism might profit; and those books of Livy, for which the classic student has so long sorrowed without hope. Among these precious tomes I observed the original manuscript of the Koran, and also that of the Mormon Bible, in Joe Smith's authentic autograph. Alexander's copy of the Iliad was also there, enclosed in the jewelled casket of Darius, still fragrant of the perfumes which the Persian kept in it.

Opening an iron-clasped volume, bound in black leather, I discovered it to be Cornelius Agrippa's book of magic; and it was rendered still more interesting by the fact that many flowers, ancient and modern, were pressed between its leaves. Here was a rose from Eve's bridal bower, and all those red and white roses which were plucked in the garden of the Temple, by the partizans of York and Lancaster. Here was Halleck's Wild Rose of Alloway. Cowper had contributed a Sensitive Plant, and Wordsworth an Eglantine, and Burns a Mountain Daisy, and Kirke White a Star of Bethlehem, and Longfellow a Sprig of Fennel, with its yellow flowers. James Russell Lowell had given a Pressed Flower, but fragrant still, which had been shadowed in the Rhine. There was also a sprig from Southey's Holly-Tree. One of the most beautiful specimens was a Fringed Gentian, which had been plucked and preserved for immortality by Bryant. From Jones Very,—a poet whose voice is scarcely heard among us, by reason of its depth,—there was a Wind Flower and a Columbine.

As I closed Cornelius Agrippa's magic volume, an old, mildewed letter fell upon the floor; it proved to be an autograph from the Flying Dutchman to his wife. I could linger no longer among books, for the afternoon was waning, and there was yet much to see. The bare mention of a few more curiosities must suffice. The immense skull of Polyphemus was recognizable by the cavernous hollow in the centre of the forehead, where once had blazed the giant's single eye. The tub of Diogenes, Medea's cauldron, and Psyche's vase of beauty, were placed one within another. Pandora's box, without the lid, stood next, containing nothing but the girdle of Venus, which had been carelessly flung into it. A bundle of birch rods, which had been used by Shenstone's schoolmistress, were tied up with the Countess of Salisbury's garter. I knew not which to value most, a Roc's egg, as big as an ordinary hogshead, or the shell of the egg which Columbus set upon its end. Perhaps the most delicate article in the whole Museum was Queen Mab's chariot, which, to guard it from the touch of meddlesome fingers, was placed under a glass tumbler.

Several of the shelves were occupied by specimens of entomology. Feeling but little interest in the science, I noticed only Anacreon's Grasshopper and a Humble-Bee, which had been presented to the Virtuoso by Ralph Waldo Emerson.

In the part of the hall which we had now reached, I observed a curtain that descended from the ceiling to the floor in voluminous folds, of a depth, richness, and magnificence which I had never seen equalled. It was not to be doubted that this splendid, though dark and solemn veil, concealed a portion of the Museum even richer in wonders than that through which I had already passed. But, on my attempting to grasp the edge of the curtain and draw it aside, it proved to be an illusive picture.

"You need not blush," remarked the Virtuoso, "for that same curtain deceived Zeuxis. It is the celebrated painting of Parrhasius."

In a range with the curtain, there were a number of other choice pictures, by artists of ancient days. Here was the famous Cluster of Grapes by Zeuxis, so admirably depicted that it seemed as if the ripe juice were bursting forth. As to the picture of the Old Woman, by the same illustrious painter, and which was so ludicrous that he himself died with laughing at it, I cannot say that it particularly moved my risibility. Ancient humor seems to have little power over modern muscles. Here, also, was the Horse, painted by Apelles, which living horses neighed at; his first portrait of Alexander the Great, and his last unfinished picture of Venus Asleep. Each of these works of art, together with others by Parrhasius, Timanthes, Polygnotus, Apollodorus, Pausias, and Pamphilus, required more time and study than I could bestow, for the adequate perception of their merits. I shall therefore leave them undescribed and uncriticised, nor attempt to settle the question of superiority between ancient and modern art.

For the same reason I shall pass lightly over the specimens of antique sculpture, which this indefatigable and fortunate Virtuoso had dug out of the dust of fallen empires. Here was Ætion's cedar statue of Æsculapius, much decayed, and Alcon's iron statue of Hercules, lamentably rusted. Here was the statue of Victory, six feet high, which the Jupiter Olympus of Phidias had held in his hand. Here was a forefinger of the Colossus of Rhodes, seven feet in length. Here was the Venus Urania of Phidias, and other images of male and female beauty or grandeur, wrought by sculptors who appear never to have debased their souls by the sight of any meaner forms than those of gods, or godlike mortals. But the deep simplicity of these great works was not to be comprehended by a mind excited and disturbed as mine was by the various objects that had recently been presented to it. I therefore turned away, with merely a passing glance, resolving, on some future occasion, to brood over each individual statue and picture, until my inmost spirit should feel their excellence. In this department, again, I noticed the tendency to whimsical combinations and ludicrous analogies, which seemed to influence many of the arrangements of the Museum. The wooden statue, so well known as the Palladium of Troy, was placed in close apposition with the wooden head of General Jackson, which was stolen, a few years since, from the bows of the frigate Constitution.

We had now completed the circuit of the spacious hall, and found ourselves again near the door. Feeling somewhat wearied with the survey of so many novelties and antiquities, I sat down upon Cowper's sofa, while the Virtuoso threw himself carelessly into Rabelais's easy-chair. Casting my eyes upon the opposite wall, I was surprised to perceive the shadow of a man, flickering unsteadily across the wainscot, and looking as if it were stirred by some breath of air that found its way through the door or windows. No substantial figure was visible, from which this shadow might be thrown; nor, had there been such, was there any sunshine that would have caused it to darken upon the wall.

"It is Peter Schlemihl's Shadow," observed the Virtuoso, "and one of the most valuable articles in my collection."

"Methinks a shadow would have made a fitting door-keeper to such a Museum," said I, "although, indeed, yonder figure has something strange and fantastic about him, which suits well enough with many of the impressions which I have received here. Pray, who is he?"

While speaking, I gazed more scrutinizingly than before at the antiquated presence of the person who had admitted me, and who still sat on his bench, with the same restless aspect, and dim, confused, questioning anxiety, that I had noticed on my first entrance. At this moment he looked eagerly towards us, and half-starting from his seat, addressed me.

"I beseech you, kind sir," said he, in a cracked, melancholy tone, "have pity on the most unfortunate man in the world! For heaven's sake answer me a single question! Is this the town of Boston?"

"You have recognized him now," said the Virtuoso. "It is Peter Rugg, the Missing Man. I chanced to meet him, the other day, still in search of Boston, and conducted him hither; and, as he could not succeed in finding his friends, I have taken him into my service as door-keeper. He is somewhat too apt to ramble, but otherwise a man of trust and integrity."

"And—might I venture to ask," continued I, "to whom am I indebted for this afternoon's gratification?"

The Virtuoso, before replying, laid his hand upon an antique dart or javelin, the rusty steel head of which seemed to have been blunted, as if it had encountered the resistance of a tempered shield or breast-plate.

"My name has not been without its distinction in the world, for a longer period than that of any other man alive," answered he. "Yet many doubt of my existence,—perhaps you will do so, to-morrow. This dart, which I hold in my hand, was once grim Death's own weapon. It served him well for the space of four thousand years. But it fell blunted, as you see, when he directed it against my breast."

These words were spoken with the calm and cold courtesy of manner that had characterized this singular personage throughout our interview. I fancied, it is true, that there was a bitterness indefinably mingled with his tone, as of one cut off from natural sympathies, and blasted with a doom that had been inflicted on no other human being, and by the results of which he had ceased to be human. Yet, withal, it seemed one of the most terrible consequences of that doom, that the victim no longer regarded it as a calamity, but had finally accepted it as the greatest good that could have befallen him.

"You are the Wandering Jew!" exclaimed I.

The Virtuoso bowed, without emotion of any kind; for, by centuries of custom, he had almost lost the sense of strangeness in his fate, and was but imperfectly conscious of the astonishment and awe with which it affected such as are capable of death.

"Your doom is indeed a fearful one!" said I, with irrepressible feeling, and a frankness that afterwards startled me; "yet perhaps the ethereal spirit is not entirely extinct, under all this corrupted or frozen mass of earthly life. Perhaps the immortal spark may yet be rekindled by a breath of Heaven. Perhaps you may yet be permitted to die, before it is too late to live eternally. You have my prayers for such a consummation. Farewell."

"Your prayers will be in vain," replied he, with a smile of cold triumph. "My destiny is linked with the realities of earth. You are welcome to your visions and shadows of a future state; but give me what I can see, and touch, and understand, and I ask no more."

"It is indeed too late," thought I. "The soul is dead within him!" Struggling between pity and horror, I extended my hand, to which the Virtuoso gave his own, still with the habitual courtesy of a man of the world, but without a single heart-throb of human brotherhood. The touch seemed like ice, yet I know not whether morally or physically. As I departed, he bade me observe that the inner door of the hall was constructed with the ivory leaves of the gateway through which Æneas and the Sibyl had been dismissed from Hades.

The Birth-mark

IN THE LATTER PART of the last century, there lived a man of science—an eminent proficient in every branch of natural philosophy—who, not long before our story opens, had made experience of a spiritual affinity, more attractive than any chemical one. He had left his laboratory to the care of an assistant, cleared his fine countenance from the furnace-smoke, washed the stain of acids from his fingers, and persuaded a beautiful woman to become his wife. In those days, when the comparatively recent discovery of electricity, and other kindred mysteries of nature, seemed to open paths into the region of miracle, it was not unusual for the love of science to rival the love of woman, in its depth and absorbing energy. The higher intellect, the imagination, the spirit, and even the heart, might all find their congenial aliment in pursuits which, as some of their ardent votaries believed, would ascend from one step of powerful intelligence to another, until the philosopher should lay his hand on the secret of creative force, and perhaps make new worlds for himself. We know not whether Aylmer possessed this degree of faith in man's ultimate control over nature. He had devoted himself, however, too unreservedly to scientific studies, ever to be weaned from them by any second passion. His love for his young wife might prove the stronger of the two; but it could only be by intertwining itself with his love of science, and uniting the strength of the latter to its own.

Such a union accordingly took place, and was attended with truly remarkable consequences, and a deeply impressive moral. One day, very soon after their marriage, Aylmer sat gazing at his wife, with a trouble in his countenance that grew stronger, until he spoke.

"Georgiana," said he, "has it never occurred to you that the mark upon your cheek might be removed?"

"No, indeed," said she, smiling; but perceiving the seriousness of his manner, she blushed deeply. "To tell you the truth, it has been so often called a charm, that I was simple enough to imagine it might be so."

"Ah, upon another face, perhaps it might," replied her husband. "But never on yours! No, dearest Georgiana, you came so nearly perfect from the hand of Nature, that this slightest possible defect—which we hesitate whether to term a defect or a beauty—shocks me, as being the visible mark of earthly imperfection."

"Shocks you, my husband!" cried Georgiana, deeply hurt; at first reddening with momentary anger, but then bursting into tears. "Then why did you take me from my mother's side? You cannot love what shocks you!"

To explain this conversation, it must be mentioned, that, in the centre of Georgiana's left cheek, there was a singular mark, deeply interwoven, as it were, with the texture and substance of her face. In the usual state of her complexion,—a healthy, though delicate bloom,—the mark wore a tint of deeper crimson, which imperfectly defined its shape amid the surrounding rosiness. When she blushed, it gradually became more indistinct, and finally vanished amid the triumphant rush of blood, that bathed the whole cheek with its brilliant glow. But, if any shifting emotion caused her to turn pale, there was the mark again, a crimson stain upon the snow, in what Aylmer sometimes deemed an almost fearful distinctness. Its shape bore not a little similarity to the human hand, though of the smallest pigmy size. Georgiana's lovers were wont to say, that some fairy, at her birth-hour, had laid her tiny hand upon the infant's cheek, and left this impress there, in token of the magic endowments that were to give her such sway over all hearts. Many a desperate swain would have risked life for the privilege of pressing his lips to the mysterious hand. It must not be concealed, however, that the impression wrought by this fairy sign-manual varied exceedingly, according to the difference of temperament in the beholders. Some fastidious persons—but they were exclusively of her own sex—affirmed that the Bloody Hand, as they chose to call it, quite destroyed the effect of Georgiana's beauty, and rendered her countenance even hideous. But it would be as reasonable to say, that one of those small blue stains, which sometimes occur in the purest statuary marble, would convert the Eve of Powers to a monster. Masculine observers, if the birth-mark did not heighten their admiration, contented themselves with wishing it away, that the world might possess one living specimen of ideal loveliness, without the semblance of a flaw. After his marriage—for he thought little or nothing of the matter before—Aylmer discovered that this was the case with himself.

Had she been less beautiful—if Envy's self could have found aught else to sneer at—he might have felt his affection heightened by the prettiness of this mimic hand, now vaguely portrayed, now lost, now stealing forth again, and glimmering to-and-fro with every pulse of emotion that throbbed within her heart. But, seeing her otherwise so perfect, he found this one defect grow more and more intolerable, with every moment of their united lives. It was the fatal flaw of humanity, which Nature, in one shape or another, stamps ineffaceably on all her productions, either to imply that they are temporary and finite, or that their perfection must be wrought by toil and pain. The Crimson Hand expressed the ineludible gripe, in which mortality clutches the highest and purest of earthly mould, degrading them into kindred with the lowest, and even with the very brutes, like whom their visible frames return to dust. In this manner, selecting it as the symbol of his wife's liability to sin, sorrow, decay, and death, Aylmer's sombre imagination was not long in rendering the birthmark a frightful object, causing him more trouble and horror than ever Georgiana's beauty, whether of soul or sense, had given him delight.

At all the seasons which should have been their happiest, he invariably, and without intending it—nay, in spite of a purpose to the contrary—reverted to this one disastrous topic. Trifling as it at first appeared, it so connected itself with innumerable trains of thought, and modes of feeling, that it became the central point of all. With the morning twilight, Aylmer opened his eyes upon his wife's face, and recognized the symbol of imperfection; and when they sat together at the evening hearth, his eyes wandered stealthily to her cheek, and beheld, flickering with the blaze of the wood fire, the spectral Hand that wrote mortality, where he would fain have worshipped. Georgiana soon learned to shudder at his gaze. It needed but a glance, with the peculiar expression that his face often wore, to change the roses of her cheek into a deathlike paleness, amid which the Crimson Hand was brought strongly out, like a bas-relief of ruby on the whitest marble.

Late, one night, when the lights were growing dim, so as hardly to betray the stain on the poor wife's cheek, she herself, for the first time, voluntarily took up the subject.

"Do you remember, my dear Aylmer," said she, with a feeble attempt at a smile—"have you any recollection of a dream, last night, about this odious Hand?"

"None!—none whatever!" replied Aylmer, starting; but then he added in a dry, cold tone, affected for the sake of concealing the real depth of his emotion:—"I might well dream of it; for before I fell asleep, it had taken a pretty firm hold of my fancy."

"And you did dream of it," continued Georgiana, hastily; for she dreaded lest a gush of tears should interrupt what she had to say—"A terrible dream! I wonder that you can forget it. Is it possible to forget this one expression?—'It is in her heart now—we must have it out!'—Reflect, my husband; for by all means I would have you recall that dream."

The mind is in a sad note, when Sleep, the all-involving, cannot confine her spectres within the dim region of her sway, but suffers them to break forth, affrighting this actual life with secrets that perchance belong to a deeper one. Aylmer now remembered his dream. He had fancied himself, with his servant Aminadab, attempting an operation for the removal of the birth-mark. But the deeper went the knife, the deeper sank the Hand, until at length its tiny grasp appeared to have caught hold of Georgiana's heart; whence, however, her husband was inexorably resolved to cut or wrench it away.

When the dream had shaped itself perfectly in his memory, Aylmer sat in his wife's presence with a guilty feeling. Truth often finds its way to the mind close-muffled in robes of sleep, and then speaks with uncompromising directness of matters in regard to which we practise an unconscious self-deception, during our waking moments. Until now, he had not been aware of the tyrannizing influence acquired by one idea over his mind, and of the lengths which he might find in his heart to go, for the sake of giving himself peace.

"Aylmer," resumed Georgiana, solemnly, "I know not what may be the cost to both of us, to rid me of this fatal birth-mark. Perhaps its removal may cause cureless deformity. Or, it may be, the stain goes as deep as life itself. Again, do we know that there is a possibility, on any terms, of unclasping the firm gripe of this little Hand, which was laid upon me before I came into the world?"

"Dearest Georgiana, I have spent much thought upon the subject," hastily interrupted Aylmer—"I am convinced of the perfect practicability of its removal."

"If there be the remotest possibility of it," continued Georgiana, "let the attempt be made, at whatever risk. Danger is nothing to me; for life—while this hateful mark makes me the object of your horror and disgust—life is a burthen which I would fling down with joy. Either remove this dreadful Hand, or take my wretched life! You have deep science! All the world bears witness of it. You have achieved great wonders! Cannot you remove this little, little mark, which I cover with the tips of two small fingers? Is this beyond your power, for the sake of your own peace, and to save your poor wife from madness?"

"Noblest—dearest—tenderest wife!" cried Aylmer, rapturously. "Doubt not my power. I have already given this matter the deepest thought—thought which might almost have enlightened me to create a being less perfect than yourself. Georgiana, you have led me deeper than ever into the heart of science. I feel myself fully competent to render this dear cheek as faultless as its fellow; and then, most beloved, what will be my triumph, when I shall have corrected what Nature left imperfect, in her fairest work! Even Pygmalion, when his sculptured woman assumed life, felt not greater ecstasy than mine will be."

"It is resolved, then," said Georgiana, faintly smiling,—"And, Aylmer, spare me not, though you should find the birth-mark take refuge in my heart at last."

Her husband tenderly kissed her cheek—her right cheek—not that which bore the impress of the Crimson Hand.

The next day, Aylmer apprized his wife of a plan that he had formed, whereby he might have opportunity for the intense thought and constant watchfulness, which the proposed operation would require; while Georgiana, likewise, would enjoy the perfect repose essential to its success. They were to seclude themselves in the extensive apartments occupied by Aylmer as a laboratory, and where, during his toilsome youth, he had made discoveries in the elemental powers of nature, that had roused the admiration of all the learned societies in Europe. Seated calmly in this laboratory, the pale philosopher had investigated the secrets of the highest cloud-region, and of the profoundest mines; he had satisfied himself of the causes that kindled and kept alive the fires of the volcano; and had explained the mystery of fountains, and how it is that they gush forth, some so bright and pure, and others with such rich medicinal virtues, from the dark bosom of the earth. Here, too, at an earlier period, he had studied the wonders of the human frame, and attempted to fathom the very process by which Nature assimilates all her precious influences from earth and air, and from the spiritual world, to create and foster Man, her masterpiece. The latter pursuit, however, Aylmer had long laid aside, in unwilling recognition of the truth, against which all seekers sooner or later stumble, that our great creative Mother, while she amuses us with apparently working in the broadest sunshine, is yet severely careful to keep her own secrets, and, in spite of her pretended openness, shows us nothing but results. She permits us indeed, to mar, but seldom to mend, and, like a jealous patentee, on no account to make. Now, however, Aylmer resumed these half-forgotten investigations; not, of course, with such hopes or wishes as first suggested them; but because they involved much physiological truth, and lay in the path of his proposed scheme for the treatment of Georgiana.

As he led her over the threshold of the laboratory, Georgiana was cold and tremulous. Aylmer looked cheerfully into her face, with intent to reassure her, but was so startled with the intense glow of the birth-mark upon the whiteness of her cheek, that he could not re-strain a strong convulsive shudder. His wife fainted.

"Aminadab! Aminadab!" shouted Aylmer, stamping violently on the floor.

Forthwith, there issued from an inner apartment a man of low stature, but bulky frame, with shaggy hair hanging about his visage, which was grimed with the vapors of the furnace. This personage had been Aylmer's under-worker during his whole scientific career, and was admirably fitted for that office by his great mechanical readiness, and the skill with which, while incapable of comprehending a single principle, he executed all the practical details of his master's experi-ments. With his vast strength, his shaggy hair, his smoky aspect, and the indescribable earthiness that incrusted him, he seemed to repre-sent man's physical nature; while Aylmer's slender figure, and pale, intellectual face, were no less apt a type of the spiritual element.

"Throw open the door of the boudoir, Aminadab," said Aylmer, "and burn a pastille."

"Yes, master," answered Aminadab, looking intently at the lifeless form of Georgiana; and then he muttered to himself:—"If she were my wife, I'd never part with that birth-mark."

When Georgiana recovered consciousness, she found herself breathing an atmosphere of penetrating fragrance, the gentle potency of which had recalled her from her deathlike faintness. The scene around her looked like enchantment. Aylmer had converted those smoky, dingy, sombre rooms, where he had spent his brightest years in recondite pursuits, into a series of beautiful apartments, not un-fit to be the secluded abode of a lovely woman. The walls were hung with gorgeous curtains, which imparted the combination of grandeur and grace, that no other species of adornment can achieve; and as they fell from the ceiling to the floor, their rich and ponderous folds, concealing all angles and straight lines, appeared to shut in the scene

from infinite space. For aught Georgiana knew, it might be a pavil-
ion among the clouds. And Aylmer, excluding the sunshine, which
would have interfered with his chemical processes, had supplied its
place with perfumed lamps, emitting flames of various hue, but all
uniting in a soft, empurpled radiance. He now knelt by his wife's side,
watching her earnestly, but without alarm; for he was confident in his
science, and felt that he could draw a magic circle round her, within
which no evil might intrude.

"Where am I?—Ah, I remember!" said Georgiana, faintly; and she
placed her hand over her cheek, to hide the terrible mark from her
husband's eyes.

"Fear not, dearest!" exclaimed he. "Do not shrink from me! Believe
me, Georgiana, I even rejoice in this single imperfection, since it will
be such rapture to remove it."

"Oh, spare me!" sadly replied his wife—"Pray do not look at it
again. I never can forget that convulsive shudder."

In order to soothe Georgiana, and, as it were, to release her mind
from the burthen of actual things, Aylmer now put in practice some
of the light and playful secrets, which science had taught him among
its profounder lore. Airy figures, absolutely bodiless ideas, and forms
of unsubstantial beauty, came and danced before her, imprinting
their momentary footsteps on beams of light. Though she had some
indistinct idea of the method of these optical phenomena, still the illusion was almost perfect enough to warrant the belief, that her husband possessed sway over the spiritual world. Then again, when she
felt a wish to look forth from her seclusion, immediately, as if her
thoughts were answered, the procession of external existence flitted
across a screen. The scenery and the figures of actual life were perfectly represented, but with that bewitching, yet indescribable difference, which always makes a picture, an image, or a shadow, so much
more attractive than the original. When wearied of this, Aylmer bade

her cast her eyes upon a vessel, containing a quantity of earth. She did so, with little interest at first, but was soon startled, to perceive the germ of a plant, shooting upward from the soil. Then came the slender stalk—the leaves gradually unfolded themselves—and amid them was a perfect and lovely flower.

"It is magical!" cried Georgiana, "I dare not touch it."

"Nay, pluck it," answered Aylmer, "pluck it, and inhale its brief perfume while you may. The flower will wither in a few moments, and leave nothing save its brown seed-vessels—but thence may be perpetuated a race as ephemeral as itself."

But Georgiana had no sooner touched the flower than the whole plant suffered a blight, its leaves turning coal-black, as if by the agency of fire.

"There was too powerful a stimulus," said Aylmer thoughtfully.

To make up for this abortive experiment, he proposed to take her portrait by a scientific process of his own invention. It was to be effected by rays of light striking upon a polished plate of metal. Georgiana assented—but, on looking at the result, was affrighted to find the features of the portrait blurred and indefinable; while the minute figure of a hand appeared where the cheek should have been. Aylmer snatched the metallic plate, and threw it into a jar of corrosive acid.

Soon, however, he forgot these mortifying failures. In the intervals of study and chemical experiment, he came to her, flushed and exhausted, but seemed invigorated by her presence, and spoke in glowing language of the resources of his art. He gave a history of the long dynasty of the Alchemists, who spent so many ages in quest of the universal solvent, by which the Golden Principle might be elicted from all things vile and base. Aylmer appeared to believe, that, by the plainest scientific logic, it was altogether within the limits of possibility to discover this long-sought medium; but, he added, a philosopher who should go deep enough to acquire the power, would attain too lofty a wisdom to stoop to the exercise of it. Not less singular were his opinions in regard to the Elixir Vitae. He more than intimated, that it was his option to concoct a liquid that should prolong life for years— perhaps interminably—but that it would produce a discord in nature, which all the world, and chiefly the quaffer of the immortal nostrum, would find cause to curse.

"Aylmer, are you in earnest?" asked Georgiana, looking at him with amazement and fear; "it is terrible to possess such power, or even to dream of possessing it!"

"Oh, do not tremble, my love!" said her husband, "I would not wrong either you or myself by working such inharmonious effects upon our lives. But I would have you consider how trifling, in comparison, is the skill requisite to remove this little Hand."

At the mention of the birth-mark, Georgiana, as usual, shrank, as if a red-hot iron had touched her cheek.

Again Aylmer applied himself to his labors. She could hear his voice in the distant furnace-room, giving directions to Aminadab, whose harsh, uncouth, misshapen tones were audible in response, more like the grunt or growl of a brute than human speech. After hours of absence, Aylmer reappeared, and proposed that she should now examine his cabinet of chemical products, and natural treasures of the earth. Among the former he showed her a small vial, in which, he remarked, was contained a gentle yet most powerful fragrance, capable of impregnating all the breezes that blow across a kingdom. They were of inestimable value, the contents of that little vial; and, as he said so, he threw some of the perfume into the air, and filled the room with piercing and invigorating delight.

"And what is this?" asked Georgiana, pointing to a small crystal globe, containing a gold-colored liquid. "It is so beautiful to the eye, that I could imagine it the Elixir of Life."

"In one sense it is," replied Aylmer, "or rather the Elixir of Immortality. It is the most precious poison that ever was concocted in this world. By its aid, I could apportion the lifetime of any mortal at whom you might point your finger. The strength of the dose would determine whether he were to linger out years, or drop dead in the midst of a breath. No king, on his guarded throne, could keep his life, if I, in my private station, should deem that the welfare of millions justified me in depriving him of it."

"Why do you keep such a terrific drug?" inquired Georgiana in horror.

"Do not mistrust me, dearest!" said her husband, smiling; "its virtuous potency is yet greater than its harmful one. But, see! here is a powerful cosmetic. With a few drops of this, in a vase of water, freckles may be washed away as easily as the hands are cleansed. A stronger infusion would take the blood out of the cheek, and leave the rosiest beauty a pale ghost."

"Is it with this lotion that you intend to bathe my cheek?" asked Georgiana anxiously.

"Oh, no!" hastily replied her husband—"this is merely superficial. Your case demands a remedy that shall go deeper."

In his interviews with Georgiana, Aylmer generally made minute inquiries as to her sensations, and whether the confinement of the rooms, and the temperature of the atmosphere, agreed with her. These questions had such a particular drift, that Georgiana began to conjecture that she was already subjected to certain physical influences, either breathed in with the fragrant air, or taken with her food. She fancied, likewise—but it might be altogether fancy—that there was a stirring up of her system,—a strange indefinite sensation creeping through her veins, and tingling, half painfully, half pleasurably, at her heart. Still, whenever she dared to look into the mirror, there she beheld herself, pale as a white rose, and with the crimson birth-mark stamped upon her cheek. Not even Aylmer now hated it so much as she.

To dispel the tedium of the hours which her husband found it necessary to devote to the processes of combination and analysis, Georgiana turned over the volumes of his scientific library. In many dark old tomes, she met with chapters full of romance and poetry. They were the works of the philosophers of the middle ages, such as Albertus Magnus, Cornelius Agrippa, Paracelsus, and the famous friar who created the prophetic Brazen Head. All these antique naturalists stood in advance of their centuries, yet were imbued with some of their credulity, and therefore were believed, and perhaps imagined themselves, to have acquired from the investigation of nature a power above nature, and from physics a sway over the spiritual world. Hardly less curious and imaginative were the early volumes of the Transactions of the Royal Society, in which the members, knowing little of the limits of natural possibility, were continually recording wonders, or proposing methods whereby wonders might be wrought.

But, to Georgiana, the most engrossing volume was a large folio from her husband's own hand, in which he had recorded every experiment of his scientific career, with its original aim, the methods adopted for its development, and its final success or failure, with the circumstances to which either event was attributable. The book, in truth, was both the history and emblem of his ardent, ambitious, imaginative, yet practical and laborious, life. He handled physical details, as if there were nothing beyond them; yet spiritualized them all, and redeemed himself from materialism, by his strong and eager aspiration towards the infinite. In his grasp, the veriest clod of earth assumed a soul. Georgiana, as she read, reverenced Aylmer, and loved him more profoundly than ever, but with a less entire dependence on his judgment than heretofore. Much as he had accomplished, she could not but observe that his most splendid successes were almost invariably failures, if compared with the ideal at which he aimed. His brightest diamonds were the merest pebbles, and felt to be so by himself, in comparison with the inestimable gems which lay hidden beyond his reach. The volume, rich with achievements that had won renown for its author, was yet as melancholy a record as ever mortal hand had penned. It was the sad confession, and continual exemplification, of the short-comings of the composite man—the spirit burthened with clay and working in matter—and of the despair that assails the higher nature, at finding itself so miserably thwarted by the earthly part. Perhaps every man of genius, in whatever sphere, might recognize the image of his own experience in Aylmer's journal.

So deeply did these reflections affect Georgiana, that she laid her face upon the open volume, and burst into tears. In this situation she was found by her husband.

"It is dangerous to read in a sorcerer's books," said he, with a smile, though his countenance was uneasy and displeased. "Georgiana, there are pages in that volume, which I can scarcely glance over and keep my senses. Take heed lest it prove as detrimental to you!"

"It has made me worship you more than ever," said she.

"Ah! wait for this one success," rejoined he, "then worship me if you will. I shall deem myself hardly unworthy of it. But, come! I have sought you for the luxury of your voice. Sing to me, dearest!"

So she poured out the liquid music of her voice to quench the thirst of his spirit. He then took his leave, with a boyish exuberance of gaiety, assuring her that her seclusion would endure but a little longer, and that the result was already certain. Scarcely had he departed, when Georgiana felt irresistibly impelled to follow him. She had forgotten to inform Aylmer of a symptom, which, for two or three hours past, had begun to excite her attention. It was a sensation in the fatal birth-mark, not painful, but which induced a restlessness throughout her system. Hastening after her husband, she intruded, for the first time, into the laboratory.

The first thing that struck her eye was the furnace, that hot and feverish worker, with the intense glow of its fire, which, by the quantities of soot clustered above it, seemed to have been burning for ages. There was a distilling apparatus in full operation. Around the room were retorts, tubes, cylinders, crucibles, and other apparatus of chemical research. An electrical machine stood ready for immediate use. The atmosphere felt oppressively close, and was tainted with gaseous odors, which had been tormented forth by the processes of science. The severe and homely simplicity of the apartment, with its naked walls and brick pavement, looked strange, accustomed as Georgiana had become to the fantastic elegance of her boudoir. But what chiefly, indeed almost solely, drew her attention, was the aspect of Aylmer himself.

He was pale as death, anxious, and absorbed, and hung over the furnace as if it depended upon his utmost watchfulness whether the liquid, which it was distilling, should be the draught of immortal happiness or misery. How different from the sanguine and joyous mien that he had assumed for Georgiana's encouragement!

"Carefully now, Aminadab! Carefully, thou human machine! Carefully, thou man of clay!" muttered Aylmer, more to himself than his assistant. "Now, if there be a thought too much or too little, it is all over!"

"Hoh! hoh!" mumbled Aminadab—"look, master, look!"

Aylmer raised his eyes hastily, and at first reddened, then grew paler than ever, on beholding Georgiana. He rushed towards her, and seized her arm with a gripe that left the print of his fingers upon it.

"Why do you come hither? Have you no trust in your husband?" cried he impetuously. "Would you throw the blight of that fatal birthmark over my labors? It is not well done. Go, prying woman, go!"

"Nay, Aylmer," said Georgiana, with the firmness of which she possessed no stinted endowment, "it is not you that have a right to complain. You mistrust your wife! You have concealed the anxiety with which you watch the development of this experiment. Think not so unworthily of me, my husband! Tell me all the risk we run; and fear not that I shall shrink, for my share in it is far less than your own!"

"No, no, Georgiana!" said Aylmer impatiently, "it must not be."

"I submit," replied she calmly. "And, Aylmer, I shall quaff whatever draught you bring me; but it will be on the same principle that would induce me to take a dose of poison, if offered by your hand."

"My noble wife," said Aylmer, deeply moved, "I knew not the height and depth of your nature, until now. Nothing shall be concealed. Know, then, that this Crimson Hand, superficial as it seems, has clutched its grasp into your being, with a strength of which I had no previous conception. I have already administered agents powerful enough to do aught except to change your entire physical system. Only one thing remains to be tried. If that fail us, we are ruined!"

"Why did you hesitate to tell me this?" asked she.

"Because, Georgiana," said Aylmer, in a low voice, "there is danger!"

"Danger? There is but one danger—that this horrible stigma shall be left upon my cheek!" cried Georgiana. "Remove it! remove it!—whatever be the cost—or we shall both go mad!"

"Heaven knows, your words are too true," said Aylmer, sadly. "And now, dearest, return to your boudoir. In a little while, all will be tested."

He conducted her back, and took leave of her with a solemn tenderness, which spoke far more than his words how much was now at stake. After his departure, Georgiana became wrapt in musings. She considered the character of Aylmer, and did it completer justice than at any previous moment. Her heart exulted, while it trembled, at his honorable love, so pure and lofty that it would accept nothing less than perfection, nor miserably make itself contented with an earthlier nature than he had dreamed of. She felt how much more precious was such a sentiment, than that meaner kind which would have borne with the imperfection for her sake, and have been guilty of treason to holy love, by degrading its perfect idea to the level of the actual. And, with her whole spirit, she prayed, that, for a single moment, she might satisfy his highest and deepest conception. Longer than one moment, she well knew, it could not be; for his spirit was ever on the march—ever ascending—and each instant required something that was beyond the scope of the instant before.

The sound of her husband's footsteps aroused her. He bore a crystal goblet, containing a liquor colorless as water, but bright enough to be the draught of immortality. Aylmer was pale; but it seemed rather the consequence of a highly wrought state of mind, and tension of spirit, than of fear or doubt.

"The concoction of the draught has been perfect," said he, in answer to Georgiana's look. "Unless all my science have deceived me, it cannot fail."

"Save on your account, my dearest Aylmer," observed his wife, "I might wish to put off this birth-mark of mortality by relinquishing mortality itself, in preference to any other mode. Life is but a sad possession to those who have attained precisely the degree of moral advancement at which I stand. Were I weaker and blinder, it might be happiness. Were I stronger, it might be endured hopefully. But, being what I find myself, methinks I am of all mortals the most fit to die."

"You are fit for heaven without tasting death!" replied her husband. "But why do we speak of dying? The draught cannot fail. Behold its effect upon this plant!"

On the window-seat there stood a geranium, diseased with yellow blotches, which had overspread all its leaves. Aylmer poured a small quantity of the liquid upon the soil in which it grew. In a little time, when the roots of the plant had taken up the moisture, the unsightly blotches began to be extinguished in a living verdure.

"There needed no proof," said Georgiana, quietly. "Give me the goblet. I joyfully stake all upon your word."

"Drink, then, thou lofty creature!" exclaimed Aylmer, with fervid admiration. "There is no taint of imperfection on thy spirit. Thy sensible frame, too, shall soon be all perfect!"

She quaffed the liquid, and returned the goblet to his hand.

"It is grateful," said she, with a placid smile. "Methinks it is like water from a heavenly fountain; for it contains I know not what of unobtrusive fragrance and deliciousness. It allays a feverish thirst, that had parched me for many days. Now, dearest, let me sleep. My earthly senses are closing over my spirit, like the leaves round the heart of a rose, at sunset."

She spoke the last words with a gentle reluctance, as if it required almost more energy than she could command to pronounce the faint and lingering syllables. Scarcely had they loitered through her lips, ere she was lost in slumber. Aylmer sat by her side, watching her aspect with the emotions proper to a man, the whole value of whose existence was involved in the process now to be tested. Mingled with this mood, however, was the philosophic investigation, characteristic of the man of science. Not the minutest symptom escaped him. A heightened flush of the cheek—a slight irregularity of breath—a quiver of the eyelid—a hardly perceptible tremor through the frame—such were the details which, as the moments passed, he wrote down in his folio volume. Intense thought had set its stamp upon every previous page of that volume; but the thoughts of years were all concentrated upon the last.

While thus employed, he failed not to gaze often at the fatal Hand, and not without a shudder. Yet once, by a strange and unaccountable impulse, he pressed it with his lips. His spirit recoiled, however, in the very act, and Georgiana, out of the midst of her deep sleep, moved uneasily and murmured, as if in remonstrance. Again, Aylmer resumed his watch. Nor was it without avail. The Crimson Hand, which at first had been strongly visible upon the marble paleness of Georgiana's cheek now grew more faintly outlined. She remained not less pale than ever; but the birth-mark, with every breath that came and went, lost somewhat of its former distinctness. Its presence had been awful; its departure was more awful still. Watch the stain of the rainbow fading out of the sky; and you will know how that mysterious symbol passed away.

"By Heaven, it is well nigh gone!" said Aylmer to himself, in almost irrepressible ecstasy. "I can scarcely trace it now. Success! Success! And now it is like the faintest rose-color. The slightest flush of blood across her cheek would overcome it. But she is so pale!"

He drew aside the window-curtain, and suffered the light of natural day to fall into the room, and rest upon her cheek. At the same time, he heard a gross, hoarse chuckle, which he had long known as his servant Aminadab's expression of delight.

"Ah, clod! Ah, earthly mass!" cried Aylmer, laughing in a sort of frenzy. "You have served me well! Matter and Spirit—Earth and Heaven—have both done their part in this! Laugh, thing of senses! You have earned the right to laugh."

These exclamations broke Georgiana's sleep. She slowly unclosed her eyes, and gazed into the mirror, which her husband had arranged for that purpose. A faint smile flitted over her lips, when she recognized how barely perceptible was now that Crimson Hand, which had once blazed forth with such disastrous brilliancy as to scare away all their happiness. But then her eyes sought Aylmer's face, with a trouble and anxiety that he could by no means account for.

"My poor Aylmer!" murmured she.

"Poor? Nay, richest! Happiest! Most favored!" exclaimed he. "My peerless bride, it is successful! You are perfect!"

"My poor Aylmer!" she repeated, with a more than human tenderness. "You have aimed loftily!—you have done nobly! Do not repent, that, with so high and pure a feeling, you have rejected the best that earth could offer. Aylmer—dearest Aylmer—I am dying!"

Alas, it was too true! The fatal Hand had grappled with the mystery of life, and was the bond by which an angelic spirit kept itself in union with a mortal frame. As the last crimsontint of the birthmark—that sole token of human imperfection—faded from her cheek, the parting breath of the now perfect woman passed into the atmosphere, and her soul, lingering a moment near her husband, took its heavenward flight. Then a hoarse, chuckling laugh was heard again! Thus ever does the gross Fatality of Earth exult in its invariable triumph over the immortal essence, which, in this dim sphere of half-development, demands the completeness of a higher state. Yet, had Aylmer reached a profounder wisdom, he need not thus have flung away the happiness, which would have woven his mortal life of the self-same texture with the celestial. The momentary circumstance was too strong for him; he failed to look beyond the shadowy scope of Time, and living once for all in Eternity, to find the perfect Future in the present.

Egotism;* or, the Bosom-Serpent

From the Unpublished "Allegories of the Heart"

H ERE HE COMES!" shouted the boys along the street.—"Here comes the man with a snake in his bosom!"

This outcry, saluting Herkimer's ears, as he was about to enter the iron gate of the Elliston mansion, made him pause. It was not without a shudder that he found himself on the point of meeting his former acquaintance, whom he had known in the glory of youth, and whom now, after an interval of five years, he was to find the victim either of a diseased fancy, or a horrible physical misfortune.

"A snake in his bosom!" repeated the young sculptor to himself. "It must be he. No second man on earth has such a bosom-friend! And now, my poor Rosina, Heaven grant me wisdom to discharge my er-

---

* The physical fact, to which it is here attempted to give a moral signification, has been known to occur in more than one instance.

rand aright! Woman's faith must be strong indeed, since thine has not yet failed."

Thus musing, he took his stand at the entrance of the gate, and waited until the personage, so singularly announced, should make his appearance. After an instant or two, he beheld the figure of a lean man, of unwholesome look, with glittering eyes and long black hair, who seemed to imitate the motion of a snake; for, instead of walking straight forward with open front, he undulated along the pavement in a curved line. It may be too fanciful to say, that something, either in his moral or material aspect, suggested the idea that a miracle had been wrought, by transforming a serpent into a man; but so imperfectly, that the snaky nature was yet hidden, and scarcely hidden, under the mere outward guise of humanity. Herkimer remarked that his complexion had a greenish tinge over its sickly white, reminding him of a species of marble out of which he had once wrought a head of Envy, with her snaky locks.

The wretched being approached the gate, but, instead of entering, stopt short, and fixed the glitter of his eye full upon the compassionate, yet steady countenance of the sculptor.

"It gnaws me! It gnaws me!" he exclaimed.

And then there was an audible hiss, but whether it came from the apparent lunatic's own lips, or was the real hiss of a serpent, might admit of discussion. At all events, it made Herkimer shudder to his heart's core.

"Do you know me, George Herkimer?" asked the snake-possessed.

Herkimer did know him. But it demanded all the intimate and practical acquaintance with the human face, acquired by modelling actual likenesses in clay, to recognize the features of Roderick Elliston in the visage that now met the sculptor's gaze. Yet it was he. It added nothing to the wonder, to reflect that the once brilliant young man had undergone this odious and fearful change, during the no more than five brief years of Herkimer's abode at Florence. The possibility of such a transformation being granted, it was as easy to conceive it effected in a moment as in an age. Inexpressibly shocked and startled, it was still the keenest pang, when Herkimer remembered that the fate of his cousin Rosina, the ideal of gentle womanhood, was indissolubly interwoven with that of a being whom Providence seemed to have unhumanized.

"Elliston! Roderick!" cried he, "I had heard of this; but my conception came far short of the truth. What has befallen you? Why do I find you thus?"

"Oh, 'tis a mere nothing! A snake! A snake! The commonest thing in the world. A snake in the bosom—that's all," answered Roderick Elliston. "But how is your own breast?" continued he, looking the sculptor in the eye, with the most acute and penetrating glance that it had ever been his fortune to encounter. "All pure and wholesome? No reptile there? By my faith and conscience, and by the devil within me, here is a wonder! A man without a serpent in his bosom!"

"Be calm, Elliston," whispered George Herkimer, laying his hand upon the shoulder of the snake-possessed. "I have crossed the ocean to meet you. Listen!—let us be private—I bring a message from Rosina!—from your wife!"

"It gnaws me! It gnaws me!" muttered Roderick.

With this exclamation, the most frequent in his mouth, the unfortunate man clutched both hands upon his breast, as if an intolerable sting or torture impelled him to rend it open, and let out the living mischief, even were it intertwined with his own life. He then freed himself from Herkimer's grasp, by a subtle motion, and gliding through the gate, took refuge in his antiquated family residence. The sculptor did not pursue him. He saw that no available intercourse could be expected at such a moment, and was desirous, before another meeting, to inquire closely into the nature of Roderick's disease, and the circumstances that had reduced him to so lamentable a condition. He succeeded in obtaining the necessary information from an eminent medical gentleman.

Shortly after Elliston's separation from his wife—now nearly four years ago—his associates had observed a singular gloom spreading over his daily life, like those chill, grey mists that sometimes steal away the sunshine from a summer's morning. The symptoms caused them endless perplexity. They knew not whether ill health were robbing his spirits of elasticity; or whether a canker of the mind was gradually eating, as such cankers do, from his moral system into the physical frame, which is but the shadow of the former. They looked for the root of this trouble in his shattered schemes of domestic bliss—wilfully shattered by himself—but could not be satisfied of its existence there. Some thought that their once brilliant friend was in an incipient stage of insanity, of which his passionate impulses had perhaps been the forerunners; others prognosticated a general blight and gradual decline. From Roderick's own lips, they could learn nothing. More than once, it is true, he had been heard to say, clutching his hands convulsively upon his breast—"It gnaws me! It gnaws me!"—but, by different auditors, a great diversity of explanation was assigned to this ominous expression. What could it be, that gnawed the breast of Roderick Elliston? Was it sorrow? Was it merely the tooth of physical disease? Or, in his reckless course, often verging upon profligacy, if not plunging into its depths, had he been guilty of some deed, which made his bosom a prey to the deadlier fangs of remorse? There was plausible ground for each of these conjectures; but it must not be concealed that more than one elderly gentleman, the victim of good cheer and slothful habits, magisterially pronounced the secret of the whole matter to be Dyspepsia!

Meanwhile, Roderick seemed aware how generally he had become the subject of curiosity and conjecture, and, with a morbid repugnance to such notice, or to any notice whatsoever, estranged himself from all companionship. Not merely the eye of man was a horror to him; not merely the light of a friend's countenance; but even the blessed sunshine, likewise, which, in its universal beneficence, typifies the radiance of the Creator's face, expressing his love for all the creatures of his hand. The dusky twilight was now too transparent for Roderick Elliston; the blackest midnight was his chosen hour to steal abroad; and if ever he were seen, it was when the watchman's lantern gleamed upon his figure, gliding along the street, with his hands clutched upon his bosom, still muttering:—"It gnaws me! It gnaws me!" What could it be that gnawed him?

After a time, it became known that Elliston was in the habit of resorting to all the noted quacks that infested the city, or whom money would tempt to journey thither from a distance. By one of these persons, in the exultation of a supposed cure, it was proclaimed far and wide, by dint of hand-bills and little pamphlets on dingy paper, that a distinguished gentleman, Roderick Elliston, Esq., had been relieved of a SNAKE in his stomach! So here was the monstrous secret, ejected from its lurking-place into public view, in all its horrible deformity. The mystery was out; but not so the bosom-serpent. He, if it were anything but a delusion, still lay coiled in his living den. The empiric's cure had been a sham, the effect, it was supposed, of some stupefying drug, which more nearly caused the death of the patient than of the odious reptile that possessed him. When Roderick Elliston regained entire sensibility, it was to find his misfortune the town talk—the more than nine days' wonder and horror—while, at his bosom, he felt the sickening motion of a thing alive, and the gnawing of that restless fang, which seemed to gratify at once a physical appetite and a fiendish spite.

He summoned the old black servant, who had been bred up in his father's house, and was a middle-aged man while Roderick lay in his cradle.

"Scipio!" he began; and then paused, with his arms folded over his heart—"What do people say of me, Scipio?"

"Sir! my poor master! that you had a serpent in your bosom," answered the servant, with hesitation.

"And what else?" asked Roderick, with a ghastly look at the man.

"Nothing else, dear master," replied Scipio;—"only that the Doctor gave you a powder, and that the snake leapt out upon the floor."

"No, no!" muttered Roderick to himself, as he shook his head, and pressed his hands with a more convulsive force upon his breast,—"I feel him still. It gnaws me! It gnaws me!"

From this time, the miserable sufferer ceased to shun the world, but rather solicited and forced himself upon the notice of acquaintances and strangers. It was partly the result of desperation, on finding that the cavern of his own bosom had not proved deep and dark enough to hide the secret, even while it was so secure a fortress for the loathsome fiend that had crept into it. But still more, this craving for notoriety was a symptom of the intense morbidness which now pervaded his nature. All persons, chronically diseased, are egotists, whether the disease be of the mind or body; whether it be sin, sorrow, or merely the more tolerable calamity of some endless pain, or mischief among the cords of mortal life. Such individuals are made acutely conscious of a self, by the torture in which it dwells. Self, therefore, grows to be so prominent an object with them, that they cannot but present it to the face of every casual passer-by. There is a pleasure—perhaps the greatest of which the sufferer is susceptible—in displaying the wasted or ulcerated limb, or the cancer in the breast; and the fouler the crime, with so much the more difficulty does the perpetrator prevent it from thrusting up its snake-like head, to frighten the world; for it is that cancer, or that crime, which constitutes their respective individuality. Roderick Elliston, who, a little while before, had held himself so scornfully above the common lot of men, now paid full allegiance to this humiliating law. The snake in his bosom seemed the symbol of a monstrous egotism, to which every-thing was referred, and which he pampered, night and day, with a continual and exclusive sacrifice of devil-worship.

He soon exhibited what most people considered indubitable to-kens of insanity. In some of his moods, strange to say, he prided and gloried himself on being marked out from the ordinary experience of mankind, by the possession of a double nature, and a life within a life. He appeared to imagine that the snake was a divinity—not celestial, it is true, but darkly infernal—and that he thence derived an emi-nence and a sanctity, horrid, indeed, yet more desirable than what-ever ambition aims at. Thus he drew his misery around him like a re-gal mantle, and looked down triumphantly upon those whose vitals nourished no deadly monster. Oftener, however, his human nature asserted its empire over him, in the shape of a yearning for fellowship. It grew to be his custom to spend the whole day in wandering about the streets, aimlessly, unless it might be called an aim, to establish a species of brotherhood between himself and the world. With can-kered ingenuity, he sought out his own disease in every breast. Whether insane or not, he showed so keen a perception of frailty, er-ror, and vice, that many persons gave him credit for being possessed not merely with a serpent, but with an actual fiend, who imparted this evil faculty of recognizing whatever was ugliest in man's heart.

For instance, he met an individual, who, for thirty years, had cher-ished a hatred against his own brother. Roderick, amidst the throng of the street, laid his hand on this man's chest, and looking full into his forbidding face,

"How is the snake to-day?"—he inquired, with a mock expression of sympathy.

"The snake!" exclaimed the brother-hater—"What do you mean?"

"The snake! The snake! Does he gnaw you?" persisted Roderick. "Did you take counsel with him, this morning, when you should have been saying your prayers? Did he sting, when you thought of your brother's health, wealth, and good repute? Did he caper for joy, when you remembered the profligacy of his only son? And whether he stung, or whether he frolicked, did you feel his poison throughout your body and soul, converting everything to sourness and bitterness? That is the way of such serpents. I have learned the whole nature of them from my own!"

"Where is the police?" roared the object of Roderick's persecution, at the same time giving an instinctive clutch to his breast. "Why is this lunatic allowed to go at large?"

"Ha, ha!" chuckled Roderick, releasing his grasp of the man.— "His bosom-serpent has stung him then!"

Often, it pleased the unfortunate young man to vex people with a lighter satire, yet still characterized by somewhat of snake-like virulence. One day, he encountered an ambitious statesman, and gravely inquired after the welfare of his boa constrictor; for of that species, Roderick affirmed, this gentleman's serpent must needs be, since its appetite was enormous enough to devour the whole country and constitution. At another time, he stopped a close-fisted old fellow, of great wealth, but who skulked about the city, in the guise of a scarecrow, with a patched blue surtout, brown hat, and mouldy boots, scraping pence together, and picking up rusty nails. Pretending to look earnestly at this respectable person's stomach, Roderick assured him that his snake was a copperhead, and had been generated by the immense quantities of that base metal, with which he daily defiled his fingers. Again, he assaulted a man of rubicund visage, and told him that few bosom-serpents had more of the devil in them, than those that breed in the vats of a distillery. The next whom Roderick honored with his attention was a distinguished clergyman, who happened just then to be engaged in a theological controversy, where human wrath was more perceptible than divine inspiration.

"You have swallowed a snake, in a cup of sacramental wine," quoth he.

"Profane wretch!" exclaimed the divine; but nevertheless, his hand stole to his breast.

He met a person of sickly sensibility, who, on some early disappointment, had retired from the world, and thereafter held no intercourse with his fellow-men, but brooded sullenly or passionately over the irrevocable past. This man's very heart, if Roderick might be believed, had been changed into a serpent, which would finally torment both him and itself to death. Observing a married couple, whose domestic troubles were matter of notoriety, he condoled with both on having mutually taken a house-adder to their bosoms. To an envious author, who depreciated works which he could never equal, he said, that his snake was the slimiest and filthiest of all the reptile tribe, but was fortunately without a sting. A man of impure life, and a brazen face, asking Roderick if there were any serpent in his breast, he told him that there was, and of the same species that once tortured Don Rodrigo, the Goth. He took a fair young girl by the hand, and gazing sadly into her eyes, warned her that she cherished a serpent of the deadliest kind within her gentle breast; and the world found the truth of those ominous words, when, a few months afterwards, the poor girl died of love and shame. Two ladies, rivals in fashionable life, who tormented one another with a thousand little stings of womanish spite, were given to understand, that each of their hearts was a nest of diminutive snakes, which did quite as much mischief as one great one.

But nothing seemed to please Roderick better, than to lay hold of a person infected with jealousy, which he represented as an enormous green reptile, with an ice-cold length of body, and the sharpest sting of any snake save one.

"And what one is that?" asked a bystander, overhearing him.

It was a dark-browed man, who put the question; he had an eva-sive eye, which, in the course of a dozen years, had looked no mortal directly in the face. There was an ambiguity about this person's char-acter—a stain upon his reputation—yet none could tell precisely of what nature; although the city-gossips, male and female, whispered the most atrocious surmises. Until a recent period, he had followed the sea, and was, in fact, the very ship-master whom George Herkimer had encountered, under such singular circumstances, in the Grecian Archipelago.

"What bosom-serpent has the sharpest sting?" repeated this man; but he put the question as if by a reluctant necessity, and grew pale while he was uttering it.

"Why need you ask?" replied Roderick, with a look of dark intelli-gence. "Look into your own breast! Hark, my serpent bestirs himself! He acknowledges the presence of a master-fiend!"

And then, as the bystanders afterwards affirmed, a hissing sound was heard, apparently in Roderick Elliston's breast. It was said, too, that an answering hiss came from the vitals of the shipmaster, as if a snake were actually lurking there, and had been aroused by the call of its brother-reptile. If there were in fact any such sound, it might have been caused by a malicious exercise of ventriloquism, on the part of Roderick.

Thus, making his own actual serpent—if a serpent there actually was in his bosom—the type of each man's fatal error, or hoarded sin, or unquiet conscience, and striking his sting so unremorsefully into the sorest spot, we may well imagine that Roderick became the pest of the city. Nobody could elude him; none could withstand him. He grappled with the ugliest truth that he could lay his hand on, and compelled his adversary to do the same. Strange spectacle in human life, where it is the instinctive effort of one and all to hide those sad realities, and leave them undisturbed beneath a heap of superficial topics, which constitute the materials of intercourse between man and man! It was not to be tolerated that Roderick Elliston should break through the tacit compact, by which the world has done its best to secure repose, without relinquishing evil. The victims of his malicious remarks, it is true, had brothers enough to keep them in countenance; for, by Roderick's theory, every mortal bosom harbored either a brood of small serpents, or one overgrown monster, that had devoured all the rest. Still, the city could not bear this new apostle. It was demanded by nearly all, and particularly by the most respectable inhabitants, that Roderick should no longer be permitted to violate the received rules of decorum, by obtruding his own bosom-serpent to the public gaze, and dragging those of decent people from their lurking-places.

Accordingly, his relatives interfered, and placed him in a private asylum for the insane. When the news was noised abroad, it was observed that many persons walked the streets with freer countenances, and covered their breasts less carefully with their hands.

His confinement, however, although it contributed not a little to the peace of the town, operated unfavorably upon Roderick himself. In solitude, his melancholy grew more black and sullen. He spent whole days—indeed, it was his sole occupation—in communing with the serpent. A conversation was sustained, in which as it seemed, the hidden monster bore a part, though unintelligibly to the listeners, and inaudible, except in a hiss. Singular as it may appear, the sufferer had now contracted a sort of affection for his tormentor; mingled, however, with the intensest loathing and horror. Nor were such discordant emotions incompatible; each, on the contrary, imparted strength and poignancy to its opposite. Horrible love—horrible antipathy—embracing one another in his bosom, and both concentrating themselves upon a being that had crept into his vitals, or been engendered there, and which was nourished with his food, and lived upon his life, and was as intimate with him as his own heart, and yet was the foulest of all created things! But not the less was it the true type of a morbid nature.

Sometimes, in his moments of rage and bitter hatred against the snake and himself, Roderick determined to be the death of him, even at the expense of his own life. Once he attempted it by starvation. But, while the wretched man was on the point of famishing, the monster seemed to feed upon his heart, and to thrive and wax gamesome, as if it were his sweetest and most congenial diet. Then he privily took a dose of active poison, imagining that it would not fail to kill either himself, or the devil that possessed him, or both together. Another mistake; for if Roderick had not yet been destroyed by his own poisoned heart, nor the snake by gnawing it, they had little to fear from arsenic or corrosive sublimate. Indeed, the venomous pest appeared to operate as an antidote against all other poisons. The physicians tried to suffocate the fiend with tobacco-smoke. He breathed it as freely as if it were his native atmosphere. Again, they drugged their patient with opium, and drenched him with intoxicating liquors, hoping that the snake might thus be reduced to stupor, and perhaps be ejected from the stomach. They succeeded in rendering Roderick insensible; but, placing their hands upon his breast, they were inexpressibly horror-stricken to feel the monster wriggling, twining, and darting to and fro, within his narrow limits, evidently enlivened by the opium or alcohol, and incited to unusual feats of activity. Thenceforth, they gave up all attempts at cure or palliation. The doomed sufferer submitted to his fate, resumed his former loathsome affection for the bosom-fiend, and spent whole miserable days before a looking glass, with his mouth wide open, watching, in hope and horror, to catch a glimpse of the snake's head, far down within his throat. It is supposed that he succeeded; for the attendants once heard a frenzied shout, and rushing into the room, found Roderick lifeless upon the floor.

He was kept but little longer under restraint. After minute investigation, the medical directors of the asylum decided that his mental disease did not amount to insanity, nor would warrant his confinement; especially as its influence upon his spirits was unfavorable, and might produce the evil which it was meant to remedy. His eccentricities were doubtless great—he had habitually violated many of the customs and prejudices of society; but the world was not, without surer ground, entitled to treat him as a madman. On this decision of such competent authority, Roderick was released, and had returned to his native city, the very day before his encounter with George Herkimer.

As soon as possible after learning these particulars, the sculptor, together with a sad and tremulous companion, sought Elliston at his own house. It was a large, sombre edifice of wood with pilasters and a balcony, and was divided from one of the principal streets by a terrace of three elevations, which was ascended by successive flights of stone steps. Some immense old elms almost concealed the front of the mansion. This spacious and once magnificent family-residence was built by a grandee of the race, early in the past century; at which epoch, land being of small comparative value, the garden and other grounds had formed quite an extensive domain. Although a portion of the ancestral heritage had been alienated, there was still a shadowy enclosure in the rear of the mansion, where a student, or a dreamer, or a man of stricken heart, might lie all day upon the grass, amid the solitude of murmuring boughs, and forget that a city had grown up around him.

Into this retirement, the sculptor and his companion were ushered by Scipio, the old black servant, whose wrinkled visage grew almost sunny with intelligence and joy, as he paid his humble greetings to one of the two visitors.

"Remain in the arbor," whispered the sculptor to the figure that leaned upon his arm, "you will know whether, and when, to make your appearance."

"God will teach me," was the reply. "May he support me too!"

Roderick was reclining on the margin of a fountain, which gushed into the fleckered sunshine with the same clear sparkle, and the same voice of airy quietude, as when trees of primeval growth flung their shadows across its bosom. How strange is the life of a fountain, born at every moment, yet of an age coeval with the rocks, and far surpassing the venerable antiquity of a forest!

"You are come! I have expected you," said Elliston, when he became aware of the sculptor's presence.

His manner was very different from that of the preceding day— quiet, courteous, and, as Herkimer thought, watchful both over his guest and himself. This unnatural restraint was almost the only trait that betokened anything amiss. He had just thrown a book upon the grass, where it lay half-opened, thus disclosing itself to be a natural history of the serpent-tribe, illustrated by life-like plates. Near it lay that bulky volume, the Ductor Dubitantium of Jeremy Taylor, full of cases of conscience, and in which most men, possessed of a conscience, may find something applicable to their purpose.

"You see," observed Elliston, pointing to the book of serpents, while a smile gleamed upon his lips, "I am making an effort to become better acquainted with my bosom-friend. But I find nothing satisfactory in this volume. If I mistake not, he will prove to be *sui generis*, and akin to no other reptile in creation."

"Whence came this strange calamity?" inquired the sculptor.

"My sable friend, Scipio, has a story," replied Roderick, "of a snake that had lurked in this fountain—pure and innocent as it looks—ever since it was known to the first settlers. This insinuating personage once crept into the vitals of my great-grandfather, and dwelt there many years, tormenting the old gentleman beyond mortal endurance. In short, it is a family peculiarity. But, to tell you the truth, I have no faith in this idea of the snake's being an heir-loom. He is my own snake, and no man's else."

"But what was his origin?" demanded Herkimer.

"Oh! there is poisonous stuff in any man's heart, sufficient to generate a brood of serpents," said Elliston, with a hollow laugh. "You should have heard my homilies to the good townspeople. Positively, I deem myself fortunate in having bred but a single serpent. You, however, have none in your bosom, and therefore, cannot sympathize with the rest of the world. It gnaws me! It gnaws me!"

With this exclamation, Roderick lost his self-control and threw himself upon the grass, testifying his agony by intricate writhings, in which Herkimer could not but fancy a resemblance to the motions of a snake. Then, likewise, was heard that frightful hiss, which often ran through the sufferer's speech, and crept between the words and syllables, without interrupting their succession.

"This is awful indeed!" exclaimed the sculptor—"an awful infliction, whether it be actual or imaginary! Tell me, Roderick Elliston, is there any remedy for this loathsome evil?"

"Yes, but an impossible one," muttered Roderick, as he lay wallowing with his face in the grass. "Could I, for one instant, forget myself, the serpent might not abide within me. It is my diseased self-contemplation that has engendered and nourished him!"

"Then forget yourself, my husband," said a gentle voice above him—"forget yourself in the idea of another!"

Rosina had emerged from the arbor, and was bending over him, with the shadow of his anguish reflected in her countenance, yet so mingled with hope and unselfish love, that all anguish seemed but an earthly shadow and a dream. She touched Roderick with her hand. A tremor shivered through his frame. At that moment, if report be trustworthy, the sculptor beheld a waving motion through the grass, and heard a tinkling sound, as if something had plunged into the fountain. Be the truth as it might, it is certain that Roderick Elliston sat up, like a man renewed, restored to his right mind, and rescued from the fiend, which had so miserably overcome him in the battle-field of his own breast.

"Rosina!" cried he, in broken and passionate tones, but with nothing of the wild wail that had haunted his voice so long. "Forgive! Forgive!"

Her happy tears bedewed his face.

"The punishment has been severe," observed the sculptor. "Even Justice might now forgive—how much more a woman's tenderness! Roderick Elliston, whether the serpent was a physical reptile, or whether the morbidness of your nature suggested that symbol to your fancy, the moral of the story is not the less true and strong. A tremendous Egotism—manifesting itself, in your case, in the form of jealousy—is as fearful a fiend as ever stole into the human heart. Can a breast, where it has dwelt so long, be purified?"

"Oh, yes!" said Rosina, with a heavenly smile. "The serpent was but a dark fantasy, and what it typified was as shadowy as itself. The past, dismal as it seems, shall fling no gloom upon the future. To give it its due importance, we must think of it but as an anecdote in our Eternity!"

Earth's Holocaust

O NCE UPON A TIME—but whether in time past or time to
come, is a matter of little or no moment—this wide world had
become so overburthened with an accumulation of worn-out trumpery, that the inhabitants determined to rid themselves of it by a general bonfire. The site fixed upon, at the representation of the Insurance Companies, and as being as central a spot as any other on the
globe, was one of the broadest prairies of the West, where no human
habitation would be endangered by the flames, and where a vast as-
semblage of spectators might commodiously admire the show. Having a taste for sights of this kind, and imagining, likewise, that the
illumination of the bonfire might reveal some profundity of moral
truth, heretofore hidden in mist or darkness, I made it convenient
to journey thither and be present. At my arrival, although the heap
of condemned rubbish was as yet comparatively small, the torch had
already been applied. Amid that boundless plain, in the dusk of eve-

ning, like a far-off star alone in the firmament, there was merely visible one tremulous gleam, whence none could have anticipated so fierce a blaze as was destined to ensue. With every moment, however, there came foot-travellers, women holding up their aprons, men on horseback, wheelbarrows, lumbering baggage-wagons, and other vehicles great and small, and from far and near, laden with articles that were judged fit for nothing but to be burnt.

"What materials have been used to kindle the flames?" inquired I of a bystander; for I was desirous of knowing the whole process of the affair, from beginning to end.

The person whom I addressed was a grave man, fifty years old or thereabout, who had evidently come thither as a looker-on; he struck me immediately as having weighed for himself the true value of life and its circumstances, and therefore as feeling little personal interest in whatever judgment the world might form of them. Before answering my question, he looked me in the face, by the kindling light of the fire.

"Oh, some very dry combustibles," replied he, "and extremely suitable to the purpose—no other, in fact, than yesterday's newspapers, last month's magazines, and last year's withered leaves. Here, now, comes some antiquated trash, that will take fire like a handfull of shavings."

As he spoke, some rough-looking men advanced to the verge of the bonfire, and threw in, as it appeared, all the rubbish of the Herald's Office; the blazonry of coat-armor; the crests and devices of illustrious families; pedigrees that extended back, like lines of light, into the mist of the dark ages; together with stars, garters, and embroidered collars; each of which, as paltry a bauble as it might appear to the uninstructed eye, had once possessed vast significance, and was still, in truth, reckoned among the most precious of moral or material facts, by the worshippers of the gorgeous past. Mingled with this confused heap, which was tossed into the flames by armsfull at once, were innumerable badges of knighthood; comprising those of all the European sovereignties, and Napoleon's decoration of the Legion of Honor, the ribands of which were entangled with those of the ancient order of St. Louis. There, too, were the medals of our own society of Cincinnati, by means of which, as history tells us, an order of hereditary knights came near being constituted out of the king-quellers of the Revolution. And, besides, there were the patents of nobility of German counts and barons, Spanish grandees, and English peers, from the worm-eaten instrument signed by William the Conqueror, down to the bran-new parchment of the latest lord, who has received his honors from the fair hand of Victoria.

At sight of the dense volumes of smoke, mingled with vivid jets of flame, that gushed and eddied forth from this immense pile of earthly distinctions, the multitude of plebeian spectators set up a joyous shout, and clapt their hands with an emphasis that made the welkin echo. That was their moment of triumph, achieved after long ages, over creatures of the same clay and same spiritual infirmities, who had dared to assume the privileges due only to Heaven's better workmanship. But now there rushed towards the blazing heap a gray-haired man, of stately presence, wearing a coat from the breast of which some star, or other badge of rank, seemed to have been forcibly wrenched away. He had not the tokens of intellectual power in his face; but still there was the demeanor—the habitual, and almost native dignity—of one who had been born to the idea of his own social superiority, and had never felt it questioned, till that moment.

"People," cried he, gazing at the ruin of what was dearest in his eyes, with grief and wonder, but, nevertheless, with a degree of stateliness—"people, what have you done! This fire is consuming all that marked your advance from barbarism, or that could have prevented your relapse thither. We—the men of the privileged orders—were those who kept alive, from age to age, the old chivalrous spirit; the gentle and generous thought; the higher, the purer, the more refined and delicate life! With the nobles, too, you cast off the poet, the painter, the sculptor—all the beautiful arts;—for we were their patrons, and created the atmosphere in which they flourish. In abolishing the majestic distinctions of rank, society loses not only its grace, but its steadfastness—"

More he would doubtless have spoken; but here there arose an outcry, sportive, contemptuous, and indignant, that altogether drowned the appeal of the fallen nobleman; insomuch that, casting one look of despair at his own half-burnt pedigree, he shrunk back into the crowd, glad to shelter himself under his new-found insignificance.

"Let him thank his stars that we have not flung him into the same fire!" shouted a rude figure, spurning the embers with his foot. "And, henceforth, let no man dare to show a piece of musty parchment, as his warrant for lording it over his fellows! If he have strength of arm, well and good; it is one species of superiority. If he have wit, wisdom, courage, force of character, let these attributes do for him what they may. But, from this day forward, no mortal must hope for place and consideration, by reckoning up the mouldy bones of his ancestors! That nonsense is done away."

"And in good time," remarked the grave observer by my side—in a low voice however—"if no worse nonsense come in its place. But at all events, this species of nonsense has fairly lived out its life."

There was little space to muse or moralize over the embers of this time-honored rubbish; for, before it was half burnt out, there came another multitude from beyond the sea, bearing the purple robes of royalty, and the crowns, globes, and sceptres of emperors and kings. All these had been condemned as useless baubles; playthings, at best, fit only for the infancy of the world, or rods to govern and chastise it in its nonage; but with which universal manhood, at its full-grown stature, could no longer brook to be insulted. Into such contempt had these regal insignia now fallen, that the gilded crown and tinselled robes of the player-king, from Drury Lane Theatre, had been thrown in among the rest, doubtless as a mockery of his brother-monarchs, on the great stage of the world. It was a strange sight, to discern the crown-jewels of England, glowing and flashing in the midst of the fire. Some of them had been delivered down from the times of the Saxon princes; others were purchased with vast revenues, or, per-chance, ravished from the dead brows of the native potentates of Hindostan; and the whole now blazed with a dazzling lustre, as if a star had fallen in that spot, and been shattered into fragments. The splendor of the ruined monarchy had no reflection, save in those in-estimable precious-stones. But, enough on this subject! It were but te-dious to describe how the Emperor of Austria's mantle was converted to tinder, and how the posts and pillars of the French throne became a heap of coals, which it was impossible to distinguish from those of any other wood. Let me add, however, that I noticed one of the exiled Poles, stirring up the bonfire with the Czar of Russia's sceptre, which he afterwards flung into the flames.

"The smell of singed garments is quite intolerable here," observed my new acquaintance, as the breeze enveloped us in the smoke of a royal wardrobe. "Let us get to windward, and see what they are doing on the other side of the bonfire."

We accordingly passed round, and were just in time to witness the arrival of a vast procession of Washingtonians—as the votaries of temperance call themselves now-a-days—accompanied by thousands of the Irish disciples of Father Mathew, with that great apostle at their head. They brought a rich contribution to the bonfire; being nothing less than all the hogsheads and barrels of liquor in the world, which they rolled before them across the prairie.

"Now, my children," cried Father Mathew, when they reached the verge of the fire—"one shove more, and the work is done! And now let us stand off, and see Satan deal with his own liquor!"

Accordingly, having placed their wooden vessels within reach of the flames, the procession stood off at a safe distance, and soon beheld them burst into a blaze that reached the clouds, and threatened to set the sky itself on fire. And well it might. For here was the whole world's stock of spirituous liquors, which, instead of kindling a frenzied light in the eyes of individual topers as of yore, soared upward with a bewildering gleam that startled all mankind. It was the aggregate of that fierce fire, which would otherwise have scorched the hearts of millions. Meantime, numberless bottles of precious wine were flung into the blaze; which lapped up the contents as if it loved them, and grew, like other drunkards, the merrier and fiercer for what it quaffed. Never again will the insatiable thirst of the fire-fiend be so pampered! Here were the treasures of famous bon-vivants—liquors that had been tossed on ocean, and mellowed in the sun, and hoarded long in the recesses of the earth—the pale, the gold, the ruddy juice of whatever vineyards were most delicate—the entire vintage of Tokay—all mingling in one stream with the vile fluids of the common pot-house, and contributing to heighten the self-same blaze. And while it rose in a gigantic spire, that seemed to wave against the arch of the firmament, and combine itself with the light of stars, the multitude gave a shout, as if the broad earth were exulting in its deliverance from the curse of ages.

But the joy was not universal. Many deemed that human life would be gloomier than ever, when that brief illumination should sink down. While the reformers were at work, I had overheard muttered expostulations from several respectable gentlemen with red noses, and wearing gouty shoes; and a ragged worthy, whose face looked like a hearth where the fire is burnt out, now expressed his discontent more openly and boldly.

"What is this world good for," said the Last Toper, "now that we can never be jolly any more? What is to comfort the poor man in sorrow and perplexity?—how is he to keep his heart warm against the cold winds of this cheerless earth?—and what do you propose to give him, in exchange for the solace that you take away? How are old friends to sit together by the fireside, without a cheerful glass between them? A plague upon your reformation! It is a sad world, a cold world, a selfish world, a low world, not worth an honest fellow's living in, now that good-fellowship is gone forever!"

This harangue excited great mirth among the bystanders. But, preposterous as was the sentiment, I could not help commiserating the forlorn condition of the Last Toper, whose boon-companions had dwindled away from his side, leaving the poor fellow without a soul to countenance him in sipping his liquor, nor, indeed, any liquor to sip. Not that this was quite the true state of the case; for I had observed him, at a critical moment, filch a bottle of fourth-proof brandy that fell beside the bonfire, and hide it in his pocket.

The spirituous and fermented liquors being thus disposed of, the zeal of the reformers next induced them to replenish the fire with all the boxes of tea and bags of coffee in the world. And now came the planters of Virginia, bringing their crops of tobacco. These, being cast upon the heap of inutility, aggregated it to the size of a mountain, and incensed the atmosphere with such potent fragrance, that methought we should never draw pure breath again. The present sacrifice seemed to startle the lovers of the weed, more than any that they had hitherto witnessed.

"Well;—they've put my pipe out," said an old gentleman, flinging it into the flames in a pet. "What is this world coming to? Everything rich and racy—all the spice of life—is to be condemned as useless. Now that they have kindled the bonfire, if these nonsensical reformers would fling themselves into it, all would be well enough!"

"Be patient," responded a staunch conservative;—"it will come to that in the end. They will first fling us in, and finally themselves."

From the general and systematic measures of reform, I now turned to consider the individual contributions to this memorable bonfire. In many instances, these were of a very amusing character. One poor fellow threw in his empty purse, and another, a bundle of counterfeit or insolvable banknotes. Fashionable ladies threw in their last season's bonnets, together with heaps of ribbon, yellow lace, and much other half-worn milliner's ware; all of which proved even more evanescent in the fire, than it had been in the fashion. A multitude of lovers, of both sexes—discarded maids or bachelors, and couples, mutually weary of one another—tossed in bundles of perfumed letters and enamored sonnets. A hack-politician, being deprived of bread by the loss of office, threw in his teeth, which happened to be false ones. The Rev. Sydney Smith—having voyaged across the Atlantic for that sole purpose—came up to the bonfire, with a bitter grin, and threw in certain repudiated bonds, fortified though they were with the broad seal of a sovereign state. A little boy of five years old, in the premature manliness of the present epoch, threw in his playthings; a college-graduate, his diploma; an apothecary, ruined by the spread of homoeopathy, his whole stock of drugs and medicines; a physician, his library; a parson, his old sermons; and a fine gentleman of the old school, his code of manners, which he had formerly written down for the benefit of the next generation. A widow, resolving on a second marriage, slily threw in her dead husband's miniature. A young man, jilted by his mistress, would willingly have flung his own desperate heart into the flames, but could find no means to wrench it out of his bosom. An American author, whose works were neglected by the public, threw his pen and paper into the bonfire, and betook himself to some less discouraging occupation. It somewhat startled me to overhear a number of ladies, highly respectable in appearance, proposing to fling their gowns and petticoats into the flames, and assume the garb, together with the manners, duties, offices, and responsibilities, of the opposite sex.

What favor was accorded to this scheme, I am unable to say; my attention being suddenly drawn to a poor, deceived, and half-delirious girl, who, exclaiming that she was the most worthless thing alive or dead, attempted to cast herself into the fire, amid all that wrecked and broken trumpery of the world. A good man, however, ran to her rescue.

"Patience, my poor girl!" said he, as he drew her back from the fierce embrace of the destroying angel. "Be patient, and abide Heaven's will. So long as you possess a living soul, all may be restored to its first freshness. These things of matter, and creations of human fantasy, are fit for nothing but to be burnt, when once they have had their day. But your day is Eternity!"

"Yes," said the wretched girl, whose frenzy seemed now to have sunk down into deep despondency;—"yes; and the sunshine is blotted out of it!"

It was now rumored among the spectators, that all the weapons and munitions of war were to be thrown into the bonfire; with the exception of the world's stock of gunpowder, which, as the safest mode of disposing of it, had already been drowned in the sea. This intelligence seemed to awaken great diversity of opinion. The hopeful philanthropist esteemed it a token that the millenium was already come; while persons of another stamp, in whose view mankind was a breed of bull-dogs, prophesied that all the old stoutness, fervor, nobleness, generosity, and magnanimity of the race, would disappear; these qualities, as they affirmed, requiring blood for their nourishment. They comforted themselves, however, in the belief that the proposed abolition of war was impracticable, for any length of time together.

Be that as it might, numberless great guns, whose thunder had long been the voice of battle—the artillery of the Armada, the battering-trains of Marlborough, and the adverse cannon of Napoleon and Wellington—were trundled into the midst of the fire. By the continual addition of dry combustibles, it had now waxed so intense, that neither brass nor iron could withstand it. It was wonderful to behold, how those terrible instruments of slaughter melted away like playthings of wax. Then the armies of the earth wheeled around the mighty furnace, with their military music playing triumphant marches, and flung in their muskets and swords. The standard-bearers, likewise, cast one look upward at their banners, all tattered with shot-holes, and inscribed with the names of victorious fields; and giving them a last flourish on the breeze, they lowered them into the flame, which snatched them upward in its rush towards the clouds. This ceremony being over, the world was left without a single weapon in its hands, except, possibly, a few old King's arms and rusty swords, and other trophies of the Revolution, in some of our state-armories. And now the drums were beaten and the trumpets brayed all together, as a prelude to the proclamation of universal and eternal peace, and the announcement that glory was no longer to be won by blood; but that it would henceforth be the contention of the human race, to work out the greatest mutual good; and that beneficence, in the future annals of the earth, would claim the praise of valor. The blessed tidings were accordingly promulgated, and caused infinite re-joicings among those who had stood aghast at the horror and absur-dity of war.

But I saw a grim smile pass over the scarred visage of a stately old commander—by his war-worn figure and rich military dress, he might have been one of Napoleon's famous marshals—who, with the rest of the world's soldiery, had just flung away the sword, that had been familiar to his right hand for half-a-century.

"Aye, aye!" grumbled he. "Let them proclaim what they please; but, in the end, we shall find that all this foolery has only made more work for the armorers and cannon-founderies."

"Why, Sir," exclaimed I, in astonishment, "do you imagine that the human race will ever so far return on the steps of its past madness, as to weld another sword, or cast another cannon?"

"There will be no need," observed, with a sneer, one who neither felt benevolence, nor had faith in it. "When Cain wished to slay his brother, he was at no loss for a weapon."

"We shall see," replied the veteran commander.—"If I am mistaken, so much the better; but, in my opinion—without pretending to philosophize about the matter—the necessity of war lies far deeper than these honest gentlemen suppose. What! Is there a field for all the petty disputes of individuals, and shall there be no great law-court for the settlement of national difficulties? The battle-field is the only court where such suits can be tried!"

"You forget, General," rejoined I, "that, in this advanced stage of civilization, Reason and Philanthropy combined will constitute just such a tribunal as is requisite."

"Ah, I had forgotten that, indeed!" said the old warrior, as he limped away.

The fire was now to be replenished with materials that had hitherto been considered of even greater importance to the well-being of society, than the warlike munitions which we had already seen consumed. A body of reformers had travelled all over the earth, in quest of the machinery by which the different nations were accustomed to inflict the punishment of death. A shudder passed through the multitude, as these ghastly emblems were dragged forward. Even the flames seemed at first to shrink away, displaying the shape and murderous contrivance of each in a full blaze of light, which, of itself, was sufficient to convince mankind of the long and deadly error of human law. Those old implements of cruelty—those horrible monsters of mechanism—those inventions which it seemed to demand something worse than man's natural heart to contrive, and which had lurked in the dusky nooks of ancient prisons, the subject of terror-stricken legends—were now brought forth to view. Headsmen's axes, with the rust of noble and royal blood upon them, and a vast collection of halters that had choked the breath of plebeian victims, were thrown in together. A shout greeted the arrival of the guillotine, which was thrust forward on the same wheels that had borne it from one to another of the blood-stained streets of Paris. But the loudest roar of applause went up, telling the distant sky of the triumph of the earth's redemption, when the gallows made its appearance. An ill-looking fellow, however, rushed forward, and putting himself in the path of the reformers, bellowed hoarsely, and fought with brute fury to stay their progress.

It was little matter of surprise, perhaps, that the executioner should thus do his best to vindicate and uphold the machinery by which he himself had his livelihood, and worthier individuals their death. But it deserved special note, that men of a far different sphere—even of that consecrated class in whose guardianship the world is apt to trust its benevolence—were found to take the hangman's view of the question.

"Stay, my brethren!" cried one of them. "You are misled by a false philanthropy!—you know not what you do. The gallows is a heaven-oriented instrument! Bear it back, then, reverently, and set it up in its old place; else the world will fall to speedy ruin and desolation!"

"Onward, onward!" shouted a leader in the reform. "Into the flames with the accursed instrument of man's bloody policy! How can human law inculcate benevolence and love, while it persists in setting up the gallows as its chief symbol? One heave more, good friends; and the world will be redeemed from its greatest error!"

A thousand hands, that, nevertheless, loathed the touch, now lent their assistance, and thrust the ominous burthen far, far, into the centre of the raging furnace. There its fatal and abhorred image was beheld, first black, then a red coal, then ashes.

"That was well done!" exclaimed I.

"Yes; it was well done," replied—but with less enthusiasm than I expected—the thoughtful observer who was still at my side; "well done, if the world be good enough for the measure. Death, however, is an idea that cannot easily be dispensed with, in any condition between the primal innocence and that other purity and perfection, which, perchance, we are destined to attain, after travelling round the full circle. But, at all events, it is well that the experiment should now be tried."

"Too cold!—too cold!" impatiently exclaimed the young and ardent leader in this triumph. "Let the heart have its voice here, as well as the intellect. And as for ripeness—and as for progress—let mankind always do the highest, kindest, noblest thing, that, at any given period, it has attained to the perception of; and surely that thing cannot be wrong, nor wrongly timed!"

I know not whether it were the excitement of the scene, or whether the good people around the bonfire were really growing more enlightened, every instant; but they now proceeded to measures, in the full length of which I was hardly prepared to keep them company. For instance, some threw their marriage-certificates into the flames, and declared themselves candidates for a higher, holier, and more comprehensive union than that which had subsisted from the birth of time, under the form of the connubial tie. Others hastened to the vaults of banks, and to the coffers of the rich—all of which were open to the first-comer, on this fated occasion—and brought entire bales of paper-money to enliven the blaze, and tons of coin to be melted down by its intensity. Henceforth, they said, universal benevolence, uncoined and exhaustless, was to be the golden currency of the world.

At this intelligence, the bankers, and speculators in the stocks, grew pale; and a pick-pocket, who had reaped a rich harvest among the crowd, fell down in a deadly fainting-fit. A few men of business burnt their day-books and legers, the notes and obligations of their creditors, and all other evidences of debts due to themselves; while perhaps a somewhat larger number satisfied their zeal for reform with the sacrifice of any uncomfortable recollection of their own indebtment. There was then a cry, that the period was arrived, when the title-deeds of landed property should be given to the flames, and the whole soil of the earth revert to the public, from whom it had been wrongfully abstracted, and most unequally distributed among individuals. Another party demanded, that all written constitutions, set forms of government, legislative acts, statute-books, and everything else on which human invention had endeavored to stamp its arbitrary laws, should at once be destroyed, leaving the consummated world as free as the man first created.

Whether any ultimate action was taken with regard to these propositions, is beyond my knowledge; for, just then, some matters were in progress that concerned my sympathies more nearly.

"See!—see!—what heaps of books and pamphlets," cried a fellow, who did not seem to be a lover of literature. "Now we shall have a glorious blaze!"

"That's just the thing," said a modern philosopher. "Now we shall get rid of the weight of dead men's thought, which has hitherto pressed so heavily on the living intellect, that it has been incompetent to any effectual self-exertion. Well done, my lads! Into the fire with them! Now you are enlightening the world, indeed!"

"But what is to become of the Trade?" cried a frantic bookseller.

"Oh, by all means, let them accompany their merchandise," coolly observed an author. "It will be a noble funeral-pile!"

The truth was, that the human race had now reached a stage of progress, so far beyond what the wisest and wittiest men of former ages had ever dreamed of, that it would have been a manifest absurdity to allow the earth to be any longer encumbered with their poor achievements in the literary line. Accordingly, a thorough and searching investigation had swept the booksellers' shops, hawkers' stands, public and private libraries, and even the little book-shelf by the country fireside, and had brought the world's entire mass of printed paper, bound or in sheets, to swell the already mountain-bulk of our illustrious bonfire. Thick, heavy folios, containing the labors of lexicographers, commentators, and encyclopediasts, were flung in, and, falling among the embers with a leaden thump, smouldered away to ashes, like rotten wood. The small, richly-gilt, French tomes, of the last age, with the hundred volumes of Voltaire among them, went off in a brilliant shower of sparkles, and little jets of flame; while the current literature of the same nation burnt red and blue, and threw an infernal light over the visages of the spectators, converting them all to the aspect of parti-colored fiends. A collection of German stories emitted a scent of brimstone. The English standard authors made excellent fuel, generally exhibiting the properties of sound oak logs. Milton's works, in particular, sent up a powerful blaze, gradually reddening into a coal, which promised to endure longer than almost any other material of the pile. From Shakspeare there gushed a flame of such marvellous splendor, that men shaded their eyes as against the sun's meridian glory; nor, even when the works of his own elucidators were flung upon him, did he cease to flash forth a dazzling radiance, from beneath the ponderous heap. It is my belief, that he is still blazing as fervidly as ever.

"Could a poet but light a lamp at that glorious flame," remarked I, "he might then consume the midnight oil to some good purpose."

"That is the very thing which modern poets have been too apt to do—or, at least, to attempt," answered a critic. "The chief benefit to be expected from this conflagration of past literature, undoubtedly is, that writers will henceforth be compelled to light their lamps at the sun or stars."

"If they can reach so high," said I. "But that task requires a giant, who may afterwards distribute the light among inferior men. It is not every one that can steal the fire from Heaven, like Prometheus; but when once he had done the deed, a thousand hearths were kindled by it."

It amazed me much to observe, how indefinite was the proportion between the physical mass of any given author, and the property of brilliant and long-continued combustion. For instance, there was not a quarto volume of the last century—nor, indeed, of the present— that could compete, in that particular, with a child's little gilt-covered book, containing Mother Goose's Melodies. The Life and Death of Tom Thumb outlasted the biography of Marlborough. An epic—indeed, a dozen of them—was converted to white ashes, before the single sheet of an old ballad was half-consumed. In more than one case, too, when volumes of applauded verse proved incapable of anything better than a stifling smoke, an unregarded ditty of some nameless bard—perchance, in the corner of a newspaper—soared up among the stars, with a flame as brilliant as their own. Speaking of the properties of flame, methought Shelley's poetry emitted a purer light than almost any other productions of his day; contrasting beautifully with the fitful and lurid gleams, and gushes of black vapor, that flashed and eddied from the volumes of Lord Byron. As for Tom Moore, some of his songs diffused an odor like a burning pastille.

I felt particular interest in watching the combustion of American authors, and scrupulously noted, by my watch, the precise number of moments that changed most of them from shabbily-printed books to indistinguishable ashes. It would be invidious, however, if not perilous, to betray these awful secrets; so that I shall content myself with observing, that it was not invariably the writer most frequent in the public mouth, that made the most splendid appearance in the bonfire. I especially remember, that a great deal of excellent inflammability was exhibited in a thin volume of poems by Ellery Channing; although, to speak the truth, there were certain portions that hissed and spluttered in a very disagreeable fashion. A curious phenomenon occurred, in reference to several writers, native as well as foreign. Their books, though of highly respectable figure, instead of bursting into a blaze, or even smouldering out their substance in smoke, suddenly melted away, in a manner that proved them to be ice.

If it be no lack of modesty to mention my own works, it must here be confessed, that I looked for them with fatherly interest, but in vain. Too probably, they were changed to vapor by the first action of the heat; at best, I can only hope, that, in their quiet way, they contributed a glimmering spark or two to the splendor of the evening.

"Alas, and woe is me!" thus bemoaned himself a heavy-looking gentleman in green spectacles. "The world is utterly ruined, and there is nothing to live for any longer! The business of my life is snatched from me. Not a volume to be had for love or money!"

"This," remarked the sedate observer beside me, "is a bookworm—one of those men who are born to gnaw dead thoughts. His clothes, you see, are covered with the dust of libraries. He has no inward fountain of ideas; and, in good earnest, now that the old stock is abolished, I do not see what is to become of the poor fellow. Have you no word of comfort for him?"

"My dear Sir," said I to the desperate book-worm, "is not Nature better than a book?—is not the human heart deeper than any system of philosophy?—is not life replete with more instruction than past observers have found it possible to write down in maxims? Be of good cheer! The great book of Time is still spread wide open before us; and, if we read it aright, it will be to us a volume of eternal Truth."

"Oh, my books, my books, my precious, printed books!" reiterated the forlorn book-worm. "My only reality was a bound volume; and now they will not leave me even a shadowy pamphlet!"

In fact, the last remnant of the literature of all the ages was now descending upon the blazing heap, in the shape of a cloud of pamphlets from the press of the New World. These, likewise, were consumed in the twinkling of an eye, leaving the earth, for the first time since the days of Cadmus, free from the plague of letters—an enviable field for the authors of the next generation!

"Well!—and does anything remain to be done?" inquired I, somewhat anxiously. "Unless we set fire to the earth itself, and then leap boldly off into infinite space, I know not that we can carry reform to any further point."

"You are vastly mistaken, my good friend," said the observer. "Believe me, the fire will not be allowed to settle down, without the addition of fuel that will startle many persons, who have lent a willing hand thus far."

Nevertheless, there appeared to be a relaxation of effort, for a little time, during which, probably, the leaders of the movement were considering what should be done next. In the interval, a philosopher threw his theory into the flames; a sacrifice, which, by those who knew how to estimate it, was pronounced the most remarkable that had yet been made. The combustion, however, was by no means brilliant. Some indefatigable people, scorning to take a moment's ease, now employed themselves in collecting all the withered leaves and fallen boughs of the forest, and thereby recruited the bonfire to a greater height than ever. But this was mere by-play.

"Here comes the fresh fuel that I spoke of," said my companion.

To my astonishment, the persons who now advanced into the vacant space, around the mountain of fire, bore surplices and other priestly garments, mitres, crosiers, and a confusion of popish and protestant emblems, with which it seemed their purpose to consummate this great Act of Faith. Crosses, from the spires of old cathedrals, were cast upon the heap, with as little remorse as if the reverence of centuries, passing in long array beneath the lofty towers, had not looked up to them as the holiest of symbols. The font, in which infants were consecrated to God; the sacramental vessels, whence Piety had received the hallowed draught; were given to the same destruction. Perhaps it most nearly touched my heart, to see, among these devoted relics, fragments of the humble communion-tables and undecorated pulpits, which I recognized as having been torn from the meeting-houses of New-England. Those simple edifices might have been permitted to retain all of sacred embellishment that their Puritan founders had bestowed, even though the mighty structure of St. Peter's had sent its spoils to the fire of this terrible sacrifice. Yet I felt that these were but the externals of religion, and might most safely be relinquished by spirits that best knew their deep significance.

"All is well," said I, cheerfully. "The wood-paths shall be the aisles of our cathedral—the firmament itself shall be its ceiling! What needs an earthly roof between the Deity and his worshipper? Our faith can well afford to lose all the drapery that even the holiest men have thrown around it, and be only the more sublime in its simplicity."

"True," said my companion. "But will they pause here?"

The doubt, implied in his question, was well-founded. In the general destruction of books, already described, a holy volume—that stood apart from the catalogue of human literature, and yet, in one sense, was at its head—had been spared. But the Titan of innovation—angel or fiend, double in his nature, and capable of deeds befitting both characters—at first shaking down only the old and rotten shapes of things, had now, as it appeared, laid his terrible hand upon the main pillars, which supported the whole edifice of our moral and spiritual state. The inhabitants of the earth had grown too enlightened to define their faith within a form of words, or to limit the spiritual by any analogy to our material existence. Truths, which the Heavens trembled at, were now but a fable of the world's infancy. Therefore, as the final sacrifice of human error, what else remained, to be thrown upon the embers of that awful pile, except the Book, which, though a celestial revelation to past ages, was but a voice from a lower sphere, as regarded the present race of man? It was done! Upon the blazing heap of falsehood and worn-out truth—things that the earth had never needed, or had ceased to need, or had grown childishly weary of—fell the ponderous church-Bible, the great old volume, that had lain so long on the cushions of the pulpit, and whence the pastor's solemn voice had given holy utterances, on so many a Sabbath-day. There, likewise, fell the family-Bible, which the long-buried patriarch had read to his children—in prosperity or sorrow, by the fireside, and in the summer-shade of trees—and had bequeathed downward, as the heirloom of generations. There fell the bosom-Bible, the little volume that had been the soul's friend of some sorely tried Child of Dust, who thence took courage, whether his trial were for life or death, steadfastly confronting both, in the strong assurance of Immortality.

All these were flung into the fierce and riotous blaze; and then a mighty wind came roaring across the plain, with a desolate howl, as if it were the angry lamentation of the Earth for the loss of Heaven's sunshine; and it shook the gigantic pyramid of flame, and scattered the cinders of half-consumed abominations around upon the spectators.

"This is terrible!" said I, feeling that my cheek grew pale, and seeing a like change in the visages about me.

"Be of good courage yet," answered the man with whom I had so often spoken. He continued to gaze steadily at the spectacle, with a singular calmness, as if it concerned him merely as an observer.—"Be of good courage—nor yet exult too much; for there is far less both of good and evil, in the effect of this bonfire, than the world might be willing to believe."

"How can that be?" exclaimed I, impatiently.—"Has it not consumed everything? Has it not swallowed up, or melted down, every human or divine appendage of our mortal state, that had substance enough to be acted on by fire? Will there be anything left us, tomorrow morning, better or worse than a heap of embers and ashes?"

"Assuredly there will," said my grave friend. "Come hither tomorrow morning—or whenever the combustible portion of the pile shall be quite burnt out—and you will find among the ashes everything really valuable that you have seen cast into the flames. Trust me; the world of tomorrow will again enrich itself with the gold and diamonds, which have been cast off by the world of to-day. Not a truth is destroyed—nor buried so deep among the ashes, but it will be raked up at last."

This was a strange assurance. Yet I felt inclined to credit it; the more especially as I beheld, among the wallowing flames, a copy of the Holy Scriptures, the pages of which, instead of being blackened into tinder, only assumed a more dazzling whiteness, as the fingermarks of human imperfection were purified away. Certain marginal notes and commentaries, it is true, yielded to the intensity of the fiery test, but without detriment to the smallest syllable that had flamed from the pen of inspiration.

"Yes;—there is the proof of what you say," answered I, turning to the observer. "But, if only what is evil can feel the action of the fire, then, surely, the conflagration has been of inestimable utility. Yet, if I understand aright, you intimate a doubt whether the world's expectation of benefit will be realized by it."

"Listen to the talk of these worthies," said he, pointing to a group in front of the blazing pile.—"Possibly, they may teach you something useful, without intending it."

The persons, whom he indicated, consisted of that brutal and most earthy figure, who had stood forth so furiously in defence of the gallows—the hangman, in short—together with the Last Thief and the Last Murderer; all three of whom were clustered about the Last Toper. The latter was liberally passing the brandy-bottle, which he had rescued from the general destruction of wines and spirits. This little convivial party seemed at the lowest pitch of despondency; as considering that the purified world must needs be utterly unlike, the sphere that they had hitherto known, and therefore but a strange and desolate abode for gentlemen of their kidney.

"The best counsel for all of us, is," remarked the hangman, "that— as soon as we have finished the last drop of liquor—I help you, my three friends, to a comfortable end upon the nearest tree, and then hang myself on the same bough. This is no world for us, any longer."

"Poh, poh, my good fellows!" said a dark-complexioned personage, who now joined the group—his complexion was indeed fearfully dark; and his eyes glowed with a redder light than that of the bonfire—"Be not so cast down, my dear friends; you shall see good days yet. There is one thing that these wiseacres have forgotten to throw into the fire, and without which all the rest of the conflagration is just nothing at all—yes; though they had burnt the earth itself to a cinder!"

"And what may that be?" eagerly demanded the Last Murderer.

"What, but the human heart itself!" said the dark-visaged stranger, with a portentous grin. "And, unless they hit upon some method of purifying that foul cavern, forth from it will re-issue all the shapes of wrong and misery—the same old shapes, or worse ones—which they have taken such a vast deal of trouble to consume to ashes. I have stood by, this live-long night, and laughed in my sleeve at the whole business. Oh, take my word for it, it will be the old world yet!"

This brief conversation supplied me with a theme for lengthened thought. How sad a truth—if true it were—that Man's age-long endeavor for perfection had served only to render him the mockery of the Evil Principle, from the fatal circumstance of an error at the very root of the matter! The Heart—the Heart—there was the little, yet boundless sphere, wherein existed the original wrong, of which the crime and misery of this outward world were merely types. Purify that inner sphere; and the many shapes of evil that haunt the outward, and which now seem almost our only realities, will turn to shadowy phantoms, and vanish of their own accord. But, if we go no deeper than the Intellect, and strive, with merely that feeble instrument, to discern and rectify what is wrong, our whole accomplishment will be a dream; so unsubstantial, that it matters little whether the bonfire, which I have so faithfully described, were what we choose to call a real event, and a flame that would scorch the finger—or only a phosphoric radiance, and a parable of my own brain!

The Artist of the Beautiful

A N ELDERLY MAN, with his pretty daughter on his arm, was passing along the street, and emerged from the gloom of the cloudy evening into the light that fell across the pavement from the window of a small shop. It was a projecting window; and on the inside were suspended a variety of watches,—pinchbeck, silver, and one or two of gold,—all with their faces turned from the street, as if churlishly disinclined to inform the wayfarers what o'clock it was. Seated within the shop, sidelong to the window, with his pale face bent earnestly over some delicate piece of mechanism, on which was thrown the concentrated lustre of a shade-lamp, appeared a young man.

"What can Owen Warland be about"? muttered old Peter Hovenden,—himself a retired watchmaker, and the former master of this same young man, whose occupation he was now wondering at. "What can the fellow be about? These six months past, I have never come by his shop without seeing him just as steadily at work as now.

It would be a flight beyond his usual foolery to seek for the Perpetual Motion. And yet I know enough of my old business to be certain, that what he is now so busy with is no part of the machinery of a watch."

"Perhaps, father," said Annie, without showing much interest in the question, "Owen is inventing a new kind of time-keeper. I am sure he has ingenuity enough."

"Poh, child! he has not the sort of ingenuity to invent anything better than a Dutch toy," answered her father, who had formerly been put to much vexation by Owen Warland's irregular genius. "A plague on such ingenuity! All the effect that ever I knew of it, was to spoil the accuracy of some of the best watches in my shop. He would turn the sun out of its orbit, and derange the whole course of time, if, as I said before, his ingenuity could grasp anything bigger than a child's toy!"

"Hush, father! he hears you," whispered Annie, pressing the old man's arm. "His ears are as delicate as his feelings, and you know how easily disturbed they are. Do let us move on."

So Peter Hovenden and his daughter Annie plodded on, without further conversation, until, in a by-street of the town, they found themselves passing the open door of a blacksmith's shop. Within was seen the forge, now blazing up, and illuminating the high and dusky roof, and now confining its lustre to a narrow precinct of the coal-strewn floor, according as the breath of the bellows was puffed forth, or again inhaled into its vast leathern lungs. In the intervals of brightness, it was easy to distinguish objects in remote corners of the shop, and the horse-shoes that hung upon the wall; in the momentary gloom, the fire seemed to be glimmering amidst the vagueness of unenclosed space. Moving about in this red glare and alternate dusk, was the figure of the blacksmith, well worthy to be viewed in so picturesque an aspect of light and shade, where the bright blaze struggled with the black night, as if each would have snatched his comely strength from the other. Anon, he drew a white-hot bar of iron from the coals, laid it on the anvil, uplifted his arm of might, and was soon enveloped in the myriads of sparks which the strokes of his hammer scattered into the surrounding gloom.

"Now, that is a pleasant sight," said the old watchmaker. "I know what it is to work in gold, but give me the worker in iron, after all is said and done. He spends his labor upon a reality. What say you, daughter Annie?"

"Pray don't speak so loud, father," whispered Annie. "Robert Danforth will hear you."

"And what if he should hear me?" said Peter Hovenden; "I say again, it is a good and a wholesome thing to depend upon main strength and reality, and to earn one's bread with the bare and brawny arm of a blacksmith. A watchmaker gets his brain puzzled by his wheels within a wheel, or loses his health or the nicety of his eyesight, as was my case; and finds himself, at middle age, or a little after, past labor at his own trade, and fit for nothing else, yet too poor to live at his ease. So, I say once again, give me main strength for my money. And then, how it takes the nonsense out of a man! Did you ever hear of a blacksmith being such a fool as Owen Warland, yonder?"

"Well said, uncle Hovenden!" shouted Robert Danforth, from the forge, in a full, deep, merry voice, that made the roof re-echo. "And what says Miss Annie to that doctrine? She, I suppose, will think it a genteeler business to tinker up a lady's watch, than to forge a horse-shoe or make a gridiron!"

Annie drew her father onward, without giving him time for reply.

But we must return to Owen Warland's shop, and spend more meditation upon his history and character than either Peter Hovenden, or probably his daughter Annie, or Owen's old schoolfellow, Robert Danforth, would have thought due to so slight a subject. From the time that his little fingers could grasp a pen-knife, Owen had been remarkable for a delicate ingenuity, which sometimes produced pretty shapes in wood, principally figures of flowers and birds, and sometimes seemed to aim at the hidden mysteries of mechanism. But it was always for purposes of grace, and never with any mockery of the useful. He did not, like the crowd of schoolboy artizans, construct little windmills on the angle of a barn, or watermills across the neighboring brook. Those who discovered such peculiarity in the boy, as to think it worth their while to observe him closely, sometimes saw reason to suppose that he was attempting to imitate the beautiful movements of Nature, as exemplified in the flight of birds or the activity of little animals. It seemed, in fact, a new development of the love of the Beautiful, such as might have made him a poet, a painter, or a sculptor, and which was as completely refined from all utilitarian coarseness, as it could have been in either of the fine arts. He looked with singular distaste at the stiff and regular processes of ordinary machinery. Being once carried to see a steam-engine, in the expectation that his intuitive comprehension of mechanical principles would be gratified, he turned pale, and grew sick, as if something monstrous and unnatural had been presented to him. This horror was partly owing to the size and terrible energy of the Iron Laborer; for the character of Owen's mind was microscopic, and tended naturally to the minute, in accordance with his diminutive frame, and the marvellous smallness and delicate power of his fingers. Not that his sense of beauty was thereby diminished into a sense of prettiness. The Beautiful Idea has no relation to size, and may be as perfectly developed in a space too minute for any but microscopic investigation, as within the ample verge that is measured by the arc of the rainbow. But, at all events, this characteristic minuteness in his objects and accomplishments made the world even more incapable, than it might otherwise have been, of appreciating Owen Warland's genius. The boy's relatives saw nothing better to be done—as perhaps there was not—than to bind him apprentice to a watchmaker, hoping that his strange ingenuity might thus be regulated, and put to utilitarian purposes.

Peter Hovenden's opinion of his apprentice has already been expressed. He could make nothing of the lad. Owen's apprehension of the professional mysteries, it is true, was inconceivably quick. But he altogether forgot or despised the grand object of a watchmaker's business, and cared no more for the measurement of time than if it had been merged into eternity. So long, however, as he remained under his old master's care, Owen's lack of sturdiness made it possible, by strict injunctions and sharp oversight, to restrain his creative eccentricity within bounds. But when his apprenticeship was served out, and he had taken the little shop which Peter Hovenden's failing eyesight compelled him to relinquish, then did people recognize how unfit a person was Owen Warland to lead old blind Father Time along his daily course. One of his most rational projects was, to connect a musical operation with the machinery of his watches, so that all the harsh dissonances of life might be rendered tuneful, and each flitting moment fall into the abyss of the Past in golden drops of harmony. If a family-clock was entrusted to him for repair—one of those tall, ancient clocks that have grown nearly allied to human nature, by measuring out the lifetime of many generations—he would take upon himself to arrange a dance or funeral procession of figures, across its venerable face, representing twelve mirthful or melancholy hours. Several freaks of this kind quite destroyed the young watchmaker's credit with that steady and matter-of-fact class of people who hold the opinion that time is not to be trifled with, whether considered as the medium of advancement and prosperity in this world, or preparation for the next. His custom rapidly diminished—a misfortune, however, that was probably reckoned among his better accidents by Owen Warland, who was becoming more and more absorbed in a secret occupation, which drew all his science and manual dexterity into itself, and likewise gave full employment to the characteristic tendencies of his genius. This pursuit had already consumed many months.

After the old watchmaker and his pretty daughter had gazed at him, out of the obscurity of the street, Owen Warland was seized with a fluttering of the nerves, which made his hand tremble too violently to proceed with such delicate labor as he was now engaged upon.

"It was Annie herself!" murmured he. "I should have known it, by this throbbing of my heart, before I heard her father's voice. Ah, how it throbs! I shall scarcely be able to work again on this exquisite mechanism to-night. Annie—dearest Annie—thou shouldst give firmness to my heart and hand, and not shake them thus; for if I strive to put the very spirit of Beauty into form, and give it motion, it is for thy sake alone. Oh, throbbing heart, be quiet! If my labor be thus thwarted, there will come vague and unsatisfied dreams, which will leave me spiritless to-morrow."

As he was endeavoring to settle himself again to his task, the shop-door opened, and gave admittance to no other than the stalwart figure which Peter Hovenden had paused to admire, as seen amid the light and shadow of the blacksmith's shop. Robert Danforth had brought a little anvil of his own manufacture, and peculiarly constructed, which the young artist had recently bespoken. Owen examined the article, and pronounced it fashioned according to his wish.

"Why, yes," said Robert Danforth, his strong voice filling the shop as with the sound of a bass-viol, "I consider myself equal to anything in the way of my own trade; though I should have made but a poor figure at yours, with such a fist as this,"—added he, laughing, as he laid his vast hand beside the delicate one of Owen. "But what then? I put more main strength into one blow of my sledge-hammer, than all that you have expended since you were a 'prentice. Is not that the truth?"

"Very probably," answered the low and slender voice of Owen. "Strength is an earthly monster. I make no pretensions to it. My force, whatever there may be of it, is altogether spiritual."

"Well; but, Owen, what are you about!" asked his old schoolfellow, still in such a hearty volume of tone that it made the artist shrink; especially as the question related to a subject so sacred as the absorbing dream of his imagination. "Folks do say, that you are trying to discover the Perpetual Motion."

"The Perpetual Motion?—nonsense!" replied Owen Warland, with a movement of digust; for he was full of little petulances. "It can never be discovered! It is a dream that may delude men whose brains are mystified with matter, but not me. Besides, if such a discovery were possible, it would not be worth my while to make it, only to have the secret turned to such purposes as are now effected by steam and water-power. I am not ambitious to be honored with the paternity of a new kind of cotton-machine."

"That would be droll enough!" cried the blacksmith, breaking out into such an uproar of laughter, that Owen himself, and the bell-glasses on his work-board, quivered in unison. "No, no, Owen! No child of yours will have iron joints and sinews. Well, I won't hinder you any more. Good night, Owen, and success; and if you need any assistance, so far as a downright blow of hammer upon anvil will answer the purpose, I'm your man!"

And with another laugh, the man of main strength left the shop.

"How strange it is," whispered Owen Warland to himself, leaning his head upon his hand, "that all my musings, my purposes, my passion for the Beautiful, my consciousness of power to create it—a finer, more ethereal power, of which this earthly giant can have no conception—all, all, look so vain and idle, whenever my path is crossed by Robert Danforth! He would drive me mad, were I to meet him often. His hard, brute force darkens and confuses the spiritual element within me. But I, too, will be strong in my own way. I will not yield to him!"

He took from beneath a glass, a piece of minute machinery, which he set in the condensed light of his lamp, and, looking intently at it through a magnifying glass, proceeded to operate with a delicate instrument of steel. In an instant, however, he fell back in his chair, and clasped his hands, with a look of horror on his face, that made its small features as impressive as those of a giant would have been.

"Heaven! What have I done!" exclaimed he. "The vapor!—the influence of that brute force!—it has bewildered me, and obscured my perception. I have made the very stroke—the fatal stroke—that I have dreaded from the first! It is all over—the toil of months—the object of my life! I am ruined!"

And there he sat, in strange despair, until his lamp flickered in the socket, and left the Artist of the Beautiful in darkness.

Thus it is, that ideas which grow up within the imagination, and appear so lovely to it, and of a value beyond whatever men call valuable, are exposed to be shattered and annihilated by contact with the Practical. It is requisite for the ideal artist to possess a force of character that seems hardly compatible with its delicacy; he must keep his faith in himself, while the incredulous world assails him with its utter disbelief; he must stand up against mankind and be his own sole disciple, both as respects his genius, and the objects to which it is directed.

For a time, Owen Warland succumbed to this severe, but inevitable test. He spent a few sluggish weeks, with his head so continually resting in his hands, that the townspeople had scarcely an opportunity to see his countenance. When, at last, it was again uplifted to the light of day, a cold, dull, nameless change was perceptible upon it. In the opinion of Peter Hovenden, however, and that order of sagacious understandings who think that life should be regulated, like clockwork, with leaden weights, the alteration was entirely for the better. Owen now indeed, applied himself to business with dogged industry. It was marvellous to witness the obtuse gravity with which he would inspect the wheels of a great, old silver watch; thereby delighting the owner, in whose fob it had been worn till he deemed it a portion of his own life, and was accordingly jealous of its treatment. In consequence of the good report thus acquired, Owen Warland was invited by the proper authorities to regulate the clock in the church-steeple. He succeeded so admirably in this matter of public interest, that the merchants gruffly acknowledged his merits on 'Change; the nurse whispered his praises, as she gave the potion in the sick-chamber; the lover blessed him at the hour of appointed interview; and the town in general thanked Owen for the punctuality of dinner-time. In a word, the heavy weight upon his spirits kept everything in order, not merely within his own system, but wheresoever the iron accents of the church-clock were audible. It was a circumstance, though minute, yet characteristic of his present state, that, when employed to engrave names or initials on silver spoons, he now wrote the requisite letters in the plainest possible style; omitting a variety of fanciful flourishes, that had heretofore distinguished his work in this kind.

One day, during the era of this happy transformation, old Peter Hovenden came to visit his former apprentice.

"Well, Owen," said he, "I am glad to hear such good accounts of you from all quarters; and especially from the town-clock yonder, which speaks in your commendation every hour of the twenty-four. Only get rid altogether of your nonsensical trash about the Beautiful—which I, nor nobody else, nor yourself to boot, could never understand—only free yourself of that, and your success in life is as sure as daylight. Why, if you go on in this way, I should even venture to let you doctor this precious old watch of mine; though, except my daughter Annie, I have nothing else so valuable in the world."

"I should hardly dare touch it, sir," replied Owen in a depressed tone; for he was weighed down by his old master's presence.

"In time," said the latter, "in time, you will be capable of it."

The old watchmaker, with the freedom naturally consequent on his former authority, went on inspecting the work which Owen had in hand at the moment, together with other matters that were in progress. The artist, meanwhile, could scarcely lift his head. There was nothing so antipodal to his nature as this man's cold, unimaginative sagacity, by contact with which everything was converted into a dream, except the densest matter of the physical world. Owen groaned in spirit, and prayed fervently to be delivered from him.

"But what is this?" cried Peter Hovenden abruptly, taking up a dusty bell-glass, beneath which appeared a mechanical something, as delicate and minute as the system of a butterfly's anatomy. "What have we here! Owen, Owen! there is witchcraft in these little chains, and wheels, and paddles! See! with one pinch of my finger and thumb, I am going to deliver you from all future peril."

"For Heaven's sake," screamed Owen Warland, springing up with wonderful energy, "as you would not drive me mad—do not touch it! The slightest pressure of your finger would ruin me for ever."

"Aha, young man! And is it so?" said the old watchmaker, looking at him with just enough of penetration to torture Owen's soul with the bitterness of worldly criticism. "Well; take your own course. But I warn you again, that in this small piece of mechanism lives your evil spirit. Shall I exorcise him?"

"You are my Evil Spirit," answered Owen, much excited—"you, and the hard, coarse world! The leaden thoughts and the despondency that you fling upon me are my clogs. Else, I should long ago have achieved the task that I was created for."

Peter Hovenden shook his head, with the mixture of contempt and indignation which mankind, of whom he was partly a representative, deem themselves entitled to feel towards all simpletons who seek other prizes than the dusty ones along the highway. He then took his leave with an uplifted finger, and a sneer upon his face, that haunted the artist's dreams for many a night afterwards. At the time of his old master's visit, Owen was probably on the point of taking up the relinquished task; but, by this sinister event, he was thrown back into the state whence he had been slowly emerging.

But the innate tendency of his soul had only been accumulating fresh vigor, during its apparent sluggishness. As the summer advanced, he almost totally relinquished his business, and permitted Father Time, so far as the old gentleman was represented by the clocks and watches under his control, to stray at random through human life, making infinite confusion among the train of bewildered hours. He wasted the sunshine, as people said, in wandering through the woods and fields, and along the banks of streams. There, like a child, he found amusement in chasing butterflies, or watching the motions of water-insects. There was something truly mysterious in the intentness with which he contemplated these living playthings, as they sported on the breeze; or examined the structure of an imperial insect whom he had imprisoned. The chase of butterflies was an apt emblem of the ideal pursuit in which he had spent so many golden hours. But, would the Beautiful Idea ever be yielded to his hand, like the butterfly that symbolized it? Sweet, doubtless, were these days, and congenial to the artist's soul. They were full of bright conceptions, which gleamed through his intellectual world, as the butterflies gleamed through the outward atmosphere, and were real to him for the instant, without the toil, and perplexity, and many disappointments, of attempting to make them visible to the sensual eye. Alas, that the artist, whether in poetry or whatever other material, may not content himself with the inward enjoyment of the Beautiful, but must chase the flitting mystery beyond the verge of his ethereal domain, and crush its frail being in seizing it with a material grasp! Owen Warland felt the impulse to give external reality to his ideas, as irresistibly as any of the poets or painters, who have arrayed the world in a dimmer and fainter beauty, imperfectly copied from the richness of their visions.

The night was now his time for the slow process of recreating the one Idea, to which all his intellectual activity referred itself. Always at the approach of dusk, he stole into the town, locked himself within his shop, and wrought with patient delicacy of touch, for many hours. Sometimes he was startled by the rap of the watchman, who, when all the world should be asleep, had caught the gleam of lamp-light through the crevices of Owen Warland's shutters. Daylight, to the morbid sensibility of his mind, seemed to have an intrusiveness that interfered with his pursuits. On cloudy and inclement days, therefore, he sat with his head upon his hands, muffling, as it were, his sensitive brain in a mist of indefinite musings; for it was a relief to escape from the sharp distinctness with which he was compelled to shape out his thoughts, during his nightly toil.

From one of these fits of torpor, he was aroused by the entrance of Annie Hovenden, who came into the shop with the freedom of a customer, and also with something of the familiarity of a childish friend. She had worn a hole through her silver thimble, and wanted Owen to repair it.

"But I don't know whether you will condescend to such a task," said she, laughing, "now that you are so taken up with the notion of putting spirit into machinery."

"Where did you get that idea, Annie?" said Owen, starting in surprise.

"Oh, out of my own head," answered she, "and from something that I heard you say, long ago, when you were but a boy, and I a little child. But, come! will you mend this poor thimble of mine?"

"Anything for your sake, Annie," said Owen Warland—"anything; even were it to work at Robert Danforth's forge."

"And that would be a pretty sight!" retorted Annie, glancing with imperceptible slightness at the artist's small and slender frame. "Well; here is the thimble."

"But that is a strange idea of yours," said Owen, "about the spiritualization of matter!"

And then the thought stole into his mind, that this young girl possessed the gift to comprehend him, better than all the world beside. And what a help and strength would it be to him, in his lonely toil, if he could gain the sympathy of the only being whom he loved! To persons whose pursuits are insulated from the common business of life—who are either in advance of mankind, or apart from it—there often comes a sensation of moral cold, that makes the spirit shiver, as if it had reached the frozen solitudes around the pole. What the prophet, the poet, the reformer, the criminal, or any other man, with human yearnings, but separated from the multitude by a peculiar lot, might feel, poor Owen Warland felt.

"Annie," cried he, growing pale as death at the thought, "how gladly would I tell you the secret of my pursuit! You, methinks, would estimate it rightly. You, I know, would hear it with a reverence that I must not expect from the harsh, material world."

"Would I not? to be sure I would!" replied Annie Hovenden, lightly laughing. "Come; explain to me quickly what is the meaning of this little whirligig, so delicately wrought that it might be a plaything for Queen Mab. See; I will put it in motion."

"Hold," exclaimed Owen, "hold!"

Annie had but given the slightest possible touch, with the point of a needle, to the same minute portion of complicated machinery which has been more than once mentioned, when the artist seized her by the wrist with a force that made her scream aloud. She was affrighted at the convulsion of intense rage and anguish that writhed across his features. The next instant he let his head sink upon his hands.

"Go, Annie," murmured he, "I have deceived myself, and must suffer for it. I yearned for sympathy—and thought—and fancied—and dreamed—that you might give it me. But you lack the talisman, Annie, that should admit you into my secrets. That touch has undone the toil of months, and the thought of a lifetime! It was not your fault, Annie—but you have ruined me!"

Poor Owen Warland! He had indeed erred, yet pardonably; for if any human spirit could have sufficiently reverenced the processes so sacred in his eyes, it must have been a woman's. Even Annie Hovenden, possibly, might not have disappointed him, had she been enlightened by the deep intelligence of love.

The artist spent the ensuing winter in a way that satisfied any persons, who had hitherto retained a hopeful opinion of him, that he was, in truth, irrevocably doomed to inutility as regarded the world, and to an evil destiny on his own part. The decease of a relative had put him in possession of a small inheritance. Thus freed from the necessity of toil, and having lost the steadfast influence of a great purpose—great, at least to him—he abandoned himself to habits from which, it might have been supposed, the mere delicacy of his organization would have availed to secure him. But when the ethereal portion of a man of genius is obscured, the earthly part assumes an influence the more uncontrollable, because the character is now thrown off the balance to which Providence had so nicely adjusted it, and which, in coarser natures, is adjusted by some other method. Owen Warland made proof of whatever show of bliss may be found in riot. He looked at the world through the golden medium of wine, and contemplated the visions that bubble up so gaily around the brim of the glass, and that people the air with shapes of pleasant madness, which so soon grow ghostly and forlorn. Even when this dismal and inevitable change had taken place, the young man might still have continued to quaff the cup of enchantments, though its vapor did but shroud life in gloom, and fill the gloom with spectres that mocked at him. There was a certain irksomeness of spirit, which, being real, and the deepest sensation of which the artist was now conscious, was more intolerable than any fantastic miseries and horrors that the abuse of wine could summon up. In the latter case, he could remember, even out of the midst of his trouble, that all was but a delusion; in the former, the heavy anguish was his actual life.

From this perilous state, he was redeemed by an incident which more than one person witnessed, but of which the shrewdest could not explain nor conjecture the operation on Owen Warland's mind. It was very simple. On a warm afternoon of spring, as the artist sat among his riotous companions, with a glass of wine before him, a splendid butterfly flew in at the open window, and fluttered about his head.

"Ah!" exclaimed Owen, who had drank freely, "Are you alive again, child of the sun, and playmate of the summer breeze, after your dismal winter's nap! Then it is time for me to be at work!"

And leaving his unemptied glass upon the table, he departed, and was never known to sip another drop of wine.

And now, again, he resumed his wanderings in the woods and fields. It might be fancied that the bright butterfly, which had come so spiritlike into the window, as Owen sat with the rude revellers, was indeed a spirit, commissioned to recall him to the pure, ideal life that had so etherealized him among men. It might be fancied, that he went forth to seek this spirit, in its sunny haunts; for still, as in the summer-time gone by, he was seen to steal gently up, wherever a butterfly had alighted, and lose himself in contemplation of it. When it took flight, his eyes followed the winged vision, as if its airy track would show the path to heaven. But what could be the purpose of the unseasonable toil, which was again resumed, as the watchman knew by the lines of lamp-light through the crevices of Owen Warland's shutters? The townspeople had one comprehensive explanation of all these singularities. Owen Warland had gone mad! How universally efficacious—how satisfactory, too, and soothing to the injured sensibility of narrowness and dullness—is this easy method of accounting for whatever lies beyond the world's most ordinary scope! From Saint Paul's days, down to our poor little Artist of the Beautiful, the same talisman has been applied to the elucidation of all mysteries in the words or deeds of men, who spoke or acted too wisely or too well. In Owen Warland's case, the judgment of his townspeople may have been correct. Perhaps he was mad. The lack of sympathy—that contrast between himself and his neighbors, which took away the restraint of example—was enough to make him so. Or, possibly, he had caught just so much of ethereal radiance as served to bewilder him, in an earthly sense, by its intermixture with the common daylight.

One evening, when the artist had returned from a customary ramble, and had just thrown the lustre of his lamp on the delicate piece of work, so often interrupted, but still taken up again, as if his fate were embodied in its mechanism, he was surprised by the entrance of old Peter Hovenden. Owen never met this man without a shrinking of the heart. Of all the world, he was most terrible, by reason of a keen understanding, which saw so distinctly what it did see, and disbelieved so uncompromisingly in what it could not see. On this occasion, the old watchmaker had merely a gracious word or two to say.

"Owen, my lad," said he, "we must see you at my house to-morrow night."

The artist began to mutter some excuse.

"Oh, but it must be so," quoth Peter Hovenden, "for the sake of the days when you were one of the household. What, my boy, don't you know that my daughter Annie is engaged to Robert Danforth? We are making an entertainment, in our humble way, to celebrate the event."

"Ah!" said Owen.

That little monosyllable was all he uttered; its tone seemed cold and unconcerned, to an ear like Peter Hovenden's; and yet there was in it the stifled outcry of the poor artist's heart, which he compressed within him like a man holding down an evil spirit. One slight outbreak, however, imperceptible to the old watchmaker, he allowed himself. Raising the instrument with which he was about to begin his work, he let it fall upon the little system of machinery that had, anew, cost him months of thought and toil. It was shattered by the stroke!

Owen Warland's story would have been no tolerable representation of the troubled life of those who strive to create the Beautiful, if, amid all other thwarting influences, love had not interposed to steal the cunning from his hand. Outwardly, he had been no ardent or enterprising lover; the career of his passion had confined its tumults and vicissitudes so entirely within the artist's imagination, that Annie herself had scarcely more than a woman's intuitive perception of it. But, in Owen's view, it covered the whole field of his life. Forgetful of the time when she had shown herself incapable of any deep response, he had persisted in connecting all his dreams of artistical success with Annie's image; she was the visible shape in which the spiritual power that he worshipped, and on whose altar he hoped to lay a not unworthy offering, was made manifest to him. Of course he had deceived himself; there were no such attributes in Annie Hovenden as his imagination had endowed her with. She, in the aspect which she wore to his inward vision, was as much a creation of his own, as the mysterious piece of mechanism would be were it ever realized. Had he become convinced of his mistake through the medium of successful love; had he won Annie to his bosom, and there beheld her fade from angel into ordinary woman, the disappointment might have driven him back, with concentrated energy, upon his sole remaining object. On the other hand, had he found Annie what he fancied, his lot would have been so rich in beauty, that, out of its mere redundancy, he might have wrought the Beautiful into many a worthier type than he had toiled for. But the guise in which his sorrow came to him, the sense that the angel of his life had been snatched away and given to a rude man of earth and iron, who could neither need nor appreciate her ministrations; this was the very perversity of fate, that makes human existence appear too absurd and contradictory to be the scene of one other hope or one other fear. There was nothing left for Owen Warland but to sit down like a man that had been stunned.

He went through a fit of illness. After his recovery, his small and slender frame assumed an obtuser garniture of flesh than it had ever before worn. His thin cheeks became round; his delicate little hand, so spiritually fashioned to achieve fairy task-work, grew plumper than the hand of a thriving infant. His aspect had a childishness, such as might have induced a stranger to pat him on the head—pausing, however, in the act, to wonder what manner of child was here. It was as if the spirit had gone out of him, leaving the body to flourish in a soft of vegetable existence. Not that Owen Warland was idiotic. He could talk, and not irrationally. Somewhat of a babbler, indeed, did people begin to think him; for he was apt to discourse at wearisome length, of marvels of mechanism that he had read about in books, but which he had learned to consider as absolutely fabulous. Among them he enumerated the Man of Brass, constructed by Albertus Magnus, and the Brazen Head of Friar Bacon; and, coming down to later times, the automata of a little coach and horses, which, it was pretended, had been manufactured for the Dauphin of France; together with an insect that buzzed about the ear like a living fly, and yet was but a contrivance of minute steel springs. There was a story, too, of a duck that waddled, and quacked, and ate; though, had any honest citizen purchased it for dinner, he would have found himself cheated with the mere mechanical apparition of a duck.

"But all these accounts," said Owen Warland, "I am now satisfied, are mere impositions."

Then, in a mysterious way, he would confess that he once thought differently. In his idle and dreamy days, he had considered it possible, in a certain sense, to spiritualize machinery; and to combine with the new species of life and motion, thus produced, a beauty that should attain to the ideal which Nature has proposed to herself, in all her creatures, but has never taken pains to realize. He seemed, however, to retain no very distinct perception either of the process of achieving this object, or of the design itself.

"I have thrown it all aside now," he would say. "It was a dream, such as young men are always mystifying themselves with. Now that I have acquired a little common sense, it makes me laugh to think of it."

Poor, poor, and fallen Owen Warland! These were the symptoms that he had ceased to be an inhabitant of the better sphere that lies unseen around us. He had lost his faith in the invisible, and now prided himself, as such unfortunates invariably do, in the wisdom which rejected much that even his eye could see, and trusted confidently in nothing but what his hand could touch. This is the calamity of men whose spiritual part dies out of them, and leaves the grosser understanding to assimilate them more and more to the things of which alone it can take cognizance. But, in Owen Warland, the spirit was not dead, nor past away; it only slept.

How it awoke again, is not recorded. Perhaps, the torpid slumber was broken by a convulsive pain. Perhaps, as in a former instance, the butterfly came and hovered about his head, and reinspired him—as, indeed, this creature of the sunshine had always a mysterious mission for the artist—reinspired him with the former purpose of his life.

Whether it were pain or happiness that thrilled through his veins, his first impulse was to thank Heaven for rendering him again the being of thought, imagination, and keenest sensibility, that he had long ceased to be.

"Now for my task," said he. "Never did I feel such strength for it as now."

Yet, strong as he felt himself, he was incited to toil the more diligently, by an anxiety lest death should surprise him in the midst of his labors. This anxiety, perhaps, is common to all men who set their hearts upon anything so high, in their own view of it, that life becomes of importance only as conditional to its accomplishment. So long as we love life for itself, we seldom dread the losing it. When we desire life for the attainment of an object, we recognize the frailty of its texture. But, side by side with this sense of insecurity, there is a vital faith in our invulnerability to the shaft of death, while engaged in any task that seems assigned by Providence as our proper thing to do, and which the world would have cause to mourn for, should we leave it unaccomplished. Can the philosopher, big with the inspiration of an idea that is to reform mankind, believe that he is to be beckoned from this sensible existence, at the very instant when he is mustering his breath to speak the word of light? Should he perish so, the weary ages may pass away—the world's whole life-sand may fall, drop by drop—before another intellect is prepared to develope the truth that might have been uttered then. But history affords many an example, where the most precious spirit, at any particular epoch manifested in human shape, has gone hence untimely, without space allowed him, so far as mortal judgment could discern, to perform his mission on the earth. The prophet dies; and the man of torpid heart and sluggish brain lives on. The poet leaves his song half sung, or finishes it, beyond the scope of mortal ears, in a celestial choir. The painter—as Allston did—leaves half his conception on the canvass, to sadden us with its imperfect beauty, and goes to picture forth the whole, if it be no irreverence to say so, in the hues of Heaven. But, rather, such in-complete designs of this life will be perfected nowhere. This so fre-quent abortion of man's dearest projects must be taken as a proof, that the deeds of earth, however etherealized by piety or genius, are without value, except as exercises and manifestations of the spirit. In Heaven, all ordinary thought is higher and more melodious than Mil-ton's song. Then, would he add another verse to any strain that he had left unfinished here?

But to return to Owen Warland. It was his fortune, good or ill, to achieve the purpose of his life. Pass we over a long space of intense thought, yearning effort, minute toil, and wasting anxiety, succeeded by an instant of solitary triumph; let all this be imagined; and then behold the artist, on a winter evening, seeking admittance to Robert Danforth's fireside circle. There he found the Man of Iron, with his massive substance thoroughly warmed and attempered by domestic influences. And there was Annie, too, now transformed into a ma-tron, with much of her husband's plain and sturdy nature, but im-bued, as Owen Warland still believed, with a finer grace, that might enable her to be the interpreter between Strength and Beauty. It hap-pened, likewise, that old Peter Hovenden was a guest, this evening, at his daughter's fireside; and it was his well-remembered expression of keen, cold criticism, that first encountered the artist's glance.

"My old friend Owen!" cried Robert Danforth, starting up, and compressing the artist's delicate fingers within a hand that was accus-tomed to gripe bars of iron. "This is kind and neighborly, to come to us at last! I was afraid your Perpetual Motion had bewitched you out of the remembrance of old times."

"We are glad to see you!" said Annie, while a blush reddened her matronly cheek. "It was not like a friend, to stay from us so long."

"Well, Owen," inquired the old watchmaker, as his first greeting, "how comes on the Beautiful? Have you created it at last?"

The artist did not immediately reply, being startled by the apparition of a young child of strength, that was tumbling about on the carpet; a little personage who had come mysteriously out of the infinite, but with something so sturdy and real in his composition that he seemed moulded out of the densest substance which earth could supply. This hopeful infant crawled towards the new-comer, and setting himself on end—as Robert Danforth expressed the posture—stared at Owen with a look of such sagacious observation, that the mother could not help exchanging a proud glance with her husband. But the artist was disturbed by the child's look, as imagining a resemblance between it and Peter Hovenden's habitual expression. He could have fancied that the old watchmaker was compressed into this baby-shape, and was looking out of those baby-eyes, and repeating—as he now did—the malicious question:

"The Beautiful, Owen! How comes on the Beautiful? Have you succeeded in creating the Beautiful?"

"I have succeeded," replied the artist, with a momentary light of triumph in his eyes, and a smile of sunshine, yet steeped in such depth of thought that it was almost sadness. "Yes, my friends, it is the truth. I have succeeded!"

"Indeed!" cried Annie, a look of maiden mirthfulness peeping out of her face again. "And is it lawful, now, to inquire what the secret is?"

"Surely; it is to disclose it, that I have come," answered Owen Warland. "You shall know, and see, and touch, and possess, the secret! For Annie—if by that name I may still address the friend of my boyish years—Annie, it is for your bridal gift that I have wrought this spiritualized mechanism, this harmony of motion, this Mystery of Beauty! It comes late, indeed; but it is as we go onward in life, when objects begin to lose their freshness of hue, and our souls their delicacy of perception, that the spirit of Beauty is most needed. If—forgive me, Annie—if you know how to value this gift, it can never come too late!"

He produced, as he spoke, what seemed a jewel-box. It was carved richly out of ebony by his own hand, and inlaid with a fanciful tracery of pearl, representing a boy in pursuit of a butterfly, which, elsewhere, had become a winged spirit, and was flying heavenward; while the boy, or youth, had found such efficacy in his strong desire, that he ascended from earth to cloud, and from cloud to celestial atmosphere, to win the Beautiful. This case of ebony the artist opened, and bade Annie place her finger on its edge. She did so, but almost screamed, as a butterfly fluttered forth, and alighting on her finger's tip, sat waving the ample magnificence of its purple and gold-speckled wings, as if in prelude to a flight. It is impossible to express by words the glory, the splendor, the delicate gorgeousness, which were softened into the beauty of this object. Nature's ideal butterfly was here realized in all its perfection; not in the pattern of such faded insects as flit among earthly flowers, but of those which hover across the meads of Paradise, for child-angels and the spirits of departed infants to disport themselves with. The rich down was visible upon its wings; the lustre of its eyes seemed instinct with spirit. The firelight glimmered around this wonder—the candles gleamed upon it—but it glistened apparently by its own radiance, and illuminated the finger and outstretched hand on which it rested, with a white gleam like that of precious stones. In its perfect beauty, the consideration of size was entirely lost. Had its wings overarched the firmament, the mind could not have been more filled or satisfied.

"Beautiful! Beautiful!" exclaimed Annie. "Is it alive? Is it alive?"

"Alive? To be sure it is," answered her husband. "Do you suppose any mortal has skill enough to make a butterfly,—or would put himself to the trouble of making one, when any child may catch a score of them in a summer's afternoon? Alive? Certainly! But this pretty box is undoubtedly of our friend Owen's manufacture; and really it does him credit."

At this moment, the butterfly waved its wings anew, with a motion so absolutely lifelike that Annie was startled, and even awe-stricken; for, in spite of her husband's opinion, she could not satisfy herself whether it was indeed a living creature, or a piece of wondrous mechanism.

"Is it alive?" she repeated, more earnestly than before.

"Judge for yourself," said Owen Warland, who stood gazing in her face with fixed attention.

The butterfly now flung itself upon the air, fluttered round Annie's head, and soared into a distant region of the parlor, still making itself perceptible to sight by the starry gleam in which the motion of its wings enveloped it. The infant on the floor, followed its course with his sagacious little eyes. After flying about the room, it returned, in a spiral curve, and settled again on Annie's finger.

"But is it alive?" exclaimed she again; and the finger, on which the gorgeous mystery had alighted, was so tremulous that the butterfly was forced to balance himself with his wings. "Tell me if it be alive, or whether you created it?"

"Wherefore ask who created it, so it be beautiful?" replied Owen Warland. "Alive? Yes, Annie; it may well be said to possess life, for it absorbed my own being into itself; and in the secret of that butterfly, and in its beauty—which is not merely outward, but deep as its whole system—is represented the intellect, the imagination, the sensibility, the soul, of an Artist of the Beautiful! Yes, I created it. But"—and here his countenance somewhat changed—"this butterfly is not now to me what it was when I beheld it afar off, in the daydreams of my youth."

"Be it what it may, it is a pretty plaything," said the blacksmith, grinning with childlike delight. "I wonder whether it would condescend to alight on such a great clumsy finger as mine? Hold it hither, Annie!"

By the artist's direction, Annie touched her finger's tip to that of her husband; and, after a momentary delay, the butterfly fluttered from one to the other. It preluded a second flight by a similar, yet not precisely the same waving of wings, as in the first experiment; then, ascending from the blacksmith's stalwart finger, it rose in a gradually enlarging curve to the ceiling, made one wide sweep around the room, and returned with an undulating movement to the point whence it had started.

"Well, that does beat all nature!" cried Robert Danforth, bestowing the heartiest praise that he could find expression for; and, indeed, had he paused there, a man of finer words and nicer perception, could not easily have said more. "That goes beyond me, I confess! But what then? There is more real use in one downright blow of my sledgehammer, than in the whole five years' labor that our friend Owen has wasted on this butterfly!"

Here the child clapped his hands, and made a great babble of indistinct utterance, apparently demanding that the butterfly should be given him for a plaything.

Owen Warland, meanwhile, glanced sidelong at Annie, to discover whether she sympathized in her husband's estimate of the comparative value of the Beautiful and the Practical. There was, amid all her kindness towards himself, amid all the wonder and admiration with which she contemplated the marvelous work of his hands, and incarnation of his idea, a secret scorn; too secret, perhaps, for her own consciousness, and perceptible only to such intuitive discernment as that of the artist. But Owen, in the latter stages of his pursuit, had risen out of the region in which such a discovery might have been torture. He knew that the world, and Annie as the representative of the world, whatever praise might be bestowed, could never say the fitting word, nor feel the fitting sentiment which should be the perfect recompense of an artist who, symbolizing a lofty moral by a material trifle—converting what was earthly, to spiritual gold—had won the Beautiful into his handiwork. Not at this latest moment, was he to learn that the reward of all high performance must be sought within itself, or sought in vain. There was, however, a view of the matter, which Annie, and her husband, and even Peter Hovenden, might fully have understood, and which would have satisfied them that the toil of years had here been worthily bestowed. Owen Warland might have told them, that this butterfly, this plaything, this bridal-gift of a poor watchmaker to a blacksmith's wife, was, in truth, a gem of art that a monarch would have purchased with honors and abundant wealth, and have treasured it among the jewels of his kingdom, as the most unique and wondrous of them all! But the artist smiled, and kept the secret to himself.

"Father," said Annie, thinking that a word of praise from the old watchmaker might gratify his former apprentice, "do come and admire this pretty butterfly!"

"Let us see," said Peter Hovenden, rising from his chair, with the sneer upon his face that always made people doubt, as he himself did, in everything but a material existence. "Here is my finger for it to alight upon. I shall understand it better when once I have touched it."

But, to the increased astonishment of Annie, when the tip of her father's finger was pressed against that of her husband, on which the butterfly still rested, the insect drooped its wings, and seemed on the point of falling to the floor. Even the bright spots of gold upon its wings and body, unless her eyes deceived her, grew dim, and the glowing purple took a dusky hue, and the starry lustre that gleamed around the blacksmith's hand, became faint, and vanished.

"It is dying! it is dying!" cried Annie, in alarm.

"It has been delicately wrought," said the artist calmly. "As I told you, it has imbibed a spiritual essence—call it magnetism, or what you will. In an atmosphere of doubt and mockery, its exquisite susceptibility suffers torture, as does the soul of him who instilled his own life into it. It has already lost its beauty; in a few moments more, its mechanism would be irreparably injured."

"Take away your hand, father!" entreated Annie, turning pale. "Here is my child; let it rest on his innocent hand. There, perhaps, its life will revive, and its colors grow brighter than ever."

Her father, with an acrid smile, withdrew his finger. The butterfly then appeared to recover the power of voluntary motion; while its hues assumed much of their original lustre, and the gleam of starlight, which was its most ethereal attribute, again formed a halo round about it. At first, when transferred from Robert Danforth's hand to the small finger of the child, this radiance grew so powerful that it positively threw the little fellow's shadow back against the wall. He, meanwhile, extended his plump hand as he had seen his father and mother do, and watched the waving of the insect's wings, with infantine delight. Nevertheless, there was a certain odd expression of sagacity, that made Owen Warland feel as if here were old Peter Hovenden, partially, and but partially, redeemed from his hard scepticism into childish faith.

"How wise the little monkey looks!" whispered Robert Danforth to his wife.

"I never saw such a look on a child's face," answered Annie, admiring her own infant, and with good reason, far more than the artistic butterfly. "The darling knows more of the mystery than we do."

As if the butterfly, like the artist, were conscious of something not entirely congenial in the child's nature, it alternately sparkled and grew dim. At length, it arose from the small hand of the infant with an airy motion, that seemed to bear it upward without an effort; as if the ethereal instincts, with which its master's spirit had endowed it, impelled this fair vision involuntarily to a higher sphere. Had there been no obstruction, it might have soared into the sky, and grown immortal. But its lustre gleamed upon the ceiling; the exquisite texture of its wings brushed against that earthly medium; and a sparkle or two, as of star-dust, floated downward and lay glimmering on the carpet. Then the butterfly came fluttering down, and instead of returning to the infant, was apparently attracted towards the artist's hand.

"Not so, not so!" murmured Owen Warland, as if his handiwork could have understood him. "Thou hast gone forth out of thy master's heart. There is no return for thee!"

With a wavering movement, and emitting a tremulous radiance, the butterfly struggled, as it were, towards the infant, and was about to alight upon his finger. But, while it still hovered in the air, the little Child of Strength, with his grand-sire's sharp and shrewd expression in his face, made a snatch at the marvellous insect, and compressed it in his hand. Annie screamed! Old Peter Hovendon burst into a cold and scornful laugh. The blacksmith, by main force, unclosed the infant's hand, and found within the palm a small heap of glittering fragments, whence the Mystery of Beauty had fled for ever. And as for Owen Warland, he looked placidly at what seemed the ruin of his life's labor, and which was yet no ruin. He had caught a far other butterfly than this. When the artist rose high enough to achieve the Beautiful, the symbol by which he made it perceptible to mortal senses became of little value in his eyes, while his spirit possessed itself in the enjoyment of the Reality.

Rappaccini's Daughter

From the Writings of Aubépine

W E D O N O T R E M E M B E R to have seen any translated specimens of the productions of M. de l'Aubépine; a fact the less to
be wondered at, as his very name is unknown to many of his own
countrymen, as well as to the student of foreign literature. As a writer,
he seems to occupy an unfortunate position between the Transcendentalists (who, under one name or another, have their share in all the
current literature of the world), and the great body of pen-and-ink
men who address the intellect and sympathies of the multitude. If not
too refined, at all events too remote, too shadowy and unsubstantial
in his modes of development, to suit the taste of the latter class, and
yet too popular to satisfy the spiritual or metaphysical requisitions of
the former, he must necessarily find himself without an audience; except here and there an individual, or possibly an isolated clique. His
writings, to do them justice, are not altogether destitute of fancy and
originality; they might have won him greater reputation but for an

inveterate love of allegory, which is apt to invest his plots and characters with the aspect of scenery and people in the clouds, and to steal away the human warmth out of his conceptions. His fictions are sometimes historical, sometimes of the present day, and sometimes, so far as can be discovered, have little or no reference either to time or space. In any case, he generally contents himself with a very slight embroidery of outward manners,—the faintest possible counterfeit of real life,—and endeavors to create an interest by some less obvious peculiarity of the subject. Occasionally, a breath of nature, a raindrop of pathos and tenderness, or a gleam of humor, will find its way into the midst of his fantastic imagery, and make us feel as if, after all, we were yet within the limits of our native earth. We will only add to this very cursory notice, that M. de l'Aubépine's productions, if the reader chance to take them in precisely the proper point of view, may amuse a leisure hour as well as those of a brighter man; if otherwise, they can hardly fail to look excessively like nonsense.

Our author is voluminous; he continues to write and publish with as much praiseworthy and indefatigable prolixity, as if his efforts were crowned with the brilliant success that so justly attends those of Eugene Sue. His first appearance was by a collection of stories, in a long series of volumes, entitled *"Contes deux fois racontées."* The titles of some of his more recent works (we quote from memory) are as follows:—*"Le Voyage Céleste à Chemin de Fer"* 3 tom. 1838. *"Le nouveau Père Adam et la nouvelle Mère Eve"* 2 tom. 1839. *"Roderic; ou le Serpent à l'estomac"* 2 tom. 1840. *"Le Culte du Feu"* a folio volume of ponderous research into the religion and ritual of the old Persian Ghebers, published in 1841. *"La Soirée du Chateau en Espagne,"* 1 tom. 8vo. 1842; and *"L'Artiste du Beau; ou le Papillon Mécanique,"* 5 tom. 4to. 1843. Our somewhat wearisome perusal of this startling catalogue of volumes has left behind it a certain personal affection and sympathy, though by no means admiration, for M. de l'Aubépine; and we would fain do the little in our power towards introducing him favorably to the American public. The ensuing tale is a translation of his *"Beatrice; ou la Belle Empoisonneuse,"* recently published in *"La Revue Anti-Aristocratique."* This journal, edited by the Comte de Bearhaven, has, for some years past, led the defence of liberal principles and popular rights, with a faithfulness and ability worthy of all praise.

A young man, named Giovanni Guasconti, came, very long ago, from the more southern region of Italy, to pursue his studies at the University of Padua. Giovanni, who had but a scanty supply of gold ducats in his pocket, took lodgings in a high and gloomy chamber of an old edifice, which looked not unworthy to have been the palace of a Paduan noble, and which, in fact, exhibited over its entrance the armorial bearings of a family long since extinct. The young stranger, who was not unstudied in the great poem of his country, recollected that one of the ancestors of this family, and perhaps an occupant of this very mansion, had been pictured by Dante as a partaker of the immortal agonies of his Inferno. These reminiscences and associations, together with the tendency to heart-break natural to a young man for the first time out of his native sphere, caused Giovanni to sigh heavily, as he looked around the desolate and ill-furnished apartment.

"Holy Virgin, Signor," cried old dame Lisabetta, who, won by the youth's remarkable beauty of person, was kindly endeavoring to give the chamber a habitable air, "what a sigh was that to come out of a young man's heart! Do you find this old mansion gloomy? For the love of heaven, then, put your head out of the window, and you will see as bright sunshine as you have left in Naples."

Guasconti mechanically did as the old woman advised, but could not quite agree with her that the Paduan sunshine was as cheerful as that of southern Italy. Such as it was, however, it fell upon a garden beneath the window, and expended its fostering influences on a variety of plants, which seemed to have been cultivated with exceeding care.

"Does this garden belong to the house?" asked Giovanni.

"Heaven forbid, Signor!—unless it were fruitful of better potherbs than any that grow there now," answered old Lisabetta. "No; that garden is cultivated by the own hands of Signor Giacomo Rappaccini, the famous Doctor, who, I warrant him, has been heard of as far as Naples. It is said that he distils these plants into medicines that are as potent as a charm. Oftentimes you may see the Signor Doctor at work, and perchance the Signora his daughter, too, gathering the strange flowers that grow in the garden."

The old woman had now done what she could for the aspect of the chamber, and, commending the young man to the protection of the saints, took her departure.

Giovanni still found no better occupation than to look down into the garden beneath his window. From its appearance, he judged it to be one of those botanic gardens, which were of earlier date in Padua than elsewhere in Italy, or in the world. Or, not improbably, it might once have been the pleasure-place of an opulent family; for there was the ruin of a marble fountain in the centre, sculptured with rare art, but so wofully shattered that it was impossible to trace the original design from the chaos of remaining fragments. The water, however, continued to gush and sparkle into the sunbeams as cheerfully as ever. A little gurgling sound ascended to the young man's window, and made him feel as if the fountain were an immortal spirit, that sung its song unceasingly, and without heeding the vicissitudes around it; while one century embodied it in marble, and another scattered the perishable garniture on the soil. All about the pool into which the water subsided, grew various plants, that seemed to require a plentiful supply of moisture for the nourishment of gigantic leaves, and, in some instances, flowers gorgeously magnificent. There was one shrub in particular, set in a marble vase in the midst of the pool, that bore a profusion of purple blossoms, each of which had the lustre and richness of a gem; and the whole together made a show so resplendent that it seemed enough to illuminate the garden, even had there been no sunshine. Every portion of the soil was peopled with plants and herbs, which, if less beautiful, still bore tokens of assiduous care; as if all had their individual virtues, known to the scientific mind that fostered them. Some were placed in urns, rich with old carving, and others in common garden-pots; some crept serpent-like along the ground, or climbed on high, using whatever means of ascent was offered them. One plant had wreathed itself round a statue of Vertumnus, which was thus quite veiled and shrouded in a drapery of hanging foliage, so happily arranged that it might have served a sculptor for a study.

While Giovanni stood at the window, he heard a rustling behind a screen of leaves, and became aware that a person was at work in the garden. His figure soon emerged into view, and showed itself to be that of no common laborer, but a tall, emaciated, sallow, and sickly-looking man, dressed in a scholar's garb of black. He was beyond the middle term of life, with grey hair, a thin grey beard, and a face singularly marked with intellect and cultivation, but which could never, even in his more youthful days, have expressed much warmth of heart.

Nothing could exceed the intentness with which this scientific gardener examined every shrub which grew in his path; it seemed as if he was looking into their inmost nature, making observations in regard to their creative essence, and discovering why one leaf grew in this shape, and another in that, and wherefore such and such flowers differed among themselves in hue and perfume. Nevertheless, in spite of this deep intelligence on his part, there was no approach to intimacy between himself and these vegetable existences. On the contrary, he avoided their actual touch, or the direct inhaling of their odors, with a caution that impressed Giovanni most disagreeably; for the man's demeanor was that of one walking among malignant influences, such as savage beasts, or deadly snakes, or evil spirits, which, should he allow them one moment of license, would wreak upon him some terrible fatality. It was strangely frightful to the young man's imagination, to see this air of insecurity in a person cultivating a garden, that most simple and innocent of human toils, and which had been alike the joy and labor of the unfallen parents of the race. Was this garden, then, the Eden of the present world?—and this man, with such a perception of harm in what his own hands caused to grow, was he the Adam?

The distrustful gardener, while plucking away the dead leaves or pruning the too luxuriant growth of the shrubs, defended his hands with a pair of thick gloves. Nor were these his only armor. When, in his walk through the garden, he came to the magnificent plant that hung its purple gems beside the marble fountain, he placed a kind of mask over his mouth and nostrils, as if all this beauty did but conceal a deadlier malice. But finding his task still too dangerous, he drew back, removed the mask, and called loudly, but in the infirm voice of a person affected with inward disease:

"Beatrice!—Beatrice!"

"Here am I, my father! What would you?" cried a rich and youthful voice from the window of the opposite house; a voice as rich as a tropical sunset, and which made Giovanni, though he knew not why, think of deep hues of purple or crimson, and of perfumes heavily delectable.—"Are you in the garden?"

"Yes, Beatrice," answered the gardener, "and I need your help."

Soon there emerged from under a sculptured portal the figure of a young girl, arrayed with as much richness of taste as the most splendid of the flowers, beautiful as the day, and with a bloom so deep and vivid that one shade more would have been too much. She looked redundant with life, health, and energy; all of which attributes were bound down and compressed, as it were, and girdled tensely, in their luxuriance, by her virgin zone. Yet Giovanni's fancy must have grown morbid, while he looked down into the garden; for the impression which the fair stranger made upon him was as if here were another flower, the human sister of those vegetable ones, as beautiful as they —more beautiful than the richest of them—but still to be touched only with a glove, nor to be approached without a mask. As Beatrice came down the garden path, it was observable that she handled and inhaled the odor of several of the plants, which her father had most sedulously avoided.

"Here, Beatrice," said the latter,—"see how many needful offices require to be done to our chief treasure. Yet, shattered as I am, my life might pay the penalty of approaching it so closely as circumstances demand. Henceforth, I fear, this plant must be consigned to your sole charge."

"And gladly will I undertake it," cried again the rich tones of the young lady, as she bent towards the magnificent plant, and opened her arms as if to embrace it. "Yes, my sister, my splendor, it shall be Beatrice's task to nurse and serve thee; and thou shalt reward her with thy kisses and perfumed breath, which to her is as the breath of life!"

Then, with all the tenderness in her manner that was so strikingly expressed in her words, she busied herself with such attentions as the plant seemed to require; and Giovanni, at his lofty window, rubbed his eyes, and almost doubted whether it were a girl tending her favorite flower, or one sister performing the duties of affection to another. The scene soon terminated. Whether Doctor Rappaccini had finished his labors in the garden, or that his watchful eye had caught the stranger's face, he now took his daughter's arm and retired. Night was already closing in; oppressive exhalations seemed to proceed from the plants, and steal upward past the open window; and Giovanni, closing the lattice, went to his couch, and dreamed of a rich flower and beautiful girl. Flower and maiden were different and yet the same, and fraught with some strange peril in either shape.

But there is an influence in the light of morning that tends to rectify whatever errors of fancy, or even of judgment, we may have incurred during the sun's decline, or among the shadows of the night, or in the less wholesome glow of moonshine. Giovanni's first movement on starting from sleep, was to throw open the window, and gaze down into the garden which his dreams had made so fertile of mysteries. He was surprised, and a little ashamed, to find how real and matter-of-fact an affair it proved to be, in the first rays of the sun, which gilded the dew-drops that hung upon leaf and blossom, and, while giving a brighter beauty to each rare flower, brought everything within the limits of ordinary experience. The young man rejoiced, that, in the heart of the barren city, he had the privilege of overlooking this spot of lovely and luxuriant vegetation. It would serve, he said to himself, as a symbolic language, to keep him in communion with Nature. Neither the sickly and thought-worn Doctor Giacomo Rappaccini, it is true, nor his brilliant daughter, were now visible; so that Giovanni could not determine how much of the singularity which he attributed to both, was due to their own qualities, and how much to his wonder-working fancy. But he was inclined to take a most rational view of the whole matter.

In the course of the day, he paid his respects to Signor Pietro Baglioni, professor of medicine in the University, a physician of eminent repute, to whom Giovanni had brought a letter of introduction. The Professor was an elderly personage, apparently of genial nature, and habits that might almost be called jovial; he kept the young man to dinner, and made himself very agreeable by the freedom and liveliness of his conversation, especially when warmed by a flask or two of Tuscan wine. Giovanni, conceiving that men of science, inhabitants of the same city, must needs be on familiar terms with one another, took an opportunity to mention the name of Doctor Rappaccini. But the Professor did not respond with so much cordiality as he had anticipated.

"Ill would it become a teacher of the divine art of medicine," said Professor Pietro Baglioni, in answer to a question of Giovanni, "to withhold due and well-considered praise of a physician so eminently skilled as Rappaccini. But, on the other hand, I should answer it but scantily to my conscience, were I to permit a worthy youth like yourself, Signor Giovanni, the son of an ancient friend, to imbibe erroneous ideas respecting a man who might hereafter chance to hold your life and death in his hands. The truth is, our worshipful Doctor Rappaccini has as much science as any member of the faculty—with perhaps one single exception—in Padua, or all Italy. But there are certain grave objections to his professional character."

"And what are they?" asked the young man.

"Has my friend Giovanni any disease of body or heart, that he is so inquisitive about physicians?" said the Professor, with a smile. "But as for Rappaccini, it is said of him—and I, who know the man well, can answer for its truth—that he cares infinitely more for science than for mankind. His patients are interesting to him only as subjects for some new experiment. He would sacrifice human life, his own among the rest, or whatever else was dearest to him, for the sake of adding so much as a grain of mustard-seed to the great heap of his accumulated knowledge."

"Methinks he is an awful man, indeed," remarked Guasconti,

mentally recalling the cold and purely intellectual aspect of Rappaccini. "And yet, worshipful Professor, is it not a noble spirit? Are there many men capable of so spiritual a love of science?"

"God forbid," answered the Professor, somewhat testily—"at least, unless they take sounder views of the healing art than those adopted by Rappaccini. It is his theory, that all medicinal virtues are comprised within those substances which we term vegetable poisons. These he cultivates with his own hands, and is said even to have produced new varieties of poison, more horribly deleterious than Nature, without the assistance of this learned person, would ever have plagued the world withal. That the Signor Doctor does less mischief than might be expected, with such dangerous substances, is undeniable. Now and then, it must be owned, he has effected—or seemed to effect—a marvellous cure. But, to tell you my private mind, Signor Giovanni, he should receive little credit for such instances of success—they being probably the work of chance—but should be held strictly accountable for his failures, which may justly be considered his own work."

The youth might have taken Baglioni's opinions with many grains of allowance, had he known that there was a professional warfare of long continuance between him and Doctor Rappaccini, in which the latter was generally thought to have gained the advantage. If the reader be inclined to judge for himself, we refer him to certain blackletter tracts on both sides, preserved in the medical department of the University of Padua.

"I know not, most learned Professor," returned Giovanni, after musing on what had been said of Rappaccini's exclusive zeal for science—"I know not how dearly this physician may love his art; but surely there is one object more dear to him. He has a daughter."

"Aha!" cried the Professor with a laugh. "So now our friend Giovanni's secret is out. You have heard of this daughter, whom all the young men in Padua are wild about, though not half a dozen have ever had the good hap to see her face. I know little of the Signora Beatrice, save that Rappaccini is said to have instructed her deeply in his science, and that, young and beautiful as fame reports her, she is already qualified to fill a professor's chair. Perchance her father destines her for mine! Other absurd rumors there be, not worth talking about, or listening to. So now, Signor Giovanni, drink off your glass of Lacryma."

Guasconti returned to his lodgings somewhat heated with the wine he had quaffed, and which caused his brain to swim with strange fantasies in reference to Doctor Rappaccini and the beautiful Beatrice. On his way, happening to pass by a florist's, he bought a fresh bouquet of flowers.

Ascending to his chamber, he seated himself near the window, but within the shadow thrown by the depth of the wall, so that he could look down into the garden with little risk of being discovered. All beneath his eye was a solitude. The strange plants were basking in the sunshine, and now and then nodding gently to one another, as if in acknowledgment of sympathy and kindred. In the midst, by the shattered fountain, grew the magnificent shrub, with its purple gems clustering all over it; they glowed in the air, and gleamed back again out of the depths of the pool, which thus seemed to overflow with colored radiance from the rich reflection that was steeped in it. At first, as we have said, the garden was a solitude. Soon, however,—as Giovanni had half-hoped, half-feared, would be the case,—a figure appeared beneath the antique sculptured portal, and came down between the rows of plants, inhaling their various perfumes, as if she were one of those beings of old classic fable, that lived upon sweet odors. On again beholding Beatrice, the young man was even startled to perceive how much her beauty exceeded his recollection of it; so brilliant, so vivid was its character, that she glowed amid the sunlight, and, as Giovanni whispered to himself, positively illuminated the more shadowy intervals of the garden path. Her face being now more revealed than on the former occasion, he was struck by its expression of simplicity and sweetness; qualities that had not entered into his idea of her character, and which made him ask anew, what manner of mortal she might be. Nor did he fail again to observe, or imagine, an analogy between the beautiful girl and the gorgeous shrub that hung its gem-like flowers over the fountain; a resemblance which Beatrice seemed to have indulged a fantastic humor in heightening, both by the arrangement of her dress and the selection of its hues.

Approaching the shrub, she threw open her arms, as with a passionate ardor, and drew its branches into an intimate embrace; so intimate, that her features were hidden in its leafy bosom, and her glistening ringlets all intermingled with the flowers.

"Give me thy breath, my sister," exclaimed Beatrice; "for I am faint with common air! And give me this flower of thine, which I separate with gentlest fingers from the stem, and place it close beside my heart."

With these words, the beautiful daughter of Rappaccini plucked one of the richest blossoms of the shrub, and was about to fasten it in her bosom. But now, unless Giovanni's draughts of wine had bewildered his senses, a singular incident occurred. A small orange-colored reptile, of the lizard or chameleon species, chanced to be creeping along the path, just at the feet of Beatrice. It appeared to Giovanni—but, at the distance from which he gazed, he could scarcely have seen anything so minute—it appeared to him, however, that a drop or two of moisture from the broken stem of the flower descended upon the lizard's head. For an instant, the reptile contorted itself violently, and then lay motionless in the sunshine. Beatrice observed this remarkable phenomenon, and crossed herself, sadly, but without surprise; nor did she therefore hesitate to arrange the fatal flower in her bosom. There it blushed, and almost glimmered with the dazzling effect of a precious stone, adding to her dress and aspect the one appropriate charm, which nothing else in the world could have supplied. But Giovanni, out of the shadow of his window, bent forward and shrank back, and murmured and trembled.

"Am I awake? Have I my senses?" said he to himself. "What is this being?—beautiful, shall I call her?—or inexpressibly terrible?"

Beatrice now strayed carelessly through the garden, approaching closer beneath Giovanni's window, so that he was compelled to thrust his head quite out of its concealment in order to gratify the intense and painful curiosity which she excited. At this moment, there came a beautiful insect over the garden wall; it had perhaps wandered through the city and found no flowers nor verdure among those antique haunts of men, until the heavy perfumes of Doctor Rappaccini's shrubs had lured it from afar. Without alighting on the flowers, this winged brightness seemed to be attracted by Beatrice, and lingered in the air and fluttered about her head. Now, here it could not be but that Giovanni Guasconti's eyes deceived him. Be that as it might, he fancied that while Beatrice was gazing at the insect with childish delight, it grew faint and fell at her feet;—its bright wings shivered; it was dead—from no cause that he could discern, unless it were the atmosphere of her breath. Again Beatrice crossed herself and sighed heavily, as she bent over the dead insect.

An impulsive movement of Giovanni drew her eyes to the window. There she beheld the beautiful head of the young man—rather a Grecian than an Italian head, with fair, regular features, and a glistening of gold among his ringlets—gazing down upon her like a being that hovered in midair. Scarcely knowing what he did, Giovanni threw down the bouquet which he had hitherto held in his hand.

"Signora," said he, "there are pure and healthful flowers. Wear them for the sake of Giovanni Guasconti!"

"Thanks, Signor," replied Beatrice, with her rich voice, that came forth as it were like a gush of music; and with a mirthful expression half childish and half woman-like. "I accept your gift, and would fain recompense it with this precious purple flower; but if I toss it into the air, it will not reach you. So Signor Guasconti must even content himself with my thanks."

She lifted the bouquet from the ground, and then as if inwardly ashamed at having stepped aside from her maidenly reserve to respond to a stranger's greeting, passed swiftly homeward through the garden. But, few as the moments were, it seemed to Giovanni when she was on the point of vanishing beneath the sculptured portal, that his beautiful bouquet was already beginning to wither in her grasp. It was an idle thought; there could be no possibility of distinguishing a faded flower from a fresh one at so great a distance.

For many days after this incident, the young man avoided the window that looked into Doctor Rappaccini's garden, as if something ugly and monstrous would have blasted his eye-sight, had he been betrayed into a glance. He felt conscious of having put himself, to a certain extent, within the influence of an unintelligible power, by the communication which he had opened with Beatrice. The wisest course would have been, if his heart were in any real danger, to quit his lodgings and Padua itself, at once; the next wiser, to have accustomed himself, as far as possible, to the familiar and day-light view of Beatrice; thus bringing her rigidly and systematically within the limits of ordinary experience. Least of all, while avoiding her sight, ought Giovanni to have remained so near this extraordinary being, that the proximity and possibility even of intercourse, should give a kind of substance and reality to the wild vagaries which his imagination ran riot continually in producing. Guasconti had not a deep heart—or at all events, its depths were not sounded now—but he had a quick fancy, and an ardent southern temperament, which rose every instant to a higher fever-pitch. Whether or no Beatrice possessed those ter-

rible attributes—that fatal breath—the affinity with those so beautiful and deadly flowers—which were indicated by what Giovanni had
witnessed, she had at least instilled a fierce and subtle poison into his
system. It was not love, although her rich beauty was a madness to
him; nor horror, even while he fancied her spirit to be imbued with
the same baneful essence that seemed to pervade her physical frame;
but a wild offspring of both love and horror that had each parent in
it, and burned like one and shivered like the other. Giovanni knew
not what to dread; still less did he know what to hope; yet hope and
dread kept a continual warfare in his breast, alternately vanquishing
one another and starting up afresh to renew the contest. Blessed are
all simple emotions, be they dark or bright! It is the lurid intermixture of the two that produces the illuminating blaze of the infernal
regions.

Sometimes he endeavored to assuage the fever of his spirit by a
rapid walk through the streets of Padua, or beyond its gates; his footsteps kept time with the throbbings of his brain, so that the walk was
apt to accelerate itself to a race. One day, he found himself arrested;
his arm was seized by a portly personage who had turned back on
recognizing the young man, and expended much breath in overtak-
ing him.

"Signor Giovanni!—stay, my young friend!" cried he. "Have you
forgotten me? That might well be the case, if I were as much altered as
yourself."

It was Baglioni, whom Giovanni had avoided, ever since their first
meeting, from a doubt that the Professor's sagacity would look too
deeply into his secrets. Endeavoring to recover himself, he stared forth
wildly from his inner world into the outer one, and spoke like a man
in a dream:

"Yes; I am Giovanni Guasconti. You are Professor Pietro Baglioni.
Now let me pass!"

"Not yet—not yet, Signor Giovanni Guasconti," said the Professor, smiling, but at the same time scrutinizing the youth with an earnest glance.—"What; did I grow up side by side with your father, and shall his son pass me like a stranger, in these old streets of Padua? Stand still, Signor Giovanni; for we must have a word or two, before we part."

"Speedily, then, most worshipful Professor, speedily!" said Giovanni, with feverish impatience. "Does not your worship see that I am in haste?"

Now, while he was speaking, there came a man in black along the street, stooping and moving feebly, like a person in inferior health. His face was all overspread with a most sickly and sallow hue, but yet so pervaded with an expression of piercing and active intellect, that an observer might easily have overlooked the merely physical attributes, and have seen only this wonderful energy. As he passed, this person exchanged a cold and distant salutation with Baglioni, but fixed his eyes upon Giovanni with an intentness that seemed to bring out whatever was within him worthy of notice. Nevertheless, there was a peculiar quietness in the look, as if taking merely a speculative, not a human, interest in the young man.

"It is Doctor Rappaccini!" whispered the Professor, when the stranger had passed.—"Has he ever seen your face before?"

"Not that I know," answered Giovanni, starting at the name.

"He *has* seen you!—he must have seen you!" said Baglioni, hastily. "For some purpose or other, this man of science is making a study of you. I know that look of his! It is the same that coldly illuminates his face, as he bends over a bird, a mouse, or a butterfly, which, in pursuance of some experiment, he has killed by the perfume of a flower;—a look as deep as Nature itself, but without Nature's warmth of love. Signor Giovanni, I will stake my life upon it, you are the subject of one of Rappaccini's experiments!"

"Will you make a fool of me?" cried Giovanni, passionately. "*That,* Signor Professor, were an untoward experiment."

"Patience, patience!" replied the imperturbable Professor.—"I tell thee, my poor Giovanni, that Rappaccini has a scientific interest in thee. Thou hast fallen into fearful hands! And the Signora Beatrice? What part does she act in this mystery?"

But Guasconti, finding Baglioni's pertinacity intolerable, here broke away, and was gone before the Professor could again seize his arm. He looked after the young man intently, and shook his head.

"This must not be," said Baglioni to himself. "The youth is the son of my old friend, and shall not come to any harm from which the arcana of medical science can preserve him. Besides, it is too insufferable an impertinence in Rappaccini, thus to snatch the lad out of my own hands, as I may say, and make use of him for his infernal experiments. This daughter of his! It shall be looked to. Perchance, most learned Rappaccini, I may foil you where you little dream of it!"

Meanwhile, Giovanni had pursued a circuitous route, and at length found himself at the door of his lodgings. As he crossed the threshold, he was met by old Lisabetta, who smirked and smiled, and was evidently desirous to attract his attention; vainly, however, as the ebullition of his feelings had momentarily subsided into a cold and dull vacuity. He turned his eyes full upon the withered face that was puckering itself into a smile, but seemed to behold it not. The old dame, therefore, laid her grasp upon his cloak.

"Signor!—Signor!" whispered she, still with a smile over the whole breadth of her visage, so that it looked not unlike a grotesque carving in wood, darkened by centuries—"Listen, Signor! There is a private entrance into the garden!"

"What do you say?" exclaimed Giovanni, turning quickly about, as if an inanimate thing should start into feverish life.—"A private entrance into Doctor Rappaccini's garden!"

"Hush! hush!—not so loud!" whispered Lisabetta, putting her hand over his mouth. "Yes; into the worshipful Doctor's garden, where you may see all his fine shrubbery. Many a young man in Padua would give gold to be admitted among those flowers."

Giovanni put a piece of gold into her hand.

"Show me the way," said he.

A surmise, probably excited by his conversation with Baglioni, crossed his mind, that this interposition of old Lisabetta might perchance be connected with the intrigue, whatever were its nature, in which the Professor seemed to suppose that Doctor Rappaccini was involving him. But such a suspicion, though it disturbed Giovanni, was inadequate to restrain him. The instant that he was aware of the possibility of approaching Beatrice, it seemed an absolute necessity of his existence to do so. It mattered not whether she were angel or demon; he was irrevocably within her sphere, and must obey the law that whirled him onward, in ever lessening circles, towards a result which he did not attempt to foreshadow. And yet, strange to say, there came across him a sudden doubt, whether this intense interest on his part were not delusory—whether it were really of so deep and positive a nature as to justify him in now thrusting himself into an incalculable position—whether it were not merely the fantasy of a young man's brain, only slightly, or not at all, connected with his heart!

He paused—hesitated—turned half about—but again went on. His withered guide led him along several obscure passages, and finally undid a door, through which, as it was opened, there came the sight and sound of rustling leaves, with the broken sunshine glimmering among them. Giovanni stepped forth, and forcing himself through the entanglement of a shrub that wreathed its tendrils over the hidden entrance, he stood beneath his own window, in the open area of Doctor Rappaccini's garden.

How often is it the case, that, when impossibilities have come to

pass, and dreams have condensed their misty substance into tangible
realities, we find ourselves calm, and even coldly self-possessed, amid
circumstances which it would have been a delirium of joy or agony
to anticipate! Fate delights to thwart us thus. Passion will choose his
own time to rush upon the scene, and lingers sluggishly behind, when
an appropriate adjustment of events would seem to summon his appearance. So was it now with Giovanni. Day after day, his pulses had
throbbed with feverish blood, at the improbable idea of an interview
with Beatrice, and of standing with her, face to face, in this very garden, basking in the Oriental sunshine of her beauty, and snatching
from her full gaze the mystery which he deemed the riddle of his own
existence. But now there was a singular and untimely equanimity
within his breast. He threw a glance around the garden to discover if
Beatrice or her father were present, and perceiving that he was alone,
began a critical observation of the plants.

The aspect of one and all of them dissatisfied him; their gorgeousness seemed fierce, passionate, and even unnatural. There was hardly
an individual shrub which a wanderer, straying by himself through a
forest, would not have been startled to find growing wild, as if an un-
earthly face had glared at him out of the thicket. Several, also, would
have shocked a delicate instinct by an appearance of artificialness, indicating that there had been such commixture, and, as it were, adul-
tery of various vegetable species, that the production was no longer
of God's making, but the monstrous offspring of man's depraved
fancy, glowing with only an evil mockery of beauty. They were probably the result of experiment, which, in one or two cases, had succeeded in mingling plants individually lovely into a compound possessing the questionable and ominous character that distinguished
the whole growth of the garden. In fine, Giovanni recognized but two
or three plants in the collection, and those of a kind that he well knew
to be poisonous. While busy with these contemplations, he heard the

rustling of a silken garment, and turning, beheld Beatrice emerging from beneath the sculptured portal.

Giovanni had not considered with himself what should be his deportment; whether he should apologize for his intrusion into the garden, or assume that he was there with the privity, at least, if not by the desire, of Doctor Rappaccini or his daughter. But Beatrice's manner placed him at his ease, though leaving him still in doubt by what agency he had gained admittance. She came lightly along the path, and met him near the broken fountain. There was surprise in her face, but brightened by a simple and kind expression of pleasure.

"You are a connoisseur in flowers, Signor," said Beatrice with a smile, alluding to the bouquet which he had flung her from the window. "It is no marvel, therefore, if the sight of my father's rare collection has tempted you to take a nearer view. If he were here, he could tell you many strange and interesting facts as to the nature and habits of these shrubs, for he has spent a life-time in such studies, and this garden is his world."

"And yourself, lady"—observed Giovanni—"if fame says true— you, likewise, are deeply skilled in the virtues indicated by these rich blossoms, and these spicy perfumes. Would you deign to be my instructress, I should prove an apter scholar than if taught by Signor Rappaccini himself."

"Are there such idle rumors?" asked Beatrice, with the music of a pleasant laugh. "Do people say that I am skilled in my father's science of plants? What a jest is there! No; though I have grown up among these flowers, I know no more of them than their hues and perfume; and sometimes, methinks I would fain rid myself of even that small knowledge. There are many flowers here, and those not the least brilliant, that shock and offend me, when they meet my eye. But, pray, Signor, do not believe these stories about my science. Believe nothing of me save what you see with your own eyes."

"And must I believe all that I have seen with my own eyes?" asked Giovanni pointedly, while the recollection of former scenes made him shrink. "No, Signora, you demand too little of me. Bid me believe nothing, save what comes from your own lips."

It would appear that Beatrice understood him. There came a deep flush to her cheek; but she looked full into Giovanni's eyes, and responded to his gaze of uneasy suspicion with a queen-like haughtiness.

"I do so bid you, Signor!" she replied. "Forget whatever you may have fancied in regard to me. If true to the outward senses, still it may be false in its essence. But the words of Beatrice Rappaccini's lips are true from the depths of the heart outward. Those you may believe!"

A fervor glowed in her whole aspect, and beamed upon Giovanni's consciousness like the light of truth itself. But while she spoke, there was a fragrance in the atmosphere around her, rich and delightful, though evanescent, yet which the young man, from an indefinable reluctance, scarcely dared to draw into his lungs. It might be the odor of the flowers. Could it be Beatrice's breath, which thus embalmed her words with a strange richness, as if by steeping them in her heart? A faintness passed like a shadow over Giovanni, and flitted away; he seemed to gaze through the beautiful girl's eyes into her transparent soul, and felt no more doubt or fear.

The tinge of passion that had colored Beatrice's manner vanished; she became gay, and appeared to derive a pure delight from her communion with the youth, not unlike what the maiden of a lonely island might have felt, conversing with a voyager from the civilized world. Evidently her experience of life had been confined within the limits of that garden. She talked now about matters as simple as the daylight or summer-clouds, and now asked questions in reference to the city, or Giovanni's distant home, his friends, his mother, and his sisters; questions indicating such seclusion, and such lack of familiarity with modes and forms, that Giovanni responded as if to an infant. Her spirit gushed out before him like a fresh rill, that was just catching its first glimpse of the sunlight, and wondering at the reflections of earth and sky which were flung into its bosom. There came thoughts, too, from a deep source, and fantasies of a gem-like brilliancy, as if diamonds and rubies sparkled upward among the bubbles of the fountain. Ever and anon, there gleamed across the young man's mind a sense of wonder, that he should be walking side by side with the being who had so wrought upon his imagination—whom he had idealized in such hues of terror—in whom he had positively witnessed such manifestations of dreadful attributes—that he should be conversing with Beatrice like a brother, and should find her so human and so maiden-like. But such reflections were only momentary; the effect of her character was too real, not to make itself familiar at once.

In this free intercourse, they had strayed through the garden, and now, after many turns among its avenues, were come to the shattered fountain, beside which grew the magnificent shrub with its treasury of glowing blossoms. A fragrance was diffused from it, which Giovanni recognized as identical with that which he had attributed to Beatrice's breath, but incomparably more powerful. As her eyes fell upon it, Giovanni beheld her press her hand to her bosom, as if her heart were throbbing suddenly and painfully.

"For the first time in my life," murmured she, addressing the shrub, "I had forgotten thee!"

"I remember, Signora," said Giovanni, "that you once promised to reward me with one of these living gems for the bouquet, which I had the happy boldness to fling to your feet. Permit me now to pluck it as a memorial of this interview."

He made a step towards the shrub, with extended hand. But Beatrice darted forward, uttering a shriek that went through his heart like a dagger. She caught his hand, and drew it back with the whole force of her slender figure. Giovanni felt her touch thrilling through his fibres.

"Touch it not!" exclaimed she, in a voice of agony. "Not for thy life! It is fatal!"

Then, hiding her face, she fled from him, and vanished beneath the sculptured portal. As Giovanni followed her with his eyes, he beheld the emaciated figure and pale intelligence of Doctor Rappaccini, who had been watching the scene, he knew not how long, within the shadow of the entrance.

No sooner was Guasconti alone in his chamber, than the image of Beatrice came back to his passionate musings, invested with all the witchery that had been gathering around it ever since his first glimpse of her, and now likewise imbued with a tender warmth of girlish womanhood. She was human: her nature was endowed with all gentle and feminine qualities; she was worthiest to be worshipped; she was capable, surely, on her part, of the height and heroism of love. Those tokens, which he had hitherto considered as proofs of a frightful peculiarity in her physical and moral system, were now either forgotten, or, by the subtle sophistry of passion, transmuted into a golden crown of enchantment, rendering Beatrice the more admirable, by so much as she was the more unique. Whatever had looked ugly, was now beautiful; or, if incapable of such a change, it stole away and hid itself among those shapeless half-ideas, which throng the dim region beyond the daylight of our perfect consciousness. Thus did he spend the night, nor fell asleep, until the dawn had begun to awake the slumbering flowers in Doctor Rappaccini's garden, whither Giovanni's dreams doubtless led him. Up rose the sun in his due season, and flinging his beams upon the young man's eyelids, awoke him to a sense of pain. When thoroughly aroused, he became sensible of a burning and tingling agony in his hand—in his right hand—the very hand which Beatrice had grasped in her own, when he was on the point of plucking one of the gem-like flowers. On the back of that hand there was now a purple print, like that of four small fingers, and the likeness of a slender thumb upon his wrist.

Oh, how stubbornly does love—or even that cunning semblance of love which flourishes in the imagination, but strikes no depth of root into the heart—how stubbornly does it hold its faith, until the moment come, when it is doomed to vanish into thin mist! Giovanni wrapt a handkerchief about his hand, and wondered what evil thing had stung him, and soon forgot his pain in a reverie of Beatrice.

After the first interview, a second was in the inevitable course of what we call fate. A third; a fourth; and a meeting with Beatrice in the garden was no longer an incident in Giovanni's daily life, but the whole space in which he might be said to live; for the anticipation and memory of that ecstatic hour made up the remainder. Nor was it otherwise with the daughter of Rappaccini. She watched for the youth's appearance, and flew to his side with confidence as unreserved as if they had been playmates from early infancy—as if they were such playmates still. If, by any unwonted chance, he failed to come at the appointed moment, she stood beneath the window, and sent up the rich sweetness of her tones to float around him in his chamber, and echo and reverberate throughout his heart—"Giovanni! Giovanni! Why tarriest thou? Come down!"—And down he hastened into that Eden of poisonous flowers.

But, with all this intimate familiarity, there was still a reserve in Beatrice's demeanor, so rigidly and invariably sustained, that the idea of infringing it scarcely occurred to his imagination. By all appreciable signs, they loved; they had looked love, with eyes that conveyed the holy secret from the depths of one soul into the depths of the other, as if it were too sacred to be whispered by the way; they had even spoken love, in those gushes of passion when their spirits darted forth in articulated breath, like tongues of long-hidden flame; and yet there had been no seal of lips, no clasp of hands, nor any slightest caress, such as love claims and hallows. He had never touched one of the gleaming ringlets of her hair; her garment—so marked was the physical barrier between them—had never been waved against him by a breeze. On the few occasions when Giovanni had seemed tempted to overstep the limit, Beatrice grew so sad, so stern, and withal wore such a look of desolate separation, shuddering at itself, that not a spoken word was requisite to repel him. At such times, he was startled at the horrible suspicions that rose, monster-like, out of the caverns of his heart, and stared him in the face; his love grew thin and faint as the morning-mist; his doubts alone had substance. But when Beatrice's face brightened again, after the momentary shadow, she was transformed at once from the mysterious, questionable being, whom he had watched with so much awe and horror; she was now the beautiful and unsophisticated girl, whom he felt that his spirit knew with a certainty beyond all other knowledge.

A considerable time had now passed since Giovanni's last meeting with Baglioni. One morning, however, he was disagreeably surprised by a visit from the Professor, whom he had scarcely thought of for whole weeks, and would willingly have forgotten still longer. Given up, as he had long been, to a pervading excitement, he could tolerate no companions, except upon condition of their perfect sympathy with his present state of feeling. Such sympathy was not to be expected from Professor Baglioni.

The visitor chatted carelessly, for a few moments, about the gossip of the city and the University, and then took up another topic.

"I have been reading an old classic author lately," said he, "and met with a story that strangely interested me. Possibly you may remember it. It is of an Indian prince, who sent a beautiful woman as a present to Alexander the Great. She was as lovely as the dawn, and gorgeous as the sunset; but what especially distinguished her was a certain rich perfume in her breath—richer than a garden of Persian roses. Alexander, as was natural to a youthful conqueror, fell in love at first sight with this magnificent stranger. But a certain sage physician, happening to be present, discovered a terrible secret in regard to her."

"And what was that?" asked Giovanni, turning his eyes downward to avoid those of the Professor.

"That this lovely woman," continued Baglioni, with emphasis, "had been nourished with poisons from her birth upward, until her whole nature was so imbued with them, that she herself had become the deadliest poison in existence. Poison was her element of life. With that rich perfume of her breath, she blasted the very air. Her love would have been poison!—her embrace death! Is not this a marvellous tale?"

"A childish fable," answered Giovanni, nervously starting from his chair. "I marvel how your worship finds time to read such nonsense, among your graver studies."

"By the bye," said the Professor, looking uneasily about him, "what singular fragrance is this in your apartment? Is it the perfume of your gloves? It is faint, but delicious, and yet, after all, by no means agreeable. Were I to breathe it long, methinks it would make me ill. It is like the breath of a flower—but I see no flowers in the chamber."

"Nor are there any," replied Giovanni, who had turned pale as the Professor spoke; "nor, I think, is there any fragrance, except in your worship's imagination. Odors, being a sort of element combined of the sensual and the spiritual, are apt to deceive us in this manner. The recollection of a perfume—the bare idea of it—may easily be mistaken for a present reality."

"Aye; but my sober imagination does not often play such tricks," said Baglioni; "and were I to fancy any kind of odor, it would be that of some vile apothecary drug, wherewith my fingers are likely enough to be imbued. Our worshipful friend Rappaccini, as I have heard, tinctures his medicaments with odors richer than those of Araby. Doubtless, likewise, the fair and learned Signora Beatrice would minister to her patients with draughts as sweet as a maiden's breath. But wo to him that sips them!"

Giovanni's face evinced many contending emotions. The tone in which the Professor alluded to the pure and lovely daughter of Rappaccini was a torture to his soul; and yet, the intimation of a view of her character, opposite to his own, gave instantaneous distinctness to a thousand dim suspicions, which now grinned at him like so many demons. But he strove hard to quell them, and to respond to Baglioni with a true lover's perfect faith.

"Signor Professor," said he, "you were my father's friend—perchance, too, it is your purpose to act a friendly part towards his son. I would fain feel nothing towards you, save respect and deference. But I pray you to observe, Signor, that there is one subject on which we must not speak. You know not the Signora Beatrice. You cannot, therefore, estimate the wrong—the blasphemy, I may even say—that is offered to her character by a light or injurious word."

"Giovanni!—my poor Giovanni!" answered the Professor, with a calm expression of pity, "I know this wretched girl far better than yourself. You shall hear the truth in respect to the poisoner Rappaccini, and his poisonous daughter. Yes; poisonous as she is beautiful! Listen; for even should you do violence to my grey hairs, it shall not silence me. That old fable of the Indian woman has become a truth, by the deep and deadly science of Rappaccini, and in the person of the lovely Beatrice!"

Giovanni groaned and hid his face.

"Her father," continued Baglioni, "was not restrained by natural affection from offering up his child, in this horrible manner, as the victim of his insane zeal for science. For—let us do him justice—he is as true a man of science as ever distilled his own heart in an alembic.

What, then, will be your fate? Beyond a doubt, you are selected as the material of some new experiment. Perhaps the result is to be death— perhaps a fate more awful still! Rappaccini, with what he calls the interest of science before his eyes, will hesitate at nothing."

"It is a dream!" muttered Giovanni to himself, "surely it is a dream!"

"But," resumed the Professor, "be of good cheer, son of my friend! It is not yet too late for the rescue. Possibly, we may even succeed in bringing back this miserable child within the limits of ordinary nature, from which her father's madness has estranged her. Behold this little silver vase! It was wrought by the hands of the renowned Benvenuto Cellini, and is well worthy to be a love-gift to the fairest dame in Italy. But its contents are invaluable. One little sip of this antidote would have rendered the most virulent poisons of the Borgias innocuous. Doubt not that it will be as efficacious against those of Rappaccini. Bestow the vase, and the precious liquid within it, on your Beatrice, and hopefully await the result."

Baglioni laid a small, exquisitely wrought silver phial on the table, and withdrew, leaving what he had said to produce its effect upon the young man's mind.

"We will thwart Rappaccini yet!" thought he, chuckling to himself, as he descended the stairs. "But, let us confess the truth of him, he is a wonderful man!—a wonderful man indeed! A vile empiric, however, in his practice, and therefore not to be tolerated by those who respect the good old rules of the medical profession!"

Throughout Giovanni's whole acquaintance with Beatrice, he had occasionally, as we have said, been haunted by dark surmises as to her character. Yet, so thoroughly had she made herself felt by him as a simple, natural, most affectionate and guileless creature, that the image now held up by Professor Baglioni, looked as strange and incredible, as if it were not in accordance with his own original conception.

True, there were ugly recollections connected with his first glimpses of the beautiful girl; he could not quite forget the bouquet that withered in her grasp, and the insect that perished amid the sunny air, by no ostensible agency, save the fragrance of her breath. These incidents, however, dissolving in the pure light of her character, had no longer the efficacy of facts, but were acknowledged as mistaken fantasies, by whatever testimony of the senses they might appear to be substantiated. There is something truer and more real, than what we can see with the eyes, and touch with the finger. On such better evidence, had Giovanni founded his confidence in Beatrice, though rather by the necessary force of her high attributes, than by any deep and generous faith, on his part. But, now, his spirit was incapable of sustaining itself at the height to which the early enthusiasm of passion had exalted it; he fell down, grovelling among earthly doubts, and defiled therewith the pure whiteness of Beatrice's image. Not that he gave her up; he did but distrust. He resolved to institute some decisive test that should satisfy him, once for all, whether there were those dreadful peculiarities in her physical nature, which could not be supposed to exist without some corresponding monstrosity of soul. His eyes, gazing down afar, might have deceived him as to the lizard, the insect, and the flowers. But if he could witness, at the distance of a few paces, the sudden blight of one fresh and healthful flower in Beatrice's hand, there would be room for no further question. With this idea, he hastened to the florist's, and purchased a bouquet that was still gemmed with the morning dew-drops.

It was now the customary hour of his daily interview with Beatrice. Before descending into the garden, Giovanni failed not to look at his figure in the mirror; a vanity to be expected in a beautiful young man, yet, as displaying itself at that troubled and feverish moment, the token of a certain shallowness of feeling and insincerity of character. He did gaze, however, and said to himself, that his features had never before possessed so rich a grace, nor his eyes such vivacity, nor his cheeks so warm a hue of superabundant life.

"At least," thought he, "her poison has not yet insinuated itself into my system. I am no flower to perish in her grasp!"

With that thought, he turned his eyes on the bouquet, which he had never once laid aside from his hand. A thrill of indefinable horror shot through his frame, on perceiving that those dewy flowers were already beginning to droop; they wore the aspect of things that had been fresh and lovely, yesterday. Giovanni grew white as marble, and stood motionless before the mirror, staring at his own reflection there, as at the likeness of something frightful. He remembered Baglioni's remark about the fragrance that seemed to pervade the chamber. It must have been the poison in his breath! Then he shuddered— shuddered at himself! Recovering from his stupor, he began to watch, with curious eye, a spider that was busily at work, hanging its web from the antique cornice of the apartment, crossing and re-crossing the artful system of interwoven lines, as vigorous and active a spider as ever dangled from an old ceiling. Giovanni bent towards the insect, and emitted a deep, long breath. The spider suddenly ceased its toil; the web vibrated with a tremor originating in the body of the small artizan. Again Giovanni sent forth a breath, deeper, longer, and imbued with a venomous feeling out of his heart; he knew not whether he were wicked or only desperate. The spider made a convulsive gripe with his limbs, and hung dead across the window.

"Accursed! Accursed!" muttered Giovanni, addressing himself. "Hast thou grown so poisonous, that this deadly insect perishes by thy breath?"

At that moment, a rich, sweet voice came floating up from the garden:—

"Giovanni! Giovanni! It is past the hour! Why tarriest thou! Come down!"

"Yes," muttered Giovanni again. "She is the only being whom my breath may not slay! Would that it might!"

He rushed down, and in an instant, was standing before the bright and loving eyes of Beatrice. A moment ago, his wrath and despair had been so fierce that he could have desired nothing so much as to wither her by a glance. But, with her actual presence, there came influences which had too real an existence to be at once shaken off; recollections of the delicate and benign power of her feminine nature, which had so often enveloped him in a religious calm; recollections of many a holy and passionate outgush of her heart, when the pure fountain had been unsealed from its depths, and made visible in its transparency to his mental eye; recollections which, had Giovanni known how to estimate them, would have assured him that all this ugly mystery was but an earthly illusion, and that, whatever mist of evil might seem to have gathered over her, the real Beatrice was a heavenly angel. Incapable as he was of such high faith, still her presence had not utterly lost its magic. Giovanni's rage was quelled into an aspect of sullen insensibility. Beatrice, with a quick spiritual sense, immediately felt that there was a gulf of blackness between them, which neither he nor she could pass. They walked on together, sad and silent, and came thus to the marble fountain, and to its pool of water on the ground, in the midst of which grew the shrub that bore gem-like blossoms. Giovanni was affrighted at the eager enjoyment—the appetite, as it were—with which he found himself inhaling the fragrance of the flowers.

"Beatrice," asked he abruptly, "whence came this shrub?"

"My father created it," answered she, with simplicity.

"Created it! created it!" repeated Giovanni. "What mean you, Beatrice?"

"He is a man fearfully acquainted with the secrets of nature," replied Beatrice; "and, at the hour when I first drew breath, this plant sprang from the soil, the offspring of his science, of his intellect, while I was but his earthly child. Approach it not!" continued she, observing with terror that Giovanni was drawing nearer to the shrub. "It has qualities that you little dream of. But I, dearest Giovanni,—I grew up and blossomed with the plant, and was nourished with its breath. It was my sister, and I loved it with a human affection: for—alas! hast thou not suspected it? there was an awful doom."

Here Giovanni frowned so darkly upon her that Beatrice paused and trembled. But her faith in his tenderness reassured her, and made her blush that she had doubted for an instant.

"There was an awful doom," she continued,—"the effect of my father's fatal love of science—which estranged me from all society of my kind. Until Heaven sent thee, dearest Giovanni, Oh! how lonely was thy poor Beatrice!"

"Was it a hard doom?" asked Giovanni, fixing his eyes upon her.

"Only of late have I known how hard it was," answered she tenderly. "Oh, yes; but my heart was torpid, and therefore quiet."

Giovanni's rage broke forth from his sullen gloom like a lightning-flash out of a dark cloud.

"Accursed one!" cried he, with venomous scorn and anger. "And finding thy solitude wearisome, thou hast severed me, likewise, from all the warmth of life, and enticed me into thy region of unspeakable horror!"

"Giovanni!" exclaimed Beatrice, turning her large bright eyes upon his face. The force of his words had not found its way into her mind; she was merely thunder-struck.

"Yes, poisonous thing!" repeated Giovanni, beside himself with passion. "Thou hast done it! Thou hast blasted me! Thou hast filled my veins with poison! Thou hast made me as hateful, as ugly, as loathsome and deadly a creature as thyself,—a world's wonder of hideous monstrosity! Now—if our breath be happily as fatal to ourselves as to all others—let us join our lips in one kiss of unutterable hatred, and so die!"

"What has befallen me?" murmured Beatrice, with a low moan out of her heart, "Holy Virgin pity me, a poor heartbroken child!"

"Thou! Dost thou pray?" cried Giovanni, still with the same fiendish scorn. "Thy very prayers, as they come from thy lips, taint the atmosphere with death. Yes, yes; let us pray! Let us to church, and dip our fingers in the holy water at the portal! They that come after us will perish as by a pestilence. Let us sign crosses in the air! It will be scattering curses abroad in the likeness of holy symbols!"

"Giovanni," said Beatrice calmly, for her grief was beyond passion, "why dost thou join thyself with me thus in those terrible words? I, it is true, am the horrible thing thou namest me. But thou!—what hast thou to do, save with one other shudder at my hideous misery, to go forth out of the garden and mingle with thy race, and forget that there ever crawled on earth such a monster as poor Beatrice?"

"Dost thou pretend ignorance?" asked Giovanni, scowling upon her. "Behold! This power have I gained from the pure daughter of Rappaccini!"

There was a swarm of summer-insects flitting through the air, in search of the food promised by the flower-odors of the fatal garden. They circled round Giovanni's head, and were evidently attracted towards him by the same influence which had drawn them, for an instant, within the sphere of several of the shrubs. He sent forth a breath among them, and smiled bitterly at Beatrice, as at least a score of the insects fell dead upon the ground.

"I see it! I see it!" shrieked Beatrice. "It is my father's fatal science! No, no, Giovanni; it was not I! Never, never! I dreamed only to love thee, and be with thee a little time, and so to let thee pass away, leaving but thine image in mine heart. For, Giovanni—believe it—though my body be nourished with poison, my spirit is God's creature, and craves love as its daily food. But my father!—he has united us in this fearful sympathy. Yes; spurn me!—tread upon me!—kill me! Oh, what is death, after such words as thine? But it was not I! Not for a world of bliss would I have done it!"

Giovanni's passion had exhausted itself in its outburst from his lips. There now came across him a sense, mournful, and not without tenderness, of the intimate and peculiar relationship between Beatrice and himself. They stood, as it were, in an utter solitude, which would be made none the less solitary by the densest throng of human life. Ought not, then, the desert of humanity around them to press this insulated pair closer together? If they should be cruel to one another, who was there to be kind to them? Besides, thought Giovanni, might there not still be a hope of his returning within the limits of ordinary nature, and leading Beatrice—the redeemed Beatrice—by the hand? Oh, weak, and selfish, and unworthy spirit, that could dream of an earthly union and earthly happiness as possible, after such deep love had been so bitterly wronged as was Beatrice's love by Giovanni's blighting words! No, no; there could be no such hope. She must pass heavily, with that broken heart, across the borders of Time—she must bathe her hurts in some fount of Paradise, and forget her grief in the light of immortality—and *there* be well!

But Giovanni did not know it.

"Dear Beatrice," said he, approaching her, while she shrank away, as always at his approach, but now with a different impulse—"dearest Beatrice, our fate is not yet so desperate. Behold! There is a medicine, potent, as a wise physician has assured me, and almost divine in its efficacy. It is composed of ingredients the most opposite to those by which thy awful father has brought this calamity upon thee and me. It is distilled of blessed herbs. Shall we not quaff it together, and thus be purified from evil?"

"Give it me!" said Beatrice, extending her hand to receive the little silver phial which Giovanni took from his bosom. She added, with a peculiar emphasis: "I will drink—but do thou await the result."

She put Baglioni's antidote to her lips; and, at the same moment, the figure of Rappaccini emerged from the portal, and came slowly towards the marble fountain. As he drew near, the pale man of science seemed to gaze with a triumphant expression at the beautiful youth and maiden, as might an artist who should spend his life in achieving a picture or a group of statuary, and finally be satisfied with his success. He paused—his bent form grew erect with conscious power, he spread out his hands over them, in the attitude of a father imploring a blessing upon his children. But those were the same hands that had thrown poison into the stream of their lives! Giovanni trembled. Beatrice shuddered nervously, and pressed her hand upon her heart.

"My daughter," said Rappaccini, "thou art no longer lonely in the world! Pluck one of those precious gems from thy sister shrub, and bid thy bridegroom wear it in his bosom. It will not harm him now! My science, and the sympathy between thee and him, have so wrought within his system, that he now stands apart from common men, as thou dost, daughter of my pride and triumph, from ordinary women. Pass on, then, through the world, most dear to one another, and dreadful to all besides!"

"My father," said Beatrice, feebly—and still, as she spoke, she kept her hand upon her heart—"wherefore didst thou inflict this miserable doom upon thy child?"

"Miserable!" exclaimed Rappaccini. "What mean you, foolish girl? Dost thou deem it misery to be endowed with marvellous gifts, against which no power nor strength could avail an enemy? Misery, to be able to quell the mightiest with a breath? Misery, to be as terrible as thou art beautiful? Wouldst thou, then, have preferred the condition of a weak woman, exposed to all evil, and capable of none?"

"I would fain have been loved, not feared," murmured Beatrice, sinking down upon the ground.—"But now it matters not; I am going, father, where the evil, which thou hast striven to mingle with my being, will pass away like a dream—like the fragrance of these poisonous flowers, which will no longer taint my breath among the flowers of Eden. Farewell, Giovanni! Thy words of hatred are like lead within my heart—but they, too, will fall away as I ascend. Oh, was there not, from the first, more poison in thy nature than in mine?"

To Beatrice—so radically had her earthly part been wrought upon by Rappaccini's skill—as poison had been life, so the powerful antidote was death. And thus the poor victim of man's ingenuity and of thwarted nature, and of the fatality that attends all such efforts of perverted wisdom, perished there, at the feet of her father and Giovanni. Just at that moment, Professor Pietro Baglioni looked forth from the window, and called loudly, in a tone of triumph mixed with horror, to the thunder-stricken man of science:

"Rappaccini! Rappaccini! And is *this* the upshot of your experiment?"

The Old Manse

The Author Makes the Reader Acquainted with His Abode

B ETWEEN TWO TALL GATE-POSTS of rough-hewn stone, (the gate itself having fallen from its hinges, at some unknown epoch,) we beheld the gray front of the old parsonage, terminating the vista of an avenue of black-ash trees. It was now a twelvemonth since the funeral procession of the venerable clergyman, its last inhabitant, had turned from that gate-way towards the village burying-ground. The wheel-track, leading to the door, as well as the whole breadth of the avenue, was almost overgrown with grass, affording dainty mouthfuls to two or three vagrant cows, and an old white horse, who had his own living to pick up along the roadside. The glimmering shadows, that lay half-asleep between the door of the house and the public highway, were a kind of spiritual medium, seen through which, the edifice had not quite the aspect of belonging to the material world. Certainly it had little in common with those ordinary abodes, which stand so imminent upon the road that every passer-by can thrust his head, as it were, into the domestic circle. From these quiet windows, the figures of passing travellers looked too remote and dim to disturb the sense of privacy. In its near retirement, and accessible seclusion, it was the very spot for the residence of a clergyman; a man not estranged from human life, yet enveloped, in the midst of it, with a veil woven of intermingled gloom and brightness. It was worthy to have been one of the time-honored parsonages of England, in which, through many generations, a succession of holy occupants pass from youth to age, and bequeath each an inheritance of sanctity to pervade the house and hover over it, as with an atmosphere.

Nor, in truth, had the old Manse ever been prophaned by a lay occupant, until that memorable summer-afternoon when I entered it as my home. A priest had built it; a priest had succeeded to it; other priestly men, from time to time, had dwelt in it; and children, born in its chambers, had grown up to assume the priestly character. It was awful to reflect how many sermons must have been written there. The latest inhabitant alone—he, by whose translation to Paradise the dwelling was left vacant—had penned nearly three thousand discourses, besides the better, if not the greater number, that gushed living from his lips. How often, no doubt, had he paced to-and-fro along the avenue, attuning his meditations, to the sighs and gentle murmurs, and deep and solemn peals of the wind, among the lofty tops of the trees! In that variety of natural utterances, he could find something accordant with every passage of his sermon, were it of tenderness or reverential fear. The boughs over my head seemed shadowy with solemn thoughts, as well as with rustling leaves. I took shame to myself for having been so long a writer of idle stories, and ventured to hope that wisdom would descend upon me with the falling leaves of the avenue; and that I should light upon an intellectual treasure in the old Manse, well worth those hoards of long-hidden gold, which people seek for in moss-grown houses. Profound treatises of morality;—a layman's unprofessional, and therefore unprejudiced views of religion;—histories, (such as Bancroft might have written, had he taken up his abode here, as he once purposed,) bright with picture, gleaming over a depth of philosophic thought;—these were the works that might fitly have flowed from such a retirement. In the humblest event, I resolved at least to achieve a novel, that should evolve some deep lesson, and should possess physical substance enough to stand alone.

In furtherance of my design, and as if to leave me no pretext for not fulfilling it, there was, in the rear of the house, the most delightful little nook of a study that ever afforded its snug seclusion to a scholar. It was here that Emerson wrote 'Nature'; for he was then an inhabitant of the Manse, and used to watch the Assyrian dawn and the Paphian sunset and moonrise, from the summit of our eastern hill. When I first saw the room, its walls were blackened with the smoke of unnumbered years, and made still blacker by the grim prints of Puritan ministers that hung around. These worthies looked strangely like bad angels, or, at least, like men who had wrestled so continually and so sternly with the devil, that somewhat of his sooty fierceness had been imparted to their own visages. They had all vanished now. A cheerful coat of paint, and golden-tinted paper-hangings, lighted up the small apartment; while the shadow of a willow-tree, that swept against the overhanging eaves, attempered the cheery western sunshine. In place of the grim prints, there was the sweet and lovely head of one of Raphael's Madonnas, and two pleasant little pictures of the Lake of Como. The only other decorations were a purple vase of flowers, always fresh, and a bronze one containing graceful ferns. My books (few, and by no means choice; for they were chiefly such waifs as chance had thrown in my way) stood in order about the room, seldom to be disturbed.

The study had three windows, set with little, old-fashioned panes of glass, each with a crack across it. The two on the western side looked, or rather peeped, between the willow-branches, down into the orchard, with glimpses of the river through the trees. The third, facing northward, commanded a broader view of the river, at a spot where its hitherto obscure waters gleam forth into the light of history. It was at this window that the clergyman, who then dwelt in the Manse, stood watching the outbreak of a long and deadly struggle between two nations; he saw the irregular array of his parishioners on the farther side of the river, and the glittering line of the British, on the hither bank. He awaited, in an agony of suspense, the rattle of the musketry. It came—and there needed but a gentle wind to sweep the battle-smoke around this quiet house.

Perhaps the reader—whom I cannot help considering as my guest in the old Manse, and entitled to all courtesy in the way of sight-showing—perhaps he will choose to take a nearer view of the memorable spot. We stand now on the river's brink. It may well be called the Concord—the river of peace and quietness—for it is certainly the most unexcitable and sluggish stream that ever loitered, imperceptibly, towards its eternity, the sea. Positively, I had lived three weeks beside it, before it grew quite clear to my perception which way the current flowed. It never has a vivacious aspect, except when a north-western breeze is vexing its surface, on a sunshiny day. From the incurable indolence of its nature, the stream is happily incapable of becoming the slave of human ingenuity, as is the fate of so many a wild, free mountain-torrent. While all things else are compelled to subserve some useful purpose, it idles its sluggish life away, in lazy liberty, without turning a solitary spindle, or affording even water-power enough to grind the corn that grows upon its banks. The torpor of its movement allows it nowhere a bright pebbly shore, nor so much as a narrow strip of glistening sand, in any part of its course. It slumbers between broad prairies, kissing the long meadow-grass, and bathes the overhanging boughs of elder-bushes and willows, or the roots of elms and ash-trees, and clumps of maples. Flags and rushes grow along its plashy shore; the yellow water-lily spreads its broad, flat leaves on the margin; and the fragrant white pond-lily abounds, generally selecting a position just so far from the river's brink, that it cannot be grasped, save at the hazard of plunging in.

It is a marvel whence this perfect flower derives its loveliness and perfume, springing, as it does, from the black mud over which the river sleeps, and where lurk the slimy eel, and speckled frog, and the mud turtle, whom continual washing cannot cleanse. It is the very same black mud out of which the yellow lily sucks its obscene life and noisome odor. Thus we see, too, in the world, that some persons assimilate only what is ugly and evil from the same moral circumstances which supply good and beautiful results—the fragrance of celestial flowers—to the daily life of others.

The reader must not, from any testimony of mine, contract a dislike towards our slumberous stream. In the light of a calm and golden sunset, it becomes lovely beyond expression; the more lovely for the quietude that so well accords with the hour, when even the wind, after blustering all day long, usually hushes itself to rest. Each tree and rock, and every blade of grass, is distinctly imaged, and, however unsightly in reality, assumes ideal beauty in the reflection. The minutest things of earth, and the broad aspect of the firmament, are pictured equally without effort, and with the same felicity of success. All the sky glows downward at our feet; the rich clouds float through the unruffled bosom of the stream, like heavenly thoughts through a peaceful heart. We will not, then, malign our river as gross and impure, while it can glorify itself with so adequate a picture of the heaven that broods above it; or, if we remember its tawny hue and the muddiness of its bed, let it be a symbol that the earthliest human soul has an infinite spiritual capacity, and may contain the better world within its depths. But, indeed, the same lesson might be drawn out of any mud-puddle in the streets of a city—and, being taught us everywhere, it must be true.

Come; we have pursued a somewhat devious track, in our walk to the battle-ground. Here we are, at the point where the river was crossed by the old bridge, the possession of which was the immedi-ate object of the contest. On the hither side, grow two or three elms, throwing a wide circumference of shade, but which must have been planted at some period within the threescore years and ten, that have passed since the battle-day. On the farther shore, overhung by a clump of elder-bushes, we discern the stone abutment of the bridge. Look-ing down into the river, I once discovered some heavy fragments of the timbers, all green with half-a-century's growth of water-moss; for, during that length of time, the tramp of horses and human footsteps have ceased, along this ancient highway. The stream has here about the breadth of twenty strokes of a swimmer's arm; a space not too wide, when the bullets were whistling across. Old people, who dwell hereabouts, will point out the very spots, on the western bank, where our countrymen fell down and died; and, on this side of the river, an obelisk of granite has grown up from the soil that was fertilized with British blood. The monument, not more than twenty feet in height, is such as it befitted the inhabitants of a village to erect, in illustration of a matter of local interest, rather than what was suitable to commemo-rate an epoch of national history. Still, by the fathers of the village this famous deed was done; and their descendants might rightfully claim the privilege of building a memorial.

A humbler token of the fight, yet a more interesting one than the granite obelisk, may be seen close under the stonewall, which sep-arates the battle-ground from the precincts of the parsonage. It is the grave—marked by a small, moss-grown fragment of stone at the head, and another at the foot—the grave of two British soldiers, who were slain in the skirmish, and have ever since slept peacefully where Zechariah Brown and Thomas Davis buried them. Soon was their warfare ended;—a weary night-march from Boston—a rattling volley of musketry across the river;—and then these many years of rest! In the long procession of slain invaders, who passed into eternity from the battle-fields of the Revolution, these two nameless soldiers led the way.

Lowell, the poet, as we were once standing over this grave, told me a tradition in reference to one of the inhabitants below. The story has something deeply impressive, though its circumstances cannot altogether be reconciled with probability. A youth, in the service of the clergyman, happened to be chopping wood, that April morning, at the back door of the Manse; and when the noise of battle rang from side to side of the bridge, he hastened across the intervening field, to see what might be going forward. It is rather strange, by the way, that this lad should have been so diligently at work, when the whole population of town and county were startled out of their customary business, by the advance of the British troops. Be that as it might, the tradition says that the lad now left his task, and hurried to the battle-field, with the axe still in his hand. The British had by this time retreated—the Americans were in pursuit—and the late scene of strife was thus deserted by both parties. Two soldiers lay on the ground; one was a corpse; but, as the young New-Englander drew nigh, the other Briton raised himself painfully upon his hands and knees, and gave a ghastly stare into his face. The boy—it must have been a nervous impulse, without purpose, without thought, and betokening a sensitive and impressible nature, rather than a hardened one—the boy uplifted his axe, and dealt the wounded soldier a fierce and fatal blow upon the head.

I could wish that the grave might be opened; for I would fain know whether either of the skeleton soldiers have the mark of an axe in his skull. The story comes home to me like truth. Oftentimes, as an intellectual and moral exercise, I have sought to follow that poor youth through his subsequent career, and observe how his soul was tortured by the blood-stain, contracted, as it had been, before the long custom of war had robbed human life of its sanctity, and while it still seemed murderous to slay a brother man. This one circumstance has borne more fruit for me, than all that history tells us of the fight.

Many strangers come, in the summer-time, to view the battle-ground. For my own part, I have never found my imagination much excited by this, or any other scene of historic celebrity; nor would the placid margin of the river have lost any of its charm for me, had men never fought and died there. There is a wilder interest in the tract of land—perhaps a hundred yards in breadth—which extends between the battle-field and the northern face of our old Manse, with its contiguous avenue and orchard. Here, in some unknown age, before the white man came, stood an Indian village, convenient to the river, whence its inhabitants must have drawn so large a part of their subsistence. The site is identified by the spear and arrow-heads, the chisels, and other implements of war, labor, and the chase, which the plough turns up from the soil. You see a splinter of stone, half hidden beneath a sod; it looks like nothing worthy of note; but, if you have faith enough to pick it up—behold a relic! Thoreau, who has a strange faculty of finding what the Indians have left behind them, first set me on the search; and I afterwards enriched myself with some very perfect specimens, so rudely wrought that it seemed almost as if chance had fashioned them. Their great charm consists in this rudeness, and in the individuality of each article, so different from the productions of civilized machinery, which shapes everything on one pattern. There is an exquisite delight, too, in picking up, for one's self, an arrow-head that was dropt centuries ago, and has never been handled

since, and which we thus receive directly from the hand of the red
hunter, who purposed to shoot it at his game, or at an enemy. Such an
incident builds up again the Indian village, amid its encircling forest,
and recalls to life the painted chiefs and warriors, the squaws at their
household toil, and the children sporting among the wigwams; while
the little wind-rocked papoose swings from the branch of a tree. It
can hardly be told whether it is a joy or a pain, after such a momentary vision, to gaze around in the broad daylight of reality, and see
stone-fences, white houses, potatoe-fields, and men doggedly hoeing,
in their shirt-sleeves and homespun pantaloons. But this is nonsense.
The old Manse is better than a thousand wigwams.

The old Manse! We had almost forgotten it, but will return thither
through the orchard. This was set out by the last clergyman, in the
decline of his life, when the neighbors laughed at the hoary-headed
man for planting trees, from which he could have no prospect of
gathering fruit. Even had that been the case, there was only so much
the better motive for planting them, in the pure and unselfish hope of
benefitting his successors—an end so seldom achieved by more ambitious efforts. But the old minister, before reaching his patriarchal
age of ninety, ate the apples from this orchard during many years,
and added silver and gold to his annual stipend, by disposing of the
superfluity. It is pleasant to think of him, walking among the trees in
the quiet afternoons of early autumn, and picking up here and there
a windfall; while he observes how heavily the branches are weighed
down, and computes the number of empty flour-barrels that will be
filled by their burthen. He loved each tree, doubtless, as if it had been
his own child. An orchard has a relation to mankind, and readily con-
nects itself with matters of the heart. The trees possess a domestic
character; they have lost the wild nature of their forest-kindred, and
have grown humanized by receiving the care of man, as well as by
contributing to his wants. There is so much individuality of character,

too, among apple-trees, that it gives them an additional claim to be
the objects of human interest. One is harsh and crabbed in its manifestations; another gives us fruit as mild as charity. One is churlish
and illiberal, evidently grudging the few apples that it bears; another
exhausts itself in free-hearted benevolence. The variety of grotesque
shapes, into which apple-trees contort themselves, has its effect on
those who get acquainted with them; they stretch out their crooked
branches, and take such hold of the imagination that we remember
them as humorists and odd fellows. And what is more melancholy
than the old apple-trees, that linger about the spot where once stood
a homestead, but where there is now only a ruined chimney, rising
out of a grassy and weed-grown cellar? They offer their fruit to every
wayfarer—apples that are bitter-sweet with the moral of time's vicissitude.

I have met with no other such pleasant trouble in the world, as
that of finding myself, with only the two or three mouths which it was
my privilege to feed, the sole inheritor of the old clergyman's wealth
of fruits. Throughout the summer, there were cherries and currants;
and then came Autumn, with this immense burthen of apples, dropping them continually from his over-laden shoulders, as he trudged
along. In the stillest afternoon, if I listened, the thump of a great apple
was audible, falling without a breath of wind, from the mere necessity of perfect ripeness. And, besides, there were pear-trees, that flung
down bushels upon bushels of heavy pears, and peach-trees, which,
in a good year, tormented me with peaches, neither to be eaten nor
kept, nor, without labor and perplexity, to be given away. The idea
of an infinite generosity and exhaustless bounty, on the part of our
Mother Nature, was well worth obtaining through such cares as these.
That feeling can be enjoyed in perfection only by the natives of the
summer islands, where the breadfruit, the cocoa, the palm, and the
orange, grow spontaneously, and hold forth the ever-ready meal; but,

likewise, almost as well, by a man long habituated to city-life, who plunges into such a solitude as that of the old Manse, where he plucks the fruit of trees that he did not plant, and which therefore, to my heterodox taste, bear the closest resemblance to those that grew in Eden. It has been an apophthegm, these five thousand years, that toil sweetens the bread it earns. For my part, (speaking from hard experience, acquired while belaboring the rugged furrows of Brook Farm,) I relish best the free gifts of Providence.

Not that it can be disputed, that the light toil, requisite to cultivate a moderately sized garden, imparts such zest to kitchen-vegetables as is never found in those of the market-gardener. Childless men, if they would know something of the bliss of paternity, should plant a seed— be it squash, bean, Indian corn, or perhaps a mere flower, or worthless weed—should plant it with their own hands, and nurse it from infancy to maturity, altogether by their own care. If there be not too many of them, each individual plant becomes an object of separate interest. My garden, that skirted the avenue of the Manse, was of precisely the right extent. An hour or two of morning labor was all that it required. But I used to visit and re-visit it, a dozen times a day, and stand in deep contemplation over my vegetable progeny, with a love that nobody could share nor conceive of, who had never taken part in the process of creation. It was one of the most bewitching sights in the world, to observe a hill of beans thrusting aside the soil, or a row of early peas, just peeping forth sufficiently to trace a line of delicate green. Later in the season, the humming-birds were attracted by the blossoms of a peculiar variety of bean; and they were a joy to me, those little spiritual visitants, for deigning to sip airy food out of my nectar-cups. Multitudes of bees used to bury themselves in the yellow blossoms of the summer-squashes. This, too, was a deep satisfaction; although, when they had laden themselves with sweets, they flew away to some unknown hive, which would give back nothing in requital of what my garden had contributed. But I was glad thus to fling a benefaction upon the passing breeze, with the certainty that somebody must profit by it, and that there would be a little more honey in the world, to allay the sourness and bitterness which mankind is always complaining of. Yes, indeed; my life was the sweeter for that honey.

Speaking of summer-squashes, I must say a word of their beautiful and varied forms. They presented an endless diversity of urns and vases, shallow or deep, scalloped or plain, moulded in patterns which a sculptor would do well to copy, since Art has never invented anything more graceful. A hundred squashes in the garden were worthy—in my eyes, at least—of being rendered indestructible in marble. If ever Providence (but I know it never will) should assign me a superfluity of gold, part of it shall be expended for a service of plate, or most delicate porcelain, to be wrought into the shapes of summer-squashes, gathered from vines which I will plant with my own hands. As dishes for containing vegetables, they would be peculiarly appropriate.

But, not merely the squeamish love of the Beautiful was gratified by my toil in the kitchen-garden. There was a hearty enjoyment, likewise, in observing the growth of the crook-necked winter squashes, from the first little bulb, with the withered blossom adhering to it, until they lay strewn upon the soil, big, round fellows, hiding their heads beneath the leaves, but turning up their great yellow rotundities to the noontide sun. Gazing at them, I felt that, by my agency, something worth living for had been done. A new substance was borne into the world. They were real and tangible existences, which the mind could seize hold of and rejoice in. A cabbage, too,—especially the early Dutch cabbage, which swells to a monstrous circumference, until its ambitious heart often bursts asunder,—is a matter to be proud of, when we can claim a share with the earth and sky in producing it. But, after all, the hugest pleasure is reserved, until these vegetable children of ours are smoking on the table, and we, like Saturn, make a meal of them.

What with the river, the battle-field, the orchard, and the garden, the reader begins to despair of finding his way back into the old Manse. But, in agreeable weather, it is the truest hospitality to keep him out of doors. I never grew quite acquainted with my habitation, till a long spell of sulky rain had confined me beneath its roof. There could not be a more sombre aspect of external Nature, than as then seen from the windows of my study. The great willow-tree had caught, and retained among its leaves, a whole cataract of water, to be shaken down, at intervals, by the frequent gusts of wind. All day long, and for a week together, the rain was drip-drip-dripping and splash-splash-splashing from the eaves, and bubbling and foaming into the tubs beneath the spouts. The old, unpainted shingles of the house and outbuildings were black with moisture; and the mosses, of ancient growth upon the walls, looked green and fresh, as if they were the newest things and after-thought of Time. The usually mirrored surface of the river was blurred by an infinity of rain-drops; the whole landscape had a completely water-soaked appearance, conveying the impression that the earth was wet through, like a sponge; while the summit of a wooded hill, about a mile distant, was enveloped in a dense mist, where the demon of the tempest seemed to have his abiding-place, and to be plotting still direr inclemencies.

Nature has no kindness—no hospitality—during a rain. In the fiercest heat of sunny days, she retains a secret mercy, and welcomes the wayfarer to shady nooks of the woods, whither the sun cannot penetrate; but she provides no shelter against her storms. It makes us shiver to think of those deep, umbrageous recesses—those overshadowing banks—where we found such enjoyment during the sultry afternoons. Not a twig of foliage there, but would dash a little shower into our faces. Looking reproachfully towards the impenetrable sky—if sky there be, above that dismal uniformity of cloud—we are apt to murmur against the whole system of the universe, since it involves the extinction of so many summer days, in so short a life, by the hissing and spluttering rain. In such spells of weather—and, it is to be supposed, such weather came—Eve's bower in Paradise must have been but a cheerless and aguish kind of shelter, nowise comparable to the old parsonage, which had resources of its own, to beguile the week's imprisonment. The idea of sleeping on a couch of wet roses!

Happy the man who, in a rainy day, can betake himself to a huge garret, stored, like that of the Manse, with lumber that each generation has left behind it, from a period before the Revolution. Our garret was an arched hall, dimly illuminated through small and dusty windows; it was but a twilight at the best; and there were nooks, or rather caverns of deep obscurity, the secrets of which I never learned, being too reverent of their dust and cobwebs. The beams and rafters, roughly hewn, and with strips of bark still on them, and the rude masonry of the chimneys, made the garret look wild and uncivilized; an aspect unlike what was seen elsewhere, in the quiet and decorous old house. But, on one side, there was a little white-washed apartment, which bore the traditionary title of the Saints' Chamber, because holy men, in their youth, had slept, and studied, and prayed there. With its elevated retirement, its one window, its small fireplace, and its closet, convenient for an oratory, it was the very spot where a young man might inspire himself with solemn enthusiasm, and cherish saintly dreams. The occupants, at various epochs, had left brief records and ejaculations, inscribed upon the walls. There, too, hung a tattered and shrivelled roll of canvass, which, on inspection, proved to be the forcibly wrought picture of a clergyman, in wig, band, and gown, holding a Bible in his hand. As I turned his face towards the light, he eyed me with an air of authority such as men of his profession seldom assume, in our days. The original had been pastor of the parish, more than a century ago, a friend of Whitefield, and almost his equal in fervid eloquence. I bowed before the effigy of the dignified divine, and felt as if I had now met face to face with the ghost, by whom, as there was reason to apprehend, the Manse was haunted.

Houses of any antiquity, in New England, are so invariably possessed with spirits, that the matter seems hardly worth alluding to. Our ghost used to heave deep sighs in a particular corner of the parlor; and sometimes rustled paper, as if he were turning over a sermon, in the long upper entry;—where, nevertheless, he was invisible, in spite of the bright moonshine that fell through the eastern window. Not improbably, he wished me to edit and publish a selection from a chest full of manuscript discourses, that stood in the garret. Once, while Hillard and other friends sat talking with us in the twilight, there came a rustling noise, as of a minister's silk gown, sweeping through the very midst of the company, so closely as almost to brush against the chairs. Still, there was nothing visible. A yet stranger business was that of a ghostly servant-maid, who used to be heard in the kitchen, at deepest midnight, grinding coffee, cooking, ironing—performing, in short, all kinds of domestic labor—although no traces of anything accomplished could be detected, the next morning. Some neglected duty of her servitude—some ill-starched ministerial band—disturbed the poor damsel in her grave, and kept her at work without any wages.

But, to return from this digression. A part of my predecessor's library was stored in the garret; no unfit receptacle, indeed, for such dreary trash as comprised the greater number of volumes. The old books would have been worth nothing at an auction. In this venerable garret, however, they possessed an interest quite apart from their literary value, as heirlooms, many of which had been transmitted down through a series of consecrated hands, from the days of the mighty

Puritan divines. Autographs of famous names were to be seen, in faded ink, on some of their fly-leaves; and there were marginal observations, or interpolated pages closely covered with manuscript, in illegible short-hand, perhaps concealing matter of profound truth and wisdom. The world will never be the better for it. A few of the books were Latin folios, written by Catholic authors; others demolished Papistry as with a sledgehammer, in plain English. A dissertation on the book of Job—which only Job himself could have had patience to read—filled at least a score of small, thickset quartos, at the rate of two or three volumes to a chapter. Then there was a vast folio Body of Divinity; too corpulent a body, it might be feared, to comprehend the spiritual element of religion. Volumes of this form dated back two hundred years, or more, and were generally bound in black leather, exhibiting precisely such an appearance as we should attribute to books of enchantment. Others, equally antique, were of a size proper to be carried in the large waistcoat-pockets of old times; diminutive, but as black as their bulkier brethren, and abundantly interfused with Greek and Latin quotations. These little old volumes impressed me as if they had been intended for very large ones, but had been unfortunately blighted, at an early stage of their growth.

The rain pattered upon the roof, and the sky gloomed through the dusty garret-windows; while I burrowed among these venerable books, in search of any living thought, which should burn like a coal of fire, or glow like an inextinguishable gem, beneath the dead trumpery that had long hidden it. But I found no such treasure; all was dead alike; and I could not but muse deeply and wonderingly upon the humiliating fact, that the works of man's intellect decay like those of his hands. Thought grows mouldy. What was good and nourishing food for the spirits of one generation, affords no sustenance for the next. Books of religion, however, cannot be considered a fair test of the enduring and vivacious properties of human thought; because such books so seldom really touch upon their ostensible subject, and have therefore so little business to be written at all. So long as an un-lettered soul can attain to saving grace, there would seem to be no deadly error in holding theological libraries to be accumulations of, for the most part, stupendous impertinence.

Many of the books had accrued in the latter years of the last cler-gyman's lifetime. These threatened to be of even less interest than the elder works, a century hence, to any curious inquirer who should then rummage among them, as I was doing now. Volumes of the Liberal Preacher and Christian Examiner, occasional sermons, con-troversial pamphlets, tracts, and other productions of a like fugitive nature, took the place of the thick and heavy volumes of past time. In a physical point of view, there was much the same difference as be-tween a feather and a lump of lead; but, intellectually regarded, the specific gravity of old and new was about upon a par. Both, also, were alike frigid. The elder books, nevertheless, seemed to have been ear-nestly written, and might be conceived to have possessed warmth, at some former period; although, with the lapse of time, the heated masses had cooled down even to the freezing point. The frigidity of the modern productions, on the other hand, was characteristic and inherent, and evidently had little to do with the writer's qualities of mind and heart. In fine, of this whole dusty heap of literature, I tossed aside all the sacred part, and felt myself none the less a Chris-tian for eschewing it. There appeared no hope of either mounting to the better world on a Gothic staircase of ancient folios, or of flying thither on the wings of a modern tract.

Nothing, strange to say, retained any sap, except what had been written for the passing day and year, without the remotest preten-sion or idea of permanence. There were a few old newspapers, and still older almanacs, which reproduced, to my mental eye, the ep-ochs when they had issued from the press, with a distinctness that was altogether unaccountable. It was as if I had found bits of magic looking-glass among the books, with the images of a vanished century in them. I turned my eyes towards the tattered picture, abovementioned, and asked of the austere divine, wherefore it was that he and his brethren, after the most painful rummaging and groping into their minds, had been able to produce nothing half so real, as these newspaper scribblers and almanac-makers had thrown off, in the effervescence of a moment. The portrait responded not; so I sought an answer for myself. It is the Age itself that writes newspapers and almanacs, which therefore have a distinct purpose and meaning, at the time, and a kind of intelligible truth for all times; whereas, most other works—being written by men who, in the very act, set themselves apart from their age—are likely to possess little significance when new, and none at all, when old. Genius, indeed, melts many ages into one, and thus effects something permanent, yet still with a similarity of office to that of the more ephemeral writer. A work of genius is but the newspaper of a century, or perchance of a hundred centuries.

Lightly as I have spoken of these old books, there yet lingers with me a superstitious reverence for literature of all kinds. A bound volume has a charm in my eyes, similar to what scraps of manuscript possess, for the good Mussulman. He imagines, that those windwafted records are perhaps hallowed by some sacred verse; and I, that every new book, or antique one, may contain the 'Open Sesame'—the spell to disclose treasures, hidden in some unsuspected cave of Truth. Thus, it was not without sadness, that I turned away from the library of the old Manse.

Blessed was the sunshine when it came again, at the close of another stormy day, beaming from the edge of the western horizon; while the massive firmament of clouds threw down all the gloom it could, but served only to kindle the golden light into a more brilliant glow, by the strongly contrasted shadows. Heaven smiled at the earth, so long unseen, from beneath its heavy eyelid. Tomorrow for the hill-tops and the wood-paths!

Or it might be that Ellery Channing came up the avenue, to join me in a fishing-excursion on the river. Strange and happy times were those, when we cast aside all irksome forms and straight-laced habitudes, and delivered ourselves up to the free air, to live like the Indians or any less conventional race, during one bright semi-circle of the sun. Rowing our boat against the current, between wide meadows, we turned aside into the Assabeth. A more lovely stream than this, for a mile above its junction with the Concord, has never flowed on earth—nowhere, indeed, except to lave the interior regions of a poet's imagination. It is sheltered from the breeze by woods and a hill-side; so that elsewhere there might be a hurricane, and here scarcely a ripple across the shaded water. The current lingers along so gently, that the mere force of the boatman's will seems sufficient to propel his craft against it. It comes flowing softly through the midmost privacy and deepest heart of a wood, which whispers it to be quiet, while the stream whispers back again from its sedgy borders, as if river and wood were hushing one another to sleep. Yes; the river sleeps along its course, and dreams of the sky, and of the clustering foliage, amid which fall showers of broken sunlight, imparting specks of vivid cheerfulness, in contrast with the quiet depth of the prevailing tint. Of all this scene, the slumbering river has a dream-picture in its bosom. Which, after all, was the most real—the picture, or the original?—the objects palpable to our grosser senses, or their apotheosis in the stream beneath? Surely, the disembodied images stand in closer relation to the soul. But, both the original and the reflection had here an ideal charm; and, had it been a thought more wild, I could have fancied that this river had strayed forth out of the rich scenery of my companion's inner world;—only the vegetation along its banks should then have had an Oriental character.

Gentle and unobtrusive as the river is, yet the tranquil woods seem hardly satisfied to allow it passage. The trees are rooted on the very verge of the water, and dip their pendent branches into it. At one spot, there is a lofty bank, on the slope of which grow some hemlocks, declining across the stream, with outstretched arms, as if resolute to take the plunge. In other places, the banks are almost on a level with the water; so that the quiet congregation of trees set their feet in the flood, and are fringed with foliage down to the surface. Cardinal-flowers kindle their spiral flames, and illuminate the dark nooks among the shrubbery. The pond-lily grows abundantly along the margin; that delicious flower which, as Thoreau tells me, opens its virgin bosom to the first sunlight, and perfects its being through the magic of that genial kiss. He has beheld beds of them unfolding in due succession, as the sunrise stole gradually from flower to flower; a sight not to be hoped for, unless when a poet adjusts his inward eye to a proper focus with the outward organ. Grape-vines, here and there, twine themselves around shrub and tree, and hang their clusters over the water, within reach of the boatman's hand. Oftentimes, they unite two trees of alien race in an inextricable twine, marrying the hemlock and the maple against their will, and enriching them with a purple offspring, of which neither is the parent. One of these ambitious parasites has climbed into the upper branches of a tall white-pine, and is still ascending from bough to bough, unsatisfied, till it shall crown the tree's airy summit with a wreath of its broad foliage and a cluster of its grapes.

The winding course of the stream continually shut out the scene behind us, and revealed as calm and lovely a one before. We glided from depth to depth, and breathed new seclusion at every turn. The shy kingfisher flew from the withered branch, close at hand, to another at a distance, uttering a shrill cry of anger or alarm. Ducks— that had been floating there, since the preceding eve—were startled at our approach, and skimmed along the glassy river, breaking its dark surface with a bright streak. The pickerel leaped from among the lily-pads. The turtle, sunning itself upon a rock, or at the root of a tree, slid suddenly into the water with a plunge. The painted Indian, who paddled his canoe along the Assabeth, three hundred years ago, could hardly have seen a wilder gentleness, displayed upon its banks and reflected in its bosom, than we did. Nor could the same Indian have prepared his noontide meal with more simplicity. We drew up our skiff at some point where the overarching shade formed a natural bower, and there kindled a fire with the pine-cones and decayed branches that lay strewn plentifully around. Soon, the smoke ascended among the trees, impregnated with a savory incense, not heavy, dull, and surfeiting, like the steam of cookery within doors, but sprightly and piquant. The smell of our feast was akin to the woodland odors with which it mingled; there was no sacrilege committed by our intrusion there; the sacred solitude was hospitable, and granted us free leave to cook and eat, in the recess that was at once our kitchen and banquetting-hall. It is strange what humble offices may be performed, in a beautiful scene, without destroying its poetry. Our fire, red-gleaming among the trees, and we beside it, busied with culinary rites and spreading out our meal on a moss-grown log, all seemed in unison with the river gliding by, and the foliage rustling over us. And, what was strangest, neither did our mirth seem to disturb the propriety of the solemn woods; although the hobgoblins of the old wilderness, and the will-of-the-whisps that glimmered in the marshy places, might have come trooping to share our table-talk, and have added their shrill laughter to our merriment. It was the very spot in which to utter the extremest nonsense, or the profoundest wisdom—or that ethereal product of the mind which partakes of both, and may become one or the other, in correspondence with the faith and insight of the auditor.

So, amid sunshine and shadow, rustling leaves, and sighing waters, up-gushed our talk, like the babble of a fountain. The evanescent spray was Ellery's; and his, too, the lumps of golden thought, that lay glimmering in the fountain's bed, and brightened both our faces by the reflection. Could he have drawn out that virgin gold, and stamped it with the mint-mark that alone gives currency, the world might have had the profit, and he the fame. My mind was the richer, merely by the knowledge that it was there. But the chief profit of those wild days, to him and me, lay—not in any definite idea—not in any angular or rounded truth, which we dug out of the shapeless mass of problematical stuff—but in the freedom which we thereby won from all custom and conventionalism, and fettering influences of man on man. We were so free to-day, that it was impossible to be slaves again tomorrow. When we crossed the threshold of a house, or trod the thronged pavements of a city, still the leaves of the trees, that overhung the Assabeth, were whispering to us—'Be free! Be free!' Therefore, along that shady river-bank, there are spots, marked with a heap of ashes and half-consumed brands, only less sacred in my remembrance than the hearth of a household-fire.

And yet how sweet—as we floated homeward adown the golden river, at sunset—how sweet was it to return within the system of human society, not as to a dungeon and a chain, but as to a stately edifice, whence we could go forth at will into statelier simplicity! How gently, too, did the sight of the old Manse—best seen from the river, overshadowed with its willow, and all environed about with the foliage of its orchard and avenue—how gently did its gray, homely aspect rebuke the speculative extravagances of the day! It had grown sacred, in connection with the artificial life against which we inveighed; it had been a home, for many years, in spite of all; it was my home, too;—and, with these thoughts, it seemed to me that all the artifice and conventionalism of life was but an impalpable thinness upon its surface, and that the depth below was none the worse for it. Once, as we turned our boat to the bank, there was a cloud in the shape of an immensely gigantic figure of a hound, couched above the house, as if keeping guard over it. Gazing at this symbol, I prayed that the upper influences might long protect the institutions that had grown out of the heart of mankind.

If ever my readers should decide to give up civilized life, cities, houses, and whatever moral or material enormities, in addition to these, the perverted ingenuity of our race has contrived,—let it be in the early autumn. Then, Nature will love him better than at any other season, and will take him to her bosom with a more motherly tenderness. I could scarcely endure the roof of the old house above me, in those first autumnal days. How early in the summer, too, the prophecy of autumn comes!—earlier in some years than in others,—sometimes, even in the first weeks of July. There is no other feeling like what is caused by this faint, doubtful, yet real perception, if it be not rather a foreboding, of the year's decay—so blessedly sweet and sad, in the same breath.

Did I say that there was no feeling like it? Ah, but there is a half-acknowledged melancholy, like to this, when we stand in the perfected vigor of our life, and feel that Time has now given us all his flowers, and that the next work of his never idle fingers must be—to steal them, one by one, away!

I have forgotten whether the song of the cricket be not as early a token of autumn's approach, as any other;—that song, which may be called an audible stillness; for, though very loud and heard afar, yet the mind does not take note of it as a sound; so completely is its individual existence merged among the accompanying characteristics of the season. Alas, for the pleasant summer-time! In August, the grass is still verdant on the hills and in the vallies; the foliage of the trees is as dense as ever, and as green; the flowers gleam forth in richer abundance along the margin of the river, and by the stone-walls, and deep among the woods; the days, too, are as fervid now as they were a month ago;—and yet, in every breath of wind, and in every beam of sunshine, we hear the whispered farewell, and behold the parting smile, of a dear friend. There is a coolness amid all the heat; a mildness in the blazing noon. Not a breeze can stir, but it thrills us with the breath of autumn. A pensive glory is seen in the far, golden gleams, among the shadows of the trees. The flowers—even the brightest of them, and they are the most gorgeous of the year—have this gentle sadness wedded to their pomp, and typify the character of the delicious time, each within itself. The brilliant cardinal-flower has never seemed gay to me.

Still later in the season, Nature's tenderness waxes stronger. It is impossible not to be fond of our Mother now; for she is so fond of us! At other periods, she does not make this impression on me, or only at rare intervals; but, in these genial days of autumn, when she has perfected her harvests, and accomplished every needful thing that was given her to do, then she overflows with a blessed superfluity of love. She has leisure to caress her children now.

It is good to be alive, at such times. Thank heaven for breath!—yes, for mere breath!—when it is made up of a heavenly breeze like this! It comes with a real kiss upon our cheeks; it would linger fondly around us, if it might; but, since it must be gone, it embraces us with its whole kindly heart, and passes onward, to embrace likewise the next thing that it meets. A blessing is flung abroad, and scattered far and wide over the earth, to be gathered up by all who choose. I recline upon the still unwithered grass, and whisper to myself:—'Oh, perfect day!—Oh, beautiful world!—Oh, beneficent God!' And it is the promise of a blissful Eternity; for our Creator would never have made such lovely days, and have given us the deep hearts to enjoy them, above and beyond all thought, unless we were meant to be immortal. This sunshine is the golden pledge thereof. It beams through the gates of Paradise, and shows us glimpses far inward.

By-and-by—in a little time—the outward world puts on a drear austerity. On some October morning, there is a heavy hoar-frost on the grass, and along the tops of the fences; and, at sunrise, the leaves fall from the trees of our avenue without a breath of wind, quietly descending by their own weight. All summer long, they have murmured like the noise of waters; they have roared loudly, while the branches were wrestling with the thunder-gust; they have made music, both glad and solemn; they have attuned my thoughts by their quiet sound, as I paced to-and-fro beneath the arch of intermingling boughs. Now, they can only rustle under my feet. Henceforth, the gray parsonage begins to assume a larger importance, and draws to its fireside—for the abomination of the air-tight stove is reserved till wintry weather—draws closer and closer to its fireside the vagrant impulses, that had gone wandering about, through the summer.

When summer was dead and buried, the old Manse became as lonely as a hermitage. Not that ever—in my time, at least—it had been thronged with company; but, at no rare intervals, we welcomed some friend out of the dusty glare and tumult of the world, and rejoiced to share with him the transparent obscurity that was flung over us. In one respect, our precincts were like the Enchanted Ground, through which the pilgrim travelled on his way to the Celestial City. The guests, each and all, felt a slumberous influence upon them; they fell asleep in chairs, or took a more deliberate siesta on the sofa, or were seen stretched among the shadows of the orchard, looking up dreamily through the boughs. They could not have paid a more acceptable compliment to my abode, nor to my own qualities as a host. I held it as a proof, that they left their cares behind them, as they passed between the stone gate-posts, at the entrance of our avenue; and that the so powerful opiate was the abundance of peace and quiet, within and all around us. Others could give them pleasure and amusement, or instruction—these could be picked up anywhere— but it was for me to give them rest—rest, in a life of trouble. What better could be done for those weary and world-Worn spirits?—for him, whose career of perpetual action was impeded and harassed by the rarest of his powers, and the richest of his acquirements?—for another, who had thrown his ardent heart, from earliest youth, into the strife of politics, and now, perchance, began to suspect that one lifetime is too brief for the accomplishment of any lofty aim?—for her, on whose feminine nature had been imposed the heavy gift of intellectual power, such as a strong man might have staggered under, and with it the necessity to act upon the world?—in a word, not to multiply instances, what better could be done for anybody, who came within our magic circle, than to throw the spell of a tranquil spirit over him? And when it had wrought its full effect, then we dismissed him, with but misty reminiscences, as if he had been dreaming of us.

Were I to adopt a pet idea, as so many people do, and fondle it in my embraces to the exclusion of all others, it would be, that the great want which mankind labors under, at this present period, is—sleep! The world should recline its vast head on the first convenient pillow, and take an agelong nap. It has gone distracted, through a morbid activity, and, while preternaturally wide-awake, is nevertheless tormented by visions, that seem real to it now, but would assume their true aspect and character, were all things once set right by an interval of sound repose. This is the only method of getting rid of old delusions, and avoiding new ones—of regenerating our race, so that it might in due time awake, as an infant out of dewy slumber—of restoring to us the simple perception of what is right, and the single-hearted desire to achieve it; both of which have long been lost, in consequence of this weary activity of brain, and torpor or passion of the heart, that now afflicts the universe. Stimulants, the only mode of treatment hitherto attempted, cannot quell the disease; they do but heighten the delirium.

Let not the above paragraph ever be quoted against the author; for, though tinctured with its modicum of truth, it is the result and expression of what he knew, while he was writing, to be but a distorted survey of the state and prospects of mankind. There were circumstances around me, which made it difficult to view the world precisely as it exists; for, serene and sober as was the old Manse, it was necessary to go but a little way beyond its threshold, before meeting with stranger moral shapes of men than might have been encountered elsewhere, in a circuit of a thousand miles.

These hobgoblins of flesh and blood were attracted thither by the wide-spreading influence of a great original Thinker, who had his earthly abode at the opposite extremity of our village. His mind acted upon other minds, of a certain constitution, with wonderful magnetism, and drew many men upon long pilgrimages, to speak with him face to face. Young visionaries—to whom just so much of insight had been imparted, as to make life all a labyrinth around them—came to seek the clue that should guide them out of their self-involved bewilderment. Gray-headed theorists—whose systems, at first air, had finally imprisoned them in an iron frame-work—travelled painfully to his door, not to ask deliverance, but to invite this free spirit into their own thraldom. People that had lighted on a new thought, or a thought that they fancied new, came to Emerson, as the finder of a glittering gem hastens to a lapidary, to ascertain its quality and value. Uncertain, troubled, earnest wanderers, through the midnight of the moral world, beheld his intellectual fire, as a beacon burning on a hill-top, and, climbing the difficult ascent, looked forth into the surrounding obscurity, more hopefully than hitherto. The light revealed objects unseen before—mountains, gleaming lakes, glimpses of a creation among the chaos—but also, as was unavoidable, it attracted bats and owls, and the whole host of night-birds, which flapped their dusky wings against the gazer's eyes, and sometimes were mistaken for fowls of angelic feather. Such delusions always hover nigh, whenever a beacon-fire of truth is kindled.

For myself, there had been epochs of my life, when I, too, might have asked of this prophet the master-word, that should solve me the riddle of the universe; but now, being happy, I felt as if there were no question to be put, and therefore admired Emerson as a poet of deep beauty and austere tenderness, but sought nothing from him as a philosopher. It was good, nevertheless, to meet him in the wood-paths, or sometimes in our avenue, with that pure, intellectual gleam diffused about his presence, like the garment of a shining-one; and he so quiet, so simple, so without pretension, encountering each man alive as if expecting to receive more than he could impart. And, in truth, the heart of many an ordinary man had, perchance, inscriptions which he could not read. But it was impossible to dwell in his vicinity, without inhaling, more or less, the mountain-atmosphere of his lofty thought, which, in the brains of some people, wrought a singular giddiness—new truth being as heady as new wine. Never was a poor little country village infested with such a variety of queer, strangely dressed, oddly behaved mortals, most of whom took upon themselves to be important agents of the world's destiny, yet were simply bores of a very intense water. Such, I imagine, is the invariable character of persons who crowd so closely about an original thinker, as to draw in his unuttered breath, and thus become imbued with a false originality. This triteness of novelty is enough to make any man, of common sense, blaspheme at all ideas of less than a century's standing; and pray that the world may be petrified and rendered immovable, in precisely the worst moral and physical state that it ever yet arrived at, rather than be benefitted by such schemes of such philosophers.

And now, I begin to feel—and perhaps should have sooner felt—that we have talked enough of the old Manse. Mine honored reader, it may be, will vilify the poor author as an egotist, for babbling through so many pages about a moss-grown country parsonage, and his life within its walls, and on the river, and in the woods,—and the influences that wrought upon him, from all these sources. My conscience, however, does not reproach me with betraying anything too sacredly individual to be revealed by a human spirit, to its brother or sister spirit. How narrow—how shallow and scanty too—is the stream of thought that has been flowing from my pen, compared with the broad tide of dim emotions, ideas, and associations, which swell around me from that portion of my existence! How little have I told!—and, of that little, how almost nothing is even tinctured with any quality that makes it exclusively my own! Has the reader gone wandering, hand in hand with me, through the inner passages of my being, and have we groped together into all its chambers, and examined their treasures or their rubbish? Not so. We have been standing on the green sward, but just within the cavern's mouth, where the common sunshine is free to penetrate, and where every footstep is therefore free to come. I have appealed to no sentiment or sensibilities, save such as are diffused among us all. So far as I am a man of really individual attributes, I veil my face; nor am I, nor have ever been, one of those supremely hospitable people, who serve up their own hearts delicately fried, with brain-sauce, as a tidbit for their beloved public.

Glancing back over what I have written, it seems but the scattered reminiscences of a single summer. In fairy-land, there is no measurement of time; and, in a spot so sheltered from the turmoil of life's ocean, three years hastened away with a noiseless flight, as the breezy sunshine chases the cloud-shadows across the depths of a still valley. Now came hints, growing more and more distinct, that the owner of the old house was pining for his native air. Carpenters next appeared, making a tremendous racket among the outbuildings, strewing the green grass with pine-shavings and chips of chestnut joists, and vexing the whole antiquity of the place with their discordant renovations. Soon, moreover, they divested our abode of the veil of woodbine, which had crept over a large portion of its southern face. All the aged mosses were cleaned unsparingly away; and there were horrible whispers about brushing up the external walls with a coat of paint—a purpose as little to my taste, as might be that of rouging the venerable cheeks of one's grandmother. But the hand that renovates is always more sacrilegious than that which destroys. In fine, we gathered up our household goods, drank a farewell cup of tea in our pleasant little breakfast-room—delicately fragrant tea, an unpurchaseable luxury, one of the many angel-gifts that had fallen like dew upon us—and passed forth between the tall stone gate-posts, as uncertain as the wandering Arabs where our tent might next be pitched. Providence took me by the hand, and—an oddity of dispensation which, I trust, there is no irreverence in smiling at—has led me, as the newspapers announce while I am writing, from the Old Manse into a Custom-House! As a storyteller, I have often contrived strange vicissitudes for my imaginary personages, but none like this.

The treasure of intellectual gold, which I hoped to find in our secluded dwelling, had never come to light. No profound treatise of ethics—no philosophic history—no novel, even, that could stand, unsupported, on its edges. All that I had to show, as a man of letters, were these few tales and essays, which had blossomed out like flowers in the calm summer of my heart and mind. Save editing (an easy task) the journal of my friend of many years, the African Cruiser, I had done nothing else. With these idle weeds and withering blossoms, I have intermixed some that were produced long ago—old, faded things, reminding me of flowers pressed between the leaves of a book—and now offer the bouquet, such as it is, to any whom it may please. These fitful sketches, with so little of external life about them, yet claiming no profundity of purpose,—so reserved, even while they sometimes seem so frank,—often but half in earnest, and never, even when most so, expressing satisfactorily the thoughts which they profess to image—such trifles, I truly feel, afford no solid basis for a literary reputation. Nevertheless, the public—if my limited number of readers, whom I venture to regard rather as a circle of friends, may be termed a public—will receive them the more kindly, as the last offering, the last collection of this nature, which it is my purpose ever to put forth. Unless I could do better, I have done enough in this kind. For myself, the book will always retain one charm, as reminding me of the river, with its delightful solitudes, and of the avenue, the garden, and the orchard, and especially the dear old Manse, with the little study on its western side, and the sunshine glimmering through the willow-branches while I wrote.

Let the reader, if he will do me so much honor, imagine himself my guest, and that, having seen whatever may be worthy of notice, within and about the old Manse, he has finally been ushered into my study. There, after seating him in an antique elbow-chair, an heirloom of the house, I take forth a roll of manuscript, and intreat his attention to the following tales:—an act of personal inhospitality, however, which I never was guilty of, nor ever will be, even to my worst enemy.

Ethan Brand

A Chapter from an Abortive Romance

B ARTRAM, THE LIME-BURNER, a rough, heavy-looking man, begrimed with charcoal, sat watching his kiln, at nightfall, while his little son played at building houses with the scattered fragments of marble; when, on the hill-side below them, they heard a roar of laughter, not mirthful, but slow, and even solemn, like a wind shaking the boughs of the forest.

"Father, what is that?" asked the little boy, leaving his play, and pressing betwixt his father's knees.

"Oh, some drunken man, I suppose," answered the lime-burner;— "some merry fellow from the bar-room in the village, who dared not laugh loud enough within doors, lest he should blow the roof of the house off. So here he is, shaking his jolly sides, at the foot of Graylock."

"But, father," said the child, more sensitive than the obtuse, middle-aged clown, "he does not laugh like a man that is glad. So the noise frightens me!"

"Don't be a fool, child!" cried his father, gruffly. "You will never make a man, I do believe; there is too much of your mother in you. I have known the rustling of a leaf startle you. Hark! Here comes the merry fellow now. You shall see that there is no harm in him."

Bartram and his little son, while they were talking thus, sat watching the same lime-kiln that had been the scene of Ethan Brand's solitary and meditative life, before he began his search for the Unpardonable Sin. Many years, as we have seen, had now elapsed, since that portentous night when the IDEA was first developed. The kiln, however, on the mountainside, stood unimpaired, and was in nothing changed, since he had thrown his dark thoughts into the intense glow of its furnace, and melted them, as it were, into the one thought that took possession of his life. It was a rude, round, tower-like structure, about twenty feet high, heavily built of rough stones, and with a hillock of earth heaped about the larger part of its circumference; so that blocks and fragments of marble might be drawn by cart-loads, and thrown in at the top. There was an opening at the bottom of the tower, like an oven-mouth, but large enough to admit a man in a stooping posture, and provided with a massive iron door. With the smoke and jets of flame issuing from the chinks and crevices of this door, which seemed to give admittance into the hillside, it resembled nothing so much as the private entrance to the infernal regions, which the shepherds of the Delectable Mountains were accustomed to show to pilgrims.

There are many such lime-kilns in that tract of country, for the purpose of burning the white marble which composes a large part of the substance of the hills. Some of them, built years ago, and long deserted, with weeds growing in the vacant round of the interior, which is open to the sky, and grass and wild flowers rooting themselves into the chinks of the stones, look already like relics of antiquity, and may yet be overspread with the lichens of centuries to come. Others, where the lime-burner still feeds his daily and night-long fire, afford points

of interest to the wanderer among the hills, who seats himself on a
log of wood or a fragment of marble, to hold chat with the solitary
man. It is a lonesome, and, when the character is inclined to thought,
may be an intensely thoughtful occupation; as it proved in the case of
Ethan Brand, who had mused to such strange purpose, in days gone
by, while the fire in this very kiln was burning.

The man, who now watched the fire, was of a different order, and
troubled himself with no thoughts save the very few that were requisite to his business. At frequent intervals he flung back the clashing
weight of the iron door, and, turning his face from the insufferable
glare, thrust in huge logs of oak, or stirred the immense brands with
a long pole. Within the furnace, was seen the curling and riotous
flames, and the burning marble, almost molten with the intensity of
heat; while, without, the reflection of the fire quivered on the dark
intricacy of the surrounding forest, and showed, in the foreground,
a bright and ruddy little picture of the hut, the spring beside its
door, the athletic and coal-begrimed figure of the lime-burner, and
the half-frightened child, shrinking into the protection of his father's
shadow. And when, again, the iron door was closed, then re-appeared
the tender light of the half-full moon, which vainly strove to trace out
the indistinct shapes of the neighboring mountains; and, in the upper sky, there was a flitting congregation of clouds, still faintly tinged
with the rosy sunset, though, thus far down into the valley, the sunshine had vanished long and long ago.

The little boy now crept still closer to his father, as footsteps were
heard ascending the hill-side, and a human form thrust aside the
bushes that clustered beneath the trees.

"Halloo! who is it?" cried the lime-burner, vexed at his son's timid-
ity, yet half-infected by it. "Come forward, and show yourself, like a
man; or I'll fling this chunk of marble at your head!"

"You offer me a rough welcome," said a gloomy voice, as the unknown man drew nigh. "Yet I neither claim nor desire a kinder one, even at my own fireside."

To obtain a distincter view, Bartram threw open the iron door of the kiln, whence immediately issued a gush of fierce light, that smote full upon the stranger's face and figure. To a careless eye, there appeared nothing very remarkable in his aspect, which was that of a man in a coarse, brown, country-made suit of clothes, tall and thin, with the staff and heavy shoes of a wayfarer. As he advanced, he fixed his eyes, which were very bright, intently upon the brightness of the furnace, as if he beheld, or expected to behold, some object worthy of note within it.

"Good evening, stranger," said the lime-burner, "whence come you, so late in the day?"

"I come from my search," answered the wayfarer; "for, at last, it is finished."

"Drunk, or crazy!" muttered Bartram to himself. "I shall have trouble with the fellow. The sooner I drive him away, the better."

The little boy, all in a tremble, whispered to his father, and begged him to shut the door of the kiln, so that there might not be so much light; for that there was something in the man's face which he was afraid to look at, yet could not look away from. And, indeed, even the lime-burner's dull and torpid sense began to be impressed by an indescribable something in that thin, rugged, thoughtful visage, with the grizzled hair hanging wildly about it, and those deeply sunken eyes, which gleamed like fires within the entrance of a mysterious cavern. But, as he closed the door, the stranger turned towards him, and spoke in a quiet, familiar way, that made Bartram feel as if he were a sane and sensible man, after all.

"Your task draws to an end, I see," said he. "This marble has already been burning three days. A few hours more will convert the stone to lime."

"Why, who are you?" exclaimed the lime-burner. "You seem as well acquainted with my business as I myself."

"And well I may be," said the stranger, "for I followed the same craft, many a long year; and here, too, on this very spot. But you are a new comer in these parts. Did you never hear of Ethan Brand?"

"The man that went in search of the Unpardonable Sin?" asked Bartram, with a laugh.

"The same," answered the stranger. "He has found what he sought, and therefore he comes back again."

"What! then you are Ethan Brand, himself?" cried the lime-burner in amazement. "I am a new comer here, as you say; and they call it eighteen years since you left the foot of Graylock. But, I can tell you, the good folks still talk about Ethan Brand, in the village yonder, and what a strange errand took him away from his lime-kiln. Well, and so you have found the Unpardonable Sin?"

"Even so!" said the stranger, calmly.

"If the question is a fair one," proceeded Bartram, "where might it be?"

Ethan Brand laid his finger on his own heart. "Here!" replied he.

And then, without mirth in his countenance, but as if moved by an involuntary recognition of the infinite absurdity of seeking throughout the world for what was the closest of all things to himself, and looking into every heart, save his own, for what was hidden in no other breast, he broke into a laugh of scorn. It was the same slow, heavy laugh, that had almost appalled the lime-burner, when it heralded the wayfarer's approach.

The solitary mountain-side was made dismal by it. Laughter, when out of place, mistimed, or bursting forth from a disordered state of feeling, may be the most terrible modulation of the human voice. The laughter of one asleep, even if it be a little child—the madman's laugh—the wild, screaming laugh of a born idiot, are sounds that we sometimes tremble to hear, and would always willingly forget. Poets have imagined no utterance of fiends or hobgoblins so fearfully appropriate as a laugh. And even the obtuse lime-burner felt his nerves shaken, as this strange man looked inward at his own heart, and burst into laughter that rolled away into the night, and was indistinctly reverberated among the hills.

"Joe," said he to his little son, "scamper down to the tavern in the village, and tell the jolly fellows there that Ethan Brand has come back, and that he has found the Unpardonable Sin!"

The boy darted away on his errand, to which Ethan Brand made no objection, nor seemed hardly to notice it. He sat on a log of wood, looking steadfastly at the iron door of the kiln. When the child was out of sight, and his swift and light footsteps ceased to be heard, treading first on the fallen leaves, and then on the rocky mountain-path, the lime-burner began to regret his departure. He felt that the little fellow's presence had been a barrier between his guest and himself, and that he must now deal, heart to heart, with a man who, on his own confession, had committed the only crime for which Heaven could afford no mercy. That crime, in its indistinct blackness, seemed to overshadow him. The lime-burner's own sins rose up within him, and made his memory riotous with a throng of evil shapes that asserted their kindred with the Master Sin, whatever it might be, which it was within the scope of man's corrupted nature to conceive and cherish. They were all of one family; they went to and fro between his breast and Ethan Brand's, and carried dark greetings from one to the other.

Then Bartram remembered the stories which had grown traditionary in reference to this strange man, who had come upon him like a shadow of the night, and was making himself at home in his old place, after so long absence that the dead people, dead and buried for years, would have had more right to be at home, in any familiar spot, than he. Ethan Brand, it was said, had conversed with Satan himself, in the lurid blaze of this very kiln. The legend had been matter of mirth heretofore, but looked grisly now. According to this tale, before Ethan Brand departed on his search, he had been accustomed to evoke a fiend from the hot furnace of the lime-kiln, night after night, in order to confer with him about the Unpardonable Sin; the Man and the Fiend each laboring to frame the image of some mode of guilt, which could neither be atoned for, nor forgiven. And, with the first gleam of light upon the mountain-top, the fiend crept in at the iron door, there to abide in the intensest element of fire, until again summoned forth to share in the dreadful task of extending man's possible guilt beyond the scope of Heaven's else infinite mercy.

While the lime-burner was struggling with the horror of these thoughts, Ethan Brand rose from the log and flung open the door of the kiln. The action was in such accordance with the idea in Bartram's mind, that he almost expected to see the Evil One issue forth, red-hot from the raging furnace.

"Hold, hold!" cried he, with a tremulous attempt to laugh; for he was ashamed of his fears, although they overmastered him. "Don't, for mercy's sake, bring out your devil now!"

"Man!" sternly replied Ethan Brand, "what need have I of the devil? I have left him behind me on my track. It is with such half-way sinners as you that he busies himself. Fear not, because I open the door. I do but act by old custom, and am going to trim your fire, like a lime-burner, as I was once."

He stirred the vast coals, thrust in more wood, and bent forward to gaze into the hollow prison-house of the fire, regardless of the fierce glow that reddened upon his face. The lime-burner sat watching him, and half suspected his strange guest of a purpose, if not to evoke a fiend, at least to plunge bodily into the flames, and thus vanish from the sight of man. Ethan Brand, however, drew quietly back, and closed the door of the kiln.

"I have looked," said he, "into many a human heart that was seven times hotter with sinful passions than yonder furnace is with fire. But I found not there what I sought. No; not the Unpardonable Sin!"

"What is the Unpardonable Sin?" asked the lime-burner; and then he shrank farther from his companion, trembling lest his question should be answered.

"It is a sin that grew within my own breast," replied Ethan Brand, standing erect, with the pride that distinguishes all enthusiasts of his stamp. "A sin that grew nowhere else! The sin of an intellect that triumphed over the sense of brotherhood with man, and reverence for God, and sacrificed everything to its own mighty claims! The only sin that deserves a recompense of immortal agony! Freely, were it to do again, would I incur the guilt. Unshrinkingly, I accept the retribution!"

"The man's head is turned," muttered the lime-burner to himself. "He may be a sinner, like the rest of us—nothing more likely—but I'll be sworn, he is a madman, too."

Nevertheless, he felt uncomfortable at his situation, alone with Ethan Brand on the wild mountain-side, and was right glad to hear the rough murmur of tongues, and the footsteps of what seemed a pretty numerous party, stumbling over the stones, and rustling through the underbrush. Soon appeared the whole lazy regiment that was wont to infest the village tavern, comprehending three or four individuals who had drunk flip beside the bar-room fire, through all the winters, and smoked their pipes beneath the stoop, through all the summers since Ethan Brand's departure. Laughing boisterously, and mingling all their voices together in unceremonious talk, they now burst into the moonshine and narrow streaks of fire-light that illuminated the open space before the lime-kiln. Bartram set the door ajar again, flooding the spot with light, that the whole company might get a fair view of Ethan Brand, and he of them.

There, among other old acquaintances, was a once ubiquitous man, now almost extinct, but whom we were formerly sure to encounter at the hotel of every thriving village throughout the country. It was the stage-agent. The present specimen of the genus was a wilted and smoke-dried man, wrinkled and red-nosed, in a smartly cut, brown, bob-tailed coat, with brass buttons, who, for a length of time unknown, had kept his desk and corner in the bar-room, and was still puffing what seemed to be the same cigar that he had lighted twenty years before. He had great fame as a dry joker, though, perhaps, less on account of any intrinsic humor, than from a certain flavor of brandy-toddy and tobacco-smoke, which impregnated all his ideas and expressions, as well as his person. Another well-remembered, though strangely-altered face was that of Lawyer Giles, as people still called him in courtesy; an elderly ragamuffin, in his soiled shirt-sleeves and tow-cloth trowsers. This poor fellow had been an attorney, in what he called his better days, a sharp practitioner, and in great vogue among the village litigants; but flip, and sling, and toddy, and cocktails, imbibed at all hours, morning, noon, and night, had caused him to slide from intellectual, to various kinds and degrees of bodily labor, till, at last, to adopt his own phrase, he slid into a soap-vat. In other words, Giles was now a soap-boiler, in a small way. He had come to be but the fragment of a human being, a part of one foot having been chopped off by an axe, and an entire hand torn away by the devilish gripe of a steam-engine. Yet, though the corporeal hand was gone, a spiritual member remained; for, stretching forth the stump, Giles steadfastly averred, that he felt an invisible thumb and fingers, with as vivid a sensation as before the real ones were amputated. A maimed and miserable wretch he was; but one, nevertheless, whom the world could not trample on, and had no right to scorn, either in this or any previous stage of his misfortunes, since he had still kept up the courage and spirit of a man, asked nothing in charity, and, with his one hand—and that the left one—fought a stern battle against want and hostile circumstances.

Among the throng, too, came another personage, who, with certain points of similarity to Lawyer Giles, had more of difference. It was the village Doctor, a man of some fifty years, whom, at an earlier period of his life, we should have introduced as paying a professional visit to Ethan Brand, during the latter's supposed insanity. He was now a purple-visaged, rude, and brutal, yet half-gentlemanly figure, with something wild, ruined, and desperate in his talk, and in all the details of his gesture and manners. Brandy possessed this man like an evil spirit, and made him as surly and savage as a wild beast, and as miserable as a lost soul; but there was supposed to be in him such wonderful skill, such native gifts of healing, beyond any which medical science could impart, that society caught hold of him, and would not let him sink out of its reach. So, swaying to and fro upon his horse, and grumbling thick accents at the bedside, he visited all the sick chambers for miles about among the mountain towns; and sometimes raised a dying man, as it were, by miracle, or, quite as often, no doubt, sent his patient to a grave that was dug many a year too soon. The Doctor had an everlasting pipe in his mouth, and, as somebody said, in allusion to his habit of swearing, it was always alight with hell-fire.

These three worthies pressed forward, and greeted Ethan Brand, each after his own fashion, earnestly inviting him to partake of the contents of a certain black bottle; in which, as they averred, he would find something far better worth seeking for, than the Unpardonable Sin. No mind, which has wrought itself, by intense and solitary meditation, into a high state of enthusiasm, can endure the kind of contact with low and vulgar modes of thought and feeling, to which Ethan Brand was now subjected. It made him doubt—and, strange to say, it was a painful doubt—whether he had indeed found the Unpardonable Sin, and found it within himself. The whole question on which he had exhausted life, and more than life, looked like a delusion.

"Leave me," he said bitterly, "ye brute beasts, that have made yourselves so, shrivelling up your souls with fiery liquors! I have done with you. Years and years ago, I groped into your hearts and found nothing there for my purpose. Get ye gone!"

"Why, you uncivil scoundrel," cried the fierce Doctor, "is that the way you respond to the kindness of your best friends? Then let me tell you the truth. You have no more found the Unpardonable Sin than yonder boy Joe has. You are but a crazy fellow—I told you so, twenty years ago—neither better nor worse than a crazy fellow, and the fit companion of old Humphrey, here!"

He pointed to an old man, shabbily dressed, with long white hair, thin visage, and unsteady eyes. For some years past, this aged person had been wandering about among the hills, inquiring of all travellers whom he met, for his daughter. The girl, it seemed, had gone off with a company of circus-performers; and, occasionally, tidings of her came to the village, and fine stories were told of her glittering appearance, as she rode on horseback in the ring, or performed marvellous feats on the tight-rope.

The white-haired father now approached Ethan Brand, and gazed unsteadily into his face.

"They tell me you have been all over the earth," said he, wringing his hands with earnestness. "You must have seen my daughter; for she makes a grand figure in the world, and everybody goes to see her. Did she send any word to her old father, or say when she is coming back?"

Ethan Brand's eye quailed beneath the old man's. That daughter, from whom he so earnestly desired a word of greeting, was the Esther of our tale; the very girl whom, with such cold and remorseless purpose, Ethan Brand had made the subject of a psychological experiment, and wasted, absorbed, and perhaps annihilated her soul, in the process.

"Yes," murmured he, turning away from the hoary wanderer; "it is no delusion. There is an Unpardonable Sin!"

While these things were passing, a merry scene was going forward in the area of cheerful light, besides the spring and before the door of the hut. A number of the youth of the village, young men and girls, had hurried up the hill-side, impelled by curiosity to see Ethan Brand, the hero of so many a legend familiar to their childhood. Finding nothing, however, very remarkable in his aspect—nothing but a sunburnt wayfarer, in plain garb and dusty shoes, who sat looking into the fire, as if he fancied pictures among the coals—these young people speedily grew tired of observing him. As it happened, there was other amusement at hand. An old German Jew, travelling with a diorama on his back, was passing down the mountain-road towards the village, just as the party turned aside from it; and, in hopes of eking out the profits of the day, the showman had kept them company to the lime-kiln.

"Come, old Dutchman," cried one of the young men, "let us see your pictures, if you can swear they are worth looking at!"

"Oh, yes, Captain," answered the Jew—whether as a matter of courtesy or craft, he styled everybody Captain—"I shall show you, indeed, some very superb pictures!"

So, placing his box in a proper position, he invited the young men and girls to look through the glass orifices of the machine, and proceeded to exhibit a series of the most outrageous scratchings and daubings, as specimens of the fine arts, that ever an itinerant showman had the face to impose upon his circle of spectators. The pictures were worn out, moreover, tattered, full of cracks and wrinkles, dingy with tobacco-smoke, and otherwise in a most pitiable condition. Some purported to be cities, public edifices, and ruined castles, in Europe; others represented Napoleon's battles, and Nelson's sea-fights; and in the midst of these would be seen a gigantic, brown, hairy hand—which might have been mistaken for the Hand of Destiny, though, in truth, it was only the showman's—pointing its forefinger to various scenes of the conflict, while its owner gave historical illustrations. When, with much merriment at its abominable deficiency of merit, the exhibition was concluded, the German bade little Joe put his head into the box. Viewed through the magnifying glasses, the boy's round, rosy visage assumed the strangest imaginable aspect of an immense, Titanic child, the mouth grinning broadly, and the eyes, and every other feature, overflowing with fun at the joke. Suddenly, however, that merry face turned pale, and its expression changed to horror; for this easily impressed and excitable child had become sensible that the eye of Ethan Brand was fixed upon him through the glass.

"You make the little man to be afraid, Captain," said the German Jew, turning up the dark and strong outline of his visage, from his stooping posture. "But, look again; and, by chance, I shall cause you to see somewhat that is very fine, upon my word!"

Ethan Brand gazed into the box for an instant, and then starting back, looked fixedly at the German. What had he seen? Nothing, apparently; for a curious youth, who had peeped in, almost at the same moment, beheld only a vacant space of canvass.

"I remember you now," muttered Ethan Brand to the showman.

"Ah, Captain," whispered the Jew of Nuremberg, with a dark smile, "I find it to be a heavy matter in my show-box—this Unpardonable Sin! By my faith, Captain, it has wearied my shoulders, this long day, to carry it over the mountain."

"Peace!" answered Ethan Brand, sternly, "or get thee into the furnace yonder!"

The Jew's exhibition had scarcely concluded, when a great, elderly dog—who seemed to be his own master, as no person in the company laid claim to him—saw fit to render himself the object of public notice. Hitherto, he had shown himself a very quiet, well-disposed old dog, going round from one to another, and, by way of being sociable, offering his rough head to be patted by any kindly hand that would take so much trouble. But, now, all of a sudden, this grave and venerable quadruped, of his own mere notion, and without the slightest suggestion from anybody else, began to run round after his tail, which, to heighten the absurdity of the proceeding, was a great deal shorter than it should have been. Never was seen such headlong eagerness in pursuit of an object that could not possibly be attained; never was heard such a tremendous outbreak of growling, snarling, barking, and snapping—as if one end of the ridiculous brute's body were at deadly and most unforgivable enmity with the other. Faster and faster, roundabout went the cur; and faster and still faster fled the unapproachable brevity of his tail; and louder and fiercer grew his yells of rage and animosity; until, utterly exhausted, and as far from the goal as ever, the foolish old dog ceased his performance as suddenly as he had begun it. The next moment, he was as mild, quiet, sensible, and respectable in his deportment, as when he first scraped acquaintance with the company.

As may be supposed, the exhibition was greeted with universal laughter, clapping of hands, and shouts of encore; to which the canine performer responded by wagging all that there was to wag of his tail, but appeared totally unable to repeat his very successful effort to amuse the spectators.

Meanwhile, Ethan Brand had resumed his seat upon the log; and, moved, it might be, by a perception of some remote analogy between his own case and that of this self-pursuing cur, he broke into the awful laugh, which, more than any other token, expressed the condition of his inward being. From that moment, the merriment of the party was at an end; they stood aghast, dreading lest the inauspicious sound should be reverberated around the horizon, and that mountain would thunder it to mountain, and so the horror be prolonged upon their ears. Then, whispering one to another, that it was late—that the moon was almost down—that the August night was growing chill—they hurried homeward, leaving the lime-burner and little Joe to deal as they might with their unwelcome guest. Save for these three human beings, the open space on the hill-side was a solitude, set in a vast gloom of forest. Beyond that darksome verge, the fire-light glimmered on the stately trunks and almost black foliage of pines, intermixed with the lighter verdure of sapling oaks, maples, and poplars, while, here and there, lay the gigantic corpses of dead trees, decaying on the leaf-strewn soil. And it seemed to little Joe—a timorous and imaginative child—that the silent forest was holding its breath, until some fearful thing should happen.

Ethan Brand thrust more wood into the fire, and closed the door of the kiln; then looking over his shoulder at the lime-burner and his son, he bade, rather than advised, them to retire to rest.

"For myself I cannot sleep," said he. "I have matters that it concerns me to meditate upon. I will watch the fire, as I used to do in the old time."

"And call the devil out of the furnace to keep you company, I suppose," muttered Bartram, who had been making intimate acquaintance with the black bottle above-mentioned. "But watch, if you like, and call as many devils as you like! For my part, I shall be all the better for a snooze. Come, Joe!"

As the boy followed his father into the hut, he looked back to the wayfarer, and the tears came into his eyes; for his tender spirit had an intuition of the bleak and terrible loneliness in which this man had enveloped himself.

When they had gone, Ethan Brand sat listening to the crackling of the kindled wood, and looking at the little spirts of fire that issued through the chinks of the door. These trifles, however, once so familiar, had but the slightest hold of his attention; while deep within his mind, he was reviewing the gradual, but marvellous change, that had been wrought upon him by the search to which he had devoted himself. He remembered how the night-dew had fallen upon him—how the dark forest had whispered to him—how the stars had gleamed upon him—a simple and loving man, watching his fire in the years gone by, and ever musing as it burned. He remembered with what tenderness, with what love and sympathy for mankind, and what pity for human guilt and wo, he had first begun to contemplate those ideas which afterwards became the inspiration of his life; with what reverence he had then looked into the heart of man, viewing it as a temple originally divine, and however desecrated, still to be held sacred by a brother; with what awful fear he had deprecated the success of his pursuit, and prayed that the Unpardonable Sin might never be revealed to him. Then ensued that vast intellectual development, which, in its progress, disturbed the counterpoise between his mind and heart. The Idea that possessed his life had operated as a means of education; it had gone on cultivating his powers to the highest point of which they were susceptible; it had raised him from the level of an unlettered laborer, to stand on a star-light eminence, whither the philosophers of the earth, laden with the lore of universities, might vainly strive to clamber after him. So much for the intellect! But where was the heart? That, indeed, had withered—had contracted—had hardened—had perished! It had ceased to partake of the universal throb. He had lost his hold of the magnetic chain of humanity. He was no longer a brother-man, opening the chambers or the dungeons of our common nature by the key of holy sympathy, which gave him a right to share in all its secrets; he was now a cold observer, looking on mankind as the subject of his experiment, and, at length, converting man and woman to be his puppets, and pulling the wires that moved them to such degrees of crime as were demanded for his study.

Thus Ethan Brand became a fiend. He began to be so from the moment that his moral nature had ceased to keep the pace of improvement with his intellect. And now, as his highest effort and inevitable development—as the bright and gorgeous flower, and rich, delicious fruit of his life's labor—he had produced the Unpardonable Sin!

"What more have I to seek? What more to achieve?" said Ethan Brand to himself. "My task is done, and well done!"

Starting from the log with a certain alacrity in his gait, and ascending the hillock of earth that was raised against the stone circumference of the lime-kiln, he thus reached the top of the structure. It was a space of perhaps ten feet across, from edge to edge, presenting a view of the upper surface of the immense mass of broken marble with which the kiln was heaped. All these innumerable blocks and fragments of marble were red-hot, and vividly on fire, sending up great spouts of blue flame, which quivered aloft and danced madly, as within a magic circle, and sank and rose again, with continual and multitudinous activity. As the lonely man bent forward over this terrible body of fire, the blasting heat smote up against his person with a breath that, it might be supposed, would have scorched and shrivelled him up in a moment.

Ethan Brand stood erect and raised his arms on high. The blue flames played upon his face, and imparted the wild and ghastly light which alone could have suited its expression; it was that of a fiend on the verge of plunging into his gulf of intensest torment.

"Oh, Mother Earth," cried he, "who art no more my Mother, and into whose bosom this frame shall never be resolved! Oh, mankind, whose brotherhood I have cast off, and trampled thy great heart beneath my feet! Oh, stars of Heaven, that shone on me of old, as if to light me onward and upward!—farewell all, and forever! Come, deadly element of Fire—henceforth my familiar friend! Embrace me as I do thee!"

That night the sound of a fearful peal of laughter rolled heavily through the sleep of the lime-burner and his little son; dim shapes of horror and anguish haunted their dreams, and seemed still present in the rude hovel when they opened their eyes to the daylight.

"Up, boy, up!" cried the lime-burner, staring about him. "Thank Heaven, the night is gone at last; and rather than pass such another, I would watch my lime-kiln, wide awake, for a twelvemonth. This Ethan Brand, with his humbug of an Unpardonable Sin, has done me no such mighty favor in taking my place!"

He issued from the hut, followed by little Joe, who kept fast hold of his father's hand. The early sunshine was already pouring its gold upon the mountain-tops, and though the valleys were still in shadow, they smiled cheerfully in the promise of the bright day that was hastening onward. The village, completely shut in by hills, which swelled away gently about it, looked as if it had rested peacefully in the hollow of the great hand of Providence. Every dwelling was distinctly visible; the little spires of the two churches pointed upward, and caught a fore-glimmering of brightness from the sun-gilt skies upon their gilded weathercocks. The tavern was astir, and the figure of the old, smoke-dried stage-agent, cigar in mouth, was seen beneath the stoop. Old Graylock was glorified with a golden cloud upon his head. Scattered, likewise, over the breasts of the surrounding mountains, there were heaps of hoary mist, in fantastic shapes, some of them far down into the valley, others high up towards the summits, and still others, of the same family of mist or cloud, hovering in the gold radiance of the upper atmosphere. Stepping from one to another of the clouds that rested on the hills, and thence to the loftier brotherhood that sailed in air, it seemed almost as if a mortal man might thus ascend into the heavenly regions. Earth was so mingled with sky that it was a daydream to look at it.

To supply that charm of the familiar and homely, which Nature so readily adopts into a scene like this, the stagecoach was rattling down the mountain-road, and the driver sounded his horn; while echo caught up the notes and intertwined them into a rich, and varied, and elaborate harmony, of which the original performer could lay claim to little share. The great hills played a concert among themselves, each contributing a strain of airy sweetness.

Little Joe's face brightened at once.

"Dear father," cried he, skipping cheerily to and fro, "that strange man is gone, and the sky and the mountains all seem glad of it!"

"Yes," growled the lime-burner with an oath, "but he has let the fire go down, and no thanks to him, if five hundred bushels of lime are not spoilt. If I catch the fellow hereabouts again I shall feel like tossing him into the furnace!"

With his long pole in his hand he ascended to the top of the kiln. After a moment's pause he called to his son.

"Come up here, Joe!" said he.

So little Joe ran up the hillock and stood by his father's side. The marble was all burnt into perfect, snow-white lime. But on its surface, in the midst of the circle—snow-white too, and thoroughly converted into lime—lay a human skeleton, in the attitude of a person who, after long toil, lies down to long repose. Within the ribs—strange to say—was the shape of a human heart.

"Was the fellow's heart made of marble?" cried Bartram, in some perplexity at this phenomenon. "At any rate, it is burnt into what looks like special good lime; and, taking all the bones together, my kiln is half a bushel the richer for him."

So saying, the rude lime-burner lifted his pole, and letting it fall upon the skeleton, the relics of Ethan Brand were crumbled into fragments.

Selected Bibliography

Hawthorne's Writings

The Centenary Edition of the Works of Nathaniel Hawthorne, edited by William Charvat, Roy Harvey Pearce, Claude M. Simpson, Thomas Woodson, and others. 23 vols. Columbus: Ohio State University Press, 1962–1997.

Biographies

Hawthorne, Julian. *Nathaniel Hawthorne and His Wife: A Biography.* 3rd. ed. 2 vols. Boston: James R. Osgood, 1885.

Miller, Edwin H. *Salem Is My Dwelling Place: A Life of Nathaniel Hawthorne.* Iowa City: University of Iowa Press, 1991.

Moore, Margaret B. *The Salem World of Nathaniel Hawthorne.* Columbia, Mo.: University of Missouri Press, 1998.

Turner, Arlin. *Nathaniel Hawthorne: A Biography.* New York: Oxford University Press, 1980.

Wineapple, Brenda. *Hawthorne: A Life.* New York: Alfred A. Knopf, 2003.

Critical Studies

Adams, Richard P. "Hawthorne's *Provincial Tales.*" *New England Quarterly* 30 (1957): 39–57.

Arac, Jonathan. *Commissioned Spirits: The Shaping of Social Motion in Dickens, Carlyle, Melville, and Hawthorne.* New Brunswick, N.J.: Rutgers University Press, 1979.

Baym, Nina. *The Shape of Hawthorne's Career.* Ithaca: Cornell University Press, 1976.

Bell, Millicent. *Hawthorne's View of the Artist.* Albany: State University of New York Press, 1962.

Bellis, Peter. *Writing Revolution: Aesthetics and Politics in Hawthorne, Whitman, and Thoreau.* Athens, GA.: University of Georgia Press, 2003.

Bensick, Carol Marie. *La Nouvelle Beatrice: Renaissance and Romance in "Rappaccini's Daughter."* New Brunswick, N.J.: Rutgers University Press, 1985.

Brodhead, Richard H. *The School of Hawthorne.* New York, Oxford University Press, 1986.

Cagidemetrio, Alide. *Fictions of the Past: Hawthorne and Melville.* Amherst: University of Massachusetts Press, 1992.

Colacurcio, Michael J. *The Province of Piety: Moral History in Hawthorne's Early Tales.* Cambridge: Harvard University Press, 1984.

Crews, Frederick. *The Sins of the Fathers: Hawthorne's Psychological Themes.* New York: Oxford University Press, 1966.

Crowley, J. Donald. "The Artist as Mediator: The Rationale of Hawthorne's Large-Scale Revisions in His Collected Tales and Sketches," in *Hawthorne and Melville in the Berkshires,* ed. Howard P. Vincent. Kent, Ohio: Kent State University Press, 1968, pp. 79–88.

Doubleday, Neal Frank. *Hawthorne's Early Tales: A Critical Study.* Durham, N.C.: Duke University Press, 1972.

Erlich, Gloria. *Family Themes and Hawthorne's Fiction.* New Brunswick, N.J.: Rutgers University Press, 1984.

Fogle, Richard Harter. *Hawthorne's Fiction: The Light and the Dark.* Norman: University of Oklahoma Press, 1964.

Gollin, Rita K. *Nathaniel Hawthorne and the Truth of Dreams.* Baton Rouge: Louisiana State University Press, 1979.

Hoffman, Daniel. *Form and Fable in American Fiction.* New York: Oxford University Press, 1965.

James, Henry. *Hawthorne,* in *Literary Criticism: Essays on Literature; American and English Writers,* ed. Leon Edel and Mark Wilson. New York: Library of America, 1984.

Lawrence, D. H. *Studies in Classic American Literature.* New York: Viking Press, 1964 reprint.

Male, Roy R. *Hawthorne's Tragic Vision.* New York: W. W. Norton, 1964 reprint.

Martin, Terrence. "The Method of Hawthorne's Tales," in *Hawthorne Centenary Essays,* ed. Roy Harvey Pearce. Columbus: Ohio State University Press, 1964.

McCall, Dan. *Citizens of Somewhere Else: Nathaniel Hawthorne and Henry James.* Ithaca: Cornell University Press, 1999.

McDonald, John J. "'The Old Manse' and Its Mosses: The Inception and Development of *Mosses from an Old Manse," Texas Studies in Literature and Language* 16 (1974): 74–108.

Melville, Herman. "Hawthorne and His Mosses" and Letter from April 16?, 1851. Reprinted in Herman Melville, *Tales, Poems, and Other Writings,* ed. by John Bryant. New York: The Modern Library, 2001.

Michaels, Walter Benn. "Romance and Real Estate." In *The American Renaissance Reconsidered,* ed. by Walter Benn Michaels and Donald E. Pease. Baltimore: Johns Hopkins University Press, 1984.

Pfister, Joel. *The Production of Personal Life: Class, Gender, and the Psychological in Hawthorne's Fiction.* Stanford: Stanford University Press, 1991.

Reynolds, David. *Beneath the American Renaissance: The Subversive Imagination in the Age of Emerson and Melville.* New York: Alfred A. Knopf, 1988.

Stein, William Bysshe. *Hawthorne's Faust: A Study of the Devil Archetype.* Gainesville: University of Florida Press, 1953.

Sundquist, Eric J. *Home as Found: Authority and Genealogy in Nineteenth-Century American Fiction.* Baltimore: Johns Hopkins University Press, 1979.

Swann, Charles. *Nathaniel Hawthorne: Tradition and Revolution.* Cambridge: Cambridge University Press, 1991.

Trollope, Anthony. "The Genius of Nathaniel Hawthorne." *North American Review* 129, no. 274 (September 1879): 203–222.

Waggoner, Hyatt H. *Hawthorne: A Critical Study.* Cambridge: Harvard University Press, 1955.

Collections of Essays

Bell, Millicent, ed. *Hawthorne and the Real: Bicentennial Essays*. Columbus: Ohio State University Press, 2004.

——— *New Essays on Hawthorne's Major Tales*. Cambridge: Cambridge University Press, 1993.

Cohen, Bernard, ed. *The Recognition of Nathaniel Hawthorne: Selected Criticism Since 1828*. Ann Arbor: University of Michigan Press, 1969.

Crowley, J. Donald, ed. *Hawthorne: The Critical Heritage*. London: Routledge and Kegan Paul, 1970; 1997.

Lee, A. Robert, ed. *Nathaniel Hawthorne: New Critical Essays*. Totowa, N.J.: Barnes and Noble, 1982.

Millington, Richard H., ed. *The Cambridge Companion to Nathaniel Hawthorne*. New York: Cambridge University Press, 2004.

Pearce, Roy Harvey, ed. *Hawthorne: Centenary Essays*. Columbus: Ohio State University Press, 1964.

Reynolds, Larry J., ed. *Historical Guide to Nathaniel Hawthorne*. New York: Oxford University Press, 2001.